Claire Rayner was born in London in 1931. She trained as a nurse at the Royal Northern Hospital, London; qualified and was State Registered in 1954 when she was awarded the hospital Gold Medal for outstanding achievement. She then studied midwifery at Guy's Hospital and at the Whittington Hospital where she was Sister in the Paediatric Department.

She married in 1957 and turned to writing in 1960 when the birth of her first child ended her nursing career. She now has three children, Amanda, Adam and Jay.

Claire Rayner is the author of some eighty books including not only fiction, but also an extremely broad range of medical subjects, from sex education for children and adults, to home nursing, family health, and baby and childcare. Among her fiction is the twelve-volume novel sequence 'The Performers', which she completed in 1986 with *Seven Dials*.

GW00371284

Also by Claire Rayner in Sphere Books:

REPRISE
JUBILEE: POPPY CHRONICLES VOL I

MADDIE

Claire Rayner

SPHERE BOOKS LIMITED

A SPHERE BOOK

First published in Great Britain by Michael Joseph Ltd 1988
Published by Sphere Books Ltd 1990

Printed and bound in Great Britain by
Richard Clay Ltd, Bungay, Suffolk

ISBN 0 7474 0215 X

Sphere Books Ltd
A Division of
Macdonald & Co (Publishers) Ltd
27 Wrights Lane, London W8 5TZ
A member of Maxwell Pergamon Publishing Corporation plc

For
Eileen Atkins
with gratitude for her inspiring
performance as Medea at
The Young Vic, London 1986

ACKNOWLEDGEMENTS

The author is grateful for the assistance given with research by Friern Barnet Hospital, London; The University Archives, The University of Liverpool, custodians of the records of the Cunard Shipping Line; John McCormick, Bostonian, now of London, England; Mr and Mrs Storer Prebble Ware, Bostonians, now of Roanoke, Virginia; The London Library; The London Museum; The Imperial War Museum; The Archivist, British Rail; and other sources too numerous to mention.

1

December 1948

Maddie, dancing. Maddie with her new dress floating in peach froth around her slender ankles. Maddie in her silver strappy high-heeled sandals and real nylon stockings, going to be nineteen in just another ninety minutes and dancing at her own special party with her own special man. The most beautiful man she had ever seen in all her life holding her in his strong arms, his handsome well-shaped head with its thick frosting of deep gold hair bent so elegantly over her own dark curls. Oh, to be Maddie is very heaven.

And then the music stops, the most expensive music Daddy could buy, Joe Loss, the very best society band there is, and the froth of Maddie's tulle skirt settles gently after the last twirl to the dying notes of 'Nature Boy' and slowly, unwillingly, she lets go of her beautiful man, sliding her hand down the smoothness of his dinner jacket, shyly looking up at him, her lashes dark against her soft young skin, smiling tremulously.

'Er, thank you,' he says, courteous, of course, voice deep and interesting, of course. American? How incredible, American! 'That was great. A good band, hmm?'

'A wonderful band,' she says breathlessly. 'I love dancing to it, don't you?'

'Yes –' He is moving away, backwards, slowly, but still moving away, and she says quickly, 'It would be nice to go on dancing –' but he is going now, smiling politely, his face so handsome under the thick fair hair, and she gets more anxious still and says, 'Er – don't you want to dance again? We don't have to go into the Paul Jones if we don't want to –'

'A little later perhaps –' He is almost gone and she wants to run after him, but knows she can't, because nice girls don't ever do that, and she calls, 'Be sure to find me, then –' and smiles, cheekily, pertly, in the way that girls are allowed to but still be considered nice and he smiles vaguely and says, 'Why – yes – of course – what did you say your name was?'

Maddie, later, sitting by Daddy, watching and clapping as some of the men start dancing a violent Cossack dance to show off how vigorous and young they are, in spite of being fifty or more, and she teasing Daddy because he isn't dancing too, until he gets up and pretends to cuff her and then goes into the middle of the men and dances better than any of them, his arms folded high and ferocious in front of him, his knees bent the most and his feet kicking out the furthest as he shows them all that Alfred Braham is better than all of them at everything. Not only is this the best party anywhere in London this New Year's Eve, not only is his daughter, whose birthday party it is, the most beautiful and the most expensively dressed, not only is the food the most lavish anyone has seen since before the war — smoked salmon, roast chickens, real shell eggs, boiled and piled high, an incredible array — but he can dance more aggressively than the youngest and strongest of them. Alfred Braham is the *best*.

And Maddie applauds him loudly and thinks so too, except that she knows he is also the best at other things she does not like so well. Like getting his own way and spoiling her fun. But she is good at dealing with him, for hasn't she had the practice? And later still, when Big Ben's New Year chimes have been counted out and 1949 and her nineteenth birthday have been given a raucous welcome, she sits with him as he drinks more of his own good brandy than any of his guests and gets steadily more morose, until he is weeping for his poor dead Bessie, the way he has wept on Maddie's birthday for as long as she can remember.

'I'm here to look after you, even if Mummy isn't,' she murmurs into Alfred's ear, as he sits beside her, slumped and red-faced, sweating in the lights, as everyone else goes on dancing. 'It's all right — I'm here —'

And he clutches her hand and looks at her with tears in his eyes and says thickly, 'Where would I be without my little ones? My little Maddie, my crazy boy Ambrose? Where would I be without you two? Eh? A man is his children, that's all a man is, his children. Only the best for you, my darlings, only the best for Alfred Braham's children.'

And then he cheers up as he always does and she can talk to him and soothe him more and find out what she wants to know,

2

without him knowing she is interested. If he thought she was interested that would be the end of it, the way it had been when she had liked David Henney, the accountant's son. Alfred had soon got rid of David, and his father too, shouting furiously at the bewildered man that he wasn't going to put up with snakes in his woodpile, not he, until the Henneys had scuttled away and left Alfred where he wanted to be, the only man Maddie ever showed any interest in. Oh, she had learned a lot from that, last year. It had made her angry then, though it hadn't hurt all that much to see David go away. But it would hurt to see this one sent away, so that mustn't be allowed to happen.

So she makes Daddy tell her about everyone at the party, every single one of them, and watches and listens as he stares round the room, the biggest room the Curzon Hotel could provide, pointing out the importance of the guests he has assembled to celebrate the birthday with his brandy and whisky and smoked salmon and real shell eggs, boiled and piled high, a sight no one can remember seeing in London for the past nine years.

'Assistant Chief Commissioner Scotland Yard,' Alfred says dreamily and blows smoke from his big cigar across the room at the tall man in the corner talking to a group of people in army uniform, brigadiers and colonels. 'That's who that is, eating on the black market like a good'n.'

'Do they know it's black-market stuff they're eating?' Maddie is distracted for a moment from her real interest, looking at the well-fed, well-pleased-with-themselves men eating the sort of food ordinary people in London hadn't seen through all the long bleak years since September 1939 had destroyed an old world to cobble up a violent new and eternally hungry one. 'Don't they care?'

He laughed fatly then, still staring dreamily through the smoke of his cigar.

''Course they know, and 'course they don't care. Getting caught doin' it, *this* they care about – but as long as it's my nosh they're eating then they aren't in any trouble, right? It's me that has to care. And I don't, because I got my friends in the right places. In Scotland Yard and Whitehall and the House of Commons and anywhere it's useful to have friends. Look, that chap there, that's Sidney Stanley – yeah, Stanley himself! All

3

that fuss about his Lynskey Tribunal and he still has the time to come to one of my parties. Wouldn't miss it, that's the truth of it, wouldn't miss it. We've done a lot of business, him and me, one way and another, so how could he not be here? They think they've caught him and his deals, that bunch of blue-nosed prissy — agh, judges, who cares for lousy judges like Lynskey? Stanley don't and I don't. I just care about looking after number one, and number one's kids. And that's why all these people are here to help celebrate your birthday, dolly —' And he blinks at her with round oily tears in his eyes, pleased to be sad on so happy an occasion.

'And who else is there?' Maddie says hastily, not wanting him to wander off down that well-trodden and therefore boring path. 'Tell me about the rest.'

At once he brightens. 'The rest? Well, there's Joey Lynn, related to the Salmon family he is, very useful fella — and there's the girl from Korda's studio — the one that was all over the *News of the World* last week — and that chap's very high up at the BBC and the girl he's talking to is one of the Rank starlets —'

'And that's Jennifer Foster, isn't it, talking to someone over there in the corner? Ambrose told me she's been through half the House of Commons — or they've been through her —'

'Don't talk like that.' Alfred Braham looks sourly reproving then, biting hard on his cigar. 'I don't like to hear a young girl talk of things like that — and anyway, it isn't. She's from the American Embassy, that's all. No one special —'

'Are they both from the Embassy?' It works every time, Maddie is thinking, every time. Talk about something else and he tells me what I really want to hear. Please make it work this time. 'The chap as well?'

'What? Oh, no, not him. American though. His dad's a friend of mine. Mind you, not seen the old man for years. We were in the trenches together, would you believe, thirty-odd years ago. I've done my share of fighting and never you let anyone forget it. I did my bit the first time round, so this time, I stayed in London, got on with essential war work, moving supplies around.' And he laughs, moistly, and chews his cigar and Maddie bites her tongue, wanting to prompt him and not

4

daring to take the chance, still praying he'll go on and talk about what he should be talking about. And at last someone listens to her prayers, and Alfred laughs again and says, 'But, I'll tell you, dolly, the strokes me and old Timothy pulled back there in France – fed half the bleedin' regiment on the sugar stick, we did, and came out smellin' of roses.'

'Timothy?' It should be safe to push him now, now that he's launched on remembering strokes and deals. These are his favourite things to talk about.

And he talks of strokes and deals, and also of dodges and wheezes, laughing and nodding at her and she listens and waits and thinks of dancing again with that man with the beautiful face and the thick golden hair, and feels her tulle dress whisper around her ankles and shivers a little with the excitement of it all. And then at last, he's telling her, as Daddy always does eventually, telling her what she needs to know.

'– so what can I say when he wants to send the boy over, to keep things quiet a while? No need to go into it, but it was a nasty little fuss, I gather. But the boy's been behaving well enough since he got here, so he's learned from it, and that's always what it's all about, learning from what happens, eh dolly? And he's learned, has young Jay Kincaid, he's learned. And working in the business for me, now. And over there, next to him, see that fella? The one with the handlebar moustache? Now I can tell you a thing or two about *him* –'

But Maddie doesn't have to listen any more. She can look at him and know him and plan for the future with him. Jay Kincaid, lovely wonderful Jay Kincaid, the most beautiful man she has ever seen in all her life.

October 1986

Annie could hear the bulldozers at work long before she could see them. They grunted and rumbled like angry old men, sending little showers of stones rattling down the scrubby bank beside the road as she drove the last hundred yards to the great iron gates. There had once been matching railings all along the edge of the bank but they had been taken away to make wartime munitions; the square brick pillars and low wall in which they had been embedded were still visible, dilapidated now after almost fifty years of weathering but still there, like toothless gums. She had never seen the railings herself. Their past existence and loss were just part of the things she knew about Greenhill without knowing how she knew. It sometimes seemed to her that the place had seeped into her very bones by some sort of osmotic process, that she'd been going in and out of these gates and on to the ill-kept gravel drive for so long that she was as much a part of it as were the nurses and the medical staff and the buildings themselves.

And the patients, she thought then, as she eased the car past the awkward corner from Damsel Lane, remembering to check in her side mirror for the huge bramble that always tried to scrape her paintwork as she came past. And the patients. I ought to be in here myself, all the time, not just wandering in and out as though I were normal and well –

'Shut up,' she said aloud as at last the car straightened itself on the driveway and left the bramble behind. 'Shut up –' And she concentrated on the drive ahead and on her bladder, which was beginning to clamour for attention. I'm late and I hate walking in there after they've all arrived, so that they all sit and stare at me, but if I don't pee first it'll give them something much more disgusting to stare at – damn the commuters, damn the motorway, damn this place, damn me –

She could see the bulldozers now, dirty great yellow and red painted creatures with maws like the prehistoric animals on the children's TV cartoon shows, chewing up the ground that had once been the garden while the tall crane swung its great iron ball at the walls of the East Pavilion. There were piles of rubble where yesterday there had been the familiar red brick squareness with its high small windows and its heavy front door, and upturned yellow earth and dirty stones where once there had been a square of grass and some straggling but gaudy geraniums. Little clouds of brick dust hung in the golden October air, lit by the brightness of the morning sun to a glittering richness that made a little spurt of anger lift in her. It was all wrong that destruction should be beautiful; it should look as ugly as it was, and as cruel as it was.

And then she saw the little knot of people standing clustered on the path beside the Pavilion watching the work, and felt so much more angry that it was like physical nausea. There they stood, forlorn and silent, each wrapped in the loneliness of their

6

ailment, watching home disappear. These were the old stagers; she recognised them as being as much a part of Greenhill as the iron gates and the battered brick pillars. Here they had been patients for years and years, living in the East Pavilion as nurses and doctors had come and gone, staying there for ever and ever. Only now for ever and ever had ended, and they had been turfed out to make room for red and yellow bulldozers with big maws, and cranes with swinging iron balls. It was hateful and cruel and I loathe this place and I don't know why I come here and I want to pee. And she put her foot down savagely on the accelerator and the little car leapt towards the administrative building on the far side of the grounds.

And of course the car park there was full and she had to turn back to the one by the West Pavilion – which at least still looked the same; with curtains flapping at the barred windows to hide their ugliness, and the garden that surrounded it neat and tidy and blazing with late dahlias and asters – and then run all the way back to Admin. By which time the finding of a loo had become imperative and she was breathless. But there was nothing she could do about being late. She knew the meeting was to start at ten sharp, but it was hardly her fault that the M25 had been so clotted with traffic – and such clottish drivers in charge of it, too, she thought furiously – that she had been held up all the way. She had started out early enough, heaven knows –

By the time she had emerged from the old Senior Administrative Staff Washroom, that sat on the ground floor in all its mahogany and brass bedecked splendour, and gone hurrying up the stairs to the boardroom she was as tense as a steel guy-rope, every fibre twanging inside her head. It's being late, and seeing the East Pavilion reduced to rubble, that's what it is, she told herself as she stood poised for a moment by the closed door, hearing the voices murmuring on the other side of its glass panels, it's just that I've got myself into a state. Nothing to do with last night and the dreams and – and she took a deep breath and pushed open the door.

'Sorry I'm late,' she said brusquely as she closed the door behind her with a snap and walked purposefully to the empty chair that waited at the end of the table. 'Heavy traffic on the motorway,' and she sat down with a little thump, rattling the chair rather imperiously, and bent her head to stare at the agenda that lay on the table in front of her.

'Not at all, Miss Matthews,' Mr Gresham said brightly and smiled at her even more brightly, but she wasn't looking at him and he sighed softly and returned to his own notes. 'Sister Barber, you were just saying?'

Betty Barber launched herself into a prolonged whimper about the sort of locker accommodation being provided for the nursing staff at the Pattison Way hostel on the Larcombe Estate on the other side of the motorway, and Joe Labosky detached his attention from the meeting gratefully, and carefully, in case she should notice, looked sideways down the table.

There she sat, her dark head, with the thick glossy hair pinned into an untidy bun on the top of it, bent as far as it could be over the agenda – which she could have read a dozen times by now – and her eyes very deliberately lowered. And he felt his chest tighten a little as he stared at her.

She wasn't looking at all well, he decided. And a word his mother had been used to use came into his head: peaky. That was it, she looked peaky. Pale, except under her eyes where there were smudges of violet shadow, and her mouth drooped so that she seemed about to weep. But then she nearly always looked like that, as though she were on the edge of giving way to some vast grief that was pushing at her from within. She had looked like that as long as he had known her and he remembered, as he almost always did whenever he saw her, the first time they had met.

She had been standing defensively beside her mother, staring at him with her eyes wide and suspicious, and that downturned sad mouth, and as he had walked into her living room she had said abruptly, 'There is no need for you to be here. I told Dr Weightman that, but he thought he knew better. Well, no one knows my mother better than I do; and she doesn't need *you*.'

'Perhaps not,' he had said equably, standing there in the doorway of the cluttered room, very aware of Dr Weightman behind him, moving from one foot to the other in an agony of annoyance and embarrassment. 'But if you attack me so ferociously before I even say good morning, you make me wonder if perhaps *you* need me.'

8

She had made an odd little sound between her teeth at that, the sort of irritable exclamation that mothers make when their children have said something absurd and he had smiled and held out his hand. 'I'm Joe Labosky. I haven't come to make a nuisance of myself. I came because Dr Weightman thought I might be useful to you.'

'I don't need anything,' she had said, trying to ignore the outstretched hand, but then as her intrinsic good manners overcame her sulkiness had held out her own and they had shaken in a perfunctory way. He could still remember how her hand had felt; hot and dry and a little tremulous.

'I see a great many families facing dilemmas like yours, Miss Brady,' and he had quirked his head, needing very much to make her smile back at him, to disarm her hostility in any way he could.

But that hadn't worked. 'My name is Annie Brady *Matthews*,' she had said loudly, and her hand had come down protectively on the shoulder of the woman in the chair. 'My mother is named Brady. *Miss* Jennifer Brady.' And he heard the challenge in her voice and though he was fascinated to know why she had made such an issue over their names and their marital status he didn't rise to it.

'I'm sorry, Miss Matthews. Now, is it possible to discuss this situation and see what I can do about it?'

Dr Weightman had bounced forwards at that. 'It was my suggestion you should do a domiciliary for Mrs – er – Miss Brady, Dr Labosky,' he said, his rather high-pitched voice filling the room with fussiness. 'I told Miss Matthews that I could not go on being responsible for either her mother's care or her own unless she agreed, so that was why I called you, though I have to say Miss Matthews has not been at all cooperative, not at all. To tell the truth, you've made matters often worse than they need be, Miss Matthews, and I'm not afraid to say so, if others are –'

'I'd rather *you* told me about it all,' Joe had said, and he had walked into the room and hooked a chair forward with one foot and sat down in front of the still silent woman in the big armchair. 'Or will you tell me, Miss Brady?'

'Miss Brady is in no state to –' Dr Weightman had started and then the woman in the armchair had stirred and lifted her head, which hitherto had been slumped forwards on her chest, and looked at Joe, and said in a thick hoarse voice, 'Tell you what?'

He had felt rather than seen Annie's amazement as he carefully fixed his gaze on the older woman and smiled at her. She had looked back at him with dull glazed eyes the colour of pebbles at the bottom of a peaty stream, brown with flecks of amber in them, and her puffy cheeks had moved a little as she worked her mouth, as though she were about to speak again. She was heavy with the collected weight of years spent sitting doing nothing; she exuded torpor, Joe had thought, and felt irritation stir in him. Why do they let it happen to these people, he had thought then. *Why?* They need to be prodded, encouraged, made to try to go on living as much life as they have, not left to rot in chairs like this, and he had looked up at Annie beside the armchair, the words of criticism already forming on his lips. But they died there when he saw her face; she was staring down at her mother with an expression that was so full of pain and distress, and yet of anger and frustration, that he was once again fascinated. Heaven knew he saw enough cases like this; as a consultant in geriatric psychiatry he went to case after case of Alzheimer's disease and he thought he knew every nuance of family reaction to it. But this household was different.

It wasn't just the look of the room in which they were, with its great clutter of furniture and ornaments and gewgaws of all kinds, ranging from the very good to the frankly appalling, nor was it the look of the patient herself, with her great mane of dark red hair cascading in curls down her shoulders and her wrapper of clearly very expensive feather-trimmed blue silk. It was the girl, with her square-shouldered straightbacked stance and her sharp-edged profile. She had a strong nose with a small curve on the bridge, and those drooping lips were wonderfully shaped. She looks a little, just a little, like my Barbara, he had thought and then, furious that such an idea could escape from the depths of his mind, had slammed it back and bolted the door on it.

'How do you feel, Miss Brady?' he had said then, gently, looking again at the woman in the chair. 'Tell me that.' But the flash of responsiveness had gone. She was sitting staring into the

10

middle distance, her lips still working, but there was no glint of awareness in her expression at all.

So, he had had no choice but to talk to the girl, and he had straightened his back and without turning his head had said kindly but with authority, 'Dr Weightman, there is no need to keep you here. I shall come back to your surgery, if I may, to deal with the paperwork, but now just leave me here to talk to Miss Matthews –' and though the little GP had tried to protest, had clearly wanted to be part of the importance of the Consultation With The Specialist, Joe had won and he had gone away and the two of them had sat there listening as his car went chugging noisily down the street outside, and the woman in the chair sat and moved her lips soundlessly, talking to herself inside her head but patently unaware of them.

'I'd rather have tea,' Joe had said then, and grinned at Annie. 'This is the point at which most people offer me coffee, but I'd rather have tea. Earl Grey if you have it and I suspect you do.' He had looked very deliberately round the room at the ormolu clock and the lustre vases with the crystal drops over the mantel with its old-fashioned open fire, at the red plush covered furniture and the peach mirrors, and then grinned. 'And herb teas too, I'll bet.'

She had reddened suddenly and said brusquely, 'This isn't me. It's Jen. She never threw – throws anything away.' She looked round too, and then turned back to stare at him. 'And what does it have to do with you anyway? The way this room looks is none of your business –'

'Oh, but it is.' He had leaned back in his chair and stretched out his legs. 'I'm a psychiatrist and that means I'm trained to look at everything about my patients. Environment, clothes –'

'We are not your patients. So this room is none of your concern.'

'But you are and it is. Like it or not, I am here because your GP has asked me to make a domiciliary visit and assess your needs as a carer, and your mother's as a sufferer from Alzheimer's disease.'

She had frowned sharply then and said, 'Alzheimer's – what are you talking about?'

'Your mother's illness,' he had said and then added quickly as

11

he looked at her blank face, 'You have been told, haven't you? what your mother's illness is?'

'Dr Weightman didn't say she was ill. He said it was just one of those things – that she's just getting on a bit and having a few problems, that's all –'

'How old is your mother, Miss Matthews?'

'Jen? She's –' She frowned. 'Why do you want to know? I'm not cooperating with all this nonsense, you know. Jen's all right. She's just – just –' And her hand closed on the heavy shoulder beside her and she had bent her head to look at the silent figure sitting there.

'She isn't old at all, is she? Looking at her – and at you – I'd guess fifty or so. Am I right?'

'Fifty-two,' she said grudgingly after a long silence.

'Precisely. Of course she isn't getting on and of course this isn't just one of those things. It's an illness called Alzheimer's disease. It's a tragedy, and I'm very sad for her – and for you – but it won't be made less tragic by telling you lies about it. Weightman should have explained –' He had stopped, angered at the way the need to protect a colleague came welling up in him, and then had gone on impulsively, 'The man's a fool. Has he made you think that she's going mad or something of the sort? She isn't. She's suffering from premature senility. Very premature. There's no stigma attached to it, it's not something you will inherit and there's not a lot we can do about the disease, though we can help her be more comfortable. And we can help you cope and stop you suffering more than you need. At least Weightman brought me here. Give him credit for that.'

She had stared at him with her face blank, and after a long moment had said, 'I'll get you some tea. And there is some Earl Grey –' And he had grinned and said easily, 'Thank you. No milk or sugar –' and watched her go to the kitchen and took a deep breath of relief. Now he could begin to get somewhere.

And that, he remembered now, watching her covertly down the table in the big boardroom, had been the breaking of the barriers. Once she had been told what she needed to know about her mother, he had been able to find out from her what he needed to know to help them both, and as he had picked it out, with painstaking effort, over the next three years, so his anger for her had grown.

12

She has been abused by life, he had told himself passionately once, sitting beside her in his consulting room at Greenhill, once she had agreed to come there to see him, wickedly abused. But she won't admit that; not she. As far as she is concerned, this is how it has to be. That damned fatalism of hers; will she ever be rid of it, ever take her life in her own hands and start to live it? She's almost — and now he squinted down the table at her, and worked it out: just over six months since her mother's death on Easter Monday, and then the three years before that; she's almost thirty-three. No age, but it's high time, for all that, that she started to be what she was meant to be. Someone who can laugh and be witty company all the time and not just in tantalising flashes, someone who will take control of her own reins — and he picked up his pencil and began to doodle with some ferocity on his agenda sheet.

And it's high time, he added severely to himself, that I stopped allowing myself to be so obsessed with a patient. High time I put her to one side of my mind where all the rest of my work lives. And high time I sorted out my own needs too. It's been six years since Barbara died; but as ever that emergent thought was immediately pushed back into the deepest part of his mind. He couldn't cope with it any other way.

Jennifer, he said to himself as Betty Barber still droned on. That pathetic stupid fool of a woman, why had she done it? Bad enough she had sacrificed her own life on the altar of her bloody obsession, but to give up her child's as well? That had not been steadfastness and passion, as no doubt she thought it was; that had been selfish and stupid and downright wicked, and he lifted his brows as he thought that. Psychiatrists don't believe in the existence of good and evil, remember? he told himself. But it made no difference. Jennifer Brady had been wicked in her dealings with her daughter, and the sooner Annie admitted that truth the better chance she would have of coming out of this dreadful miasma of depression in which she had lived for so many years. For all her life, in fact.

He had often tried to visualise Jennifer Brady as she must have been before her memory and her speech and her initiative had crumbled away with the death of her brain and nerve cells; that incredible red hair and the strong Irish profile with its crisp-cut jawline and its imperious nose, so like Annie's own, and the brown and amber eyes; she must have been a beauty. It's no wonder the man had wanted her, no wonder he had tried to hang on to her for so long. It would have been interesting to know Colin Matthews, interesting to see what it was in him that could inspire the sort of devotion that Jennifer had given him. Had he been good looking? Witty? Sexually attractive? There was no way of knowing, for Annie flatly refused to talk of him and had destroyed all his photographs after he had died, long before Joe had known her. But he must have had some very special quality when a girl who looked like Jennifer Brady must have done willingly immured herself for the whole of her life in a little suburban house for love of him and never ever spoke to another man again. Nor apparently had she ever made any attempt to get Matthews away from his wife and his other children. She had, it seemed, been content to be his mistress, a silent, adoring, uncomplaining, secret mistress, who had wrapped her entire existence around his occasional visits, and had made her daughter, Colin's daughter, treat him in the same uncritical worshipful way.

No wonder Annie was so bitter and angry now, Joe thought, and again lifted his head to look at her. Her father had died before she had found the anger in her to fight back, to tell him what she thought of him and his fatherhood, which added up to no more than his name on her birth certificate and an occasional toy brought when he thought of it. Never at Christmas or on birthdays when it would have been blessedly normal and something to show off to the other children at school, but only at odd times that suited him, when the thing had to be hidden away, kept secret for fear someone would realise, Jennifer would tell the solemn little girl, for fear someone would know their business. Poor sad little Annie, and looking now at adult Annie, with her downcast eyes and her drooping mouth and her sulky expression Joe felt tears rise in him, tears of regret for her, and loathing for Colin; her long dead father, and fury for Jennifer's stupidity and, he could not deny, for himself, because he found the girl so interesting.

'Oh, damn it all to hell and back,' he muttered under his breath and pressed so hard on his doodling pencil that he broke the point.

'Yes, Dr Labosky?' Gresham's voice was raised and there was

14

a note in it that made it clear that he had repeated his words more than once already, and Joe lifted his head, startled, to find them all looking at him, even Annie.

'I'm sorry?' he said and blinked at Gresham. 'I was thinking – what did you say?'

'I wondered if you had any ideas about what we might do in this situation. Perhaps if I recap? Yes – it might help us all –' And he beamed round the table at them and ruffled his papers. 'Just to set out the problems, then. And after that we can go round everyone and see what answers you all have to this particular dilemma.'

And he began to talk, and this time Joe listened.

2

April 1949

Maddie crying. Maddie with furious tears streaking her face because she couldn't make him see how important it all was, and Jay smiling at her, his face creased and amused, and she for one moment hating him for that. It would be so much easier if she could hate him all the time, a little part of her mind had thought. So much easier to hurt a person you hate than to make a person you love do what you want him to do.

A person you love; and now Maddie sniffed and rubbed at her eyes with a handkerchief, wanting to show him the sort of face she should, the sort of face the magazines said a girl should show; smile gently, never be sulky, don't nag or cajole or flirt obviously, men hate that, the magazines said. Just be sweet and funny and above all vivacious. And, Maddie thought now, it isn't vivacious to cry. It makes men despise you.

But the magazines must have got it wrong, because he was leaning forwards and saying, 'Now don't you go spoiling your pretty little face that way! I had no notion it mattered so much.'

And now her tears stopped without any effort at all, and she could look up at him and smile brilliantly. 'Matter? Of course it matters! I want to do it more than I want to do anything in this whole world!'

'But why? It's only a show, after all!'

'Only a show? How can you say that, when it's the greatest thing that's come to London for, oh, years! And you an American and this a show all the way from Broadway – well, I just don't understand you!'

Does he believe me? Does he think it's just the show? Please let him think that, please, because once he does and we go, then I can make it all happen my way –

'Well, I guess I'm not that crazy about Broadway shows, not having the chance to see many.'

'Nor do I – and that's *why* I'm so crazy about them. Is it such

16

a very long way from Boston to New York? I mean, couldn't you have gone to shows there if you wanted to?'

'Oh, it's not that far. It's just that I never thought it worth the trouble, just for the theatre.' She loved the way he said theatre, shifting the emphasis subtly, so that he sounded like someone in a film, like Frederic March or even Franchot Tone, so shivery exciting. 'A ball game now – that I'd go to New York for. I'd go all the way to the West Coast, like my Pa, for that.'

'And yet you won't take me to the theatre in London, and it's only just down the road!'

She smiled as vivaciously as she could, but wondered if she ought to cry instead after all. And wondering that made her look worried and he grinned again, that lazy easy sort of grin he had and said, 'Well, if it's so important, I guess I could.' And at once she jumped up and clapped her hands and ran round the table to lean over and hug him.

It was all beginning to work as it should. It had taken her weeks to get to know where he was all day and where he lived and to find ways to get to know him. She couldn't possibly ask Daddy, so she had to try all her girlfriends, one after the other, and it hadn't been easy because obviously none of them must know why it mattered. None of them could be trusted not to go after him themselves or to sneak to her father, bitches that they were, so she had to be so careful, go out to tea with even the silliest ones, gossip with them about all the things they were doing and where they went. So boring. But it had been worth it, in the end. Shirley had known him, because he was staying in a flat with her brother David, who also did some work for Alfred Braham, as did Shirley's father come to that. Was there anyone in London who didn't have business connections with him? Maddie wondered, and was glad the answer was probably no. It might make it harder in one way to get to know a man she wanted to, because of the risk of her father finding out her interest, but it also made it easier in other ways. It gave her some power, for a start. People wanted to please Alfred's daughter as much as they wanted to please Alfred. A pleased Alfred was a generous man. A displeased Alfred was uncomfortable to have around.

Even for me, she thought then, sitting again in her chair on the other side of the small table and beaming at Jay. Even for me. If he knew I was here taking afternoon tea at the Ritz with a man, what would he say? What would he do? Not good things. So he mustn't know.

And Jay mustn't know, not yet, how important it was to keep quiet. He'd have to be taught that, and she cast around for a lie to use now to make sure he kept his tongue between his teeth, and smiled again, not vivaciously this time, but cheekily.

'Now, Jay, there's just one thing. You mustn't tell a soul where you got the tickets from.'

He looked blank. 'But I haven't got the tickets,' he said and then frowned. 'You said you had.'

Oh, but you are even more beautiful when you frown. The way your eyebrows cock in the middle, the way your mouth curves down at the corners and the shadows get darker in the cleft in your chin. So beautiful, oh, so beautiful!

She laughed, making it sound as much like a cascade, a tinkling cascade for preference, as she could. 'Dear man, I know you haven't! I have! I managed it through – well, never mind. I have my little ways, and they wouldn't be mine any more if I told you, would they? But my father would be so mad if I had first-night tickets and didn't get some for him. He likes the theatre too, you see. But I don't want to go with him – I mean, he's a lovely father to me, but you know how it is! A girl likes –' And now was the time to dip her head and smile and look up at him swiftly from beneath lowered lashes, '– a girl likes to choose her own company. So not a word to anyone about my getting the tickets, hmm? What Daddy doesn't know doesn't hurt him.'

'Listen, I don't want no trouble with your Pa. He's kind of – I work for him, you see. My old man'd cut up real rough if there were any troubles here. Bad enough what happened at home –'

Her eyes sharpened and she stared at him, but trying to look casual. 'Oh? What did happen?'

'I'm not telling a little girl like you such things! Pollute your young mind, then your Pa'd really get mad.' But his laughter wasn't as easy as it might have been. He looked a bit sulky, and she knew that wouldn't help at all.

'Daddy won't mind what I do or who I do it with!' she said and gave another of her brilliant smiles. 'It's only if he thinks I'm neglecting him. And even with my own ways and means I can't get more than two tickets for a show like *Brigadoon* and if he knew I'd decided to share them with you instead of him, then he'd be hurt. I'm not trying to avoid trouble for me, you see – I just don't want to hurt the dear old buffer's feelings.'

'As long as that's all it is. Bad enough the fight with your brother – he got pretty shirty over that –'

'Oh, Ambrose!' She waved her hand airily, dismissing Ambrose, but watching him carefully for all that. Please don't be frightened, dear, dear Jay, don't be frightened by anything. Just look at me, think of me, love me. 'He's always doing that.'

'Doing what?'

'Getting drunk at parties, making a scene. Been doing it for years. Daddy used to be able to do things to stop him, but not any more, not since he got some of his own money.'

'What money?' Jay leaned forward now, and looked closely at her, and Maddie lifted her chin to match the way her belly lifted with sudden excitement. 'Is your brother a rich man like your Pa?'

'Not rich, exactly. Not according to Daddy. It's money he got from my mother's will, when he was twenty-one. That was almost two years ago. I'll get my share when I'm twenty-one, New Year's Eve – well, Day, really, 1951. For ever to wait! But Ambrose has got his and spent most of it, Daddy says. He says he'll be skint in another year, the way he's going and then Daddy'll be able to sort him out properly. He just laughs, because he says sooner or later Ambrose'll have to do it his way, and a chap has to sow his wild oats. It's what makes a man a man.'

'I wish my Pa thought that way,' Jay said with more feeling than she had heard in his voice before. 'Sending me to this lousy country to shiver and half starve and no decent bourbon anywhere, and all because of –' He had shrugged then and leaned back. 'So your Dad isn't mad at me for hitting Ambrose?'

'Oh, he didn't like that much. But he knows what Ambrose is like, and he won't be really angry at you. Even if he is, he'll get over it. But let's not let him know I'd rather be at the theatre with you than with him.' And again she laughed her special silvery laugh. It had been worth practising that because now he grinned at her, a really nice friendly look and again she shivered with the excitement of it.

'You're a funny kid, you know,' he said. 'You remind me of my sister Bernie. One minute she's all over me and the next she's laughing and kicking her heels up like some colt. A real kid –'

She was devastated. All this effort to make him notice her, to get to know him properly, to make him love her, and all he could say was that? Where had she gone wrong?

'I'm not a kid. I'm –'

'Sure.' He grinned even wider. 'Nineteen. So old!'

'And you? Are you so old?'

'Six years more than you are, my child! Twenty-five soon – another six weeks –' And now he stopped grinning. 'And not a goddamned thing to call my own. It's crazy. There's my Pa loaded with it, and what have I got? I have to beg him for every lousy cent and if he says go away, I have to go away. I tell you, it's a lousy business being my age – a kid like you, what can you know what it's like?'

'It's not easy being my father's daughter either,' she said then, not pretending now, not acting any more, not trying at all to impress him or catch his fancy. Just talking. 'There's only us, me and Ambrose, and with Ambrose doing all his wild-oats stuff, it's really only me as far as Daddy's concerned. He's in charge, you see. I have to wriggle and slide and cheat to live any of my own life. And really I do love him. I mean, I don't hate him or anything. I just have to –' She shrugged, 'cheat a little. That's the way it is. For me as well as for you.'

He smiled at her, now. A warm nice smile, not a grin that mocked at her or a polite grimace just because she was talking at him. A real look-at-us-we're-together-and-we-like-it sort of smile, and she felt her own face crease to match and contemplated the bubble of accord that hung in the air between them. It was the first such moment since she had first seen him facing her when the Paul Jones music had stopped at her birthday party, and he had been there, brought by chance, magical wonderful chance, to be her partner. She had known then what he was to be, that he was not just the most beautiful man she had ever seen but also the most important one she would ever know.

It was beginning, the rest of her life was beginning. It could only get better and better from now on.

October 1986

There's nothing useful I can do here, Annie thought as Gresham's voice, light, cheerful and oh so reasonable, went on and on, nothing at all. I should never have agreed to come on this damned committee in the first place, and now I'm here, I should have the sense to say so, and get up and go. And she imagined herself doing just that; getting to her feet, pushing back her chair, saying in ringing tones, 'I've had enough of this. It's a waste of time and I'm bored. I'm going. Goodbye.' And she'd go and never look at Joe Labosky at all, leaving him sitting there staring after her –

The image was so strong that she actually felt her thigh muscles tense beneath the table; but she didn't get up. As usual the inertia that filled her was too heavy to allow her to do anything. And after all, what did it matter where she was, or what she did? What did it matter whether she was interested or bored? She couldn't imagine ever being interested in anything again, and for a moment she tried to remember if there had ever been a time when living had been amusing, purposeful, worth the effort, but again the dead inertia swamped her, and she just sat and listened.

Down the table Joe Labosky leaned forwards and so moved into her line of vision and she looked at him and he winked outrageously, and she found herself almost smiling back, almost against her will. He made her angry, the way he meddled, had done ever since the day he had first come marching into the living room at the old house, so full of himself, but it was hard to dislike him. He looked so ridiculous for a start; all that fluffy dark hair curling all over his head and the long chin and the big mouth that was more often than not curved upwards; how could anyone dislike him? But he was often irritating and this morning was no exception, because he was talking about her now.

'As I see it, this is something our patients' representative could help deal with. You say there are just these three patients you're concerned about?'

'I'm concerned about them all,' Gresham said, reprovingly.

'But yes, there are just the three for whom we have no disposal plans at present and need help –'

'Disposal?' Joe said, and there was a sardonic note in his voice. 'You make it sound as though you'd be just as happy to polish 'em off with a shot of something lethal and pop 'em into the incinerator.'

Gresham reddened but managed to laugh lightly. 'Always so witty, Dr Labosky – you know quite well what I mean.' He tapped the file in front of him. 'This came up from the Department labelled as you see it – Disposal – and it refers entirely to where patients are to be sent when we close the West Pavilion. Forty-six to the neighbouring boroughs –' He flashed another of his emollient smiles round the table then. 'And I do think someone might have congratulated me with my fiddling of the books on this, you know,' he said with mock petulance. 'To find forty-six patients with family addresses outside this borough and make them another authority's problem – it really is the cheapest and most satisfactory way to deal with disposal. And –' he added hastily as he caught Joe's eyes on him again, 'a most compassionate and – er – humane way to solve the problem. It means patients will be nearer their families and there'll be more visiting and presents and so forth for them –'

'Oh, come off it, Gresham,' Joe said, but there was no malice in his tone, 'you know as well as I do that most of the addresses you got hold of are long since forgotten by the patients who are supposed to have come from them, and certainly the people who live in them now won't be taking any responsibility. That's a bit of bureaucratic fiddling you've been up to, and let's not pretend it's been anything else.'

Gresham grinned, disarmingly. 'And it's got us well off the hook, hasn't it? So it can't be all bad. And the patients won't come to any harm in other hospitals.'

'Until they want to sell 'em off like this one,' growled the tall black man at the far end of the table. He was sitting very upright, very neat in his grey suit and tightly knotted blue tie and glittering white shirt. 'Where will they go then?'

'I'm afraid that isn't part of my remit, Mr Oliver. I simply have to make sure that all the patients currently at Greenhill are dispersed. With your help, of course. What happens to them afterwards can't be our concern – we've far too much to worry about as it is. I can't impress too much on all of you how urgent

22

this matter is. If the developers can't get in here to complete clearance of the site by the end of the financial year in April there's a real risk the deal will collapse. There's a time clause in the contract – and that means a fifteen million pound development up in flames, the DHSS in one hell of a state –'

'Well, I'll tell you, Mr Gresham, that that is no part of my worry.' Mr Oliver stuck his chin forwards and looked ferocious. 'I was asked to serve on this here committee to represent the interests of the non-medical staff –'

'And the non-*secretarial* staff –' murmured the large woman in red on the far side of the table.

'– and the non-secretarial, all right, Mrs Franey, I won't make no claim to your fancy ladies – I repeat, the other non-medical staff, but that don't mean I'm not interested in the patients or that my people aren't. That's what you senior types with fancy ideas about how important you are always do – forget porters and cleaners and suchlike. They don't care about patients, you think, but I'm here to tell you that the members of my union, and our brother unions, we care about the patients more than some of you lot do, and I say –'

'Come, Mr Oliver, no need to get aerated.' Gresham smiled easily at him down the table. 'No one doubts for a moment your commitment to your work or to the welfare of the patients at Greenhill. But we must be practical – and –' And he looked pointedly at the clock on the wall above his head, twisting himself elegantly in his chair, 'and we really must get on. As I was saying, forty-six to neighbouring boroughs. Thirty to the hostel at Pattison Way on the Larcombe Estate and another thirty to the Foster's Walk hostel on the Norbury Corners Estate. No, Miss Barber, not now. We'll deal with the matter of the nursing accommodation and arrangements later, after the meeting. No need to waste everyone's valuable time with minutiae, is there? Then there are twenty-three patients to be discharged home to the care of their families –'

'And I'd like to know just how much support is going to be provided for them too. Not the patients – the families. As far as I can tell, this business of being put back into the community means lumbering some poor bloody woman somewhere with all the work and the headaches and –'

'Yes, Mr Fordyce, we know your views on the matter. We've

23

heard them often and have digested them carefully.' Mr Gresham's veneer was beginning to wear a little thin now and he almost glowered at the man in pugnaciously casual clothes who was sitting on the far side of him. 'You must not think that the nursing staff has a monopoly of caring, you know. There are those amongst us who are just as concerned for the happiness and welfare of patients and their families as you are. And Miss Matthews who is the patients' and families' representative has made no demur to the plans we've outlined here, so I really don't think we need to go haring off down that cul de sac again. We've spent the last two meetings on it, after all –'

'Jimmy, no need to worry,' Joe said. 'The medical staff committee have been dealing with that matter in some depth. We've got a considerable commitment from the Department of Social Services for the borough, and we're pushing for more. I'll tell you after this meeting, if you'll just wait for me. Let's sort out first what these arrangements are to be, hmm? Then we can do what's necessary to make sure they're good arrangements and that they'll work to the patients' benefit.'

Joe didn't like taking over meetings like this, and rarely did it, but this morning's had been particularly heavy going and showed signs of getting worse, and using the weight of his position as the sole medical member was the only way he could think of to improve matters. It was worth doing damage to his decent democratic principles, a part of his mind thought, to get this bloody business settled for good and all. 'So, according to the arithmetic, that leaves three patients not accounted for. Tell us again who they are, Gresham.'

Gresham, who had bridled a little at the way Joe had taken control, moved his shoulders petulantly as a bird does when it is ready to preen and said a little sulkily, 'Yes. Just three. And if we can sort them out, we're really on stream for getting through in time. We've already disposed of – made arrangements for – the seven pavilions at the north side of the site and there'll just be the last two hundred patients to sort out from South Pavilion, and since most of them are under fifty, it won't be so difficult to find places. It's these old long-term people who make the real problems – no one wants them. It's even easier to dispose of – damn it, find places for – the mentally handicapped than it is for these geriatrics.'

'They aren't all geriatrics,' growled the male nurse. 'I've plenty in my ward there in West who're under sixty. Or are you suggesting that all folks o' that age are automatically geriatrics?' And he thrust his chin at Gresham who blinked and smiled and tugged on his tie, very aware suddenly of his own thirty-eight years as compared with Fordyce's fifty-seven.

'Yes, Mr Fordyce, two of these difficult cases are yours, are they not? Ah – let's see –' And he pulled the file towards him again and began rifling importantly among them. 'Ah, here we are. Jimmy Teague, on Ward Six – that is your ward, is it not, Mr Fordyce? – and Ted ah – Meakins, I think it is. Both your patients, then. And been here at Greenhill since the middle nineteen-fifties, as I see. Not been able to rehabilitate them, then, Mr Fordyce, for all your new methods of therapy?' And he looked at the pugnacious little man with a malicious glint and grinned.

'Hell, I'm not rising to bait as stinkin' as that, Gresham!' Jimmy said disgustedly. 'Those two poor bastards were ruined well before I was able to get the care of them. Both had lobotomies in the early fifties. Would you believe it, Dr Labosky? Brain surgery! Chopped their bloody brains in half and then expect us to be able to rehabilitate them! That's psychiatry for you!'

'That *was* psychiatry for you,' Joe said equably. 'Thank God fasting for the past tense. They'd stopped it before I came on the scene too, but they left their messes behind. I'm not sure there's a lot you can do with those two chaps, Gresham. I know them both well enough – and I have to tell you they're heavy going. They could never cope in a hostel and as for families of their own – who knows? Have they ever had any visitors, Jimmy?'

'Is the Pope a Catholic?' Jimmy gave a little crack of laughter. 'Not like you to ask daft questions, Dr L.'

'I thank you for the vote of confidence. No, I thought not. Well, it might be worth digging out the old records to see what we can discover about them. Maybe they too can be found to be the residents of other boroughs and Mr Gresham can do some of his magic shuffling of the books, hmm? If not – well, David Michaels at the Octagon Hospital in East Anglia is doing some research on brain-damaged individuals and I might be able to get him to take these two chaps into one of his cohorts. They'd come to no harm, Xavier,' he added hastily as the black man lifted his head sharply. 'All they do at the Octagon is try to teach brain-damaged people various skills and measure the rate at which they learn. It's stimulating and possibly therapeutic for the patients and they get excellent physical care while they're there. They've got a big grant from one of the foundations, lucky bastards, so the research'll go on for years – it'll see Teague and Meakins out. So, see what you can do, Jimmy, hmm? We'll find a solution for those two that won't upset any of you, I promise.'

'Which leaves just one problem,' Gresham said in great satisfaction. 'And that was the one –'

'Yes,' Joe said and turned his head to look at Annie. 'That was the one I thought Miss Matthews might be able to help us with.'

'I can't do anything,' Annie said abruptly, and her voice sounded harsh even in her own ears. 'I have too much to do at home –'

'What?' Joe lifted his brows at her.

'I've just moved in,' she said, trying not to sound defensive. 'You know that perfectly well. I had to sell the house when my mother died and get a flat. And now I've moved in and I've still so much to do –'

'Nothing that won't wait,' Joe said and again produced that grin of his and she felt her own lips tighten in response. 'You've been there four months already, and you should be tolerably settled by now. A brand-new flat, after all –'

He was right, of course. He always damned well was, that was the trouble. It had been he who had chivvied her into selling the old house, which was absurdly too big for her, and anyway was in the way of the new development that was happening in that part of the suburb, he who had seen to it that she had sold at a ridiculously high price and then found a new flat for her, filled with every modern convenience she could ever need, at half the price she had got for her house. What with that and the surprisingly large sum of money Jennifer had left, she was well off. 'No need to worry about money at all, any more,' Joe had said. 'A woman of independent means, that's you, more's the pity.'

And she had refused to ask him what he meant by that,

because she knew perfectly well. He wanted her to have some purpose in life, something to get up for in the mornings, to make life worth living. If she didn't have to earn her keep, what else was there? So he had made her come on to the close-down committee, as patients' representative, refusing to take no for an answer, and what could she do? The awful heaviness of her inertia worked for him against her. So here she sat, knowing she couldn't argue with him on whatever it was he wanted her to do now, any more than she had been able to unpack the massive tea chests and boxes full of Jen's things that still lay about the flat, quite untouched. Home was anything but comfortable and pleasant, so there wasn't even a desire to be there to act as spur to any resistance to him.

'So,' Joe went on inexorably, 'I'm sure you can cope with this task. I'll explain, with your permission, Gresham?' And not waiting for an answer he leaned across and picked up Gresham's file and then turned to Annie, speaking to her as though there were no one else there at all apart from themselves.

'This patient, Annie, is a woman called Maddie. As far as we can tell she was admitted to Greenhill in 1953, transferred here from a general hospital in Southampton. I can't tell you why, because the current notes don't include the information.'

'So?' Annie said. 'What has this to do with me?'

'We need the information.' Gresham could bear his exclusion no longer. 'Until we know more about her and where she came from, we can't make — er — arrangements for her further care.'

'One of the hostels?' Annie didn't want any task at all, wanted nothing more to do with this committee, this hospital, or its patients, than she had to have. She was only here because Joe Labosky had bullied her. 'Can't she go to a hostel?'

'Certainly not!' That was Betty Barber, the female nurse representative. 'She's not fit for that sort of care at all. My nurses will be on their own in that environment with no medical or para-medical backup, and that means that patients have to be fully ambient, cooperative, and with a certain amount of sense about them. This one — no way can she come to a hostel! You'd have a nursing strike on your hands if she did, and so I warn you — I've told you from the start we won't have those very sick people sent out hugger-mugger and willy-nilly this way and –'

'No one is sending anyone anywhere that is not suitable, Miss Barber,' Joe said soothingly. 'That is why I want Miss Matthews to concern herself with this patient. A patient of yours, is she not? Yes, of course – you tell Annie, will you, what the problems are?'

And he leaned back in his chair in a practised fashion and at once Betty Barber launched herself into an account of her patient. It really is too easy, Joe thought as he watched and listened, to manipulate people. Maybe I ought to give up psychiatry and go into industry and make my bloody fortune instead of sitting here in this dilapidated place allowing myself to be coerced into supporting a system of pushing patients around just so that the damned government can sell off a valuable hospital site for cash – and he made a grimace at himself and turned to watch Annie's reaction to what Betty was telling her.

'She's a helpless old thing, poor Maddie,' Betty was saying importantly. 'Well, maybe not that helpless at that. There's malice in her, and sharpness. She certainly gets her own way, which is to do nothing and get the other patients to wait on her. I can't get her to join in on any of the ward activities, she won't respond to anything, not occupational therapy or drama or music or art or anything. Just sits there in the corner day after day rocking. Never speaks, never looks at anyone. Just rocks. Done it for years, as far as I know. I've been here fifteen and it's all I've ever seen her do. Poor soul!'

'What – I mean, why is she like that? What's wrong with her?' Annie threw a sudden terrified glance at Joe and he heard the words that were in her head as loudly as if she had spoken them, and he leaned forwards at once to speak directly to her.

'There is no dementia, Annie,' he said quietly. 'No senility, no evidence of brain damage. I've checked her frequently. This is not a case of Alzheimer's or anything like that. Be sure of it. This lady has simply withdrawn herself totally. I don't believe it to be an organic problem, though some of my colleagues have thought so. She's been labelled as schizophrenia, catatonia, you name it, someone's thought of it. But I think it's totally functional. She needs to find out how to relate to someone, how

28

to speak again. She's been an elective mute for thirty-five years, but that doesn't mean she wouldn't have something to say to the right person. I think it could be you.'

'Why me? Why – haven't – I've got enough –' she began and then, suddenly aware that there were after all other people present, subsided, her face red.

'Because I think you can help her.' Joe got to his feet. 'That's why. And we need you to do it. If it isn't done now, I don't know what will happen to Maddie. She's not a suitable candidate for the Octagon, and even Gresham can't fiddle the books to dispose of her. No one can say whether she's happy or miserable, she's so unresponsive, but I can't help thinking that moving her without trying to sort out something about her would be tantamount to killing her. And though that would be one way of making sure the DHSS got their millions for this valuable development site, I doubt many of us would regard it as an ideal solution. Not even you, Gresham, hmm?' and he smiled at Gresham with such warmth that he said, 'What? Oh, yes, absolutely, Dr Labosky,' without realising what he was saying.

'She's on the ground floor of the West Pavilion, Annie. I want to talk to Mr Fordyce about the Octagon arrangements, but I'll take you over there and introduce you – for want of a better word – to Maddie if you'll just wait for me. I'm sure you'll find her a most interesting project.' And he nodded at Gresham and lifted his chin at Jimmy Fordyce, with whom he left the room as the rest of the committee got to its collective feet and went away, leaving Gresham furiously collecting his papers and aware that yet again that bloody psychiatrist had made him look – and what was worse feel – like an office boy.

And Annie, sitting staring down at her hands on her lap, was equally furious with herself for letting Joe bulldoze her once again into an action she didn't want, and not knowing what she could do about it.

I feel like the East Pavilion, she thought then, as Gresham at last left, and she was alone in the room. I'm being eaten up by a prehistoric monster, and its name is Joe Labosky.

3

August 1949

Maddie, planning. Maddie sitting up in bed in her pretty pink room in the flat overlooking Regent's Park, wrapped in her pink frilled dressing gown and drinking hot chocolate and planning. All round her there is silence; Daddy gone to the races at the White City to watch his own dogs run, his favourite way to spend an evening lately, and Ambrose out heaven knows where, no one in but Maddie, because even the housekeeper has gone to drink coffee with some of the other Displaced Persons who clean the flats in the block. A good chance to think and plan and perhaps, act. And she sips her chocolate, lovely chocolate Daddy got from America, and thinks hard.

And it is the chocolate that gives her the idea she needs and she puts down the cup on the bedside table and lies back with her hands behind her head and stares up at the ceiling, laughing inside her head. She's been brave enough to get this far, she can be brave enough to go the rest of the way. Can't she?

And then she remembers last night, and it gets difficult, because somehow it never works out precisely the way you want it to. Sometimes better, occasionally worse, but always different.

All these months of working at it. All these months of getting theatre tickets and arranging dinners in restaurants for three or four couples so that she and Jay can be one of them. All these months of asking him to come with her to sort out her car and to advise her on dealing with the mechanics, pretending she had no one to help her and praying no one would say anything in front of him that would show her father had already dealt with it all. All these months of accidentally happening to be where he was, at other people's houses and the nightclubs she had found out he liked. But it had worked eventually, and there they had been at Nancy Lewis's party on Midsummer Eve and when everyone had started necking she had drawn him to the only free sofa left and curled up there with him and at last he'd behaved as he was supposed to, holding her close and kissing her and making her feel unbelievably good. It wasn't as good yet as it was going to be, but oh, it was good enough for the present!

And at last he had started to ask her out, and she didn't have to work quite so hard at it, and they had dates like other people, when he made the plans and met her at Swan and Edgar's or at the Piccadilly Hotel, because of course it was out of the question that he should ever collect her at the flat, or bring her home afterwards, in case Daddy saw him. It was all wonderful now.

But not wonderful enough. It wasn't enough just to go out on dates; he had to be brought completely under her spell – she liked the sound of that phrase and thought it again – completely under her spell, and adore her as much as she adored him. But last night –

And now, suddenly, the chocolate she was drinking had given her an idea, showed her how she could make him hers as he was meant to be, totally and completely, and she rolled out of bed and ran into the drawing room to the telephone.

He was, glory be, there at home in his flat in St John's Wood, and she curled herself small in the armchair and breathed into the mouthpiece, 'Hello, my darling!'

'Oh, hi,' he said after a moment. 'How are you?' He sounded distant and a little flat, but that was the problem with a telephone. You couldn't touch people, make them look at you, make them really feel you were necessary to them, on the telephone.

'Lonely. How about you?'

'Mmm? Oh, no, not really. Busy in fact. Doing a few chores.'

'Like what?'

'Oh, letters home. You know, those sort of chores. My mother gets bothered if she doesn't get a letter every other day. I make her settle for one a week, but it has to be at least that. So I'd better –'

'I was thinking – you remember what I was saying to you last night?'

'Now, listen, Maddie, I told you.. You're a crazy kid, and –'

'Don't you like me? Don't you want me to be happy? And don't you want me to make *you* happy? Hmm?' She made her voice as deep and throaty as she could, and then laughed softly.

'Listen, Jay, listen to me carefully – I'm stroking you, just like I did last night. Remember? The back of your neck, first, and then your shoulders. Very soft and very light, just stroking you – feel it? And now my fingers are slipping and sliding, and I'm stroking your back, down across your shoulder blades and now I'm there – just *there* in the small of your back, just under the belt of your trousers – feel it? My fingers, soft and ve–ry smooth, stroking and touching you – feel it?'

She knew it was working, because he was so silent and she went on, talking softly, describing what she was doing and then suddenly he laughed, a thick sort of laugh and said, 'Jeez, Maddie, you are one hell of a crazy kid, the things you think of. Will you stop that?'

'Don't you like it?'

'You know damn well I do. Too much. You ought to be ashamed of yourself –'

'Why? Because I love you?'

'Listen, Maddie, I told you last night, it's crazy. You're a great girl, believe me, but I can't even begin to think about – what would your Pa say? You can't fool me, you know, with your stories. He'd go mad if he thought you had a beau. And if he found it was me you were after –'

'He'll have to face it sooner or later. I'm grown up, almost twenty now and –'

'Not for another six months. You don't get your own money for another year and a half, you're just a kid. And anyway, your family and mine – it's just not on the cards. Even if –'

'Even if nothing,' she said it quickly, scared of what he might have been meaning to say, refusing even to think about that. 'And I told you, Daddy'll have to come round. I can be patient. To get married, I mean, I can wait. Eighteen months – it's no time, not if we can be together and do things together – not like last night.' Again her voice dropped. '*More* than last night.'

'Listen, Maddie, you've got to stop this sort of talk. I tried to tell you, didn't I? But will you listen? Like hell you will. I never said a word to you, not ever, that anyone could take to mean I was saying we should –'

'I said it all,' she said immediately. 'I know. I promise I won't ever say it was your idea. It's mine. I love you. I told you, I love you and that's all there is to it. I want you more than I've ever wanted anything in the whole world, and – and I always get what I want in the end.'

Daddy had taught her that, a long time ago. If you want something, go and get it, he'd say. Never sit there and hope it'll come to you. Only schmucks do that. You have to go and make it come to you. You can do a bit of hoping along the way to keep your spirits up, but if you want it, you can have it. You've a right to it. That's what Daddy said and she knew he was right.

There was a little silence. 'I thought I knew people who were go-getters,' he said at length. 'But you're something else. And such a kid!'

'Don't call me that,' she said sharply. 'I'm a woman, not a child. Don't call me that.'

'I've never even met a woman like you. Listen, didn't anyone ever tell you men don't like ballcrushers? That they like to make the running?'

'What?'

'You see what I mean? A kid. You don't even know what you don't know. Didn't anyone ever tell you that a feller likes to get his own girls?'

'A man chases a girl until she catches him,' she sang softly and laughed. 'I don't care what other people do. I used to read about it in the magazines, listen to the girls talking, tried to do what they said, but not any more. Now I know my father's got the right idea. Make up your mind what you want and then go and get it, he says. And I want you. I love you. Don't you love me?'

'Hell, what's love? What do I know about love?' He sounded uneasy. 'A lot of silly girl talk, that's all –'

'Not so silly when it means getting married and having children and –'

'You see what I mean? You're a crazy kid, talking rubbish. I'm not marrying anyone. As for having kids – I've had enough of that, thank you very much –'

'What?'

'Never mind – look, I have to go and write letters, Maddie. Do me a favour and stop this nonsense. I can't handle it – I mean, even if it was possible, can you imagine the family rows there'd be?'

'I told you, Daddy'll get used to the idea. He'd have to.'

'I'm not so worried about him, believe me. He's your problem, not mine. I have a family of my own, remember? My mother'd go crazy if I ever admitted I'd *talked* to a girl who wasn't a Catholic. Dammit, Maddie, I never even met a Protestant till I was seventeen! Can you imagine if I went home and said, "Hi, Mom, hi Pa, meet Maddie Braham. Religion? Hell, she ain't even a Christian far as I know" – can you imagine?'

'They'd come round if they had to.' A cold wriggle of anxiety was crawling in her now. This was something new, something her chocolate idea wouldn't help at all. He'd said nothing before about religious differences. And she tried to think how her father would be if she told him Jay was a Catholic and she was going to marry him. Would he mind? Would it matter? He'd never said anything to her about religion; it was there hazily in the background as something that made the Brahams different, but not something that had ever been important and she took a sharp little breath in through her nose and said quickly, 'Listen, Jay, that doesn't matter right now. Right now what matters is money, hmm?'

'You're not bloody kidding,' he said with more feeling than he'd shown yet. 'I told you last night, money is –' and she could almost see him shake his head as the soft whistle escaped from between his teeth and pursed lips.

'Well, I have an idea about that. A very useful idea. What'd you say to making yourself about – oh, I'm not sure. At least a thousand pounds.'

'How much? A thousand – that's four thousand dollars – how?'

'Come and have a cup of hot chocolate with me, Jay. And I'll tell you *all* about it. Come right away, now. You can finish your letters later. And there's no need to worry. Daddy's out till past midnight. Plenty of time to explain it all. And for one or two other things too, maybe –'

And she laughed softly, throatily, again, and hung up the phone.

November 1986

Their feet crunched on the gravel of the path and she watched the small stones spit up under her shoes as they walked, keeping

34

her head well down. Why didn't I just sit there and refuse to get up when he came back to fetch me? Why didn't I just say, 'No, I'm going home'? I don't have to do things just because he tells me to.

'You know, there's no compulsion here, Annie,' Joe said as though she had spoken her thoughts aloud and she shifted her gaze from her own walking feet to his, alongside her. 'I want you to be willing to take on this job.'

'Really?' she said harshly. 'No compulsion? You surprise me. Listening to you in the boardroom I'd have said there was a lot of compulsion going on.'

'Well, it's not going on now. We can stop right here and you can go back to the car and drive back to the flat and just not bother with Maddie.'

'Why the change of tack?'

'No change.' He stopped walking and perforce she had to stop too. 'I said I thought you could help her. I still think so. I said it could be an interesting project for you. It could. But you have to want to.'

'Why should I?' She said it dully, still keeping her head down and staring at her feet. 'Why should I want anything? Why should it matter what I do? Why are you bothering me like this?'

'Because you can feel better than you do.' He moved forwards and turned round to stand before her and now she could see his feet in front of her as well as her own. Her shoes looked scuffed and dirty compared to his which were old and creased but well polished, and she felt a moment of shame and lifted her hand to smooth into a semblance of neatness the hair that had escaped from her bun and which was blowing round her ears, while she shuffled her feet a little, not wanting to look at her shoes. 'I feel fine,' she said.

'Don't be silly, for heaven's sake.' He sounded irritable suddenly. 'We all know that when people are depressed they try to hide the fact, but for Christ's sake, Annie, this is me, remember? I've known you long enough now, surely, to be regarded as a friend? Can't you trust me yet? Tell me the truth?'

Now she did look up, and stared at the way the wind moved his curly hair lightly and how his face was a little creased as he looked back. Creased but friendly. 'Hmm?' he said and smiled.

'Friend?' she said and put all the venom she could into the word. 'Is that what you're supposed to be?'

The corner of his mouth tightened slightly, but that was all, and after a moment he said, 'I hope so.'

'Oh,' and that was all she would say. No matter how he pushes, no matter what he does, she thought with sudden passion, I won't let him have the pleasure of hearing it. I won't. Why the hell should he feel good?

'Well, whether you know it or not, I am,' he said lightly. 'And what's more I'm a useful friend. Depressed people need friends who are psychiatrists.'

'Mad people need psychiatrists,' she said.

'Yes, so they do. But so do a lot of other people. You among 'em. So even if you can't accept my friendship, the fortunate thing is it's still there. Now, shall we go on to see Maddie? Will you help us with her? Now's the time to say one way or the other.'

Across the wide grassy slopes that led to the gates and the remains of the East Pavilion the sounds of the bulldozers came clanking at her together with the steady thwack of the iron ball being hurled at the walls, and she lifted her head and looked back. There were no watching patients now; just the workmen and their great ugly machines and beyond that the gates and the road and the tumble of suburban roofs falling down the hill towards the motorway, snaking along in the valley beneath. Somewhere down there on the far side of that ribbon of road crawling with traffic was her flat, and she suddenly saw it in all its dreariness. The newly painted walls in their buttercup yellow and the clutter of packing cases everywhere and her bed tumbled with its duvet, unmade, unwelcoming, and the kitchen with its empty refrigerator and just a packet of tea and a bottle of milk on the table, and tried to find pleasure in the thought of leaving him standing here and going back there. And because there was none to be found, deliberately called up the pain of remembering the old house, with Jennifer sitting slumped in her armchair amid all her treasures and her ornaments and her overstuffed furniture and gilded peach mirrors. But all that happened was that her eyes filled with tears of rage and pain and misery.

He paid no attention to that; he just moved back to be by her side and took her elbow and began walking again and she made no demur and went with him. Whatever they were to find in the West Pavilion, it couldn't be as bad as what she'd find if she went back to the flat. There there would be only herself with all her memories and thoughts waiting for her on the doorstep. In the West Pavilion there would be someone worse off than she was. And ugly though it was to find comfort in that, it was better than going on as she was. Somewhere deep inside her there was still a fragment of common sense, a shred of desire to feel better, and it was, she told herself drearily as they reached the paved path that ran round to the front door of the building, worth nurturing that. So she allowed him to lead her into the building, letting them in with his own key.

It smelled. That was the first thing of which she was aware, the layers of odours that assaulted her. Above all, disinfectant, raw and rough and powerful, rising from the ferociously clean tiles of the floor and from the glossy yellow paintwork of the high walls. Then there was floor polish, thick and heavy in her nostrils, and after that cooked food – glutinous greyish sort of food – and old plimsolls and sweating human bodies and, faintly, flowers, and the shock of it was so powerful that the tears came to her eyes again, actually stinging her lids.

It was as though the past six months hadn't happened, as though she had just brought Jen to the East Pavilion to spend the long weekend so that she, Annie, could go to Paris for Easter. It had taken her weeks of planning, weeks of anxiety and guilt, but Joe had said it would be all right, that the hospital would take care of Jen, there'd be no need for her to worry; and what had happened?

Not two hours after she had arrived in Paris, when she had just taken her clothes out of her weekend bag and arranged them in the neat and pretty room on the third floor of the Hotel de Pavillon in the Rue St Dominique, and was eagerly about to take the five-minute walk to the Esplanade des Invalides to start her much-longed-for holiday weekend at last, the telephone call had come, and she had stood there in the little reception area with the concierge of the hotel watching her with avid curiosity and been told that Jen had collapsed and died.

A stroke, they had said. A blessed release, they had said.

Nobody's fault, they had said. An act of God. But for Annie it hadn't been an act of God. It had been an act of Annie's and now she stood in the clean cold lobby of the West Pavilion and smelled the Greenhill smell and felt the cold hand that had held on to her ever since Paris tighten its hold, and it was all as though it had happened yesterday.

Whether he knew how she felt, she didn't know. It didn't really matter, after all. But he did the right thing, setting an arm across her shoulders so that she had to walk forwards, and so led her, without any effort, to the big double doors that led to the ground floor ward.

'No matter what we do to make these places better, they always strike horror into me,' he said, as their footsteps echoed across the tiles. 'They're hellish to come into, and they make everyone feel lousy when they come through the door. But it's never so bad in the wards themselves, is it? And they are at least all different.' And he pushed open the doors so that she could see into the ward beyond.

Quite different, of course. The ward where Jen had been and where she had died had been a long medical one, with rows of beds and lockers neat and organised like teeth in a widely open mouth. That ward had cried out its closeness to pain and death. But this one was not like that. This was a big open room with chairs set in clusters round tables with jigsaw puzzles and magazines on them. There were curtained windows and screened sections behind which red counterpaned beds, arranged in fours, could just be seen. There was a television set with a big screen flickering and muttering to itself in a far corner, and in another three men argued shrilly over a small billiard table. Old women watched the television set in one group, while another sat beside the jigsaw puzzles, staring at them but making no attempt to do anything with them. At first glance it looked ordinary enough, cheerful even, until the eye wandered and saw other details; a man standing by a window and gesticulating furiously and obscenely out of it at the trees; a woman with long grey hair straggling over her shoulders marching up and down purposefully, over and over again using the same carefully circumscribed dozen feet of floor; a girl in a corner, weeping. It was like looking at a Richard Dadd painting she thought, then; at first you think it's just prettiness and charm in fairyland and then you look closer and the faces are distorted and malevolent, and the soft colours threatening and sickly.

She turned, wanting to go now because it hadn't been like this in the ward where Jen had come to spend her last hours, so that her selfish daughter could go and enjoy herself in Paris. That ward had been what a ward should be, antiseptic and redolent of disease. This was a different sort of horror, where nothing was quite as it seemed and where decent reticence and good behaviour and politeness were peeling off like paint from a sunburned door.

But he seemed unaware of her attempt to turn away and walked on, very directly and quickly, leading her across the polished floor, past the marching old woman and the weeping girl to a chair which stood with its back to them, facing out of the window.

'Here she is, Annie,' he said cheerfully. 'Your new project. Meet Maddie.' And he took his hand from her shoulders and reached for the chair and pulled it round so that she could see the occupant.

4

August 1949

Maddie, confused. Maddie not sure that she was saying the right things, frightened she would scare him off, yet driven to say them all the same, because they were so exciting, because just using the words made the skin over her belly crawl as though he were actually touching her, even though he was in fact sitting a little remote and chill in the armchair facing her.

'Why not? This is 1949, for heaven's sake! You're sounding like – like a Victorian frump! I told you I love you! I want to give you all of myself, now and for ever –'

'If you're going to talk like that, I'm going right now,' he said, though he didn't move. 'It's all such guff – real romantic guff. Real people don't carry on that way, Maddie! You've been reading too many romantic magazines.'

'No, I have not,' she cried passionately. 'Don't make such a fool of me! I love you, for God's sake! Ever since that very first time I set eyes on you and we danced I've been crazy about you! I tried not to tell you, but it was like – it was like I was in a river and the water just went too fast for me. You're stuck with me, Jay Kincaid, whether you like it or not. And I so much want you to like it, my darling – I so much do! And you could, believe me. I can see we can't be married yet, but I have plans to make it easier for us, to get you the money you need, but until then we can be lovers the way we were surely meant to be –'

She knew, of course, that he was right. She was spouting a lot of romantic gush, letting the words tumble out of her, but it was true even if it was gush. She ached with excitement whenever he was near her, and ached even more with emptiness whenever he wasn't. Until she could make him understand how much a part of her life he was now, and always would be, there was no other comfort for her, no other way to express her feelings except in showers of flowery words.

He laughed, staring at her and she stared back, trying to see behind his eyes to what he was thinking. But all she saw was the beautiful face and the thick dark gold hair, smooth as honeyed toast.

'I've come across some girls in my time, Maddie, but none like you. D'you really believe all the things you're saying? I'll just bet that if I took you at your word and came on strong and tried to get you into bed, you'd scream blue bloody murder.'

'Try me!' she said and leapt to her feet and with shaking fingers pulled at the tie on her frilly dressing gown to take it off. To display herself in all her lovely nakedness in front of him – oh, that would be the pinnacle, the very tiptop magical pinnacle of –

'Hey, hey!' he said hastily, sitting up straight. 'None of that! Okay, okay, I'll believe you. But Jesus, girl, I'm going to have to look after you. You're not safe out –'

'I love you,' she said simply and let her fingers fall. She wanted to show herself to him, wanted him to make love to her, all the way love, too, not the silly petting they'd been doing, but that couldn't be hurried. He had to be as sure as she was, and as eager. It wouldn't be any pleasure otherwise. She didn't know how she knew that, but she was certain she was right. 'I'm safe as long as I'm with you. So please, Jay, will you agree? That one day we'll be married?'

He was still leaning forwards and staring at her. 'You're quite a girl, aren't you? If you were plain it'd be different. I'd just put it down to being over-anxious and hearing wedding bells in your sleep. God knows Boston's full of that sort and they've been after me for years. But you don't have to do that, do you? You're pretty –'

'Pretty enough for you?' she said swiftly. 'Really pretty, the sort that you'd be happy to have around you after a long time? Ten years, twenty years pretty?'

'Pretty,' he said. 'And no fool. And your Pa's got plenty of the necessary too. You don't have to come on strong like this just to get a living, do you? So it must be true, I guess. All that stuff about love –'

'It's true,' she said. 'I keep telling you, I love you –'

'What was this plan you had? The one I came here to talk about?' He leaned back abruptly and folded his arms across his chest and stared at her.

She blinked. 'You agree then? We'll be married as soon as it's practical? And until then we –'

'I agree nothing,' he said firmly.

'– and until then we are lovers,' she went on, her eyes very bright and fixed on his, and after a moment his gaze wavered and slid away.

'You're being ridiculous,' he muttered. 'I came here to talk about some moneymaking notion you had and –'

'And about the reason for making the money. So that you and I can be free of my father and of your family and do what we want to do. If it's money that you need to make you feel safe with me, all right, I'll help you make it. That's easy –' She looked scornful for a moment. 'I don't know why you make such a fuss about it. I've listened to my father long enough and often enough. Anyway, I only had to ask. He's never kept me short. And with the best part of thirty thousand due to me when I'm twenty-one –'

'Thirty thousand – around a hundred thousand dollars,' Jay said and lifted his brows. 'And your own. It's easy for you to be offhand about money. We're not all so fortunate.'

'Your father's rich, isn't he? My father said they've been making money together for years.'

'He's stinking with it,' Jay said bitterly. 'And it's all his. Every lousy cent of it. Seven of us and we all have to go to him cap in hand to ask favours. Why the hell else do you think I'm stuck here in this stinking country, short of everything that makes life worth living? Even my mother lets him treat us that way – it makes me sick –'

'If that's all the problem is, we can sort that out.' She sounded very offhand. 'I told you, I can help you make money.'

'A thousand pounds, you said. Four and a half thousand dollars –'

'That's just for starters.' She smiled at him sweetly and pulled her bare feet up to tuck them beneath her dressing gown hem, curling her arms round her knees so that she could rest her chin on them. 'I told you, I didn't know it was so important. Now I do, we'll soon sort it all out.'

'How?'

'We'll be married, then?'

He laughed. 'Oh, stop all that! Wait and see how things turn out, okay? Who can say what we'll want to do this time next year? As long as my pockets are in my father's charge, I'm in no position to make any promises. But I'll come on like Sam Goldwyn and give you a definite maybe. How's that?'

'And we become lovers?' She still sat there in the big armchair with her chin perched on her knees and her arms entwined round her legs, looking very young and vulnerable and he smiled then and shook his head.

'I got into enough trouble down that road in Boston. Why the hell do you think I'm here? I want no pregnant girls looking for obliging doctors this side of the Atlantic, thank you very much.'

She managed not to show in her face how much that hurt.

'There are ways of making sure that doesn't happen,' she said, as airily as she could. 'People don't have to get pregnant.' She knew that was so from the hints of such matters she had found in her women's magazines. Quite what they were she didn't know, but there were ways of finding out. And find out she would.

He looked genuinely shocked. 'I told you, Maddie. I'm a good Catholic! I can't use things like that. It'd be as much as I dared.'

'But if a girl gets pregnant you don't mind her finding an obliging doctor? Is that all right for good Catholics?'

'Listen, I won't even talk about it with you! Where do you get off, asking things like that? Mind your tongue, or you can go to hell with all your schemes, however much money there might be in them.' He had gone brick-red suddenly and she lifted her eyebrows at him and laughed softly.

'Nice to see I can make you take something I say really seriously. All right, I apologise if I've offended you.'

'Well, okay,' he said sulkily after a long pause. 'But watch your tongue in future. If you can. Which I'm beginning to doubt.'

'Oh, I can if I have to,' she said cheerfully and smiled at him brilliantly. 'I dare say I'll find a way to sort that out anyway. I mean, making sure I don't get pregnant. I wouldn't want that either. Not yet.'

'I'm glad to hear it.' He sounded sardonic. 'I'm beginning to think there wasn't anything you didn't want right away.'

'Just you,' she said softly. 'Just you. And you might as well give in, because you're mine now.'

'We'll see about that. Anyway, I didn't come here to talk about such stuff. If you want to tell me about the money thing, okay. Otherwise I'm heading for home to write my letters. It's been a crazy waste of time to come over here. I must have been mad.'

'Oh, no you weren't,' she said swiftly, and uncurled herself and came out of her chair in one smooth movement. 'Now just you listen to me. Chocolate, that's the thing. I heard Daddy talking to Ambrose about chocolate last week. And the thing is –' and she began to explain it all to him and, at first with little interest but then with gradually increasing absorption, he listened. And as he did, slowly the scowl that had mantled his face melted away and was replaced by a look of smooth pleasure. Because it really was going to be very simple indeed to make that thousand pounds.

November 1986

It must, Annie thought involuntarily, have been a beautiful face, once. The eyelids were wide and heavy and even though she was now clearly well into late middle age, were smooth and showed no signs of sagging. The eyes beneath them were dark brown, very rich and deep in colour, and it seemed hard to believe that they saw nothing as they stared so fixedly into the middle distance. But it was clear they did not, because when Joe bent to speak to her, putting his face very close to hers, her gaze did not flicker for one moment. She just was not seeing whatever it was she appeared to be looking at. The eyes seemed to be intelligent and yet there was no hint of any thought there.

She had a high broad forehead and that too was smooth and expressionless and beneath her eyes the cheekbones lifted high and round and were as smooth as the forehead. The mouth was wide and full and, Annie thought, must once have been what is called mobile. She could imagine it moving, quirking, the corners flicking as she spoke, but all there was now was stillness, the lips half parted over strong yellowish teeth. The hair was a thick cloud of grey frizz that stood out over her head like an aureole and where the sun from the window caught the edges they glittered silver.

44

She was wearing a sacklike dress of washed-out blue cotton and her legs, surprisingly thin ones, were encased in wrinkled brown stockings and her feet were thrust into brown slippers with folded-over edges and ridiculous red woollen pompoms on the front. She had a red cardigan with torn pockets and missing buttons draped across her shoulders and her hands, with long unmanicured nails, were clasped in her lap, and Annie stared at the extraordinarily long fingers and again seemed to see behind her immobility the movement they were clearly designed to make. They should be active hands, she thought, hands that waved round expressively when their owner talked, the fingers flickering and busy, rather than slumped there dead in her lap like a tangle of twigs from a dead tree.

'Maddie,' Joe said softly and then more loudly, 'Maddie!' but the woman showed no awareness at all, just rocking gently backwards and forwards as she had been all the time. There was no change in the rhythm of her movements, nor was there any reaction in those dark eyes.

'I've tried all sorts of ways to get a response,' Joe said. 'So have the nurses, of course. We've tried to startle her, we've delivered noises so loud they must hurt, and tried delivering mildly painful stimuli. Pinches and so forth.' He shook his head. 'She is really quite extraordinarily detached. We thought at first it was control, but no one I think could maintain that sort of control so unremittingly. It's more complex than that. She's found out how to withdraw totally, and stay there as long as she likes.'

'Like hypnosis,' Annie said, and he flicked a sharp glance at her and then nodded approvingly as though she were a medical student who had shown unexpected evidence of intelligence.

'Exactly like hypnosis. She's in some sort of self-induced trance and no one has ever been able to get her out of it. But she gets herself out when it suits her –' He looked at his watch and then across the ward towards the long table at the far end to which patients were beginning to wander in a straggling group. 'Watch this. Lunchtime.'

The woman sat and rocked, her gaze unwavering, and Annie stood and waited, passively, watching her. She was so very odd; not in the way the man still standing and making obscene

45

gestures from the window was odd, nor like the weeping girl in the corner – at whom Annie could not bear to look, her pain was so vivid – but in a remote and special way. Annie actually wanted to know what was going to happen, was interested, and that was an odd feeling. Because it had been a long time since she could remember feeling the faintest flicker of interest in anyone at all, even herself.

A nurse came in through the big double doors, pushing a high-sided chrome trolley, and the group of people at the long table seemed to waken up a little, becoming more alert, and those who had not yet reached the table moved towards it, even the man at the window. The weeping girl did not, until another nurse came into the ward and went and fetched her and led her to the table, but she went willingly enough.

A couple more nurses appeared and there was a sudden clatter as the trolley was opened and metal tureens and food containers were unlidded and the serving of the meal began. Some of the patients began to chatter now, and there was a semblance of cheerfulness about the place. Even the weeping girl had accepted a plate of food and was sitting staring at it, not weeping now, though she wasn't eating either.

'Nurse Collins!' Joe called and one of the nurses, a tall girl with a smile so wide and so tooth-filled that she looked like a television advertisement, Annie thought, detached herself from the group at the table and came across to them.

'Try and get her to join the others, nurse, will you?' Joe said softly and inclined his head at Maddie and the girl stared at him and then laughed.

'That'll be the day, Dr Labosky!' she said but obediently bent over the chair and put her hand on the woman's shoulder.

'Come on, Maddie, dinnertime! Lovely meat pie and mashed carrots today, you'll like that. And you can have some chips with it if you'll come over to the table – come on, Maddie, you must be hungry!'

There was no response at all, and the nurse shook her shoulder a little more roughly.

'Now, come on, Maddie! It's time to eat it while it's hot! I'll help you.' And with a practised twist of her shoulders the girl set her arm behind Maddie and urged her out of the chair, lifting her in strong young arms.

46

Maddie made no effort at all to cooperate. She just hung there in the nurse's arms, her head held foursquare on her shoulders, but otherwise as limp as a sack of dead rocks. Her legs flopped under her like a doll's, her arms hung, hands still clasped, in front of her and her eyes still stared at the same mid-distant point. And the nurse lifted again, grunting slightly and then, breathlessly, let her go, and Maddie settled in the chair again; like a sack full of hay this time, smoothly and lightly, until she was back in exactly the same position; and began to rock again at precisely the same speed.

Annie stared at her and then looked at Joe. 'But what happens? Surely she must eat?'

'Of course she must. And she will. Will you feed her, nurse?'

'But you know what happens if we –' the nurse began and Joe shook his head. 'Indulge me. I want to show Miss Matthews the task she is to take on. If you'd be so good –'

The nurse made a little grimace and went back to the food trolley and returned with a plate of food, the meat pie and the chips and the carrots neatly arranged, and with a knife and fork wrapped in a paper napkin in her other hand.

She sat down beside the woman's chair and smoothed the napkin over the neck of the cardigan and the blue cotton dress and then, with one more glance at Joe, in which irritation and some embarrassment seemed to vie for main components, set about forking up some of the food. She speared a chip, and tried to put it into the woman's mouth, but the lax lips remained exactly as they had been, not moving. It was as though she were totally unaware of the fork prodding at her, of the smell of the food, which was, Annie realised, far from disagreeable, however unpleasant the cooking had smelled outside, or of its warmth. She just sat oblivious.

'Ah, there you are, Cynthia!' Joe said in a cheerful voice and Annie turned her head to see a small woman neatly dressed in a grey flannel suit with a white blouse and a lacy jabot at the collar, all immaculately clean, hovering at her side. She had a large leather bag over one arm and was watching the nurse and her efforts to feed the woman in the chair with her face creased with anxiety.

'Thank you, Nurse Collins,' Joe said then. 'Let Cynthia take over then,' and the nurse made a grimace and got up, gratefully,

47

and at once the little woman in the businesslike suit scuttled to sit in the chair she had vacated.

She picked up the fork and leaning over, fixed the handle into Maddie's fingers, and at once, slowly but definitely, the hand moved and took the fork, and the head, hitherto erect, bent forwards so that the hair fell over the forehead obscuring the eyes beneath their heavy lids.

Moving slowly and neatly, Maddie began to feed herself, eating steadily until all the food was gone, and then, as the little woman who still sat beside her leaned over and took the fork from her hand and removed the plate from her lap, curled her fingers once more and settled them back where they had been. And Cynthia got to her feet and quietly went trotting over to the table to take away the empty plate and the knife and fork.

'She'll bring her some pudding and then a cup of tea, and the same thing will happen,' Joe said softly. 'And then, after that, she'll make her stand up and lead her to the lavatories and then bring her back. And there she will sit until suppertime when it'll happen again. And at bedtime Cynthia will take her to her bed and undress her and Maddie will climb in and lie there until the morning when Cynthia will get her up and dress her. It's an extraordinary thing to see, and there's no one else at all who can do it. If anyone else tries it's the way it was with Nurse Collins. Total refusal to cooperate.'

'Has Cynthia been here as long as Maddie, then?'

'Oh, no. She's been here just three months. And she'll be going next week to the hostel on the Larcombe Estate.'

'So what —'

Joe nodded. 'What did she do before? She had another patient looking after her. And when Cynthia goes she'll find someone else. I don't know how she does it, but she always does. She never asks, never says thank you, but all the years she's been here it's been this way, apparently. A total refusal to accept nurses, a willingness to accept the help of other patients, but only carefully selected patients.'

'And next week —'

He nodded again. 'Next week, when Cynthia leaves, someone else will be chosen. Or will choose to do it. Yes.'

'And you want it to be me.' She said it flatly, without any expression in her voice at all.

He hesitated for just a moment. 'It did seem to be an opportunity. If you are willing to spend the days here, getting her up in the morning, seeing that she eats, goes to the lavatory, washes and so forth – perhaps you can break down the barrier.'

'Why me?'

'Because of your own, Annie,' he said softly. And now she did look at him for a brief moment before shifting her gaze back to Maddie.

'Some of us need barriers,' she said harshly. 'She does. Maybe it would be cruel to take hers away, if she's safe inside it.'

'Maybe,' he agreed. 'If we didn't have what Gresham calls a disposal problem we might take a chance on that and let her go on as she is. After so many years of trying to get to her, and failing, it would seem the only answer. But we do have a disposal problem, so we have to do something. Don't we?'

'And the notes you mentioned? The old notes from her past time here? What about them?' Annie was still watching the woman in the chair, seeming almost mesmerized by her rhythmic motion.

'Oh, yes, we'll find them. They're part of the task, aren't they? Something the journalist in you will enjoy –'

'I'm not a journalist.'

'Of course you are. You may have been kept from it for longer than you should have been, but it's the work you were trained for. Investigative journalism must be very – exciting. A bit like investigating a patient to make a diagnosis. There are more things in common between us than you might imagine, Annie.'

'I doubt it,' she said harshly. 'All right. Where are these notes? If I'm going to do it I might as well get on with it.'

5

November 1986

Maddie, remembering. Maddie holding on as hard as she could to her vision of the way they had worked together, she and Jay, and holding on to the memory of that very first deal of all, the chocolate deal that had started it all. But the pictures kept sliding away, the pictures she needed to make it happen, and anger began to lift in her. She felt as though she was being pulled about, being prodded and shouted at, and she had to work too hard at locking all that out to hold on to her remembering, and she felt the anger grow inside her, hot and tight, and wanted to shout at them.

Not that she did, of course. She learned long ago the importance of not letting them know anything of what was struggling inside her head; never shout, never react, just be. So she didn't shout and she didn't react, and at last the proper person came and her fork was put in her hand and she could eat the tasteless stuff and then forget it and start the memories going again; and at last they left her alone.

But even after that it didn't work. She dredged deep inside her head for the pictures; there she was with Jay, sitting in her father's drawing room in the Regent's Park flat, talking to him of what she had heard when her father had spoken to Ambrose, explaining how he could, by making two telephone calls and one visit, arrange the transfer of the fifty cases of chocolate and collect the commission. She had to tell Jay that there was no need to worry; Ambrose had been told several days ago and had said he'd get on to it right away, but of course he hadn't. Indolence was Ambrose's middle name, she had to tell Jay, with all the amused big sisterly contempt she could, so if and when he did finally make the contact and was told the deal had already been struck, he wouldn't say anything, least of all to his father. He'd know it was his fault that there had been the delay, and would assume that his father had gone over his head – or behind his back, whichever way he preferred to look at it – and would forget all about it, grateful for silence. No one need ever know it was Jay who had handled it, she had to explain, so he could make the money for himself, easily. Himself and her.

But she couldn't explain, not today. Today the whole place was much too busy, somehow, and she sat there with her gaze fixed as usual, not looking at anything, but still seeing it all, and it all appeared as it always did. People, ugly stupid people, milling about aimlessly, and the nurses bustling, pretending to care but not giving a damn inside, as she knew better than anyone, but somehow it was different, today. There was a buzz and she tried to escape from it back into her memories, but knew that she was defeated. The buzz was too loud. And she sat there rocking as she always did, listening and watching with those eyes that no one ever saw flicker, but which missed very little.

What she saw was the girl again. She had been here every day now for several days, and the thing about her that was wrong was that she wasn't a patient, and she wasn't a nurse either. That made it difficult for Maddie to understand, but she knew all she had to do was sit tight and she would find out. She always did, eventually. It had always been like that. She had always got what she wanted eventually – and suddenly it was there again, the bad feeling, the one she had managed to escape for a long time now, the empty screaming desolation that warned her she was getting too close to the bad memories, the things that must never be thought about. And she rocked a little faster and a little more vigorously, struggling again to get the good memories back so that she could escape and see her Jay once again.

Annie registered the change in the rocking rhythm at once and watched covertly, not making any sign that she was aware, but slowly and almost imperceptibly the rhythm relaxed and returned to its usual steadiness, and she wondered what had caused it all, and lifted her head and looked round the ward.

She had spent five days here now and was beginning to know not just the pattern of the ward's day, and the personalities as well as the identities of all the people who lived and worked on it, but the nuances of feeling too, the unspoken and unmarked currents that flowed and eddied between patients and nurses and patients and patients. And today there was an electricity of excitement in the air, an unhappy excitement, and it made the back of her neck tingle a little.

She knew what it was. Eleven of the patients were to leave today, among them Cynthia, Maddie's self-appointed servant, and they weren't happy about it. They were to be transferred with all their belongings – and between them that added up to several cardboard boxes of books and magazines and mementoes and assorted detritus, quite apart from cases containing clothes – by bus to the hostel on the Larcombe Estate. They had had lessons in the Occupational Therapy Department in making their own meals and in dealing with their own care, but they were all frightened, even though they knew there was to be one nurse there to keep an eye on them to start with.

Six of the women who were going had been on the ward for over three years and had taken it for granted they would always be here. To be thrown out into some horrible hostel to look after themselves, they had wailed and wept, to be sent away when they weren't well! The whole ward had seemed to tremble with their fear and pain. But they were going all the same and today was the day, and Annie was unhappy for them. They should be left in peace to be where they wanted; bad enough they had been sent here in the first place and had had to learn its intricacies. Now they were here, why couldn't they be allowed to stay and feel safe and comfortable? It mattered dreadfully to feel safe and comfortable, Annie thought, and refused to remember the way Jen had looked at her when she had been lifted in her wheelchair from the ambulance and carried into the East Pavilion. She had been safe and comfortable at home in the old house. She hadn't wanted to be brought here, just so that her daughter could have her first holiday in almost ten years. What did it matter to Jen that Annie had been screaming inside her head with the hell of it, the day in, day out hell of it all? All Jen had known was that she had to move, just as the keening women here knew they had to move. And they didn't want to any more than Jen had wanted to.

Determinedly Annie bent her head over the thick pile of papers in the folder on her knee. She had a job to do; that was why she was here, not to think about Jen or these other women for whom arrangements had been made, good arrangements, accepted by the committee of which she was a member, the only possible ones under the circumstances, which were that their hospital had been sold under them. And do it she would.

'Surname Kincaid,' she read for the umpteenth time. 'Forenames Madeleine Braham, date of birth 1–1–30, admitted ex Cunard Shipping Company's SS *Carenia* via St Mary's Hospital Southampton, address on papers Larches Lodge, Stanmore Hill, Middlesex, within Greenhill's catchment area. Date of admission 17 November 1953.

'Condition on admission: well nourished female, eyes dark brown, hair dark brown, some striae on anterior abdominal wall, probably sequelae pregnancy, otherwise no blemishes. Physical examination all systems N.A.D. multip. 2? 3. Uterus bulky, relevant breast changes.

'Psychological state: totally withdrawn, not responsive to superficial pain stimuli, but clearly conscious and aware. Control considerable; muscle rigidity of voluntary muscles ++. Not catatonic. Diagnosis ?Depression ?Severe psychoneurotic state. Prognosis doubtful. Treatment: observation.'

The notes, for all their thickness, were deeply boring, Annie decided. They had tried some remedies in the early days; there had been electric shock therapy given three times and then abandoned, because there was no response at all, and they had tried to start psychotherapy, but found it impossible with a patient who never talked and never seemed to listen either, and once the new anti-depressive drugs had arrived they had tried those too, one after another, and she had never once responded to anything. Doctor after doctor had arrived at Greenhill, bright-eyed and bushy-tailed and convinced they had new ideas, new ways with psychiatric patients that would work in the most resistant of cases, and all had been defeated by Maddie.

Annie could tell that from the way the notes were. Each time the handwriting changed and the signature in the notes altered, there had been frequent examinations and copious comments, but as the weeks of each doctor's residency had passed, clearly they had lost heart and interest. Then in time the notes had become scrappy and laconic in the extreme, and several times stopped altogether; there were months on end when, it seemed, no doctor had come anywhere near Maddie. The nurses' notes were just as casual, with even longer gaps of silence. Until Joe Labosky had arrived.

Annie read his comments on Maddie with unwilling approval. He had examined her very carefully, it was clear, and his findings were listed in concise elegant English. He had been obviously concerned with her inactivity and some eight years ago had instituted regular physiotherapy, so that she got some exercise instead of sitting interminably in her chair; thus there had been a time when Maddie had been taken out of doors, and even to the hospital swimming pool and made to get into the water, and had actually moved her own muscles a little. But that had stopped when the NHS cuts had really started to bite three or four years ago and the number of physiotherapists had been cut so drastically that there was no one available any more to make Maddie walk in the garden or swim. So here she had sat in her chair for the long months doing nothing.

It was remarkable, Annie thought, that she wasn't just a lump, a blob of a woman. But she wasn't. Even beneath that shapeless cotton dress and cardigan which were hospital issue she had a neat body, soft, rather than well muscled, lax and drooping, but not totally lost, and she could, Annie found herself thinking, look quite good with a little care.

But who was to give it? It was not the hospital's job to titivate a patient. They had to provide some sort of haven, a cure if possible for whatever ailed the minds of the people who were washed up on Greenhill's shores, but pretty clothes and haircutting and suchlike fripperies? A mad idea – and anyway, why do I care? It's not as though I've bothered that much about my own appearance lately. And she smoothed her hand over her untidy head and was suddenly aware, as she had not been for a very long time, of the dismal reflection of herself she could see in the ward window.

There must be someone who belongs to her, she told herself then, determinedly keeping her head down so that the reflection couldn't be seen, and she went back to the other wadge of notes that were in the folder, labelled 'Social'.

Someone with an indecipherable signature – a young doctor? A social worker? (Did they have them in 1956? Or were they called almoners then?) Perhaps a nurse? – had gone to the house referred to in the private papers Maddie had had with her (what they were was unspecified, and they weren't in the notes) to find out more about her and, the report read, had done very poorly in his or her searches.

'House occupied by Japanese, speaking poor English, claims no knowledge of patient. House purchased by Japanese embassy last year via estate agent, no knowledge of previous owner. Neighbours deny all knowledge of previous occupants. Several say that awareness of neighbours not a feature of the district.'

And Annie grinned suddenly, a wide grin of real amusement. She knew Stanmore Hill well, with its big self-satisfied houses set back from the road, lofty and aloof in their obvious expensiveness. No, she was quite sure that neighbourliness had never been a feature of life in that cushioned corner of London. She returned to the notes.

Other searches had been made, trawling the phone books and voters' lists for people named either Kincaid or Braham, which was assumed to be a family name of some kind by the searcher since it was patently not a female forename of choice, and both searches had ended in dead scents. No one seemed to know anything about Madeleine Braham Kincaid. So the searcher – and, Annie thought, he/she was a trier, not one to give up easily at all – had gone to Cunard to study their passenger lists.

No luck there either. Mrs Madeleine Braham Kincaid had joined the ship at New York – at least we know she is married, the searcher had noted laconically – and at that point had made no special mark on the crew, not even her stewardess. But on the first day at sea the passenger in cabin twenty-three, deck C, had been found by said stewardess sitting in the corner of her bathroom curled up in a tight ball, her eyes wide open and refusing to respond to questions or to move. The stewardess had called the ship's doctor, who had suspected some sort of drug overdose and removed the passenger to his sick bay, where she had remained in the same apparently catatonic state for the remainder of the voyage. She had been transferred on docking to the nearest Southampton hospital which would accept her, and from there had been transferred to the mental hospital which served the area in which she had appeared to live. The Southampton mental hospitals would certainly not accept her, and Annie smiled again, wryly this time, almost hearing the self-satisfied pompous voice of whoever had refused the patient echoing at her through the years since he had handed down his edict. Almost thirty-five years ago he had said it, and here Maddie still sat, with no one any the wiser about the where, the who and above all the why of her situation.

Annie closed the notes and set them on the low table beside her. Every time she read them, and that had been several times now, she hoped she would find something new, something she had overlooked, a clue to the mystery that was Maddie, but it never happened and it wasn't going to now. Reading the dusty yellowing pages was a waste of time.

'So what do I do now with you?' she said softly to the woman sitting there rocking in front of her. 'Walk away like everyone else? I might as well. You're not going to help, are you?'

The rocking went on, rhythmic, unaltered, silent.

'I shouldn't have agreed in the first place.' It was odd how easy it was to talk to her, Annie thought then. All these months of being alone in that flat – she couldn't call it home – and never talking to anyone had seemed peaceful and easy. Not happy, but easy. Talking when she had to, to shopkeepers or the milkman or the garage man, or worst of all the people on Joe Labosky's bloody committee, had been an agonising business. So why was it so easy to talk now? And she said it aloud. 'Why is it easy to talk to you?'

The rocking went on and the dark eyes stared ahead, unmoving.

'Because it's like being alone,' Annie decided. 'That's what it is. I like talking to you because you won't be a pest and talk back. How does that make you feel, hmm? I'll bet you're listening in there somewhere, so think about it. I know why you don't talk to people. You hate them as much as I do. But here am I talking to you because I hate everyone and don't want an answer, so your refusal to talk which is meant to be an insult, I think, isn't to *me*. It's a pleasure. I'm talking nonsense, aren't I? Never mind, I'm only talking to you, and you don't matter because you just sit there and give nothing back and ask for nothing. I like that. I like that a lot. I don't like you, but I like that.'

And then she laughed softly. 'I hate you, you know that? I

56

hate you the way I hated –' her voice died in her throat then and she pushed her chair back irritably and stood up. Just being in this place was enough to make a person mad. Here I am talking rubbish to a dummy. Christ, I really must be as mad as everyone else here. I need disposal as much as they do –

There was a little flurry then as the big ward doors opened and two of the hospital porters came in, scrawny men in brown overalls pushing a long trolley, and at once several of the women, sitting miserably waiting for their bus, burst into noisy tears and others came clustering round to comfort them, and Annie sat down again. To walk out in the middle of all this hubbub would attract attention and that was the last thing she could cope with right now. She'd wait, let them all go, then leave in her own time. And on the way out tell that bloody man Labosky she'd done her best, and couldn't do more, and that would be an end of her visits here –

The women began to make their doleful way to the door, clutching their parcels as the nurses chivvied them along cheerfully, making soothing noises that Annie for one found deeply irritating rather than comforting, and there was an eddy of activity round the door as the few remaining patients waved goodbye and wept in sympathy as the men with the trolley loaded it with much banging about of boxes and warning cries from the owners of them. Annie watched and then jumped as someone tapped her shoulder.

'Is it you what's going to look after her dinners and that, then?' Cynthia was standing staring at her owlishly. She was wearing a small fox collar over her suit and lacy blouse now, a mean attenuated and limp thing which carried its tail in its narrow mouth to fasten itself across Cynthia's meagre bosom, and bulging brown glass eyes that Annie couldn't bear to look at.

'What?' she said stupidly.

'Her!' Cynthia said almost irritably and jerked her head at the rocking figure in the chair. 'Are you doing her food and that? Someone has to.'

'No – I don't think so –' Annie stammered and then stopped and blinked as Cynthia shook her head even more irritably and said loudly, 'You should be ashamed!'

'Ashamed? Why, what –'

'If you wasn't going to take on the job you should have said sooner so I could show someone else. But I showed you like I was showed. So I thought it was all set. I got to tell her, of course, like I was told, but once you knows how, it's easy. And you knows how, now.' And the small woman stared at her accusingly.

'How do you mean, as you were told?' Annie said, her curiosity lifting a cautious head again.

'Why, when I come here to this ward, and began to get a bit better and the other one what had looked after her left – she was a nice woman, Sally was – she said I could do it. And she showed me how and then she told Maddie so it was all right. After that Maddie wouldn't let no one else do it but me.' She smiled then, a pleased self-congratulatory little smile, and looked over her shoulder at the silent Maddie. 'She's very choosy, you see. She'll only eat for the one what she knows is right, that she's been introduced to properly, you see. Like I was by Sally and Sally told me like she was by the one before.'

She frowned then. 'She was called Mary, I think. Back in – oh, must ha' been a good ten years ago. Sally, she was here over five years before she took that cancer and had to go to the other hospital, and me –' She made a face then and almost shook herself. 'Anyway, I got to go now to the hostel and sort things out there, so you see I can't muck about, can I? You been shown what to do, and I got no time to show no one else, so all I got to do is tell Maddie, introduce you like. And you can't say you won't, really. What else you got to do, after all?'

'What else,' Annie murmured and then as the woman nodded briskly and turned away to Maddie reached out a hand to stop her. But she was too late.

'This here one, she's new, and she'll look after you now, Maddie. Me, I'm going away. What's your name, dear?' And she looked over her shoulder at Annie, bright-eyed and enquiring and then, as Annie didn't answer at once, almost snarled, 'Eh? What're you called?'

'Annie,' Annie said before stopping to think, she was so taken aback by the firm way this little woman, hitherto so meek and quiet, had taken charge, and at once Cynthia nodded and said to Maddie, 'She's called Annie, dear, and she'll look after you –' And she turned away and made her way back to the door, busily pulling on a pair of pale blue transparent nylon gloves with frills at the wrists. They looked very odd with the fox round her neck and her neat suit.

'That'll be all right now,' she said with great satisfaction. 'She'll be all right. And so will you. It's nice to have something to do, something you got to be relied on for. It makes it all right being here. It did a lot for me, that did. I dare say it'll do it for you too. Goodbye, dear. Hope you get your health back soon. It's not a bad place to fetch up, one way and another. Even if they do go and dump you in hostels –' And she bustled away to the door and was gone before Annie could stop her and tell her first that she wasn't a patient, and second that she didn't want the job of looking after Maddie, no matter what Joe Labosky said and anyway –

And then she stopped because behind her there had been a sound and she whirled and stared at Maddie and felt a sense of shock so great it was as though a light bulb had exploded in her head.

Because Maddie was staring at her. She had shifted the level of her gaze and was looking sideways. She was still rocking and her hands were still locked in her lap, but she was looking directly at Annie and there was awareness in her eyes and not a blank stare at all.

6

December 1986

'Why?' Joe said. 'I haven't the remotest idea. I'm only a psychiatrist, not a soothsayer.'

'She's your patient. You're supposed to know all about her. You told me to look after her. It's perfectly reasonable to expect you to know.'

He looked at her, at the way her head was up and her eyes were fixed on his, and wanted to cheer. She looked alert in a way she certainly had not before, and angry. And that was good. Better certainly than the dull edginess that had been so much a part of her for so long. In putting these two women together he might have wrought better than he knew, he told himself, and leaned forwards and folded his arms on the table between them.

'No one really knows what goes on inside another person's head, Annie. A psychiatrist tries to make informed guesses, and to base a therapy on those guesses, praying all the time that he's somewhere near the target, let alone the bull's-eye. Occasionally he manages to get somewhere. Most of the time he doesn't. He can only sit and make helpful noises and try a few pills and maybe make people feel a little more comfortable while they get better anyway. Most psychiatric illnesses are self-limiting, you see. No matter what we do or don't do they get better in time.'

'Really?' she said sardonically. 'Is that why there are so many people here who've been here for years and now need disposal? Did no one remember to tell them their illnesses were self-limiting? Maybe if you had you wouldn't have to worry now about where you're going to dump people.'

'Touché,' he grinned at her. 'But give me some credit, Annie. I did say *most*. Not all. And I don't claim to be the answer to anyone's problems whatever sort of illness they have. I can't be. I'm not God – who or whatever God may be. I'm just a doctor with some knowledge of what makes people tick, and how their minds work, and I try to apply some of that knowledge to the

60

people who come to me because they're unhappy – which is what mental illness usually means – and try to make them feel different.' He made a small grimace then. 'Though to tell the truth I'm expected to make the happy ones feel different, too. The ones who are so floridly mad and cheerful. I'm supposed to make them normal, poor bastards. I'd rather not, often. Why extract them from mania to give them reality? I'd rather be manic, myself. It must be rather agreeable –'

'If you know so much about what makes people tick, you must know what makes this Maddie tick,' she said abruptly. 'Why she sits there rocking like that, refusing to react to anything or anyone and then suddenly looks at me. So tell me why.'

'You're sure she did?'

'Here we go,' she said roughly. 'If it doesn't fit in with what the great doctor expects then of course it's a lie or a stupidity. I'm telling you, that woman *looked* at me, with intelligence in her eyes. She wasn't just staring the way she usually does. She looked at me. Sideways, *at* me. And I want to know why.'

'So do I,' he said and leaned back. 'I'm sorry if you thought I didn't believe what you said. I do believe you. I always have, whatever we talked about. I was only asking for confirmation. I'm sorry indeed if I offended you. I didn't mean to.'

There was a short silence and then she said wearily, 'It doesn't matter, I just get irritable, I suppose. I meant no rudeness.'

'You offered none. Look, there are two things we need to talk about. One is why Maddie showed that moment of awareness – and you say she went back to her usual state as soon as you looked at her?'

'Yes.'

'So she was caught out – that's interesting. I wonder how often she's been doing it? How often she's shown signs of awareness, I mean, that the nursing staff and I didn't see? I'm a bloody fool, you know. I never thought to interview Cynthia about her, and I should have done. Maybe she knew her better than any of us, doctors or nurses.'

'Maybe. But –'

'And the other thing to talk about is you.'

'Not at all,' she said, rough-voiced again. 'I agreed to come here to help with the committee, and I let myself be talked into helping with this patient. But that's as far as it goes, and as far as it's going to go. You've been trying to make a patient out of me for years, I know that. And I also know I'm not going to let you. You can dig away at me till you're blue. It won't get you anywhere.'

'I don't want to dig at you and I certainly don't see you as a patient. At least –' He stopped, clearly struggling to be honest. 'At least, I don't think so. I think I'm much the same with everyone. I'm nosy, you see. Deeply inquisitive. If I had my way, I'd make window curtains illegal, so I could look in every house I pass, to see how people are and how they live. I like to know about people and what they do and what they think and why, and how they feel and I have this tiresome drive to meddle if they feel bad and try to make them feel better whoever they are. You should ask some of my friends –'

'I'm not interested in meeting your friends.'

'No, I know. That's come up before, hasn't it? Well, all the same – the point I'm trying to make is that I like you. Can't help it. It happens sometimes. You just like a person. Hasn't it ever happened to you?'

'What?'

'Taking a fancy to a person and being interested in them?'

'You're trying it again – wanting to analyse me.' She said it loudly, so loudly that the nurses at the adjoining table in the canteen looked over their shoulders at them curiously and then grinned, seeing Joe Labosky sitting there. People always grinned when they saw Joe Labosky. She'd noticed that before, and it made her curiously angry to see it again.

'I've told you,' she said passionately, but in a lower voice, 'I've told you, I don't want to talk to you now or ever about me. I'm not ill, I'm not depressed. If I'm miserable that's my affair. Why the hell should you have the right to come along and try to change me? Maybe I like being depressed, if I am. And you can't be sure I am anyway. And maybe I ought to be depressed. It's like those madmen you say you ought to leave alone to be mad in peace. Why not leave depressed people alone to be in peace?'

'Because they're not,' he said simply. 'There's no peace in your life, Annie. You spend all your waking hours in a state of misery. It shows in the way you walk and the way you look and every word you say. It seems such a pity to see so interesting and capable a person in such a state of – of waste.'

'How do you know I'm interesting and capable? How can you possibly know anything at all? You looked after my mother. Fair enough. Now she's dead and there's an end of it – what do you know about me?'

'I know it's not the end of it when someone dies. It's only the beginning sometimes.'

'Oh, shut up!' She made her voice as withering as she could. 'Trotting out silly paradoxes like that – it's just a trick of speech. It doesn't mean anything.'

'It means a lot.' The angrier she got, the more patient he sounded. 'It means that when a person is dead, you can't talk to them any more, not properly. You can talk to them inside your head, of course, but they can't really answer. And if there was anything you should have said and never did, it's too late. You can't apologise and you can't explain and you can't, above all, tell them how angry you are, and how –'

She had gone crimson with fury. 'If you don't stop this sort of talk I'm leaving. I came here to talk about your patient Maddie, and that's what I'll talk about. I won't fall for this trick of yours, digging around in my mind. It may be your hobby, but it's my bloody mind. Leave it alone!'

He smiled equably. 'Very well. But thanks for listening this far. You'll remember some of the things I said –'

'Like hell I will,' she said and got to her feet. 'Look, it's obvious that there's nothing you can tell me about Maddie, so there's an end of it. I won't be back. I've done all I can with those notes, and I can't see anything further that I can do that will be of any use –'

'She looked at you,' he said softly, not getting up, sitting there at the table with his hands folded on it neatly. 'She looked at *you*. As far as I know that is the first direct contact she's made with anyone in this place for years. Maybe she did the same with Cynthia. I don't know and it wouldn't be right for Cynthia for me to go to the hostel now and start quizzing her. She's part of the past now as far as Maddie's concerned. But you're here in the present and Maddie *looked* at you. And after a very short acquaintance too. It's obvious you've had quite an effect on her, somehow. So we need you. Or rather she needs you –'

And he was furious with himself for that slip of the tongue. After her anger, the last inducement that would have any effect was a plea that he or anyone else among Greenhill's staff needed her. But the appeal to her relationship with Maddie which however short was, it seemed, forming more and more firmly, now that was different. That might work –

She stood there uncertainly for a long moment, staring down at the table, and that gave him more time to look at her without her being aware of his regard and he made the most of it.

He had not been too hopeful, after all, he told himself. There *had* been a change in her since the last time he had spoken to her. She was still depressed, heaven knew; it showed in every line of her body and in the tone of her voice, as well as in her passionate denial that she might have a problem. To say in one breath that she wasn't depressed and in the next that it was how she chose to be, and also right that she should be, taking on herself blame for her state and seeing it as a just punishment for her sins, was virtually diagnostic of the illness. But getting her to face it and to accept that she needed help was proving to be something of a hurdle.

Not that he wanted to try the usual remedies for depression for her. It would be easy enough to put her on a course of Tofranil or Norval tablets or whatever and to wait until the illness burnt itself out eventually before weaning her off them, but that was not his sort of psychiatry. He used drugs, of course he did; only an idiot took a single line and stuck to it, in his opinion. He was as scornful of the narrowness of the methods of Sargent as he was of those of Laing, while not disagreeing with either of their philosophies. It was the blinkered nature of their approach he deplored, regarding the eclectic method as the one most likely to work.

Not that he called it anything so fancy; not Joe Labosky who had no time for fancy labels. As far as he was concerned it was always horses for courses. What suited one patient would not suit another. You looked at the patient and sought a treatment to fit his or her needs, rather than taking a treatment and expecting all patients to benefit from it. And he was sure, from all he knew of Annie Matthews – Annie Brady Matthews, he corrected himself then, a little wryly – he was sure that for her, drugs would not serve. They might temporarily ease her pain a little, and soften her hard edges, but in the long term she needed to dig out the source of her distress and deal with it. And he thought again of Jennifer, and the way she had sat there lumpishly in her chair and the way Annie had hovered, furiously watchful, over her and wondered again what had happened between those two women in the past to create so painful and awkward a relationship. Because that was undoubtedly how it had been, and it was equally undoubted that it was somewhere in what had happened between them, rather than in ordinary grief, that the source of Annie's present illness lay. Which she refused to acknowledge, and refused to allow him to treat.

But it was getting easier. A small chink was appearing in her carapace of denial. First it had been her acceptance of his coaxing to join the committee and then it had stretched to take in care of Maddie. And now it was widening before his very eyes as she stood there and thought about Maddie.

'All right,' she said suddenly and sat down again and folded her hands on the table in unconscious mimicry of his own posture and looked at him. 'What do I do next?'

'Be with her as often as you can,' he said at once. 'And go on doing whatever it was that made her look at you before —'

'It might be —' she began and then stopped. And wisely he sat and waited, saying nothing to prompt her.

'It might be,' she said at length, 'that I talked to her.'

'People have talked to her before. I have,' he ventured.

'Oh, I'm sure. About the sort of things people do talk to dumb patients about. How are you? and What are you feeling like? and silly questions like that. Or Pull yourself together, and Don't be so silly, and the rest of it —' The scorn in her voice dripped like melting icicles from a dead branch. 'I didn't do that. I talked about *me*. I told her I didn't like her and that the best thing about her was that I could talk to her and not get an answer. So being insulting by refusing to answer me was really doing me a favour. Could that be why she looked at me?'

He laughed softly. 'By God, maybe it was at that. It must have been a surprise to her, if in fact she heard it. I was assuming that after so long she didn't listen either. That she had dug herself so deep into her trances that she was deaf as well as mute. Genuinely deaf, I mean.'

'She probably is sometimes,' Annie said. 'I've watched her and she's different some of the time. But when she's had something to eat, when she goes to the lavatory and to bed, she isn't like that then. She still stares, but it's a different sort of stare. Sharper, somehow –' She stopped. 'I'm only guessing.'

'It's all any of us have been doing for years. Guessing. Go on guessing, then. Go on being with her, trying to talk to her again. Will you?'

'I won't try,' she said. 'I think that makes her go away. Inside herself. I'll talk if I feel like it. Then she may hear. Otherwise –'

'Otherwise what?'

She shrugged, and the blankness settled over her again, and her shoulders drooped, so that she looked as she usually did, flat and dismal, and her hair seemed to lose a little of the added lustre it had seemed to have as her eyes hooded and her chin went down. 'Otherwise nothing,' she said after a moment. 'I've no other ideas.'

'The one you have will do fine to start with. May I come and see you both, you and Maddie, in the next couple of days?'

'You're the doctor,' she said. 'It's up to you.' And she didn't look at him again, not even when his bleep called him and he had to go and said goodbye. She just sat there at the table in the same position and he looked back as he reached the door, on his way to the telephone, and wondered. Was it a real chink he had seen open in her? Or just a temporary flash of the real Annie he was sure lived inside her there somehow? He'd have to do the same thing that she was doing with Maddie, he decided as the big double doors swished softly closed behind him. Wait and see.

It's not true, Annie told herself. It's not true. He was just talking the way doctors do talk, trying to get at you, digging you out like someone digging an oyster out of its shell –

And at once her mind slid away and she was sitting not in Greenhill's ugly staff canteen with its green washed walls and eternal smell of elderly instant coffee and burnt toast, but at a corner table at El Vino's with – what was his name? Oh, yes, Giles, that was it. A silly lovely laughing man who worked on the gossip column and who had taken her out to El Vino's because it was the first of September and at last they could eat oysters.

And he had ordered a dozen each for them and a bottle of the best Chablis and piles of brown bread and butter and while they were waiting for the wine to be served he'd told her she'd do fine on the *Record*, that she'd enjoy working with old Sidgewick on the 'Probe' desk, and it was a great opportunity for a new girl in the Street, just as it was a great opportunity for a new girl to come and eat oysters with him, Giles. And he'd leered like a dirty old man and laughed to make it clear it was just a joke and they had drunk the wine and eaten the oysters with great delight and gone back down Fleet Street arm in arm and she had been totally, deliriously happy. She was twenty and she had her first job on a national newspaper and was pretending to be a little bit in love with a raffish journalist and it was summer and everything was lovely.

Until she had gone home and found Jen sitting by the kitchen table, exactly where she had left her that morning, but now stinking of her own urine and with her fingers burned with the cigarettes she had allowed to burn down to their butts, and had known it couldn't last. Something had to be done and she called Dr Weightman and he had told her it was just one of those things, put Jen to bed, keep an eye on her and it would sort itself out.

And she had put Jen to bed and sometimes made her get up and sit in a chair but that had been that. No more oysters at El Vino's with Giles, no more excitement on the 'Probe' desk of the *Record*, and come to that, she thought now, with a sudden flash of humour, no more *Record*. That was one of the newspapers no one ever remembered any more. I wonder what happened to Giles? Where is he working now? And did he ever marry and write the great novels he told me he was going to and –

I mustn't think this way. It's silly and it's sick. It's all you've ever done, digging about in the past, remembering, remembering. What good is it? She's dead, Colin's dead, they're all dead and gone, and it just doesn't matter any more.

And as though Joe were still sitting there, she heard his voice again. '– it's too late. You can't apologise and you can't explain and above all you can't tell them how angry you are –'

She jumped to her feet, as anger welled up even more hotly, and pushed her way out of the canteen, roughly elbowing aside a covey of nurses, much to their noisy irritation, and went hurrying out of the staff quarters building across the garden to the West Pavilion. She'd have to tell Sister she wouldn't be back, that somehow, someone else must take on the problems of Maddie and her food and her other needs; she, Annie, had had enough. She wasn't going to come back and put up with all this —

And what are you going to do? She found herself standing stock still in the middle of one of the gravel paths staring out across the slope of the lawn to the view beyond the hospital as it fell away down towards the motorway in the valley. Go back there to that hateful flat? Or — and she began to weave a fantasy of herself, going back there, packing a suitcase, digging out her passport from wherever it was hidden and then taking the car to Heathrow, just along the motorway there, not very far at all, and parking it in the long-stay car park and then going, going, going, anywhere she could get a ticket to go to. She would look at the departure boards and read off the places, those magical, romantic place names, Vienna and Berlin, Palma and Madrid, Genoa and Bermuda, Rome and Paris, Frankfurt and Venice, and they would sell her a ticket. First class even: she could afford that now that Jen was dead. And off she would fly and there she would have peace of mind and start to laugh again and —

And there she would be waiting for herself in the hotel when she got there to stare back at her out of a mirror, contemptuous and sneering, and ask her what she was doing there. Wasn't it bad enough she had gone to Paris and left Jen behind to die with no one to care? Was she going to do it again, to this woman, Maddie?

But she is nothing to me, a voice in her secret mind cried passionately, nothing at all! When you left Jen and let her die here all alone, that was different, Jen was your mother, Jen was someone you loved — who loved you — and this time the little voice in her head rose to a shrill shriek so real she had to put her hands over her ears to make it go away. And the movement and the resultant muffling of the ordinary outside sounds made her realise how stupid she was being and she took a deep breath and made herself walk with carefully relaxed steps back to the West Pavilion.

Sister was hurrying through the ward as she arrived and greeted her with a wide and obviously deeply relieved smile.

'Oh, Miss Matthews, am I glad to see you! I thought perhaps you weren't well. I should have realised of course you'd let me know if you weren't coming. Poor soul, of course, had nothing! We all tried, every one of us, and she refused to take a single mouthful. Staff Nurse Cobbins got very irritable and threatened to force feed her and even that made no difference. Not that we would, of course, we don't do that sort of thing these days, it's not the kind of thing modern therapists – anyway here you are and I'm very glad. I have to go over to the Larcombe Estate – they're having all sorts of problems there, but then I told everyone they would, anyway, didn't I? You heard me at the meetings, Miss Matthews. I warned them there'd be problems and of course there are. So I must go. But I asked them to keep something for Maddie in case you got back in time, and it's in the kitchen. It can go into the microwave, you know, one minute is enough to take the chill off, I find, and then they don't burn their tongues. We wouldn't want that to happen, would we? No, of course not – well, so long Miss Matthews, I hope to be in in the morning, but the way things are at Larcombe, who can say? They've not been there a week yet, and it's exactly what I said it would be, nothing but trouble –' and she went rustling away and Annie stood in the middle of the ward looking across at Maddie in her chair, sitting and rocking and not looking at her.

But she knows I'm here, she thought then. She's waiting for me, because she knew I'd come back. And it's not just for the food. It's me she's waiting for. I know she is.

But she couldn't say how she knew.

7

January 1987

It was four weeks before Maddie spoke to her and even then Annie couldn't be sure she had. Four weeks of pushing and talking and deciding to pack it all in and still coming back to try again, four weeks during which she became more and more angry with Maddie, and yet more and more attached too.

It really was absurd the way this silent rocking woman had come to fill her life, Annie thought. She became the first thought of the morning when Annie opened her eyes to her bleak bedroom and its still lingering smell of new plaster and paint, and the last one before she fell into her lonely sleep at night. She was used to waking hours before there was any point in getting up, to lie and stare at the ceiling and push vagrant thoughts about her head, but this was different. She would wake early, as usual, but now she would think not about odd wisps of things while being furious with herself for not sleeping, but very definitely of Maddie, without minding that she was awake. And the same thing would happen as she lay curled up after climbing into bed, trying to escape into oblivion. Maddie and her silence would haunt her. She would go back through the whole of the previous day, seeking clues in her reactions – or rather non-reactions – to the flow of talk with which Annie now bombarded her, and sometimes thinking of that would actually make her smile. Because it was ridiculous the way she talked to Maddie. It was as though she had pulled a plug out of the bottom of her own mind and every thought that ever entered it immediately trickled out again as words. And Maddie would sit and rock and stare ahead with her blank brown stare, but Annie knew it wasn't as it had been used to be. She wasn't locked away; she could hear, and understand too. But she still didn't speak.

Until, one afternoon after she had eaten her lunch, and Annie, unusually tired for some reason, had sat staring out of the window and paying Maddie no attention. The ward was quiet, with just three or four of the older patients sitting at the far end staring at the muttering TV screen. A few more people had been transferred to hostels and to other places over the last few weeks and the whole place had the feeling of a seaside hotel at the end of the season; dreamy, lazy and working at half speed.

It might have been that which had made Annie so lackadaisical herself, and left her sitting in a half-doze long after Maddie had finished eating, or it might have been the fact that she was feeling rather comfortable. It had been a long time since she had been able to sit slumped as easily in a chair as she was now, and she wondered vaguely why she should be so relaxed. She was, in fact, sleeping a little better these days, and this morning had actually woken late. She had drifted into the habit of getting up at seven and leaving the flat before half past in order to get to the ward to get Maddie out of bed early and to give her breakfast, and had never needed an alarm clock. She was usually awake before five. But this morning, she had woken with a start at seven-fifteen and had had to rush to get to the ward at the usual time; and sitting now and staring out at the dying November garden she wondered a little about why that had happened.

And then realised that Maddie was looking at her. She did this more often now, although she still didn't do it when anyone else was around. Annie had never been able to demonstrate to Sister or to Joe Labosky the change in their patient, but all the same it happened, and she always knew when it did, even if she wasn't looking at her at that moment. It was as though someone had switched on a different light somewhere and changed the pattern of the shadows.

She turned her head lazily and looked at Maddie now. She was sitting in her usual position, the fork from her lunch still clutched in her hand and her plate very empty in front of her. Annie was beginning to know the sort of food Maddie liked, and today had been one of her favourites, a concoction of pasta and cheese and tomato that would have horrified any Italian cook told it was called lasagne, but which tasted well enough. Maddie had eaten all of it; there was not a scrap of waste left on the plate anywhere and Annie grinned at the sight of that.

'You like it? You can have some more if you ask for it. Mm?

Another plateful? There's plenty there. The trolley's still hot and it's over there –' and she jerked her head towards the far end of the ward where the trolley indeed still sat, ignored by the nurses who because they had so little to do found it an effort to do anything at all, and were just not bothering to start the afternoon's tidying and chivvying of patients to occupational therapy and group sessions. They were sitting smoking and gossiping in the staff room and Annie was the only non-patient in sight.

'I'll get you some more if you want it,' she said then and still Maddie's eyes were fixed on her and she leaned forwards very deliberately and stared deeply into them. 'But only if you ask for it. Say please. *Ask* for it. If you don't you can't have it. And what's more, I'm feeling bloody minded. So you shan't have pudding either unless you ask for it. It's ice cream, too. Not boring old vanilla, either. Rum and raisin. I saw it.' She leaned back with a casual air and grinned back over her shoulder at the silent woman in the chair. 'So it's up to you. Say please and I'll get it. I might even go and get you some coffee – the real coffee the nurses drink, not that muck they usually give you.'

And she closed her eyes, pleased at having been so unkind to the woman. She wanted more food; Annie had learned to identify the feelings that came from Maddie, however uncommunicative she was, and she was quite certain that a second helping of lasagne was something she wanted very much. Refusing to fetch it for her gave her a sense of pleasure, she told herself; and then opened her eyes to stare out of the window again, horrified by her own hatefulness. Was I always like this? she wondered. Did it always give me pleasure to be a bitch? Why can't I just get up and go and get the poor devil some more food? What skin is it off my nose whether she talks or not? And she was about to tense her muscles preparatory to standing up when she heard it.

It wasn't so much a word as the ghost of one. The voice sounded remote and hollow, but it was a voice all the same.

'Please,' Maddie said.

Annie sat very still and then slowly turned her head to look at her. She was still sitting as she had been, her fork clutched in her hand, the plate on her lap, and was still staring directly at Annie. Her lips were half parted, but then, they often were, and Annie couldn't remember if that was how they had been before she had closed her eyes, and she said a little stupidly, 'What? What did you say?'

Maddie stared back at her, but now there was more to her gaze than there had been, or so it seemed to Annie. She did not move a muscle or shift her eyes at all, but there was expression there now, a sort of reproach and after a moment Annie laughed.

'My God, you *did* ask, didn't you? You said please! I didn't imagine it!'

Still the dark eyes stared and this time Annie thought she saw a glint of self-satisfaction there and she grinned and got to her feet and went to pick up the plate from Maddie's lap. She stood there looking down at her and there was no movement at all. Maddie still kept her head in the same posture and after a moment Annie touched her shoulder and then went to fetch the second helping of food.

She arranged it on the plate as neatly as she could, wanting to give Maddie the extra reward of food that looked attractive as well as tasting as she liked, and took it back to her, and then sat and watched as slowly she ate it, finishing it with the same meticulousness as she had shown when she demolished the first helping she had been given.

'Ice cream?' Annie said as Maddie raised her head and again fixed her eyes on her. 'Ice cream and then coffee? Good. Would I be pushing my luck to ask for another please for them? What do you think?'

The eyes looked back at her and this time Annie saw no expression at all, and then made an irritable sound in her throat. 'I'm a bloody fool, aren't I? As if eyes ever showed any expression anyway. It's the way the muscles around the eyes look, not the damned eyes themselves. You know that, don't you, Maddie? And you think I'm a bloody fool, don't you, imagining otherwise? Well, I am. I probably imagined you spoke before too. Except I don't think I did –' She picked up the plate. 'All right, Maddie. Ice cream and coffee, coming up. Maybe when I get back you'll feel like saying thank you. You never know your luck, do you?'

'No,' Maddie said quite loudly as Annie turned away and at once she whirled and came back to crouch in front of her and

73

peer into her face, and there she squatted for a long moment.

'Well, I'm damned,' she said. 'I'm damned,' but Maddie said nothing, just sitting and looking at her. And Annie laughed and got to her feet and went and fetched the ice cream and then, as Maddie spooned it up, went and collected cups of coffee from the staff room.

The nurses had cleared the trolley and taken the patients away to their various activities now and the ward was completely empty apart from the two women sitting drinking coffee. Annie watched Maddie over the rim of her cup and tried to contain her excitement. She'd done it. She had persuaded this woman to speak, after years and years of silence. She couldn't be all bad, after all. She wasn't useless, or stupid, as she had been so certain she was. She had made Maddie speak, and she could have laughed aloud at the thought of it. But she didn't, collecting their empty cups neatly and taking them away to the kitchen before coming back to sit close to Maddie's chair and lean over her.

'You've done it now, you know,' she said conversationally. 'As long as you stayed silent no one could or would expect anything else from you. But now you've spoken and you won't be allowed to stay silent again. Had you thought of that?'

There was no response. Maddie had started to rock again and her eyes were fixed as usual on the far distance. But Annie wasn't going to allow that; she leaned over and pulled on Maddie's shoulder.

'Oh, no you don't. You're going to talk to me,' she said and shook her slightly. There was no resistance there; it was like shaking a bag of hay and Annie let go and leaned back in her chair.

'I'm sorry,' she said after a moment. 'I'm being ridiculous, aren't I? Why should you speak to me, after all? What am I to you? You don't know anything about me, after all. I'm not a nurse, you know. And I'm not a patient either.'

She looked round the ward. 'Not officially, anyway. He thinks I ought to be. The doctor who looks after you, if it's called looking after, seeing how little he seems able to do for you. He thinks I'm mad, you know. Depressed. It's the same thing, isn't it? Not in your right mind, that's what it means. They can call you disturbed or depressed or manic or crazy or

74

mad. It all adds up to the same thing. *They* are normal and *we* aren't. And I sometimes think there are a bloody sight more of us than there are of them.'

Still no response, and Annie frowned. 'Oh, bloody hell –' she said and then stopped. 'I keep saying that lately. I wonder why? It's so stupid. Say it often enough and it doesn't mean anything. Bloody, bloody, bloody, bloody. It never meant anything before and repeating it doesn't make it any better. Why do I do it, Maddie? Hmm? Is it because I used to be punished for it when I was a child? Is that why?'

The silence persisted and Annie took a deep breath. 'Listen, Maddie, I'll make a deal with you. I'll talk to you if you'll talk to me. What do you say to that? I've been talking for a bit – for a month already. But never mind. I'm more used to it than you are, so I'll start now. I'll talk to you, and then you talk to me. Fair enough?'

Maddie was looking at her now, and again there was expression there even though the muscles of the face seemed not to have moved an iota. She looked wary, Annie decided, uncertain whether to go along with what she was saying, and she grinned.

'Oh, come on, Maddie! What harm can it do? There's no one here at all, so even if you do talk and I go rushing off to tell them all, those doctors and nurses who are so full of themselves, if I go off and tell them you spoke, they won't believe me. Why should they? No one need ever know if you don't want 'em to. It's for *my* own interest I want you to talk. I don't give a damn about them and their problems. Or about yours come to that. I don't really give a damn about anything. But I'm curious about you. I want to know who you are and why you stopped talking to people. So start talking to me, just to me, and let me off my hook, hmm? I want to know if it'll work for me, you see. If I can do it then I will, if it makes me feel better. Does not talking make you feel better, Maddie? Is that why you stay so quiet?'

The lips moved, fluttering a little and the word came out like a whisper. 'No –'

'Then why? For all these years, why?'

'No,' Maddie said again and Annie frowned. Was she really responding, or just making a sound? The only word she had been sure of hearing was this 'no'; that first 'please' had been so ghostly and strange that she might have imagined it. Was Maddie actually talking or was she just making a noise?

'Listen,' Annie said firmly, 'I'll start you off. I don't want any more of these "noes", thank you very much. I want information. So here we go. I am Ann Brady Matthews. I'm usually called Annie. I'm a bastard.'

Maddie still had her eyes fixed on her and Annie laughed, a savage little sound that echoed in her own ears.

'Now I'll never know, will I, whether you're quiet because you're horrified or because you're not talking anyway. What the hell. Let's keep going. So. My mother had me with a man called Colin Matthews. Her name was Jennifer Brady. Pretty she was. Bright too. Could have done all sorts of things with her life. But not she. No, she spent it being madly in love with a selfish bastard who used her like a second car, when it was convenient and it didn't matter who saw him, and she waited for the convenient times in a silly house full of silly rubbish, raising a silly kid. And then got even sillier and died all on her own while the silly kid she'd spent her life rearing was whooping it up in Paris. That's me. Now, how's that for a nice tale to start you off? Hmm?'

Maddie wasn't rocking, she suddenly realised, and that made her feel good. It meant she was sure that she was listening. She wasn't trying to escape into her own world of trance, that was certain. So Annie went on talking and talking, waiting sometimes for some sort of response and then, not getting it, ploughing on. And on.

'All right, you want to know more? I'll tell you more. She never married him, this Colin Matthews. Shall I tell you why? His wife wouldn't let him, that was why. Or so he told Jen. That's what I called her, Jen. It was too shameful to say Mum to a woman who didn't have a wedding ring. That's what I thought when I was at school, when I was ten. I couldn't tell *her* that, of course. Could I? There she was being so brave, so bloody heroic, the stupid creature, refusing to tell a lie about being married, for all she was always so proper, and I was ashamed to call her Mum. How could I tell her that? So I pretended it was smarter to use your mother's first name at our school and the silly bitch believed me. What do you think of that? Such a snob – she used to boast to me, do you know that?

76

She'd boast about how high-class her precious Colin was with his big car and his kids at public schools. Oh, yes, he had other children. Three of them. I was never allowed to meet them of course, never even knew their names, any more than Jen did. He didn't think it was right to mix the two sides of his life. That was what he told her and the poor bitch believed him. Oh, what a poor bitch she was! Whatever he said, she believed him. And boasted about him to me. Not to anyone else, of course. We had to be refined, she said, keep ourselves to ourselves. No friends, no chat with the neighbours. Crazy. I couldn't argue either, even when she said words like "refined" in that awful Irish voice of hers. "He's so refined" she'd say.' And Annie lapsed into a cruelly accurate mock-genteel Irish accent. ' "He's *so* refined. Drives only the best of cars and has *such* a lovely house. In Northwood, you know, very smart area, very select. Nice tone to the neighbourhood." Pah –' And again Annie made the thick sound in her throat that was all she could use to show her disgust.

Maddie had lifted her head more, Annie noticed now. Her eyes were still fixed on Annie's own, but the lids were lower, which meant her chin had come up. She's listening hard, Annie thought and her chest tightened with a sort of excitement.

'So that was how it was, you see. Me going to that tatty private school – she did that for *my* sake, of course. She said his other kids, the ones we mustn't ever talk about by name, they were at expensive public schools, so she said I ought to be at a school he had to pay for as well. So she chose this awful convent, where the nuns looked at your knickers to see if you had impure thoughts, and never thought of anything but sex themselves. Wicked old harridans – I hated them –'

She was silent then, not thinking about Maddie at all now. 'That isn't fair,' she said after a moment. 'There was only one like that, and she was a pathetic thing, really. The others were all right. Civilised really, in their own way, even though I didn't like the religious stuff they shoved at me. It was the only way I could argue with Jen, you see. She went on and on about religion even though she never went to church. She thought she couldn't, seeing she'd had me, and Colin wouldn't marry her, but it didn't stop her trying to make a Catholic of me. She didn't, of course. You can't be a Catholic if you don't go to church and she couldn't take me, so there was an end to it. But that didn't stop her nagging. Until I lost my temper that day and – but we won't talk about that. Will we?'

She turned her head to look at Maddie, waiting as if for an answer and then said roughly, 'Oh, why the hell shouldn't I tell you? I lost my temper and I hit her and she had a bruise. Is that so wicked, hmm? To hit your mother? She never hit me, mind you. Thought it was vulgar, you see. Told me that only the cheap ones hit their children.' Again the imitation of the Irish accent appeared in Annie's voice. ' "The bog Irish do that. I'm not bog Irish, you know. I'm middle class, always was," she'd say. And then went and got involved with that man! How stupid can a woman be? Tell me that. How stupid can a woman be? All those years in that awful little house, collecting all her things because they were refined or pretty or whatever else it was she called 'em, and they were all awful, believe me, they were awful, garish and ugly and awful, but she said they were nice and she collected them and dreamed of him and nagged me to be a lady and reared me a bastard –'

And then she was crying as she hadn't cried for years. She hadn't cried like that when Jen had died, hadn't cried like that, it was certain, when she had heard Colin had died, long before, had never cried as she did now, thick tearing sobs pulling her ribs apart till they screamed their pain at her, and her eyes ached and her head thumped with it.

It stopped at length, of course, though she couldn't be sure how long it had gone on. Only that she had been out of control of it, and that the weeping had been the real Annie, and her body just something that the weeping needed to use. She began to breathe more normally, not sobbing so much, though occasionally a single spasm lifted her diaphragm so that she hiccupped, and she blinked to see if she could open her swollen eyes. And then moved experimentally, to see if she could lift her head from her arms where she had rested it, and realised there was a weight on it.

And she put up one hand, trembling a little with the after effects of the storm of grief that had filled her and touched the weight and then managed to lift her chin stiffly and stare at Maddie. She still sat as she always did but she had one hand held out and awkwardly set on the top of Annie's head.

8

January 1987

After that it was like a tide coming in, slow but powerful,
sometimes eddying a little and sometimes seeming to retreat but
always creeping further and further up the beach, leaving ever
deepening water behind it as the shallows were filled in and new
territory was swallowed up.

Because Maddie, once she started to talk, didn't stop. At first
her voice came haltingly, hoarse and low like a very rusty old
engine creaking unwillingly into life, but as the days went on
she became more and more fluent, and the words would come
tumbling out in a steady stream. That was when it most seemed
like a brisk sort of tide that would never turn, and there were
moments when Annie almost panicked, fearing she would be
engulfed by this woman and her history. But then she got used
to it, and it became easier, because although to begin with
Maddie talked what seemed to Annie to be gibberish, dis-
connected words and phrases interlarded with names that
meant nothing to her and which Maddie never explained,
gradually her account of herself became coherent and under-
standable.

It was a little bit, Annie would think, lying in her bed at the
flat at night and remembering the day's output of words, it was
a little bit like doing a jigsaw puzzle but cutting out the pieces as
you went along. Maddie would pour out a great gobbet of talk,
and then, painstakingly picking her questions, to avoid startling
her, going as delicately as Agag, Annie would chip away at the
mass of words, persuading Maddie to explain, to discard, to
shape what she was telling so that that piece of new information
could be fitted in with the piece that had emerged the day
before.

The comparative emptiness of the ward contributed greatly,
Annie decided, to Maddie's emergence from her years of silence.
If it had been as it had been before the determined emptying of

Greenhill by its busy efficient administrators, would she have spoken? Wouldn't the constant chatter of the other patients, the noise of occasional arguments between them, the regular press of daily ward activities, have gagged her? Wasn't Annie being presumptuous and excessively self-satisfied to think – as she sometimes did – that it was her doing that had unplugged that tide?

I mustn't get too pleased with myself, she would think, as she left Maddie safely put to bed at the end of each day, and made her way back to her car and the journey back to her bleak flat. I mustn't take credit for something that's nothing to do with me –

But Joe Labosky wouldn't have that. He had made one of his usual visits on a Tuesday morning, ostensibly to check on Maddie's progress, but in fact to see how Annie was – not that he would have let her know that for the world – and had found the two women sitting with their heads together and so wrapped up in each other that they did not notice his arrival. Usually Annie was very aware of the presence of others, and if one of the nurses appeared anywhere near their section of the ward would lean back slightly in her chair, so that Maddie, seeming to communicate instinctively, would immediately stop talking, only to start again when Annie leaned forwards in that confidential way that showed that it was safe to do so. But on this morning Maddie had been particularly verbose and picking anything useful out of what she was saying so much more difficult that all Annie's concentration was fixed on her; and when she felt Joe's hand on her shoulder and looked up to see him standing beside her she felt a lurch in her chest and belly that made her feel sick, she was so startled. At once she leaned back and equally quickly Maddie slid into her customary silence, but they were both too late. Joe had seen and, more importantly, heard.

Maddie of course would not talk while he was there. She sat as she had for as long as he had known her, erect, blank of expression, rocking silently and with unfocused gaze, and although Joe tried to persuade Annie to try to get her talking again so that he could observe what happened, she refused.

'I can't,' she said mulishly, after he had insisted she come to the ward office to discuss it. 'It's nothing to do with you. It's

80

between Maddie and me. She doesn't like to talk when anyone is there but me. So I shan't make her.'

He grinned at her. 'Really? Are you sure it isn't that you don't want her to talk to anyone but you? Have you developed a proprietary interest, Annie?'

'Like hell I have,' Annie flashed. 'If you think that, you can go to blazes. I'll stop coming here and I'll stop talking to her and –'

He lifted his hands in a posture of mock self-defence. 'Sorry, sorry! It's a bad habit of mine you'll have to forgive. Always trying to see all the possible motives behind a course of action. All right – how do you know Maddie doesn't like to talk when other people are around?'

'Because she stops doing it,' Annie said witheringly. 'It's the most obvious evidence you can have, I imagine.'

'But do you signal her when other people are around and warn her to be silent again? She can't see the bulk of the ward – it's behind her. All she can see is the window in front of her. You're the one who can see the ward, because you sit in front of her. So isn't it possible that somehow you send a warning to her, and that makes her stop?'

'I didn't see you coming today,' Annie said. 'And she stopped as soon as you arrived. So what more do you want?'

'Nothing,' he'd said. 'Nothing at all. So it's got to be you and your company that's worked this particular bit of magic. I do congratulate you, Annie. You're a remarkably successful psychiatric nurse, clearly. We should have brought you in sooner.'

'Rubbish,' Annie said sharply. 'It's nothing of the sort. Nothing to do with me, at all. It's Maddie herself. She decided the time had come to talk so she's talking –'

'But she won't when you're not there. If she won't talk to anyone but you –'

'I don't want to discuss it,' she said and got to her feet. 'She ought to hear what we talk about, when we talk about her. It's not right to go on like this behind her back.'

He looked up at her and smiled. 'Good for you, Annie.'

'Good for what?'

'For this. For Maddie. For *you*. That's what being a friend is about. It's nothing to do with listening or talking or anything of that sort, is it? It's to do with protecting the interests of a person you care about.'

' "But it was the very *best* butter," said the Mad Hatter,' Annie said making her voice sound as contemptuous as she could and turning for the door. 'Do you have to lay it on quite so thick? It doesn't impress me.'

He shook his head with an obviously exaggerated patience. 'Dear me, but you make it hard for a person to be friendly to you! Oh, well, if that's the way you want it, what can I do? Maybe abrasive will stop being your buzzword in a month or two. It's getting a bit boring though, I must say.'

She had reached the door and was almost out of it but she stopped and not turning round stood still for a moment. And then turned deliberately and said carefully, 'I'm sorry. You're quite right. I've been unnecessarily rude. I'm sorry.'

He actually looked taken aback and she could have laughed aloud at that. She had been very rude to him, but she had enjoyed it. It was like punching a cushion to speak so to him because he absorbed all her anger or her hate and whatever it was she was feeling and gave nothing disagreeable back. But it was something that had to be dealt with, she had decided, this tendency to take pleasure in being nasty. I don't have to come on like Pollyanna, all sweetness and light, she thought now, but it won't hurt me to mind my tongue. Being hateful and bitchy can be a bad habit, and no more than that. It can be just as easy to develop the habit of being polite if still remote. They'll still leave you alone if you do that. It's not that I give a damn about what he thinks. It's just that I have to start somewhere and it might as well be with him. So she repeated it. 'I'm sorry.'

'Oh,' was all he said, and suddenly she smiled and then turned and went, leaving him sitting half perched on the edge of the table in Sister's office, staring after her. Knowing she had surprised him was really very pleasant, she thought as she went back to Maddie. I really enjoyed that. I must tell Maddie all about it.

And she did.

April 1950

The important thing, Maddie told Jay, was to make yourself pleasant to people. 'It's what they remember most,' she said.

'Not what you did, but how you did it. Believe me, there'll be no problems over this deal. No one'll think you had anything to do with it. If they remember you at all it'll be just as someone pleasant. You see if I'm not right.'

She was, of course. He handled the chocolate affair, collected his thousand pounds and it all went as smoothly as the chocolate itself; smoother in fact, because as Maddie said, it was pretty lousy chocolate. It was weeks before Ambrose stirred himself to do anything about his other instructions and he made such a racket when he found it had all been dealt with already, that all anyone remembered was that Ambrose Braham was a bastard, a typical rich man's kid who threw his weight about and made a pest of himself. And they stored it up as a score to discharge some time in the future, and no one paid any attention at all to Jay. Least of all Alfred, who was too busy with other matters to be interested in Ambrose's complaints. He just found him another deal to handle and sent him off grumbling to do it.

But that was the start of it all, as Maddie would remind Jay sometimes. It had all gone so very well and he was so very excited about his new-found solvency that he took her out a good deal that spring. They went to the races, and they went to dinner dances at the Savoy Hotel and the Caprice and to parties in houses by the river, and Maddie began to glow inside, knowing it was just a matter of time now. He'd soon see it her way, and they'd be married and it would all be just as it was meant to be.

But then he began to change. Not a great deal but enough to make her start to plan again. Odd dates missed and invitations to parties set aside because he was 'too busy' and she felt him sliding away from her, and had to make a new plan that didn't involve chocolate. There wasn't any chocolate to work with anyway; Alfred had had some sort of disagreement with the American end, she found, listening to one of his conversations on the phone at the Regent's Park flat, so that avenue was closed.

But there were others, and she needed them. And when Alfred sacked yet another secretary (he was famous for that, Maddie told Jay afterwards; the girl wasn't born who could be what he wanted, which was an efficient shorthand typist, a filing clerk, *and* willing to go to bed with him without expecting any special treatment in the office next day) she moved in.

'I'm bored, Daddy,' she told him. 'So bloody bored –'

'Don't say a word like that. It ain't stylish for a decent girl.' He said it abstractedly, not really listening, trying to pick his way through a confidential letter that listed actual sums of money and therefore couldn't be entrusted to any newcomer he might find to fill the departed Polly's chair.

'Well, I am. Nothing to do all day –' She came and leaned over the back of his chair as he went on picking away at the keys, swearing when he made a mistake and savagely pulling the paper out to start again.

'Get something to do then,' he grunted. 'And get out of my way, for Christ's sake. Bad enough trying to get this out tonight without you driving me crazy –'

'Oh, here,' she said, all disingenuousness. 'For God's sake, let me do it. You're all thumbs –' And she pushed him out of the chair and sat herself down and with an expert twist of her wrist put the paper in the platen. 'Is this what you want copied? Right, let's see now –'

And she rattled through the letter with only two or three mistakes which she was able to rub out neatly enough, and he looked it over, his cigar jutting up between his teeth in what he fondly regarded as his Churchill manner, and looked at her with a great grin.

'Hey, where'd you learn to do this?'

'Honestly, Daddy, you really are the dregs sometimes. At school of course! You sent me to that bloody – sorry! – that boring finishing school and they taught us this as well as flowers and walking with a book on your head and all the rest of it. Said it was a useful thing for a naice gel to be able to do –' And she laughed. 'Though why, they never said.'

'It's bloody useful,' Alfred said and signed the letter with his sprawling carefully practised signature and then watched her as she typed the envelope and folded the letter and put it in. 'Here, come to my office and help out till I can get a girl who's got a bit more in her mind than what's between her legs. I got more stuff to sort out this week than you can shake a bloody stick at, and girls are playing up about jobs, you never saw anything like it. They want their four pound ten and a five-day week and an hour for lunch and no bloody work, that's what they want.'

She set her head to one side and grinned at him. 'Me, I'd want the hour for lunch and the five-day week and at least six pounds ten. But you'd get plenty of work for it. And keep it in the family,' she said and laughed when he chewed his cigar at her. 'Oh, come on, Daddy. You need some help and I'm bored. I might as well earn the money you give me as not, so why shouldn't I? If it doesn't work out, you can get someone else and no harm done. Make up your mind. I might change mine any minute. It might be as boring in your dreary old office as sitting around here all day.'

That settled it, of course. As soon as he thought he'd have to coax her, it was a firm decision. She started work on the following morning and it worked out exactly as she hoped it would. Better in fact.

Because it wasn't at all boring. There were people in and out of the place all the time, toiling up the three flights of stairs that led to Braham's Export Agency Ltd on the top floor of the shabby building in Great Portland Street, and they were interesting people. Some looked shady and highly unreliable, but others seemed as prosperous as Alfred himself. Once even Sidney Stanley, the famous Sidney Stanley who had so ruffled the Whitehall dovecotes when the Government's Lynskey Tribunal had looked into, amongst other things, his business dealings, came puffing into her small outer office, where she sat being secretary and receptionist and general queen of the realm of Braham's Export. He was carrying a large basket of fruit and was wrapped in a heavy black overcoat with a Persian lamb collar, and under his heavy black homburg hat his face was red and gleaming.

'Alfred around?' he asked jovially. 'Got a little something for him –'

'He's gone round to the BBC, Mr Stanley,' she said demurely. 'A friend of his there needed some information about some new records from America –'

Her father had told her to say that to all comers. He was in fact having a haircut but part of one of his present schemes included importing several thousand new record players from America. Someone there had invented a new kind of record that played much longer than the ordinary three-minute ones, and was planning to bring them over to London.

'No use, though,' Alfred had said, talking to the man who came to make him the offer, while Maddie, ostensibly bringing the petty cash book up to date, listened avidly. 'Unless we got the new sort of machines you need to play 'em. You get me those and I'll get your records on the wireless, okay? I got pals round there in Langham Place, I have, I'll get them talking about your bloody records. Just get me the gramophones.'

So Alfred was busily working up the demand for his gramophones, as he insisted on calling them, which should be arriving in the next month or so depending on freight space and the right import licences and Maddie, knowing of Sidney Stanley's supposed expertise in the area of import licences, smiled sweetly at the big man and said again, 'The BBC. No idea how long he'll be, I'm afraid.'

'Ah,' Stanley said fatly. 'Glad to hear it. It's just where he ought to be, the way things are shaping up. Very nice too. Now, dear, I'll leave this for him. Just a couple of pieces of fruit, you know, a couple of pieces. Oh, and just give him this, will you? Very confidential —' And he went away down the stairs, pretending to run lissomely, which was a lot easier than climbing up them had been, his heels rattling importantly on the shiny lino that covered the treads.

Before he had reached the bottom and slammed the glass front door behind him she had examined the fruit basket – which was surprisingly well filled and even contained a pineapple, a rare object even though it was now five years since the war had ended – and opened the envelope which was carefully marked in large letters 'Private and Confidential. For Alfred Braham Esq. *only*'. All she had to do was throw away the envelope and her father wouldn't know she hadn't been meant to see its contents.

But when she read it she decided he wouldn't see it anyway, and carefully salvaged the envelope from the wastepaper bin. This was too useful to be left to her father, or worse still to Ambrose, who was getting a little sharper these days about work since his father had started to become a little less generous with cash. This was something for her Jay.

He rose to it just as she'd hoped he would, because for the first time in all their dealings he was able to feel that he knew more than she did. Because the envelope contained an export licence for fifty thousand bottles of best Scotch whisky, currently in a warehouse at Tilbury.

All he had to do, she told him, was to go armed with this document to supervise the loading of the whisky on to a cargo carrier due to leave London for Boulogne from whence it would be trans-shipped to a liner with some available cargo space on its way to Boston. And because Jay knew the way the Boston docks worked, and the necessary fiddles needed to get the stuff ashore, the whole thing would be very easy indeed.

'And,' Maddie said, 'worth a good deal of money.'

'How much?' Jay sounded guarded then. 'Is it worth the effort? I mean, to spend the whole of two days at Tilbury when I'm supposed to be at the Great Portland Street office – how will your Pa react when he finds out I'm not there? I could go sick, I suppose, but you know how he is. Not above sending someone round to my flat to make sure I'm there –'

'He won't,' she said confidently. 'I'll see to that. It's what I'm best at, seeing Daddy does what I want him to. And more importantly doesn't do what I don't want him to. Leave that to me. The thing is, it should get you at least five thousand. And if you can't make a bit more on the side with the warehousemen and a few bottles not making it to the hold on account of they're supposed to be broken, you're not the chap I thought you were. And I know you are.'

He stared at her and shook his head. 'Jesus, Maddie, you really are – listen, this is your Pa you're screwing! How can you do it?'

'I told you. I want you.' She laughed then softly and lifted her head and whispered into his ear, 'It's you I want to be screwing.' And he pulled away from her, seeming shocked.

'Where did you learn language like that?'

She laughed again. 'With a brother and a father like mine? Don't be daft! I've got ears. And anyway, I'm not screwing Daddy.'

'What happens when he finds out you've taken this licence out of his mail? Stanley'll be expecting to be paid for it. Won't he? He doesn't go sniffing round these government offices just for the fun of hobnobbing with civil servants, does he? From all I've heard of him he's a right twister –'

'You're being so silly, Jay! I shall go and see him and tell him I made a mistake and accidentally tore up his letter or burnt it or something. I'll show him the envelope and say how I now realise I was supposed to give it direct to Daddy but I opened it by mistake and didn't think it was important because I'm so stupid. Oh, you can work it out! I'll be all pathetic and helpless and he'll feel sorry for me and he'll get me a copy of it. It has to be on file somewhere, doesn't it? And then when I get it we give it to Daddy and he pays Stanley as arranged and by the time he gets the business in hand the ship's gone and he finds the deal's been struck with someone else. It's always happening – I've heard it often enough in the weeks since I've been here. People make three set-ups of deals to sell something they've got and it goes to whoever comes up first with the best money. These days it's the way it is everywhere. Daddy'll just curse it and get on to the next deal. He's going to make a fortune out of these gramophones, you know. I wouldn't let you in on that because it's much too big and Daddy's watching every step. But he's been in booze for so long it practically runs itself and he's used to there being mistakes and things going wrong. Especially when it's supposed to be Ambrose who's dealing with it.'

'Then it's your brother you don't mind screwing.' He was watching her with fascination for her face was alight with the excitement of it all and her hands were flickering busily as she pushed home the points she was making with those elegant gestures of hers. 'Doesn't that worry you?'

She made a face. 'Ambrose? Listen, Jay, I gave up worrying about him a long time ago. He's so *stupid*. He could have half this business all to himself by now if he wanted. Daddy wanted him to have it, being the son and everything. But he's hopeless, absolutely hopeless. Daddy says Mummy could keep him in order, but since she died he says he's been impossible. So he has, too. Makes my life a misery sometimes, the way he – well, anyway, I don't give a damn about him. If he can't look out for himself then I don't see why I should. I'm looking after number one. Daddy does. Ambrose does. So I shall too. Or rather one *and* two. Me and you. You especially. I do love you, Jay –' And she leaned across the table of the small cocktail bar where they were sharing a drink and set her hand in his.

He didn't move it away, but turned his palm upwards so that her fingers slid into his grasp.

'I'm beginning to realise how much,' he said. 'To put this sort of money my way – and you think we can get away with it –'

'I'm damned sure we can,' she said at once and then leaned closer still. 'Tomorrow's time enough for business, Jay, my darling. Tomorrow. Tonight Daddy's out at Wembley till midnight. There's a boxing match. Come and have some supper. Stay late with me? Please?'

'I've got work to do tomorrow,' he said and smiled lazily at her, his face curving gloriously, Maddie thought, in the limited light of the bar. 'What good will I be to anyone if I spend a night of mad passion with you, hmm?'

'Do you want to spend some mad passion with me?'

'Any man would.' He grinned even more widely.

'I'm not interested in any man. Only in you. Go on, answer me – do you?'

'Of course I do – no, hang on there, for Christ's sake. I don't do things like that to innocent young girls, you know. Especially if they love me.'

'I'm not so bloody innocent,' she flared at him, trying to look sexually experienced but not quite sure how to. 'And it's not whether I love you that should matter. It should be don't you love me?'

'I'm beginning to think a hell of a lot of you, Maddie,' he said and suddenly he wasn't bantering any more. He took hold of both her hands now and leaned over towards her so that their faces were almost touching. 'More than just wanting to crawl into the sack with you. That'd be easy and fun and then what? No, I want more for us. A real partnership, hmm? Real togetherness – I'll take you out for supper tonight and tomorrow I'll work and get on to this deal. Let's see how this one works out and then after that – who knows? But until we know we're on the right road together, my dear impetuous Maddie, I'm going to take care of you. And that means no mad passionate love. Yet.'

And he leaned just that little bit further forwards and kissed her and her bones melted completely.

9

February 1987

A bitter February sort of day, heavy with the kind of chill that creeps into bones and makes them feel fragile, and she had to choose today to decide to walk; bloody Maddie, Annie thought sourly and tucked her chin down into her scarf. And then lifted her shoulders because the movement had exposed the back of her neck and that was cruelly cold. Having her hair cut in that mad fashion had really been just that: mad.

She thought about it as she walked slowly along beside the shuffling figure that was Maddie. She was wrapped in several layers of cardigans and sweaters and an overcoat and on her feet she was wearing an elderly pair of Annie's own Wellington boots, the only things that could be found that would fit the splayed old feet. It had been so long since Maddie had walked anywhere except between her bed and her chair and the bathroom that her feet had softened, losing their muscle tone. Now they flapped in the old boots and she put them down to the ground gingerly at each step, as though they hurt.

Well, she'll just have to put up with that, Annie thought. If she'd have agreed to come out to walk with me when I first suggested it, when the weather was in that mild phase, she'd have found it easier. To wait till now, when snow glowered over the sky like a pall and the ground was rock hard with frost, was asking for painful walking. And she was suffering it, and it served her right, Annie told herself and went back to thinking about her visit to the hairdresser and was angry once more.

Why had she done it? What had possessed her? It had been like being possessed, come to think of it. She had woken that morning feeling quite extraordinary, as though there was helium in her bones so that she floated above ground instead of plodding along as heavily as Maddie was now doing, in the way she had seemed to have done for months, even years. That morning there had seemed to be sun in the sky and softness in the air of the sort that spoke of April, even though it had been just an ordinary gloomy sort of January Saturday, and she had gone to the High Street to do her usual bits and pieces of shopping, leaving Maddie to spend the morning alone for once. And had succumbed to the most ridiculous behaviour ever.

She had been walking past the hairdresser's shop on the corner where the buses turned, a shop she had seen before and despised for its absurd over-fanciful frontage covered as it was in shimmering silvery scales that glittered as the wind moved over it, and great steamed-up glass windows and silly name: 'Heading for Heaven'. Someone had pushed the door open just as she had passed it and come out bringing with her a great wash of luscious smells and warmth and light.

It had been amazing the effect the smell had had on her; it was a concoction of flowers and herbs and heat and ammonia and bleach and coffee and sweating female bodies and it had engulfed her and made those helium-filled bones feel even lighter; and before she knew what she was doing she had walked into the shop and was asking for an immediate appointment.

She had been given it by a receptionist who looked at her with bored disdain and then, before she could change her mind, had wrapped her in a frilled pink plastic cape and taken her and plopped her down in front of a mirror where an even more disdainful young man waited to look after her.

From then on it had been impossible to change her mind even if she had wanted to, which in fact she didn't, at first. The disdainful young man talked at her about the lack of condition her hair showed, and its split ends, its dryness and general dinginess and then washed it in several highly scented unguents, covered it in coloured foam, cut it with much determined waving about of scissors and finally attacked it ferociously with hair dryer and brush and comb. And she had sat throughout in a sort of trance, watching herself being transformed, and not until he had finished and she had handed over what seemed to her an inordinately large sum of money – for it had been so long since she had been to a hairdresser that she could not remember how much it ought to cost – and walked out of the shop had she really registered what she had done.

She had gone back to the flat at once, not bothering with the shopping at all and had stared at herself in the mirror, aghast and then secretly pleased and then suddenly angry, for she hardly recognised herself. The mass of ill-pinned dark hair in a bun to which she was so accustomed had been replaced by a jagged-edge cap that shone redly in some lights – the effect of the coloured foam? she rather suspected it – and which made her face look thinner and lighter. Younger too, and she hated that and yearned to have her heavy bun back.

But that, of course, was a stupid way to think so she had tried to forget what she had done, refusing to look in a mirror even when she combed her hair, just running the teeth through the tangles and leaving it to find its own level, and pretending it just didn't matter. And it didn't, except when it was cold and she forgot her neck no longer had the heavy bun of hair that had once protected it from the chill and she felt the exposed skin shudder in the wind. Like this morning.

She looked at Maddie again. She was now walking a little more steadily, both hands still thrust into the pockets of her top coat – for she had flatly refused to budge if anyone touched her or tried to support her – and with her head up. The ward sister had set a large knitted woollen cap on her head which she had tolerated and now she glowered out from beneath its edge, set low on her forehead, at the monotone world of the wintry afternoon with her dark eyes fixed ahead and her face as expressionless as ever. And suddenly Annie laughed.

'Maddie, you've no idea how bloody ridiculous you look! That stupid hat makes you look like an upended radish and that awful coat – if you're going to come out and about with me, you're going to have to look better than that. I'll get you some new clothes. What do you say to that? Hmm?'

Maddie plodded on, but it seemed to Annie she was listening with more care than usual. It was impossible ever to know whether she was listening, because although Maddie now talked, often for hours on end, she did not converse in any way. It was not a matter of Annie asking questions or making comments and getting logical answers. It was far more that the two women embarked on a series of parallel monologues, although Annie did listen to Maddie. But Maddie seemed not to listen to Annie.

Or did she? Looking at her now Annie thought – is she listening? – and she said a little more loudly, 'I'll get you some clothes, Maddie. And I'll take you to the hairdresser. Come to *my* hairdresser. A very determined young man, knows exactly how someone should look. See what he did to me –' and she moved sharply to come and stand in front of Maddie, so that she had to stop walking and look at her.

'See what he did to me?' Annie pulled off her own cap, a rough Jules et Jim one that she had bought when she had been a schoolgirl and had never got round to throwing away. She could feel her hair blowing in the wind, stirring over her forehead, and again she shivered as the cold stroked the back of her denuded neck. 'Do you like it?'

Maddie focused her eyes on her and then let them slide into their usual glaze and Annie made an irritated noise between her teeth and crammed her cap back on her head. 'Well, all right, you don't like it. Neither do I, much. But it's done. And I dare say if I took a bit of trouble over it I'd get used to it.'

She was arguing with herself now as they started to walk again, side by side. 'I dare say it was more that I'm not used to it than anything else. And why shouldn't I try to make myself look nicer? Mmm? I may be gone thirty and useless but dammit, it's my head and my hair and there's no reason why I shouldn't make an effort, is there?'

'No,' Maddie said and this time seemed almost to smile and Annie laughed and without thinking tucked her hand into Maddie's elbow and walked alongside her, in step, feeling suddenly better again. And Maddie let her, seeming now not to mind being touched.

'Then I'll take you there and you shall have a haircut too, next time I go. And I will go. I'll get used to the way it is, won't I? If I try again –'

Across the garden, from his place in the shadow of the corner of the West Pavilion, Joe watched them and began to let hope rise a little higher in him. When he had first seen the new haircut he had been positively excited; it had always been a good sign of emergence from depression when a woman – or indeed a man, come to that – began to take an interest in personal appearance. The combination of that lightening of her depression and her success with Maddie could be all that Annie needed to bring her

93

back to a level where some sort of real communication with her might be possible —

Or so he thought, standing watching his two patients as they curved round to the other side of the garden and began to make their slow way back. Just give me the chance to make a real contact with her and maybe I won't be so lonely any more. And I must stop thinking of her as a patient. The way I feel about that damned woman, that could be a disaster.

May 1950

'Do you like it, Jay?' Maddie said again, and twisted in her chair so that he could see the other side of her head. 'It's called the gamine haircut. It's like the one Zizi Jeanmaire has. And I'm getting a pair of those Perugia boots, like stockings they're so tight on your legs, you know? And a coat like a tent — oh, I'm going to look the very best ever! Say you like it.'

'It's great,' he said but he didn't look up. 'Hey, Maddie, look at this, will you? I've been through this list till my head bursts with it and I make it four thousand dollars down. I just can't see where the cheat is. Someone's screwed me, that's for sure —'

He pushed the pile of papers at her and she sighed and got up and came round to sit beside him and look at the columns of figures. He'd kept a very painstaking account of all the work he'd done on the basis of the tips she had given him and as she ran her eyes down it she felt a twinge of unease.

'Is this the only copy of this there is?'

'Sure. Why?'

'My God, if Daddy saw this, he'd have a fit. I mean, I didn't think you'd actually put it in writing this way. It's one thing to pick up the odd job here and there for you, but quite another to see them listed.' She ran her eyes down the page again and then looked at him, almost in awe. 'My God, did I set up all of these?'

'You know quite well you did. What's the fuss? Listen, can you see why it is that the two columns don't match? I'm down four thousand dollars here —' and he leaned over and pointed and she experienced him in a great wash of soap and scent and toothpaste and cigarettes and whisky and bay rum and her skin crawled on her belly. It was hell being with him and wanting him so much, agony not to know when they'd be able at last to complete their loving. That was always how she thought of it, as completing their loving. Not just as making love or losing her virginity or anything of that sort but a completion of a thing that was meant to be whole, the finishing of a structure that had just the smallest of gaps in it. Their love was as solid to her as a brick building, but it was an unfinished building and she sat and stared at the sheet of paper in front of her, letting the words and feelings jostle in her mind, and tried to prevent herself from reaching up and pulling him down to her to force him to that completion. But if she did that he got angry. 'You make it so hard for me,' he had told her when she had done it in the past, trying to force him to make love at last. 'Don't you think I want you? It's just that it wouldn't be right. Not till we're really entitled to be together. Then – oh, then, honey, believe me, it will have been worth the waiting –'

'Maddie, for Christ's sake, if you can't see it say so, and give it back to me!' He was getting irritable now and she blinked, startled out of her reverie.

'What? Oh, yes – look, it's here. See? You were paid there in pounds and you've forgotten to change it to dollars the way you have in this column. That's why it's down. You've carried it over as pounds –'

'Jesus, I did too! Where would I be without you, Maddie? Good for you!' And he pulled the paper from her hand and corrected it, and finished the calculation, writing the totals at the end with such satisfaction that he almost flourished the pen.

'Will you look at this? In just over ten months, I've made over thirty-seven thousand dollars, quite apart from your father's salary to me. Christ, Maddie, that's real cash! I never imagined I'd ever have done so well in this lousy country. Who'd ha' thought it, the way things are here –' He laughed fatly. 'It just goes to show you, hmm? Where there's a bit of intelligence a fella can do anything –'

'It helps to have a bit of assistance too,' she said sharply and looked up at him with her brows raised. 'Listening to you people'd think it was a case of all my own work and look Mum no hands.'

'Eh? Hell, Maddie, don't look so sorry for yourself! Sure you helped. Without you I wouldn't have made a dime.' And he leaned down and pulled her to her feet and then hugged her, and swung her round so that she had to bury her face in the delicious gap between his neck and his shoulder and could inhale him until her head swam.

'Give me a kiss!' she demanded as soon as he stopped turning and lifted her face so close to his that he had to. Maybe this time? But he was as controlled as ever and kissed her lightly and set her on her feet.

'You'll make sure no one ever sees that list, Jay?' she said then, as anxiety about her father came surging back into her mind. He'd been getting very edgy lately, the old man, what with Ambrose nagging him about the troubles he was having holding on to the whisky business and the difficulties he had himself with his gramophones. He'd sold them all right, but there had been a great many complaints because of the wiring; over and over again machines had been found to be faulty and had to be sent back to London for expensive overhauling by an American electrician Alfred had managed to track down. (He had been a wartime deserter who had never found the courage or the cash to go home again.) That had eaten into the company's profit margins. Altogether Alfred was much less pleased with himself than he had been, and Maddie, still working in his office, was very aware of it. And also knew just how powerfully he would explode if he discovered what she had been doing for Jay.

'Don't worry,' Jay said easily now and sat down in the armchair by the dead fireplace. Once again they were alone in the Regent's Park flat, but not because her father was out with one of his women gambling this time. Nowadays he spent his evenings drumming up more business to make up for what seemed to be dropping cash returns. Jay repeated, 'Don't *worry*. There's no way anyone will ever see that or that anyone will ever know that you and me did business.'

He stopped then and looked at her a little sideways and then down at his hands. 'Anyway,' he said lightly, 'I won't be around for anyone to talk to, so no one'll be able to pump me, hmm?'

She lifted her chin sharply and stared at him as a wave of cold shifted from the depths of her belly slowly upwards to engulf her and make her breathing come oddly short.

'What did you say?'

'Listen, dolly, you didn't think I'd be here in England for ever, did you? I mean, damn it all, girl, I'm a foreigner here! I got a home and folks and friends I haven't seen in damn near a year. You must have known I'd have to go back to Boston sooner or later. Well, it turned out to be later, but later is here. I'm going home. I have to, believe me.'

'Why?' She was on her feet, not caring now what she said or how he might react, and she flew at him and threw her arms around his neck with such vigour that his chair nearly rocked backwards, taking them both with it. But he righted it and tried to push her away. But she clung on grimly.

'You can't, you can't! Why, Jay? What did I do? What did I say? I'm sorry, Jay, if I made you angry – I won't again, I promise – just tell me what I have to do and I'll do it, I swear to you –'

'Maddie, for Christ's sake, will you calm down? You crazy kid – I'm going home is all! No one said anything, no one did anything. Except maybe Declan –'

He had managed to push her away by now, so that she was sitting in front of him on the rug, crouching with her heels pushed into her buttocks, and she seized on that and said quickly, 'Who?'

'Declan. I told you about Declan –'

She struggled, dredging through her memory. 'Your brother –'

'Sure my brother. The bastard. I'm out of the way five minutes and he's in there creaming it all up, the lot. It's like there's only him, only one son. And there sure as hell is not –'

'I know. There's Timothy, and –' She was struggling even harder now to be calm, to salvage what she could from this dreadful situation, to distract him from his awful decision. It was the only possibility she hadn't foreseen, and she was furious with herself for being so obtuse. She had imagined another girl turning up to beguile him, had imagined him doing something stupid over one of the deals she put his way, and being caught by her father and being beaten up for it, had even imagined Ambrose finding out about what she and he were doing. But she had never imagined this.

'Yeah. And Declan. He's the one next to me. Timothy's the oldest of course. But he's married now, got his own share of the action. It's between Declan and me. And because I'm here in

London, that creep is oiling his way into everything. I know – he needn't think I don't. I may be stuck here in this god-forsaken hole but I have my contacts. I get letters –'

He was glowering now, staring down at her with his face looking solid because his expression was so aggrieved.

'I know what he's doing. And it is time he stopped. So –' He leaned back then and his face slowly smoothed itself. 'So now I've got some cash, I can go back. I've spent a bit, but I've got most of it. Thirty thousand dollars at least. Bless you, Maddie.' And he leaned forwards and kissed her with real passion, and she felt the gratitude oozing out of him and wanted to be sick. To think she had worked so hard and lied so readily to her father and brother to make him the money – to go away from her! It was enough to make her die, and not just be sick, and she pulled away from him and said shakily, 'You don't have to go. Write to your father if you think your brother's trying to cheat you. He'll tell you it's all right, won't he? He'll be like my father, won't he, wanting to take care of all of you?'

He laughed at that, sourly. 'My father? Jesus, kid, he's got seven of us! There's my four sisters, you know, and girls don't come cheap.' He laughed again. 'Believe me, there aren't many like you, with a gift for putting cash a fella's way. Most girls see to it it's the other way about. No, I've got to go back. With my father it's out of sight, out of mind. The old goat sent me here, thinks I'm okay, so Declan makes all the running. It's got to stop. And I'm going home to stop it.'

She took a deep breath. 'Take me with you, Jay. Please take me with you –'

'Are you mad? You know I can't do that!'

'You could if we were –'

'Listen, I told you. That is out of the question just yet –'

'You said, when you had enough money. Thirty thousand dollars – that's a lot of money – it's nearly ten thousand pounds. We could get married with that, and we could work for ourselves. I've learned a lot, Jay, being with Daddy. We could start our own business, export and import and all that. I can run the office, you can do the dealing the way you have been all year. No need to be secret about it any more either. Just run a proper business like Daddy's –'

She knew she was spitting into the wind, even as her tongue

ran on and on. He had a different set of plans and he was never going to change them. She would have to fit in with them, rather than expect him to change his ideas to fit in with her and beneath the surface of her mind, beneath the cold fear of losing him and the sound of words that she was spinning, her thoughts raced ahead, making their way round the maze of possibilities. He was going to America –

'It's settled, doll. Believe me, I'll send for you. Let me get home to Boston, show Pa he can't go on putting Declan in front of me, and see to it he gets the business right for me as well as the rest of 'em and then I'll talk him round to a non-Catholic daughter-in-law and I'll send for you – because, my God, Maddie, I'm going to miss you something amazing!' and he leaned over now and pulled her up so that she was sitting in his lap. 'I really am.'

His voice was a little thicker now, and his forehead a little beaded with sweat and she turned her head and looked at him and felt a new wave of feeling rise in her. He was as excited as she was; she knew it even before she felt the way his body altered beneath her buttocks, before he reached awkwardly beneath her to rearrange himself. He wanted her as badly as she had wanted him. Now, tonight, at last, they could be complete.

And she took a deep breath and scrambled down from his lap and moved away to the other side of the table.

'No,' she said. 'No, Jay. Not till we're married. We agreed that, didn't we? We said we'd be married and then we'd be together? And we *will* be married – you go to America and then when the time comes, you send for me. And then we'll be together for always.' And she smiled at him and saw the baffled look that moved across his face and the hint of anger and smiled softly. Oh, Jay, Jay, why are you so easy to see through? Why didn't I realise long ago this was the answer?

10

March 1987

'I think,' Joe said, 'the time is coming to push her a little.'

'You push her,' Annie said. 'It's not up to me.'

'You're the only person she talks to. So who else is it up to?'

'She doesn't talk to me,' Annie said. 'She talks *at* me because I just happen to be there. I don't know who she talks to actually. It's not to herself really. Or perhaps it is –' She leaned forwards and propped her elbows on the table and set her chin on her fists. 'It's odd, you know. You watch her and you'll see. She's still in a way as she was before. Sitting and staring and rocking, only now she's talking as well. But I think, you know, that really she's the same as she used to be.'

'Yes?' he prompted her gently, needing to understand what she meant while not wanting to upset her unusually communicative mood and certainly not wanting to fire her short temper. Not that it was as short as it used to be, and he held that thought close, letting it warm him. It wasn't just excessive hopefulness on his part, he was sure. She was changing in her mood and her behaviour, as well as in her appearance. The short jagged haircut had softened a little now, and it suited her well, making her face look less heavy and shadowed than it had been, and today he even suspected she'd put on some powder and lipstick. Not a great deal, but enough to make his hopes rise. So it was important not to upset her by rushing her. But of course he still needed to know about Maddie. She really was his patient.

'Well, it's a bit as though she's still in that trancelike state she used to be. Only now she's not just thinking about what happened in her life. She's talking about it too. But it's all a dreadful jumble. I must have listened to hours and hours of it, but I'm still not all that much the wiser. I'm beginning to sort out what it's all about though. I think.'

'Would it worry you to tell me?'

'Hmm?' She looked at him, puzzled. 'Why should it worry me?'

'You said once before that it wouldn't be – a friendly thing to do, to talk about Maddie behind her back. You showed some very nice ethics there.'

'Oh dear.' She reddened a little. 'I must have been in a very pompous mood that day. Though perhaps not. It is a bit tacky to talk about people behind their backs. But that day – I think I was just feeling bloodyminded. I do sometimes, I'm afraid.' And she stopped abruptly and he could have hugged her for her candour.

'Yes,' he said gently, still sitting as he had been with his arms folded. 'I had noticed.'

She grimaced. 'Well, we all have our bad days. I still do, but they're not quite as they were. I –' She stopped. 'I suppose I could apologise or something but – would you like some more tea?'

'Yes please.' It seemed the answer she wanted so he provided it, though he didn't want more tea. He watched her as she went to the servery at the far side of the staff canteen where they had been sharing lunch and tried to see in the way she looked now the girl she had been a few months ago. She had gained a little weight, which meant she was eating better, and that was good, for it suited her. She had been both heavy looking and yet gaunt and bony. But now there was more spring in the way she moved and a lightness that was agreeable to see. And he sighed softly as she made her way back to their table, carefully balancing the cups, and wished he found her less interesting than he did.

They drank the tea in silence and then she said abruptly, 'It's odd, you know, how she makes me feel. I'm not as angry as I was.'

'Why?'

'If I knew, it wouldn't be odd,' she said with a flash of her old irritability and then she laughed. 'Well, don't ask silly questions, and then I won't snap,' but there was no malice in her tone.

'You're entitled to snap if the questions are silly. And I'm afraid they usually are. Most of the things psychiatrists say and do are exceedingly silly. Meddling in people's lives as we do –' He set down his cup. 'But we've talked about that before, and it's dull. Let's meddle instead. So, you don't mind talking about Maddie now when she isn't here to listen herself?'

She shook her head. 'No. It's partly because she's changing too. She's talking a lot, as I said, but most of it's incomprehensible. I get the feeling sometimes that she goes over and over the same episodes in her life, trying to change the way they happened but not being able to. Oh, I'm explaining this badly. Look, have you ever been a daydreamer? When you were a child?'

'Daydreamer? Probably. Most children are, I imagine.'

She shook her head. 'No, not just being inattentive. I mean really daydreaming. I did.' She stopped. 'I'm supposed to be talking about Maddie, I know, but this is the only way I can explain. The thing is, I used to choose a subject to think about, a scene I was in, a place, or an event – I had lots of them. Sometimes on a stage, and sometimes being caught in a terrible mystery – all sorts of different ones. I'd sort of see myself in the situation and then let it go – let it happen and watch inside my head. Do you understand?'

'You're explaining it very well.' He wasn't sure what she was trying to get at, but it mattered to her, obviously. So it mattered to him.

'Well, sometimes I liked what happened. I'd watch the story as though it were someone else's – like a film or a play, and it was marvellous, better than real living. All the best things in my life happened inside my own head. They still do, really.'

She stopped and stared down into her cup and then, almost with a visible physical effort, dragged herself back to the here and now, lifting her head to look at him.

'But sometimes it used to happen that the story went bad. Ugly and frightening and – and I used to try to drag it round, to change it and make it fun again and to decide for myself how the story I was watching would work out. Sometimes I could. Often I couldn't, and it would all turn horrible and I'd be helpless and have to watch it all, and see myself going through hell and then I'd be miserable all day. Or I'd sleep badly or I'd get into trouble at school with the Sisters or with Jen at home. Well, the point of all this is that I think that's what happens to Maddie. She starts to have a vision of her past. Of what happened to her, and how it happened and why. And sometimes she doesn't like what she sees and tries to change it. But it won't change. And she has to keep on living it over and over again, the bad parts. And that frightens her. Can you understand?'

'I think I do. You really have developed a strong bond with her, haven't you?'

'How can I?' She sounded bitter. 'How can you have a bond with someone who only ever talks *at* you and who talks like a torrent about things you can't entirely understand, and who never explains even when you ask her to, and ignores what you say unless it's something she wants, like food or a walk or whatever? She responds to me then, well enough. But then she shuts herself up in that cupboard of her own past and talks and talks at me through the door and never hears a word I say. How can I make a bond with *that*?'

'Do you want to?'

She shrugged. 'I don't know.' Her mood was changing. She was becoming irritable again, and a dullness seemed to spread over her, the way it spreads over landscapes when clouds move over the sun. 'What does it matter what I want, anyway? It's what she wants that's important, isn't it? And you want to find out about her so that you can work out how to dispose of her.'

'It's more than that with me,' he said mildly. 'It started that way, I agree, but now I'm eaten with curiosity about Maddie. I want to know in the worst way what it is that made her become an elective mute for so many years, and why she's now talking. I think it's because of you – you say it's just that the time has come. Well, why did it come? And where do we go from here? That's the important question.'

August   October 1950

'Why do you want to go? That's the question. Just to come and tell me you feel like it – that's no reason. It costs money, you know, gallivanting. And what for? Anyway, I need you here. You've got a job now, you know. Part of the family business, you are. You wouldn't want to go off and leave me in the lurch, now would you? Forget it, sweetheart, forget it. I ain't being touched for no transatlantic ship tickets.'

And that was that. When Alfred was adamant that he wasn't going to spend money on something, then he never would. He was unmovable. If there was one thing Maddie had learned in the years of being the most important woman in his life, it was that. Before her mother had been killed in the air raids of 1940 he had been an easier man, as she remembered him. Whatever she asked for she got. But that had changed after Mummy had gone. He had indulged her, of course he had; but there were times when he dug in his heels and wouldn't be budged. And this, Maddie knew, was one of them.

So she would have to do it alone. It wouldn't be easy, but that made no difference. It still had to be done, and done quickly. Jay had told her that he was going in six weeks – he had to organise one or two things of his own, he had said importantly and refused to tell her what they were, and why was she rushing him, anyway?

'Are you trying to get rid of me sooner?' he had said, making a face at her that she found quite adorable. 'I thought you were going to miss me.'

'I shan't miss you in the slightest,' she had said airily, putting on a great show of bravado that wasn't meant to convince him and which didn't, while gleefully hugging to herself the knowledge that she wouldn't need to, and he had laughed and kissed her cheek and told her she was a crazy kid but cute with it and he was going to miss her, anyway. And she had thought, six weeks – I've got to move fast, and kissed him back and told him that of course she was going to miss him dreadfully, and he was a hateful beast not to take her with him.

Six weeks. First the passport problem. She'd been on her father's hitherto, but now she had to have her own, and it was the fact that she wanted new clothes that made that possible.

'But, Daddy,' she argued when he told her she could do her shopping in London perfectly well. 'You know it's impossible! Ever since clothes came off coupons you haven't been able to get a single interesting thing! All the shops have got are millions of dreary things for dreary people. I want the sort you used to have to buy black market – and the only place I can get them is Paris. You know it's true!'

'Oh, dammit, why can't you be like other girls and settle for what you can get? All right, all right, leave me alone already. You want Paris, you'd better have Paris.'

It had worked like a dream, reminding him how important it

was that Alfred Braham's daughter should look exciting and different and not the same as everyone else's daughter, and she held out her hand gleefully as he put a cheque for a hundred pounds into it.

'But I can't take you till the end of October, so you'll just have to be patient – no nagging,' he went on and at once she pouted and threw her arms round him and began the coaxing she knew he liked so much.

'But Daddy, that's ages away! You can't make me wait so long! If you can't go, let me go on my own, hmm? I'll ask Ruth to come with me – she's so dull she'll make sure I stay dull too. I'll be perfectly safe. Let me go, Daddy, or I'll sulk all over the office and put everything in wrong files and then where will you be?'

And Alfred, who was feeling a good deal more genial these days since fewer of his special deals seemed to be melting away under his fingers and business looked like picking up, laughed and slapped her behind and agreed. She had known that would happen, known he wouldn't be able to take her, and now she said offhandedly, 'Well, then, I suppose I'd better fix up a passport for myself then.'

'What? Yeah – suppose you had. Never thought of that. It'd be easier to wait till October –'

'Not a bit of it!' she said and hugged him once more. 'I'll get the forms and everything and you can sign 'em. So that'll be that –' and of course it was.

Getting a berth was a lot harder. Ships making the trans-atlantic crossing in the summer and autumn months were always more heavily booked than the rougher winter ones, when seasickness dogged the Atlantic and spoiled trade, and to get on to the same ship as Jay was essential. She had first to find out which ship that was and then get on it herself and in a different part of it, too. All of which was likely to prove difficult indeed.

It took her a terrifying ten days to get the information she needed out of Jay. He was being very secretive, she felt, and that drove her nearly demented with anxiety, but she didn't dare to let him know that. It might make him withdraw even more and that was not to be allowed. She had heard whispers among some of the people she met at parties that he wasn't above kicking up his heels with some of the better known easy girls, but that didn't worry her. A man spending time with tarts was to be expected. As long as he didn't love any of them, there would be no problems. And if she nagged him about tarts, then he might find her the harder to love. It wasn't easy, Maddie told herself, to be as wise and clever a woman as women were supposed to be. None of her magazines had ever told her how to handle a situation like this one. But she felt instinctively she was doing it right, and battled on.

And it paid off. On a Saturday night when they had gone dancing at the Caprice and had laughed a great deal and he had seemed to her to be closer than ever to her in mood, and had admired the pretty clothes she had brought back from her three days in Paris the week before (for having fussed so to Alfred about the need to go, she had of course been forced to make the trip even though she wasn't nearly as keen to go as she might have been) he told her casually that he was sailing on the eighth to New York, on the *Mauretania*, and she wasn't to fuss about it.

'Who's fussing?' she said lightly and smiled at him. But she made sure it was a tremulous smile that seemed to hide the threat of tears. Oh, but she was being clever and sensible; oh, but she could teach other women a thing or two. 'I know it can't be helped. As long as you keep our promise and send for me to marry me as soon as you can –'

'You know something, Maddie?' He came closer and held her so that his lips were very close to her ear as they moved through the slow foxtrot that they were dancing to, 'Some Enchanted Evening', 'I do want to marry you. I used to think it was a crazy idea, and I won't pretend I didn't. But you've got a way of growing on a man, and I'm going to miss you like the devil. I wish I could have taken you with me, believe me. But I'll have to sort things out with my Pa, and having you along'd make it tough. But let me sweeten him and then you'll be on the next ship over. It's a promise.'

And she had closed her eyes ecstatically and inclined her head a little more towards him so that he could nibble her earlobe and knew she would get what she wanted, all that she wanted. The secret of life, she whispered inside her head, is to want things and to imagine the things you want happening to you, and then to go out and make them happen. That's the secret and it's my secret and I am happy, happy, happy. Or I soon will be, when I make it all happen the way it's supposed to –

'Let me come and see you off at – where will you be sailing from? Liverpool? Southampton?'

'Southampton,' he said and looked down on her fondly. 'All right, come and see me off. If you feel you must.'

'Of course I must. I want to spend as much time as I can with you –' she murmured and looked tremulous again. It really was absurd; he was getting as easy to handle as her father was.

It took a good deal more than tremulous smiles, however, to get herself a berth and there were times when she almost despaired, as she travelled from shipping agent to shipping agent, trying to find one who had some extra leverage with Cunard. It began to look ominously true that there were no berths available at all. Until just five days before the ship was due to sail she found a man in a tatty office in Holborn who listened to her heartrending tale of a lover who had gone back to America after the war and was now waiting for her in New York, and had sent her the money for her ticket and was insisting she sail on this ship.

'He's from Nevada,' she improvised, wide-eyed and anxious as she gazed at the grubby little man who lounged behind the scarred wooden counter of the small shop. 'And he's going to be in New York to meet me that day, the fourteenth. What can I do? I can't travel from New York on my own. I'd be too scared. Please, Mister, get me on that ship. My sweetheart sent me enough money to buy a good ticket, an expensive one. Can you help?'

For an extra twenty-five pounds he managed somehow to bend all the rules and take risks to get her a berth which was as much as his job was worth, as he told her over and over again, and she accepted what he had, no longer concerned to know where in the ship it might be. If she had to share with seven seasick mothers and babies in a cabin set right over the screw, she'd do it. It was only for a few short days, anyway. Just five days out of Le Havre and then they'd be in America and she would at last be Mrs Jay Kincaid and the real living could begin. And she curled up with delight as she thought of it and began slowly and with great care to smuggle her clothes out of the

Regent's Park flat and into a cheap hotel room she had found, ready to be on her way.

She told her father casually that she was going to Southampton to see off a friend who was going to New York.

'Mary Saltash, you remember? Her dad's in the diplomatic or something. So I won't be at the office that afternoon. Can you manage without me?'

'I suppose I'll bloody have to,' he said. 'Are you giving me any choices?'

'Not really!' she said sunnily and suddenly jumped up from the table where they were sitting eating breakfast and threw her arms round him. 'I do love you, Daddy, you know. You're so good to me.'

He swivelled his eyes and glared at her. 'Hey, hey, what is all this? What are you after? You don't come the angel of the hearth like this unless you're up to something.'

Alarmed at the risk she had taken she hugged him closer and murmured into his cigar-scented hair, 'How well you know me! I spent too much money in Paris, Daddy. Ever so much too much. I need a lot more. How about three hundred pounds?'

'Three hundred – are you potty?' He pushed her arms away and turned and glared at her. 'Three hundred pounds is real money, you know! It doesn't grow on bushes with tomatoes. You must be out of your mind to get into debt like that. As bad as your brother.'

'You know that's not fair.' She was in such a delight that she had salvaged the situation so well it was all she could do to keep her face properly controlled and to look suitably repentant. 'Honestly, Daddy, when did I last ask you for so much? Hmm? I mean, for a debt? Not once to every five times Ambrose does –'

He grumbled for a long time, but of course he gave it to her in the form of a handful of crisp white fivers, since he'd earned some useful extra side money this week anyway, and she rewarded him with kisses and flattering attention and extra effort at the office, leaving everything in the best order she could manage. It wasn't going to be easy for him once she'd gone. She knew that. He'd be confused and angry and fit to be tied, so the least she could do was to make the parting as painless as possible. And that meant a perfectly clean and orderly flat – and she harried Mrs Nemethy, their daily help, mercilessly to achieve

108

that – and an office as thoroughly organised as an army barracks.

On the evening of the seventh of October she told her father she was going to the theatre with her friend Elizabeth and then in the morning to Southampton to see her friend Mary off on her travels, reminding him he'd said she could, and kissed him goodnight for the last time. It was going to be strange not seeing Daddy again for a long time, but it couldn't be helped. That was the price that had to be paid, if she was to be Mrs Jay Kincaid. He'd understand, eventually, she told herself, as she packed that night in the hotel room to which most of her belongings had now been shifted. He'd have to.

Because for herself, it was all settled. Tomorrow she was to leave her home to go to a new country to be married to the only man in the world who mattered.

11

October 1950

Three times she had been round the *Mauretania*'s deck, looking
for him. Three times along the level by the sundeck, past the
row of lifeboats, round the shuffleboard deck, returning along
the second boat deck and then back to the bow and the rows of
bleak and mostly empty deckchairs. There were a couple of
people sitting out bravely, wrapped in blankets and with blue
noses and miserable eyes peering out at the grey skies and
pitching seas that were much the same steely colour, waiting for
the moment they could go scuttling below to tell their new-
found friends that it was really lovely up on deck, bracing, you
know, so healthy and delightful. But they were the only ones.
Once the ship had eased her way out of Southampton Water
and left Ryde and Ventnor and the last traces of the Isle of
Wight vanishing behind her they would go below to the grateful
warmth of the saloons and the luscious offerings of the cocktail
bars and she would have the twilit deck to herself. Without any
sign of Jay.

Shivering a little she leaned against the rail, staring down at
the water far below as it peeled lazily away from the sides of the
great liner and tried to catch her breath which had for some
time now been sticking in her throat, so that she found herself
breathing fast and anxiously even when she wasn't moving
about. She felt a little queasy, too, her throat tightening against
the bile in her gullet as the ship shuddered against the swell of
the water, and rolled a little more heavily. But she wasn't
seasick; she was never seasick. She had crossed the Channel on
those awful bucketing little ferries quite unscathed often enough
to know that. The way she felt now was nothing to do with the
sea. It was fear, simple cold fear. She had never felt so alone, so
vulnerable or so unsure of herself as she did at this moment, and
it was the nastiest feeling she had ever had.

And it wasn't to be given in to. She lifted her chin as
resolutely as she could but that dislodged the thick woollen cap

she had pulled down over her ears against the cold, and she had to pull it on again, and that meant letting go of the rail just at the wrong moment, for the ship lurched and she went skittering along the deck and ran painfully into a stanchion that was sticking out from one of the rails. She felt the bruise begin to appear in her thigh and she rubbed it furiously, staring out over the rail at the vanishing shoreline at the same time, willing herself to keep her head, not to panic, above all not to weep. She had a deep certainty that if she once gave in to this mood of fear and loneliness she would be overwhelmed by it. Control was what she needed –

But she could not stop it happening, because as she looked at the sliver of darker grey that was the Isle of Wight and saw a few faint winking lights there, a picture of her father swam sharply into her head; Daddy with his eternal cigar and his head bent over his books on his desk, cursing because she wasn't there to sort out the letters he needed, and the great rush of guilt and longing for him that rose in her was more than she could handle; and there she stood, holding on to the rail of the ship, her head down and her shoulders hunched against the cold, weeping like a terrified three-year-old, wanting her Daddy, needing to be picked up and held close and looked after.

It was like one of her magazine stories, she decided then. It really was. Because suddenly she was being held close and warm and safe by a pair of strong arms that came round her from behind and she caught her breath as again the ship rolled, pushing her even more closely to whoever it was, so that she couldn't turn to look. But she knew the smell of him and she lifted her chin and cried, 'Jay!' as loudly as she could, and twisted herself in his grasp and looked at him.

He was blank with amazement. She looked up into those beloved familiar blue eyes and at the thick cap of dark gold hair and knew every single fleck and variation in colour, every fine line on the lightly tanned cheeks and round the eyes and knew that she was the last person he had expected to see, because of the glazed, almost fish-like expression on his face. And she laughed and lifted one hand to pull off her cap, not caring about the cold any more at all, and said softly, 'Oh, Jay –' and then, as the wind snatched the words away from her, said it more loudly, 'Oh, Jay –'

'Jesus bloody Christ, what in the name of all that's holy are you doing here?' He almost shouted it and then half shook her, for he still had his arms around her. 'You said goodbye at the dock –'

'I know,' she said and gasped a little as another roll of the ship pushed them closer together. 'I lied.'

'Christ, Maddie, you aren't stowing away or anything crazy like that, are you? Because if you are –'

'Darling, of course not! I'm not that sort of fool! I'm a passenger with a ticket! Not as fancy a passenger as you, I dare say. I had to settle for what I could get. I'm in a six-berth cabin, God help me, right down in the bowels somewhere. It was all I could get. Are you on your own?'

He was still staring at her as though she were an apparition. 'How did you –'

'Darling, you didn't think I'd give in that easily, did you? Of course I had to come too. If you're going to America, then I've got to go. If you won't take me, then I have to bring myself. It's all very simple –'

He shook his head, and then shivered as a sharper wind began to blow across the otherwise empty deck. 'Listen, we'd better go below, get out of this –'

'Not yet –' She clung to him. 'There'll be people all over the place and I have to talk to you and –' She stopped very suddenly and stared up at him. 'You didn't know it was me, standing there crying. Did you?'

'No, of course not. I told you – I thought we'd said goodbye at Southampton.'

'So you were just trying it on with me? Thought you'd get yourself a bit of skirt for the crossing? Anyone'd do, as long as she was female and available?'

He went a sudden brick-red and stood there very still and then before she could say another word, bent his head and kissed her. He'd kissed her before, of course, and she had learned a great deal about his reactions and his needs from the way he behaved when he did, but this was something totally new. He was as passionate as she had ever longed for him to be, but it wasn't a storybook passion, an imagined excitement. This was vividly real, filled not just with desire but with anger and guilt and fear and a number of other emotions besides, and as his teeth bruised her lips and his tongue forced its way into her mouth so violently and so far that it ceased to cause pleasurable pain and became frightening, a part of her mind shouted exultantly at her. She had done it. She had imagined this man being hers, wanting her as much as she wanted him, had longed for him and fantasised over him for long months, and now she knew it was true and that Daddy was right. It *was* just a case of wanting badly enough, and trying hard enough and in the end you got exactly what you desired.

She pulled away from him, using all the strength she had, pulling her lips back from her teeth and biting against his tongue – not that it was easy for the tension in him was so strong that her efforts seemed puny against the power of control he had – but she was at last able to get her head away and both hands set on his chest so that she could push him, and she did and then stood there, her elbows straight and firm so that he could not get close enough to try to kiss her again.

'That's not an answer,' she said breathlessly and stared at him with great sternness, though what she wanted to do was laugh and shout her excitement and delight and pull him close to her. But she had to be as clever in victory as she had ever been in the chase. She didn't know how she knew that, but she was as certain of it as that she stood here and that he was staring at her, with the pupils of his eyes so dilated that they looked black in the rapidly fading light, and breathing heavily as sweat appeared in a fine row of beads on his upper lip in spite of the cold.

'Tell me the truth, damn you! Were you trying it on with another girl – as you thought – only an hour or two after saying goodbye to me, and knowing how I felt?'

'I –' He swallowed and started again. 'Oh, God, Maddie, but I wanted you! I watched you go – or I thought I did, damn you – and I wanted to call you back. I had no idea how much you'd moved in on me, for Christ's sake! I thought – I'll get over her. How can I marry a girl who ain't a Catholic? Pa'd go bananas, and as for my mother – I wanted you, but it was crazy. And then I saw you go and I knew it didn't matter a damn. I don't give a shit what Pa says, and I care less what my mother says. I want you and I was going to send a cable to you or something to say come over – and I came up on deck here to talk myself out of it, because believe me, Maddie, us getting married has to be the craziest idea in the world. It'll bring me such grief from the old man – and then I saw this girl crying and I felt so lousy I thought – what the hell. And put my arms round her – and it – it was you – I tell you, Maddie, it was like some saint in heaven had done it. I was never so knocked over in my life – come here, you crazy –' And his voice thickened as he tried to pull her closer and kiss her again.

But she was too quick for him and slid out of his grasp, beneath his arm, and went half sliding, half running, along the deck towards the port side boat deck and he came lunging after her as still the ship rolled majestically and steadily onwards, settling now to a regular rhythm.

He caught up with her under the shadow of the third boat which was about what she had intended, and she laughed softly as again his arms came out and grabbed for her.

'Do you want me, Jay, my own darling? Do you? No more worrying about whether you should –'

'Want you?' He had one arm round her again, but the other hand was scrabbling at her coat, the new coat she had bought in Paris, and she laughed softly again as she felt one of the buttons give way and she seized his hand in one of her own and cried, 'Jay – for God's sake – not here – not on the deck!'

'Here – now – anywhere –' he said, and his voice sounded more like a grunt than the voice she knew and again exultation rose in her. To have brought him to this pitch – oh, it was better than she could ever have hoped for. Even in her best fantasies, it hadn't been as violent as this. He was going to hit her, and hurt her and make her suffer because he wanted her so much, and the thought of it sent a great frisson of excitement down her back that almost buckled her knees under her. But not quite. She still had some of her wits about her and she lifted her head and looked upwards and said, 'In one of the boats – you can reach. Untie it there and give me a lift up.'

He looked up too and then grinned. It was almost dark now, with just a few lights burning along the deck, but there was enough illumination to see the shape of the lifeboat above them, and he let go of her and reached up and with a swing of his legs hoisted himself up.

She couldn't see exactly what he was doing but she heard the rattle of metal-ended ropes and the heavy flap of tarpaulin and then he was hissing down at her from the darkness above and she reached up and felt his hands, and put both hers into them, and with a wrench that almost dislocated her shoulders she was up, swinging away from the rolling deck and scrambling over the edge of the lifeboat into its dark damp interior.

He pushed the way through to the centre so that they could lie across the boat between the thwarts and even before she was there, he was trying to get her down on her back and was pulling on her clothes, tugging at her expensive coat so that all the buttons burst off, and then hauling up her skirt, reaching for her as she was reaching for him. She had her first climax even before she had managed to unbutton him, but it didn't matter. There was plenty more ecstasy where that came from. There always had been.

12

April 1987

'Well, I just can't,' Annie said. 'I really do have a rotten cold and
I just can't,' and she sniffed heavily as much to prove her words
as because she needed to, although in fact her nose was running
and her eyes felt as though they'd been sandpapered.

Sister's voice clacked tinnily in her ear and she felt her lower
lip come out mulishly as she listened; damn the woman, she had
no right to go on at her like this! She wasn't a member of her
staff, and even if she were she had the right to have a cold and
stay at home, surely?

'I'm sorry,' she said sharply, and with no hint of apology in
her tone. 'But there it is, I have a cold, and someone else will
have to look after Maddie today. Just put her fork in her hand
and her plate in front of her, and as long as it's food she likes,
she'll eat it. And I'll be in again as soon as I feel fit.' And she put
the phone down as firmly as she could without being obviously
rude. The woman couldn't help being a twittering fool, and she
didn't really want to antagonise her totally. Maddie would still
need her care and if Annie rubbed her up the wrong way, maybe
she'd take it out on her –

She frowned and went back to her chair by the electric fire
and sat down and glowered at the red bars. Damn Maddie, why
the hell should it matter to her either way whether she was
victimised or not? The woman had been at Greenhill for so
many years now and survived that it was obvious the care she'd
had had been good. If it hadn't she'd have died long since, or
gone even madder, wouldn't she?

But that argument wouldn't hold up. Hadn't Maddie
changed and blossomed under her, Annie's, care in a way that
everyone said was amazing? In less than six months she had
started talking – to Annie at any rate, if not to anyone else – and
moving about of her own volition. She no longer sat and rocked
interminably in her chair, no longer looked like an unkempt

witch. The clothes that Annie had taken to her and the haircut she had arranged had taken years from her; she now looked what she was, a once handsome woman in her fifties rather than a decrepit wreck in her seventies, and could have passed a cursory inspection as a normal, if quiet, person, rather than the patently mad one she had been. And hadn't it been Annie's care that had wrought that change? And didn't that make it clear that the care she had had previously had been bad?

Yes it did, Annie thought, and was filled with a wave of self-pity; and who appreciates what I've done anyway? She sat and glared at the red bars of the fire until her already smarting eyes, cold filled, began to water and although they weren't tears of sadness, still the wetness on her cheeks made her feel lugubrious, and that was not to be borne; and she got to her feet purposefully and rubbed her eyes with her handkerchief and looked round the room. To hell with Greenhill, to hell with Joe Labosky, to hell with Maddie. Let them all see how much they needed her. She had a right to stay home and take care of her own health and her own life just for once. Let them miss her. It would do them good. And the flat really needed some attention.

She looked disgustedly at the scatter of still unpacked tea chests and shook her head irritably. This was not good enough. Efforts had to be made. And she began to pull the chests into some sort of order so that she could start taking out the contents and putting them away in the places where they were supposed to be. Better to do that than spend all her time with someone who didn't appreciate her, or really need her.

October 1950

He doesn't deserve to have me here, Maddie thought mournfully and bit into another biscuit and then put it down. Three days of devoted eating and already her skirt waistbands were making themselves felt; it had been such a shock to see so much food so lavishly provided that she had eaten like a schoolgirl out on a spree, enchanted to discover that because the ship victualled on the American side of the Atlantic, it could offer a cornucopia of goodies that even Alfred Braham hadn't been able to provide. Jay had eaten heartily too, but it seemed to show less on him, and that had irritated her too. Altogether a number of things were irritating her about Jay at a time when she ought to be lyrically happy with him.

Not that it was entirely his fault that it hadn't been possible to rearrange the cabins so that they could be together. Heaven knows he'd tried, nagging the purser and offering bribes to the stewards to rearrange the accommodation in some way, but as Maddie had found when she tried to book a ticket, the ship was packed to the gunwales; not a berth to be had anywhere. So, the only time they could make love was in the early evening, up on the boat deck after the last straggling hearties who insisted on running round the deck and doing press-ups before dinner had vanished below; and it was all much less delightful than it ought to be.

That first time, when they had stayed there in their lifeboat for two hours or more, not caring about dinner or anything else but the delight they were giving each other, it had been wonderful, and now, sitting in the forward lounge and staring out of the glassed-in deck at the heaving horizon she remembered it and felt her skin crawl under her tight waistband. He had been so urgent, so hungry, that he had made her breathless, and had fed her own need amazingly. Had they really managed to go on as long as they had? Had he really been able to make such violent and satisfactory complete love – satisfactory for both of them – fully three times? And lazily she rehearsed in her mind each episode and counted the waves of feeling that had swept her up, more than matching the waves through which the ship was rolling, and almost felt them again. Almost but not quite, and she leaned back in her seat and closed her eyes and tried again to remember, to bring the feelings back. It was amazing what she could do with just thinking about it –

'I hope you aren't feeling the sea, Miss Braham.' The voice seemed to come from behind her and she snapped her eyes open and looked upwards and backwards and saw the face upside down behind her; a silly round face with silly round eyes where the mouth should be and a silly pouting mouth in the middle of its forehead and she blinked and turned her head and the face swam sideways and came right side up. Almost as silly this way up as the wrong way, she thought, and then smiled. It was an instinctive thing to do for he was looking at her with such sheep's eyes that it would have been cruel to do otherwise.

At once the expression changed. He did indeed have a very babyish look about him in spite of the crisp uniform and the cap neatly tucked under his arm which proclaimed him one of the ship's officers, but there was no doubt that he thought she, Maddie, looked wonderful, for his fair skin developed blotches of red across the forehead and cheeks as he stared at her, and that made him more interesting to her.

'If you are feeling too much put out by the motion, Miss Braham, I know the ship's doctor has some excellent draughts you can try. I used to get seasick when I first took this job, but not any more. Not with his help.'

'No, I'm not seasick.' She smiled again as he hovered, looking anxiously at her, and said graciously, 'Won't you sit down?'

At once he flopped into the seat beside her and sat turning his cap between his fingers, and looking at her with those silly round eyes so mournfully that after a while she began to feel embarrassed and uncomfortable and that made her snap a little.

'Is there something wrong with my face?' she asked sharply. 'You do seem to be staring rather.'

'Oh, dear, I'm sorry!' he said and went even redder. 'It's just that – I was looking for you – I was wondering whether – if I could – what to say about – oh dear –' And he collapsed into silence and bent his head and began to turn his cap around even more industriously.

She was charmed. Since Jay had appeared on her horizon she hadn't bothered at all with the young men she met; there had seemed little point in London. But she hadn't forgotten how agreeable it was to have someone tongue-tied and entranced at your feet and she leaned back in her chair now to bask a little. This would show rotten old Jay what his damned poker games could do! Though it would be nicer if the boy were a little more prepossessing, or even interesting. He really did look very stupid.

'What's your name?' she asked in as friendly a voice as she could manage and he bobbed his head and glanced at her and then away again and said in a tight little voice, 'Er – I'm Allan Foss. Ship's radio officer.'

She began to revise her opinion of him. Radio officers, she felt hazily, were really quite clever. They understood a number of matters which to everyone else were incomprehensible and she sat up straighter. Perhaps he would be worth cultivating, to show Jay how stupid he was being in not spending every available moment on board with her instead of in the smoky card room trying to win money.

'How fascinating!' she said, still warm and friendly. 'Does that mean you send all the SOS messages and so forth?'

'Yes,' he said, and now he looked up at her. 'What's more to the point, I receive them all, too.'

'Oh! So if we want to know what's going on at home, we have to come and ask you?'

Amazingly he went bright red and she stared at him, nonplussed. All she had been doing was making small talk, yet there he sat looking as though she had poleaxed him, for his eyes were bulging even more and the look of misery on his hot red face was almost funny in its intensity.

'I – er – I suppose you put that notice up on the board every day about the main news from England? The one that's next to the notice about how far we went yesterday and who won the daily sweep?' she went on, wanting to make him feel better, to put him at his ease.

He nodded miserably and went on staring at her for a long time and then seemed to make up his mind about something, and hitched his chair closer to her, so that he could talk more quietly. There were only a few people in the forward lounge and most of them were asleep over their books or knitting, and those who weren't were well out of earshot. But clearly he was determined to be very secretive indeed.

'I've been worrying myself stupid over this, Miss Braham. At first it was no problem. It was a secret message and there was no reason why I should ever – and I never have, of course, said a word about what I discover and – well, the thing is I saw you in the dining saloon and I thought –' The redness which had begun to ebb away came back and he looked at her with his eyes so shining and pleading that she thought he was about to burst into tears. 'The thing is, I thought when I saw you you looked so sweet and alone and helpless and – well, I felt so sorry for you. I just have to tell you. I can't let you just – I mean I dare say I'm a fool. You've got that chap so what do you care for someone like me? And if I'm caught passing on messages – well, you can imagine – but I thought – I don't want to be selfish, you see. I

120

want to – to do what I can for you, even though there's nothing for me in being so – I mean, you'll just go away when we dock and I'll never see you again either way, so be generous, I thought, do the decent thing, even if it's all wrong and –'

He stopped and swallowed and looked at her miserably again and at once she knew what she was dealing with. Allan Foss was just such another as herself, if not so gifted. He wanted things badly and dreamed about having them. He wove great tangled stories inside his own head and lived them as vividly as he could. If he couldn't get what he wanted one way, he'd get it another. And for some reason he wanted to please her, Maddie, and she was so delighted with him for that that she leaned even closer and set her hand over his fingers which were still writhing round his cap, and smiled deeply into his eyes.

'Oh, Mr Foss,' she murmured, 'can I call you Allan? And will you tell me what all this is that's worrying you so? Don't be shy, I'll understand, truly I will.'

His fingers jerked compulsively so that he dropped his cap and with one hand he seized hers, and his skin felt damp and hot and rather disagreeable though she made no sign of noticing, and with the other he scrabbled for his lost property.

'Leave it there,' she said gently. 'You can pick it up later. Now tell me what all this is about. You aren't being very clear, you know.'

'It's very difficult – the thing is, there was a cable about you. Came in two days ago.'

Sharply she withdrew her hand and stared at him. 'What did you say?' And her voice was cold now, not at all friendly.

'Oh, I know I shouldn't have said anything!' he cried wretchedly. 'I knew you'd be livid. Any person would – other people knowing their affairs and so forth – but if I didn't tell you, how could you protect yourself? I so much want to protect you, you see. You really are – I think you're the most marvellous person, Miss Braham. I've been watching you and – really, so marvellous, so devoted, so –' He struggled for the language that would pull her inside his mind and his feelings. 'So alive and vivacious and –' He shook his head. 'I couldn't let you suffer, not for want of me telling you.'

'I'm suffering a good deal right now from not knowing what

121

the hell you're talking about,' she retorted. 'What cable, for God's sake? What about me?'

'It's your father. There's been a fuss at home.' He sounded wretched still but as he realised that he had her attention fixed on him, he gained confidence, and seemed to swell a little. 'It seems the papers are full of you, runaway heiress and so forth. I've checked with our shore people and they've let me know all about it – your father says you're under age and you've run away and he has reason to think you might be going to America. So he checked with the shipping line –'

'He shouldn't have known where I was!' she said and stared at him, her eyes wide with the shock of it all. 'I told him I was going to Wales for a few days with a friend, told him I'd be in touch at the weekend – he wasn't supposed to go and –'

'That's the thing,' Allan Foss said softly and again hitched himself closer. 'It said in the paper that he said he got this note that you were away with a friend but then the friend rang up and you weren't there and she knew nothing about you going to Wales with her so he got suspicious and thought you might be going to America. Does he – er – does he know this chap you spend all your time with?'

She stared at him, dazed at the suddenness of it all. She had been so sure she'd arranged it all so neatly; the casual note dropped in the post to say that after she'd seen her friend Mary off at Southampton some of their other friends had suggested that they all go off to a weekend cottage in Barry Island one of them had, and she'd be home the following Monday. It had all been explained simply and casually and there had been no reason for him to do more than curse her for being out of the office for so long and to tell her off when she came home. Or so he was supposed to think. It had never occurred to her that anyone would bloody well phone and tell him otherwise, and she stared blindly at Allan Foss and said loudly, 'Oh, Christ!'

Across the lounge, one of the old ladies asleep over a book woke abruptly and stared round, startled, and he set a hand over hers and pressed it warningly and after a moment the old lady closed her eyes again.

'Come to the radio cabin,' he murmured. 'I'm on duty about now, and the other chap'll be glad to go early – then we can talk. Don't worry, Miss Braham, I'm sure we'll think of something we can do to stop him –'

'Stop him what?' she said, but he was already on his feet and across the lounge, walking busily towards the door, his gait assured and his cap, which he had seized as he stood up, held in one hand and tapping irritably against his knee as he walked, and she scurried after him, her chest tight with anxiety. However much Allan Foss might be enjoying the little drama he was unfolding – and he clearly was delighted with all the excitement of it – she was alarmed. It hadn't occurred to her that her father might find out so soon where she was; he wasn't supposed to know till he got a letter from America telling him she was married. She had arranged it all so carefully – but not carefully enough. And as she went hurrying along the companionways after Foss, she felt rage against herself rise in her.

She had been stupidly arrogant, that was the thing. In all her dealings for Jay she had been ultra-careful, checking and double-checking that there was no way anyone could ever find out what she and Jay were up to. She had laid covers and then further covers for her covers so that no one could ever suspect anything. But for herself, at one of the most important times of her life, she had been careless. She should have phoned her friends, told them all to lie for her, told them to make sure they didn't inadvertently let her down. After all, hadn't she done it often enough for them? These were the people she had sworn were spending weekends at her flat when their parents called, so that they could have their illicit pleasures elsewhere, yet for herself she had failed, sailing cheerfully along into disaster, certain that she was invincible.

And the self-hatred and self-blame that had filled her thickened and curdled and turned itself round as she thought of her father hearing from some damned silly girl on the phone that she had lied to him, and instead of just being hurt and waiting till she came home to explain, had set about making searches for her, and checking shipping lines, and sending cables – how could he be so wicked to her? How could he treat her so? She wasn't his possession, after all. She was herself, Madeleine Braham, her own person. She had the right to do what she wanted when she wanted. Hadn't her father himself taught her that? Yet here he was, when she went to get what she wanted, setting out to make it hard for her, exposing her to the pity of silly round-eyed pink boys in officers' uniforms – oh, but she hated her father that moment, and knew he had to be dealt with. He had no right, no right at all – and the words went round and round in her head as she clattered down the last set of stairs to the last corridor and the door of the radio cabin, after Allan Foss.

'Wait here,' he hissed as he went in. 'Wait till Joe comes out –' and she stopped, uncertainly, not sure whether to obey him or not. She was eaten with impatience now, fed by her anger at her father. The sooner she knew what he had done the sooner she'd be able to undo it. Or better still, pay him back for his wicked unkindness to her.

She was about to ignore Foss's warning and go marching in to the radio cabin when the door opened and another young man, in the same uniform, came out and nodded affably at her as he passed her and she watched him go whistling along the corridor to disappear round a corner before pushing the door open and walking in.

The place smelled odd; that was the first thing she noticed and in time to come whenever she smelled that particular odour of crisp crackling air that always seems to hang about radio installations she was to see Foss, sitting there at his console and staring at her with his bulging eyes alight with excitement and a sort of lascivious pity. He looked more at home here, less awkward and baby-faced and she halted beside the door and stared at him as he sat importantly at his console in his shirt sleeves, a set of earphones hanging negligently about his neck, and smiling at her.

'Now, come and sit down, Miss Braham, and I'll show you all the cables we've had about you. And then you can decide what to do. Not that there's a lot you can do, I reckon. But if there's any help you need, you can count on old Allan –' And he held out his hand invitingly, and then patted the chair beside him. And slowly she came across the cluttered cabin and sat down.

13

April 1987

'Oh,' Annie said and didn't know what to say next.

'Heavens, don't look at me as though I were the rent man!' he said and grinned. 'May I come in? Or can't you believe I'm not the rent man?'

She blinked. 'The what man?'

'You clearly had a richer childhood than I did.' He followed her into the flat as at last she stood aside to make way for him. 'Where I grew up, he was the man who turned up on Friday afternoon and made my mother very bad-tempered.'

'Is that why you've come here? To make me bad-tempered?'

'Not at all. To get myself some tea. I like your Earl Grey tea. And to make sure you're all right.' He quirked his eyebrows at her and then laughed as he saw how angry she immediately looked. 'No, it's no use getting annoyed with me. You're stuck with me, and you might as well accept it. When Sister B told me you were too ill to come in to the ward today, I was concerned. I decided to risk your undoubted wrath and as soon as I'd finished at the hospital to come and see how you are. And to get that cup of tea.'

'I'm fine. I mean, I have a stinking cold —'

'I can see. Your eyes look as though they've been boiled, you poor dear.'

'Thank you for your kind encouragement. It's such a comfort when one is cheered up in ill health.'

'Oh, I can't be doing with dishing out lollipops. You must know you look as though you've been stuffed as well as boiled and to pretend you didn't would be an insult. You need tea more than I do. May I go and make it?'

'If you like.' She went back to the last tea chest. 'I want to finish this anyway.'

She went on unwrapping the last of the Worcester dinner service as he went through to her kitchen and she heard him

125

whistling as he clattered about and set the kettle to boil. It was an agreeable sound, and she sat back on her heels and stared at the blank wall in front of her and tried to imagine how it might be always to have someone around this flat, whistling and making occasional friendly noises like that, and then was angry with herself. Being alone was what she was for; after all the years of Jen and the tie of the way they had shared their lives, it was mad to contemplate any other lifestyle now she was free.

And even if she did want company, where was she to find it? Advertise for someone to move in with her? She'd seen ads like that and they made her shiver. It sounded so desperate somehow. 'Girl wanted, must be quiet non-smoker to share expenses and care of lovely two-bedroomed flat, select neighbourhood –' No, that wasn't for her. She'd live alone and like it, and the sooner Joe Labosky drank his tea and went away and left her in peace in her quiet aloneness the better.

It was good tea and he'd managed to find some biscuits too, and he came and set the tray on the empty tea chest, turning it on its side to make a handy low table, and then came and sat on the floor beside her to drink it.

'Bliss,' he said after a long silence while they drank, and she went on unwrapping Jen's special plates. 'I'm really a charwoman at heart, you know. All I ever want is a nice cuppa and a bit of a gossip.'

'I can only provide the former,' she said.

'Oh, I don't know.' He refilled his cup and held the pot up to her invitingly. 'I like talking to you. You usually start responding eventually and then you're fascinating. I dare say it wouldn't be as interesting if I didn't have to pull the words out of you with pincers.'

'There you go again, treating me like a patient.'

'Not at all,' he said vigorously. 'When will you understand that I'm the same with everyone? Listen, come and find out, will you? Just for once, accept an invitation. I'm a good cook and I make the best chicken soup in the world. My mother taught me how and all I have to do is exactly the opposite of what she did. Then it turns out perfect. And it soothes even the worst of lousy colds. I've got some really rather pleasant people coming tonight. Not at all psychiatric – he's an actor and she teaches slow readers – and they're fun. And the soup'll do you good.

And so will hearing me talk to them in exactly the same way I do to you and everyone else. Not like patients at all –'

'Why?' She had stopped her unwrapping and was sitting back on her haunches holding the last plate in her hands. Her face felt hot and sticky and she knew she was smudged with dust, but was unconcerned. 'Why on earth do you bother?'

'You silly woman,' he said after a long moment and then leaned forwards and rubbed one of the dust smudges off her cheek with the back of one forefinger. 'Because I like you.'

October 1950

She read them all, one after the other, trying to keep her face under control, though really what she wanted to do was shout and weep and then scream her fury. How dare he treat her so? Wasn't she grown up, a real *person*? He had no right to carry on as though she were still a baby –

'I shouldn't have shown them to you,' Foss said worriedly. 'I know I shouldn't. And I wouldn't have done if it hadn't been that I saw you in the dining saloon and then at the dancing and I thought – I liked you so much. I just couldn't let you suffer without knowing what was going on.'

She looked up at the glistening pale eyes and the pink forehead now dewed with a film of earnest sweat, and managed to smile. He was so transparent with his I'm-a-knight-errant-saving-a-damsel-in-distress look, but also very irritating. She wanted to snap at him, to tell him to shut up so that she could sit and think quietly about what to do next. But she couldn't do that; he'd been too kind and she tried to smile even more widely and then bent her head to read the cables.

Clearly her father had been more alarmed than she had imagined was possible. She knew he cared about her and Ambrose; who else did he have to care about, after all? She knew he was always willing to fork out money for them and liked nothing better than to show off to them, as well as through them, as he always did at their respective birthday parties, but he had never spent that much time with them. Most of her life in London had been spent alone or with her girlfriends. Her father was always out with his own cronies, dealing with business or gambling, and of course with the various girls he collected and then shed as he went through his life, and showed no taste for excessive amounts of his children's company. Ambrose, of course, was always away on his own affairs. She hardly ever saw him, and doubted her father saw much more.

Yet in spite of this semi-detached life they had all led, here he was sending off cables of inordinate length and therefore cost, pouring out his anguish at the loss of his dear beloved daughter. She was a minor, she was to be stopped. She was to be returned to her adoring father, he told the ship's captain. On no account was she to be allowed to leave the ship, but must be kept aboard till he could come after her in the next available ship and bring her home –

She lifted her head sharply and looked at Foss. 'Has the captain seen these?'

'Of course – I had to show him. Didn't I?'

'I suppose – but he's said nothing to me.'

'He won't. No need. He's just let the police know at New York – then it will be up to them. Oh, Miss Braham, I am so –'

She ignored that. 'When does the next liner make the crossing?'

'What?'

'The next ship over.' She slapped the sheets of paper in her lap. 'He says he's coming after me – when can he do that?'

'I'll check for you –' He picked up a sheaf of papers from the tangle on his desk and began to leaf through them. 'Liverpool, Montreal – Liverpool, Quebec – Liverpool, Australia, oh, here we are. There's a sailing on the 15th from Liverpool – the *Parthia*. If he takes a Cunarder of course – he might manage to get on a foreign ship – French perhaps –'

'If it's the *Parthia* – when would he get to New York?'

'Ah, the 23rd –'

'If it isn't, if it's a French ship, can he get there before we do?'

'No.' He shook his head forcefully. 'It's all planned very carefully so there's no tangle at the docks. Of course he could go to Montreal or Quebec and take a train down to New York – there are all sorts of possibilities.'

'Oh, hell – what do I have to do? I have to stop him – I can't let him come over and make everything go wrong. The police at New York – I can find a way round them. But not him – he'll know it's me whatever I try to do. What can I *do*?'

128

He stared at her and then shook his head. 'I don't know. If there's anything I can to do help – send cables or anything – I'll do it gladly. I can find a way to cover up – I'll do anything for you, Miss Braham, I never saw a girl like you ever –' And he leaned forwards clumsily and seemed about to seize her, but adroitly she shifted slightly so that all he could do was grab at her hands.

'You're terribly sweet, Mr Foss, really you are, but I just don't see –' And then she stopped and still holding both his hands firmly stared deep into his eyes as she thought, faster than she ever had. He, convinced that because she was gazing at him so intently she was thinking of him too, held on tightly and sweated happily.

'You'll send cables?' she said slowly. 'Yes, you can send cables for me. Oh, hell, I'm not sure how to – have you some paper I can work it out on?'

At once he was all efficiency and provided her with pencils and cable forms and a desk to sit at and then busied himself at his console as sounds and lights became too clamorous to be ignored. And she sat and chewed the pencil and sorted out her memories and then, as succinctly as she could, wrote her cable.

It was long and it was detailed and half an hour later, when Allan Foss had caught up with his routine work and had time to turn back to her, she was ready for him.

'Can you send this?' she asked and pushed the form into his hands, and then watched his bent head as he read it.

'Yes,' he said at length, a little unwillingly. 'I can send it. Are you sure – I mean, it seems –'

'What does it seem?'

'A bit – I mean, this is to go right to the top people. Are you going to – are you telling them – he is your father, after all, isn't he?'

She had to make up her mind swiftly, and she did, and pushing to the back of her mind any bad feelings she might have about what she was saying, sat down in the chair beside him again and leaning forwards to take both his hands in hers, began to talk, to tell him all about it.

All about the dreadful life she had led with this awful man. Yes, he was her father, but so cruel, so uncaring – and his eyes softened and gleamed with sympathy as she painted her picture in more and more vivid and true-blue colours. The way he had kept her locked up, deprived of all that made life worth living while he got richer and richer. The way she had to countenance his wicked ways and his black-marketeering – and here she dropped her gaze in shame and then bravely looked up at him again, wide-eyed and limpid. The bad, dreadfully bad, way she had felt about it all. She had fled, she told Foss, now hanging on every word she uttered, his mouth lax with the sheer excitement of it all, simply in order not to have to see his inevitable downfall. It wasn't for her own good, but for his; her poor misguided father. She had known the police were on his track because of his dealings, and would come to her for evidence and she had not wanted to give it – oh, she had so much not wanted to give it for she still loved him, wicked as he was. But if he was chasing her, he would beat her if he caught her and – and now she shuddered and faltered to a silence and he squeezed her hands in desperate damp sympathy and leaned perilously close.

She swayed gently away from him and went on earnestly, 'Do you see, Allan? What else can I do? I must yield to the law of the land – if he had left me alone then I could have saved my father even at the cost of my own conscience, but as it is – what else can I do? Will you send the cable?'

He nodded convulsively and then picked up the cable form again and turned back to his console and she sat and watched as he tapped away the long message she had prepared for the CID at Scotland Yard investigating rationing and controls abuses and frauds, the accounts of all the deals she had passed on to Jay, in every possible detail they could need, but telling them that the person they had to investigate if they were to get at the facts of the case was her brother Ambrose and giving the Regent's Park flat address.

As she watched his fingers flashing over the keys she bit her lip; when he'd finished would he see the huge holes in her hastily constructed tale? Would he start to doubt her, see what a liar she had been, tell the captain, get her locked up? And the thought of such an action on his part frightened her so much that tears began to well up in her eyes and she had to sniff to stop her nose running.

At which point he had finished the sending and turned to see her sitting there so woebegone and with tears streaking her cheeks, that with a little cry he lunged and seized her, hell bent on providing comfort for her, as well as some agreeable contact for himself. And she sobbed even more loudly and did the only thing she could do which was to bury her face in his shirt and keep her head well down so that the kiss which was clearly bursting to emerge from him could not be planted on her.

And in fact it was comforting to be able to cry like this, for all the time she had told the tale about her father she had seen his head with its crinkled half-grey hair bent over a typewriter, his cigar jutting out from his face, his corrugated forehead even more deeply lined than usual as he struggled to cope with the letters she should be doing for him, and guilt had washed over her like a flood.

And that was not all; she had found herself remembering Ambrose too. Not Ambrose as he now was, pompous and boring and unpleasant whenever he spoke to her, but as he had been when they had been children, when he had missed his mother so much and clung so warmly to her. That he had grown up to be so hateful didn't alter the fact that he had been the brother she had loved once and now she sobbed deeply and let her tears splash Allan Foss's shirt to good effect as she pushed as far away as she could her grief for the little boy she had loved once. He was dead now, and his place had been taken by a far from nice person who had done all sorts of horrid things to her and to her father, so why feel so guilty because she needed to be unkind to him? It wasn't, she told herself passionately as Allan Foss patted her back with an infuriating tattoo meant to comfort but having far from that effect, that she was doing it out of spite. It was only because she had to. To be stopped now, when she and Jay were at last on their way to being the married couple they were destined to be, would be impossible. It was necessary, indeed vital, that she do what she had done. It was not her fault. It had been forced on her, that was the thing, and she mustn't feel so bad about it –

Slowly, with a few hiccups, her tears stopped and carefully she lifted her head from Foss's shirt and stepped back at the same moment so that there was no risk of being too close and therefore kissable, and smiled at him tremulously.

'I'm sorry,' she said huskily. 'I – I lost control. Do forgive me.'

He shook his head earnestly as delicately she stepped even further away from him and began to mop her damp face with her handkerchief.

'Oh, Miss Braham, don't apologise, please. I want to help you, any way I can. I'm truly so sad for you. It's a dreadful situation to be in – to be forced into such an action – I think you're so brave.'

'Thank you,' she murmured softly and managed a watery little smile. 'You're being so kind. Oh, dear –' And she put her hand to her forehead as she saw his round eyes brighten hopefully. 'I've got such a headache now. I feel quite wrung out –'

He was all concern. 'Of course you do! I can well – look, I'll see if I can get my oppo to come and take over for a while – I can always take his night watch. He hates that – well, we all do – and then I can take you to your cabin and look after you and –'

'No, really, no,' she said, not hastily enough to offend him, but with determination. 'You've already done too much – and there are so many other people who share my cabin, you see, that –'

'I could take you to mine.' He now looked almost as determined as she felt and she managed a wan little smile and shook her head, clearly regretful.

'That sounds bliss – but I can't. I asked my friend to come with me on this journey, you see. He's – er –' Again she began to improvise. 'He's my best friend's fiancé, you see, and he agreed to help me – and if I vanish he'll get worried. And he's madly protective, you know. He promised my friend Barbara to take care of me and he's very thorough – if he can't find me where he expects me to be, why, he'll go mad. We don't want him raising a fuss, do we?'

'No,' he said, though without great conviction, but then he brightened, clearly happy to hear of Jay's status as another girl's property. 'I hope to see you some time later in the voyage, then?'

'Oh, of course!' she said and now smiled sweetly. 'Oh, of course – I'm so grateful to you, and you're really so awfully sweet. And –' she went on hastily as he stepped closer once more '– and of course there may be other cables you'll want to tell me about, mayn't there?'

132

'Oh, yes, yes, of course,' he said. 'Of course, there may well be. I'll make sure I come and tell you the moment I get any news –' She began to make her way to the door, one hand still held limply to her forehead. 'We get the main newspaper stories, you know – we need to be informed even though we're at sea. I'll let you know anything I hear that could be important to you –'

'Thank you,' she murmured and then, as if on an impulse, leaned forwards and kissed his cheek. It was safe to do so now, for the door was open and she was almost out of it, and then she pulled it closed behind her, leaving him standing in the middle of his cabin, looking ineffably pleased with himself.

It wasn't till she reached her own cabin on the lowest deck and could creep into her bunk to lie down that she really let herself think properly. She had been faced with a crisis and she had dealt with it. Surely, with that information about Ambrose, the police would be after him immediately? And surely her father would have to stay in England to look after him? Whatever she was up to, his son at risk of prison sentences must surely take precedence. Yes, she had made sure he wouldn't come after her, at least not till she was a safely married woman. So why should she feel so dreadful about it all? Why was it she was crying again, not prettily this time for a besotted man's benefit, but in great ugly tearing sobs, for her own need? Why?

14

May 1987

'You should have come. The soup was really vintage stuff. So was I. At my peak as a host. You should have been with us.'

'I told you I had that rotten cold. Why didn't you believe me? I didn't say I would come – not for a moment, and –'

'I know you didn't. I didn't expect you. I just wanted you to know what you missed. You look very nice today. Not so boiled. It could be that sweater. The colour suits you.'

'Too bright,' she said dismissively, and tried to look annoyed. He really was getting ridiculous lately, with all his chatter, but at the same time she had to admit it was agreeable to be told she looked well. And the sweater had been a gamble. She'd found it when she unpacked the last of the tea chests yesterday and decided to wear it, marvelling that she'd ever bought so vivid a thing, bright scarlet as it was, because it would look good with her grey trousers and jacket, and because it would be less trouble than washing one of the others in time for the morning. Or so she had told herself, though she had a suspicion that she was actually finding herself interested in how she looked again. It felt all wrong somehow to waste time and effort on such matters, but there it was; she was much more aware lately of her clothes and the state of her hair than she had been used to be. It was irritating and yet perhaps, a little pleasant –

'How has she been while I was away? I should have come back sooner, I suppose, but I thought –'

'Not at all. You needed to get your cold quite well. And it clearly is. It'd be a poor state of affairs if you couldn't be away for a few days from us without the place falling to pieces.'

'It's not the place I'm concerned with,' she said drily. 'Just Maddie. Has she been eating, do you know?'

'We'll have to find out. I haven't heard she wasn't, and Sister

B being what she is she'd have been nagging me stupid if there'd been any cause for concern. I dare say she'll be there now, waiting to pounce.'

He had appeared beside her in the car park this morning with such promptness that she had wondered briefly if he had been waiting to see her arrive and had deliberately joined her, but then pushed the thought aside. There was no reason why he should, after all; there could be no great pleasure to be had in walking with her from the admin. building car park to the West Pavilion even on a morning as blowy, albeit shiny, as this blustery Monday.

'Have you missed her?' he asked then as their footsteps crunched along the gravel, making a satisfactory sort of noise that she rather enjoyed and she looked up at him, startled for a moment, because she had been concentrating on the way the wind felt against her skin as well as the sounds and smells of the morning.

'Missed Maddie? Why should I? I only come here to help with her – she's nothing to do with me.'

'But you've spent a lot of time with her these past few months. By now you either hate her or –'

'Or what?'

'Or feel rather fond of her.'

'She's a job you asked me to do. That's all,' she said, and then shook her head irritably. 'Were you trying to make me fond of her? As though she were a puppy or a kitten, ideal for bringing bad-tempered women out of themselves?'

He grinned. 'I may have had something of the sort in mind once. I really can't remember. It's so long ago now. Anyway, I know better than to try to make you do anything you don't choose to do. You've taught me well, Annie! I'm not doing anything sinister in asking you how you feel about her. Just wondering. I'm fond of her myself, you see. I get a feeling of – oh, I don't know – strength, I think, from her. It takes immense strength to shut yourself up in silence for thirty-five years. Misguided but tremendous. It takes even more to start to come out of it. It may well be that underneath it all she's a ghastly woman – the sort I'd never want to invite to supper. But I suspect not, because I like her. And I was wondering if you did.'

135

October 1950

The next problem was getting off the ship. The last full day at sea, she decided, would have to be the one devoted to carrying out her plans, and she sat over dinner on the night before, silent as Jay joked and guffawed with his other neighbour and trying not to notice the way Allan Foss was staring at her from his table across the aisle and three down the line. She'd used him enough, she decided. Dodging his ardour this past couple of days had been far from easy; add any more favours to his load and he'd be demanding repayment loudly. At least there had been no more alarming cables from her father to the ship. There had been a couple from the captain to New York arranging for immigration officials and police to meet her and he had told her of those faithfully. She knew they would be there at Pier Ninety-Two, unobtrusive but watching for her. A description of her (rather a flattering one, she had been glad to read) had been sent, and now as the ship steamed stolidly on its way over the last few hundred sea miles, she had to think.

Jay leaned across and tapped her arm. 'Hey, dreamer! I said, do you want some more wine?'

'Mm? No – no thanks. I think – I'd like to go up on deck, Jay. I want to talk to you.'

He grinned lasciviously. 'So soon? Let me digest my dinner, for Christ's sake – boy, but you are one eager little lady –'

'No, not that. I mean – yes, any time we can. But I really have to speak to you.' She was keeping her voice low, very aware of the rest of the people at their table, even though most of them were too busy eating to pay any attention. 'I've got – there are problems.'

He looked suddenly blank and bent his head closer to her. 'Listen, you're not knocked up, are you? You can't be yet –'

She blinked. 'Knocked up?'

'Shh, keep your voice down. You know what I mean. I knew this'd be a problem – oh, Christ, didn't I warn you? But you said there were ways of taking care –'

'Hussh,' she said and got to her feet. 'Please excuse us,' she smiled at the rest of the table and swept away, pulling Jay behind her, desperate to get up on deck where they could talk in private, though not so desperate that she did not remember to take the way out of the saloon that led them well away from Allan Foss's table.

Outside it was dark and blowing hard and they huddled in the lee of a boat and she pulled her stole around her and stood as close to him as she could, not just for protection from the wind, but so that they would not be heard by late walkers.

'Listen, I promised you I wouldn't get pregnant, and I won't. I've been ready for us any time this past three months. I've got some special things, you see – I didn't the first time – I didn't expect – well, it was all a bit sudden, wasn't it? But I've used them since and I reckon I'm all right. We'll find out in a month or two, if not. Right now, it's not that I'm worried about. Listen Jay, I'd better explain –'

It wasn't easy, walking the narrow line between getting him to understand how important it was to do things her way and not alarming him so much that he would turn and run. That he wanted her and needed her she had no doubt now; even in just a lifeboat she had found ways to make him almost burst with excitement, and knew already how to coax him and tease him and either hold him back or push him over the edge into explosive climax when she wanted to – and as often, too. She had a control over him that was not only exciting in its own right; it added to her own sexual hunger and responsiveness. Together they had rolled and struggled and tumbled into a shared need and a shared excitement that tied them together as tightly as the boat itself was fastened to the ship. But for all that she knew his frailties better than he realised she did. Not a man to turn and fight problems, her Jay, she had told herself in the long nights when she had lain in her crowded cabin listening to other women snoring and trying to work out what to do. He needed protection and support and she had to provide it if she was to get what she wanted from life with him.

So now she told him just enough to make him understand. Her father, she said, had found out that she had gone, and had cabled the ship.

'I can get off, I think, without being caught, if you'll help. And I mustn't be stopped, any more than you must, because I don't trust Daddy. He's going to start checking the books and finding out how – what I've been doing for you. He'll know

137

where your money came from – and he'll make trouble, given half the chance. We mustn't let him.'

'You can't stop him,' Jay said and held her close as the wind howled viciously through the ropes and davits that held the boat. 'Not from three thousand miles away, for God's sake. Hell, this is a shit of a mess –'

'I know. So we have to keep out of his way. I've done what I can to stop him following us. Look, do as I say – and as soon as we're ashore we'll get married. Once you're his son-in-law, there'll be no more problems.'

'How can you know that? If he's really angry enough –'

She shook her head vigorously in the darkness. 'I'm sure I'm right. Yes, I know I made a mistake over him finding out about me going. But that was my fault, I wasn't thorough enough. But I'm not wrong about how he'll be if we get married. Believe me, Jay. Do as I say, and we'll sort it all out. Once he knows I'm your wife he'll stop being so angry about his money. He'll see it as going to me and that'll make it okay. He's never been mean with me – not with money.'

She stood there holding him and holding her breath too. Would he believe her? He had to; because although it was true up to a point that she believed Alfred would stop hunting her once they were married, she couldn't be sure, any more than she could be sure that once they reached Boston Jay wouldn't give in to his parents' view of how he should live his life. He'd talked a good deal about his home and his parents during their times together on this voyage, when he wasn't making love to her, or playing poker, which he did a great deal. And she was getting a hazy but worrying picture of people as dominating and as difficult as Alfred himself was. It wasn't going to be easy to win them round, she had begun to think, not easy at all.

But now, telling Jay of her own troubles with Alfred, it all began to fall into place as elegantly and satisfyingly as a well-constructed jigsaw puzzle. Use the problems to her own advantage, that was the thing. Push him into marrying before they got to Boston and had to face the Kincaids en masse. One Kincaid, her Jay, was easy to handle. But a houseful? She was beginning to doubt her ability there.

'So, will you do as I say, Jay? Listen, I've worked it all out.'

'I'll bet you have. You really are one crazy kid, Maddie –'

And he kissed her violently and she held on to him tightly. He had drunk rather a lot at dinner, and adding all that to the hour they had spent in the boat before changing, she hadn't expected he'd be at all amorous tonight. But the cold air was blowing the alcohol out of him and the closeness of them was bringing her back into his blood, and she felt him harden against her belly as he pushed his pelvis against her.

'In a minute, darling – very soon – listen –'

And she told him all he had to do, and then they climbed into their boat and again set it rocking, not emerging until almost midnight, while Allan Foss lugubriously patrolled cocktail bars and dance bands, cardrooms and lounges, looking for her. It was their last night at sea and he'd had such high hopes . . .

The stewardess had lost all her doubts, and was actually beginning to enjoy it all. She listened enthralled to Maddie's tale of their elopement, of the way her father ('he's a baronet – frightful snob, you know, Master of Hounds and all that, and just can't understand what it is to be young and in love. Everyone who knows him says Sir Jeffrey never loved anyone but horses') had beaten her when he discovered she was in love with her handsome American who was, of course, a war hero, and how the only way she could ever achieve happiness was to run away. And now she'd discovered that he had notified the police in America of her flight and had arranged for them to stop her at the pier and drag her from her beloved's arms.

'And oh, please, dear Enid,' Maddie said with tears in her eyes, clutching the girl's hand and staring up piteously into her rather vapid face, 'please, you can't let that happen to me! All I need is your uniform – I'll buy it from you, your spare one. You've got a spare one, haven't you? I'll give you a hundred pounds for it – that's an awful lot of money.'

It was the money more than the romantic treacle of her tale which swayed it, Maddie rather thought, and that was a comfort. Not only was it much more reliable as both bait and goad; it was easier to deal with. It was quite fun to use the language of the magazines she had once read so avidly to get what she wanted from this rather silly girl, but there was too much of a real problem to waste time on that; so dealing with a simple cash transaction made much more sense to her.

And to Enid, who duly took her to her cubbyhole full of dusters and sick bowls and gave her the uniform. It needed a little fixing to fit her because Maddie was rather bigger busted than Enid – a fact which made the girl almost back out of the whole arrangement in a sudden fit of pique – but she was soothed at the sight of the ten white five pound notes that Maddie gave her on account and agreed to go on with the arrangement.

It involved nothing very difficult after all. Maddie packed her cases early in the morning, making a small parcel out of one change of clothes, and moved them out of the way of the other frantic packers in her cabin, her passport well hidden inside one of them, as early as she could. Enid then took them to the midsection of the ship where luggage to be portered ashore was being collected amid a great hubbub, to find Jay waiting to change the labels, erasing Maddie's name and putting on his own. She had only two cases for she had brought just some of her better and more recent Paris clothes, determined to buy masses of exciting new things in America, and she was deeply glad of that decision now. Jay himself had six bags and would have fussed considerably, she suspected, if he had been saddled with an equivalent number of hers.

The next stage was for Enid to collect her shore pass from the bo'sun, using her own passport, and then to bring it to Maddie, who was waiting for her, already changed into the spare uniform, in the stewardess's cubbyhole.

'All you have to do is show that and walk off. There'll be no problems – not till tonight when they count up and discover I've not come back on board. Then they're likely to try to fuss, 'cos we're not supposed to stay ashore overnight without special permission. She's a bit fussy, the chief stewardess on this ship.'

'But you'll be all right?' Maddie was alarmed. The last thing she wanted was Enid suddenly taking fright.

'Yeah – it'll be a real treat to put one over on that old cow. I'll just go along at eleven o'clock and tell her I want some aspirin for my period or something. Then she'll say where've you been and I'll say I went ashore but that I didn't feel well so I come back again and can I have that aspirin and the morning off tomorrow and she'll moan at me and then when the bo'sun tells

140

her one of her girls is adrift she'll give him hell for being so inefficient and losing my pass, on account of I'm back on the ship, so I must have handed it in. And then tomorrow, or the next day, when I feel better an' I want to go ashore again, they'll have to make me a new pass, won't they?'

'You're a clever girl, Enid,' Maddie said admiringly. 'And so kind and nice to me. I do appreciate it, really I do.'

'Well, it's a pleasure, dearie. I mean, you having so cruel a father an' all. I always knew they was like that, those sort of people. You ought to have a mum and dad like mine, really nice ordinary people what cares for you. None of these snobs knows anything about love, do they? Not like Mum and Dad. They had ever such a romantic time they did —'

And Maddie, knowing when the time had come to pay her debts, sat and listened to Enid's interminable tale of her parents' courtship when her Dad had been a merchant seaman and her mother a housemaid in a house that was, Enid said, 'Just like your Dad's, miss — not interested in nothing but 'orses and dogs, and not people at all. I tell you, my Mum told me about them people and she'd be real glad I'm helping you. So good luck to you, miss — and God bless you —'

And her benison worked, for two hours after the *Mauretania* docked at seventeen hundred hours on Friday 14th October 1950, Madeleine Braham gave the other ten five pound notes to Enid and walked ashore past the jabbering crush of meeters and porters and customs men and taxi drivers and all the rest of the people who had business at Pier Ninety-Two, with a nod from the bo'sun who checked her shore-leave pass with a grunt and never an upward look at her, and melted into the melee of members of the ship's crew bent on a wild night on the town, and passengers who bade each other noisy farewells and haggled with porters over tips and shouted furiously about lost luggage.

It had all been almost too simple, she felt, and she looked uneasily over her shoulder to see if she was being followed, but there was no sign of anyone who was at all interested in one stewardess among so many.

So, she found a women's lavatory and changed her uniform for the clothes she had brought ashore in a paper parcel and stuffed the uniform behind the cistern and went, empty-handed, through the customs shed, to meet Jay as arranged by the taxi rank.

And there he was with the luggage and a grin on his face that threatened to split his cheeks and a hug and an exultant, 'Wow, didn't we fool 'em? Didn't we pull that one off?' And she returned his hug and said nothing at all about the way he had taken all the credit for their safe arrival. The important thing was they had arrived. She was in New York, with the man she loved, and she was going to be married to him before she left the place. And she peered out of the cab window at the towering buildings she had only ever seen on cinema screens before and didn't really believe it had happened.

But it had.

15

October 1950

It really felt rather good to be so tired. She was weary when she woke in the morning and as each hectic day went on she became even wearier, but it didn't matter. She had never known such excitement in all her life, and it built up in her to create such a dreamlike state that she seemed to float her aching feet and tired muscles everywhere she went.

The city itself was a major source of the strangeness. The first time she saw the Chrysler building with its extraordinary spire lit to a flaming bronze by the afternoon sun, she caught her breath at its strange yet so familiar beauty; and at the sight of Central Park where they rode in a horsedrawn cab, filled with trees burning with October fires of amber and gold, burnt umber and bronze and deep rich crimsons, she almost wept. But it wasn't just the beautiful that dazzled and delighted her. There was also the cheap and the ugly, the garish and the vulgar, that were so filled with vitality that they doubled up the wild excitement inside her. To walk along Fifth Avenue and Broadway, Times Square and Forty-Second Street, to see the hot dog stalls, the delis and the automats and to see the great self-confident buildings clawing their arrogant way upwards was like walking into a film. It seemed to her as though at every other corner she might bump into Ginger Rogers and Fred Astaire, or Bette Davis and George Brent, and she revelled in that, actually watching the passers-by avidly for evidence of their film fame.

But there were also the other things the films hadn't told her about, like the smell of the city, petrol fumes and dirt and hot roast chestnuts and boiling frankfurters and mustard and onions from the stalls, and the heavy reek of the subway that came rolling out of the ground like the steam from the heating system gratings set in the roads; and the colour of New York, the subtle brick and stone tones slashed by violent reds and blues and greens as people in extraordinary clothes went scuttling by, together with the yellow cabs and the long rakish cars glittering with chrome and everywhere shop windows laden with goods. It was that as much as anything that tipped the strangeness over into fantasy; to see so many things, clothes and jewellery, furniture and linens, china and crystal and silver, so freely available after the long thin years of war followed by austerity in London made her mind flip sideways and lose any sense of reality.

'We'll stay at the Algonquin,' Jay had said to her in the taxi taking them uptown from the pier. 'It's a very English hotel – you'll feel at home there.'

It wasn't at all, of course. The menus, lusciously overloaded with incredible dishes, read like greedy fairy tales to her, and she ate buttery blueberry muffins and drank coffee full of real cream better than any she had ever tasted at breakfast, and had Waldorf salad and massive shrimps for lunch, and wondered what planked steak was and what sweetcorn might taste like for dinner, and then wandered through the dark leathery lobby with its brass bells on the small round tables and deep parchment lampshades and tried to compare it with the Ritz in London. And could find no points of contact. The Algonquin was, like everything else in her life now, new and exotic and wonderful and above all, gloriously exhausting.

Jay was different too. Now he was on his own territory, he seemed far less new and exotic but still wonderful to her. He continued to be to her the most important person who ever breathed, the passion of her life, the one man who mattered, but there was no doubt that the uniqueness that had made him so remarkable in London was quite gone in New York. Every other man she looked at had his well-fed glossiness, his sleekness and air of total rightness, and most of them seemed to dress as he did, in what she discovered were Brooks Brothers' shirts with button-down collars and beautifully pressed grey flannel suits and unbelievably glossy black shoes. She felt herself to be dowdy, suddenly, in spite of her Paris clothes, when she saw him alongside the girls of the town, in their sheer nylon stockings over incredibly high-heeled shoes and deliciously tailored little suits surmounted by wisps of veiling and silk and nonsense that were the hats that were all the rage this season.

And that led to considerations of shopping and she thought about that greedily and counted her money, sadly depleted by the cost of her escape from the *Mauretania*, and told Jay she needed more.

'If I'm to be Mrs Jay Kincaid, you'll want to be proud of me,' she said, as she snuggled into his chest one morning, revelling in the sheer physical pleasure of being able to share a bed with him instead of a hard rocking lifeboat. 'After we sort out this morning about getting married, will you take me shopping? I want to know what you like, so you'll have to choose –'

'Married –' he said and put up one hand to bury his fingers in her hair, and twist the curls round, tugging gently in the way he knew she liked. 'Listen, honey, why rush? I mean, let's go to Boston, meet with the family –'

She pulled away from him and sat up so sharply that his fingers tangled in her hair and it hurt as she pushed his hand down. 'Jay! We talked about this. My father – I mean, he may be coming after us right now. If we're not married he'll – oh, I can't bear to think what he might do to you. He must know by now it was you that had the money from those deals and not Ambrose – and if he gets his hands on you – I've seen him do terrible things to people when he's angry. But if we're married, there'll be no problems, I promise you – I explained.'

'Yeah, yeah,' he mumbled and got out of bed and padded away to the bathroom and even in her anxiety she could not help but respond to the sight of his back with its smooth curves and planes and the way his buttocks, small and hard, fitted so elegantly into his thighs. Her skin crawled a little, even though they had made love only half an hour ago.

'Yeah, I know what you mean – but listen, we'll have breakfast, go shopping and then we'll talk. I can't now – too shagged.' And at the bathroom door he turned and stood, arms akimbo and legs astride, displaying himself arrogantly. He grinned as her gaze inevitably shifted downwards and he jerked his pelvis towards her in an insolent inviting gesture so that his genitals swung lewdly and then ran to the shower as she came lunging towards him from the bed.

They showered together, laughing a lot as they soaped each other and made as many lascivious movements and contacts as the small space allowed them, and went down to breakfast in great amity; but Maddie was still worried. She could almost feel the baleful influence of his family in Boston reaching across the miles – how many? She was hazy on that point – to touch and chill her and to spoil her success, and to come between her and her Jay. And that could not be borne.

On an impulse she went across the lobby to buy a paper, as Jay went into the Rose Room in search of a table for breakfast, and happening to see it there bought *The Times* of a few days ago as well as a New York paper. And found herself with the most powerful of allies.

The story was on the third page, and she read it as she sat back replete after negotiating a massive breakfast (the offer of corned beef hash on the menu had so fascinated her it had been irresistible) and felt her overfilled stomach jerk with shock as she saw the headline SON NAMES FATHER AS ACCOMPLICE IN LONDON BLACK MARKET ENQUIRY.

'Oh, God, Jay –' she murmured and spread the paper on the table between them so that they could read together.

It was a clear and comprehensive account. Clearly the police had been watching Alfred Braham and his dealings for some time, for the evidence that had been offered in court was much more wide-ranging than anything her cable had suggested. And her brother too, it seemed, had been dealing in ways she had known nothing about.

'Oh, my God, Jay, we got away just in time,' she breathed and he nodded, almost awestruck at the narrowness of their escape.

'I could have been up to my eyes in this shit,' he said after a long moment and she nodded eagerly and put one hand over his on the smudged newspaper.

'But I stopped it from happening, didn't I? I told you I'd look after you, and I did. I got you all that money and kept you out of trouble and now we're here, safe and sound, and Daddy can't come after us, can he? Not with all this trouble for Ambrose –'

And suddenly, to her own amazement, she was crying. Tears were running down her face and splashing on the newspaper and her face was twisted like a baby's as sobs choked her and he stared at her, startled, and then quickly pulled a handkerchief from his pocket and thrust it at her face.

'She just choked on her coffee,' he said hastily to the waiter who had arrived looking concerned and she kept the capacious handkerchief over her face, trying to maintain Jay's polite fiction as the waiter went away and Jay slid an arm round her shoulders and held on tight, and at last, the tears began to ease.

'What is it? The same as last time, on the ship? Crying for your Daddy?'

Convulsively she nodded, grateful for his understanding, and managed to get her breath back.

'I've treated him so badly –' she whispered. 'Haven't I?'

'Not really,' he said after a moment. 'I mean, dammit all, Maddie, you didn't tell him to run the sort of business he does! Any more than I tell my Pa. They do what they want to do. Usually it all goes great and no one ever says a word and likes the good that comes of it – but sometimes it doesn't go so good, and what can you do? It's not your fault. You only worked for him.'

She sniffed dolorously. 'All the same, if he goes to prison –' And again she shook with a deep sob.

'He won't,' Jay said with great confidence. 'Not him. He's much too clever for that. Alfred Braham, go to gaol? Pigs'll fly! He'll wriggle his way out, all right. I keep telling you, he's like my Pa –'

'Could they take me to court for being involved? And for helping you the way I did?' She lifted her chin and looked at him with red eyes. 'Could you get into trouble too?'

There was a long silence and he took his arm from her shoulders and sat and stared down at the paper, reading the account of Ambrose in court, and then took a deep breath.

'It might be better if we got married at that,' he said at length, almost casually. 'It's only you who knew what I did, and how we fixed it, right? Better we were married, if it came to anything.'

At once the last shred of her distress melted and she took hold of his arm so sharply that he winced.

'Oh, Jay, do you mean it? Can we? How long will it take to arrange it? And can I get something to wear and –' And then she stopped. 'How do you mean, if it comes to anything?'

'Law,' he said simply. 'Wives can't testify against their husbands. Or for 'em come to that. So it's better we get married, hmm? I'll go to City Hall this morning, see what we can fix up.'

And he leaned across and smiled at her and then kissed her and she dissolved with delight and excitement, but not so much she didn't wonder, just briefly, if the law about wives and testimony were the same in England as it was here in America. But never mind. Jay thought it was and that was good enough.

16

October 1950

The dreamlike state became ever more enchanting, and all she could do was beam her joy at everyone, and it was easy to do so, for the people she met did seem to be very responsive and that made her beam even more. But that was because she at last realised that that was the only possible response to give someone as hugely happy as she was. Her towering excitement and flowing good spirits dragged everyone within reach into her centre, and invested them with part of her warmth. Even Jay lost some of his usual self-absorption and laughed back at her when she turned her glittering gaze of pure bliss on him; so the next days were spent in a haze of excited happiness.

There was official business at City Hall, making the necessary arrangements for a wedding, Jay telling smooth tales about her age while warning her to keep quiet for fear her English accent would make officialdom too curious; money changing hands, forms being filled out and at last all arrangements completed for a Friday morning wedding, down to the required blood test ('What on earth is that for?' she asked Jay softly. 'Nothing that need worry you,' he had said and refused to explain), and time then to shop.

Dresses and little suits, coats and shoes and blouses and above all lingerie; wisps of nylon lace and satin that clung to her body and made her feel incredibly aware of her own sexuality; nightdresses in floating romantic chiffon that amused her hugely, for they were for posing in, never for sleeping or loving in – who needed dresses to make love? – and that most potent of symbols of luxury, nylon stockings. She ran the length of transparency through her hands and sighed with the sheer rapture of it all. Oh, to be Madeleine Braham at this moment, was to be the most successful, the most beautiful and above all the most supremely happy person in the world.

It was raining on the 28th of October, a thin biting rain, cold and dank, that threatened to creep into every corner of her, but it didn't matter. She clung to Jay's arm, very proud of the way he looked in his dark blue suit, specially bought for the occasion, and his shirt so white it almost blinded her and the handsome silk foulard tie in dark blue and crimson, and hardly heard a word the Justice said as he gabbled his way through the ritual. All she was waiting for was the magic moment when her Jay would slip a wedding ring on her finger. Then he would be hers for always and ever and she would never have to worry any more about anything. As long as they two were tied together as they were meant to be, all would be well; and for one tiny moment she had a sudden memory of her birthday party almost two years ago – could it be so short and yet so immense a time? – and the first time she had seen him, so beautiful with his thatch of glossy dark gold hair and his wonderful face; and she looked up at him now and almost wept with the delight of it, for he was even more beautiful now that she knew every plane, every pore, of his face in intimate detail.

She shook hands with the Justice and the witnesses – a couple of City Hall cleaners – and emerged on to the steps of City Hall to find the rain had stopped and she hugged his arm even closer and said gleefully, 'Hello, Mr Kincaid,' waiting for the obvious response. But he missed his cue, just smiling at her and saying, 'Hi, honey.'

'Call me Mrs Kincaid,' she commanded and he laughed. 'That isn't you, for heaven's sake! Mrs Kincaid is my mother! I can't think of you except as Maddie. Crazy kid, Maddie.'

'Well, you'll have to get used to it!' she said gaily. 'Because that's who I am now –'

'Yeah,' he said, seeming a little abstracted and then as she tugged again on his arm said, 'Listen, hon, I thought – we ought to have a honeymoon, hmm? We can't just – can we?'

'Can't just what?'

'Go back to the hotel and –'

'Go to bed?' she said mischievously. 'Why not?'

'It's an idea – but after that – No, I made a plan. We're going to London.' And he looked down at her with his eyebrows raised and his lips curved in a wicked little smile.

She felt the colour leave her face. 'What do you – Jay, are you mad? We can't –'

'*Naw*, New London, Connecticut. On Long Island Sound. It's a nice place, right by the ocean, with a hotel I stayed in once a while back. Nice place, you'll like it. Great for a honeymoon –' And she shook her head at him in mock fury and pretended to beat his chest with clenched fists. Oh, it was so wonderful to be married to a man like Jay and share the sorts of jokes married people shared, and to know that for ever and ever they'd be together . . .

He had hired a car and after lunch at the hotel and the settling of the bill – he looked a little gloomy for a moment as he contemplated the size of it – they drove north-east out of Manhattan over the river and out on the Long Island turnpike and she sat beside him, the fur collar of her new coat pulled up about her ears against the chill, and listened to banal songs about red robins and four-leaved clovers on the radio and sang inside her head: Mrs Kincaid, I'm Mrs Kincaid; Mrs Kincaid, I'm Mrs Kincaid – and it sounded and felt all that she had ever hoped it would. It didn't seem possible to be so happy.

She slept for a while, worn out with living at the very top of her emotional capacity, and woke only when they stopped for petrol – and she thought, I'll have to learn to call it gas. I'm an American now. I'm Mrs Kincaid – and went into the diner for coffee and a doughnut.

'Not much further now,' he said, and smiled a little vaguely at her. 'Another hour or so and we should be there . . .'

'Something wrong?' she said after a long pause and leaned over and touched his hand, for he was staring down into his coffee cup and paying her no attention at all.

'Mmm? Oh, no – just homesick, I guess,' and he looked up then and for the first time there was an expression in his eyes that startled her. She hadn't realised before just how smooth and carefully controlled a face he had: he wasn't one who, like her, bore his thoughts on his visage for all to see, but now he seemed troubled and – she reached for a word that would describe it and the one that came into her mind was young – he looked as young as a schoolboy and as anxious.

'But why be homesick? You're here in your own country. I'm not – and I'm not a bit homesick, I have you. That's all the home I need –'

'Oh Maddie, you do rattle on, don't you? All that guff – you

151

make me laugh –' But he didn't look all that amused and she felt a little stab of anxiety again.

'But tell me, Jay, I want to understand. How do you mean, homesick?'

'Boston's my home, Maddie. Not New York. Wouldn't you be homesick in England if you were – oh, I don't know where – Nottingham, say. That awful place I had to go to on one of the whisky deals, remember? If you were there wouldn't you be homesick for London?' She considered for a moment and then nodded and held his hand in an even warmer clasp.

'I see what you mean. But we'll go to Boston, Jay, really we will. I just, I mean, I want to meet your family and see your home. It'll be my home now, won't it? It was just – I wanted us to be married first, so that we arrived as we mean to go on –'

But he wasn't listening, staring over her shoulder into the middle distance with glazed eyes.

'I used to come home this way sometimes in the old days when I'd been in New York with some of the fellas from Harvard – we'd go down by train but we'd come back in a hired car so that one of the New York guys could take it back, and it used to be –' He shook his head in admiration of his memories. 'It was great. All those miles, going so damned fast and dodging the cops, knowing when they were around, knowing when to slow down, when to take off and really burn up the blacktop – oh, it used to be such fun.'

'How far are we from Boston then? Are we nearly there? Would you rather go there right away instead of to this hotel? I don't mind, Jay. I can pretend our honeymoon was in New York, and I had it before the wedding –' And she laughed, a soft chuckle that was meant to please him, but he shifted his eyes to look at her and said sharply, 'Hey! Don't go making gags like that to my folks, when you meet them, will you? That's all I'm in need of!'

'Of course I won't,' she said, outraged. 'Do give me credit for some sense, Jay! I know they're difficult. You've told me often enough –'

'I haven't told you the half of it,' he said shortly and jerked his head at the boy in the white cap and apron behind the diner counter who was desultorily wiping the counter with a tired rag. 'Gimme some more coffee – not the half of it, believe me.'

'Then tell me now,' she said and rested her elbow on the counter and propped her chin on her fists. 'And tell me first how far we are from Boston.'

'How far? Oh, another two, three hours. We're an hour to New London and I could pick up the road to Providence there and be home in another two hours' drive from there. If I pushed a tad –' And he grinned and looked young again in a different sort of way. Impish, she thought, and loved the word as applied to him, 'and I sure can push when I want to. I broke up one of Pa's Studebakers, pushing too much.'

He was away now, talking easily and fluently in a way she hadn't ever heard him do before, ignoring his cooling coffee and staring at her with that same wide-eyed glazed look, talking of the house his family lived in in Brookline: 'It's a handsome house, real handsome, on Commonwealth Avenue, as nice as any of those on Back Bay, in its own way. You don't have to be Back Bay or Beacon Hill to be – well, Mother likes Brookline, and so do I. It's a nice house –'

'Tell me about it. How big is it?'

'Big? Oh, big enough for all of us. Five bedrooms, two, three, bathrooms – you know. Nice front lawn – with a long drive. You know.'

She smiled, tenderly, as a mother does to an excited child. 'But I don't. I've never been to Boston.'

He laughed. 'No, I suppose – well, it's about a half-acre in front, the lawn, and at the back it's a deal bigger, with a tennis court of course and a pool for the summer. It gets lousy hot in the summer in Boston. Real humid and up in the nineties. You have to have a pool –'

'Of course,' she said and smiled even more widely. 'An essential –'

'But most summers we went down to Cape Cod, to Hyannis. Well, to Osterville, really. We have this house there, right by the ocean, white clapboard, you know, and a long verandah where we had the swings – very nice and select. Mother liked it though Pa always said the place was stuffy and too Blue Book for him –'

'Blue Book?'

'Oh, the Brahmins. The real Boston kings, you know?'

153

She didn't, but it didn't matter. Not when he was so animated and excited. 'What's it like, this place? Where is it?'

'I told you, Cape Cod. Right out on the elbow, where the big Atlantic rollers come in and the fishing and swimming are the best. Oh, we had such great summers there, the best, with wienie roasts on the beach after dark and going after the big fish in the small hours when the tide was just right, and the dances at the country club – the best of times we had, the very best –'

'You will again,' she said. 'Maybe we could have a seaside place too? In Hyannis or wherever it was? And then when we have children we can take them there –'

He blinked and came back to her, his eyes sharp now. 'What? Oh, yes, of course. But listen –' He pushed his coffee cup away and leaned across to bring his face a little closer to hers. 'Listen, about kids and all – we've got time, hmm? I mean, I don't think we ought to be rushing into anything –'

She laughed softly. 'And here was me thinking you wouldn't do anything to – what was it? Anything a good Catholic boy shouldn't do! Are you suggesting we deliberately avoid having children?'

There was a little silence and then he said, 'Yes. For a while. I can leave that to you, can't I? What you do, you do. I don't have to know everything, do I? My Pa always said that. The best way to be with a woman is not to know everything about her – and make damn sure she doesn't know all about you.'

'But I'm not just a woman, Jay. I'm your wife. I'm Mrs Kincaid – junior, if you like, to make sure it's not your mother I'm talking about.'

'There already is a Mrs Kincaid Junior,' he said after a moment, and turned on his stool, digging into his pocket for change for the coffee and doughnuts. 'My brother Timothy's wife, Rosalie. She's Mrs Kincaid Junior.'

'Then I'll have to be Mrs Jay Kincaid,' she said slowly and stood up too. 'So that they can tell us apart. What's she like, Rosalie? Shall I like her? And is Declan married? And if –'

'Declan isn't married. And as for Rosalie –' He shrugged. 'It's all a bit complicated there. They don't get along. She wants a divorce but of course Mother won't hear of it, so there it is. She has to turn out for family things but they spat a lot, she and

Tim. Oh, you should hear 'em! I reckon a divorce'd be the better of two evils, but there it is – Mother says –'

They had reached the door now and she was pulling her fur collar back around her ears against the chill night air outside. 'But it's their business, surely, isn't it?' she said lightly. 'If they want to be apart how can anyone force them to be together? I mean, I thought here in America no one cared about divorce. It's different in England, I know, but everyone's so stuffy and silly there. But here, people get divorced all the time.'

'Kincaids don't', he said shortly. 'And Rosalie's a third cousin too, Mother's side, so there it is. And anyway there's always the money. Timothy gets his allowance from Pa as long as Pa is happy to give it. If Mother gets upset, Pa sure as hell won't be so happy. So, Rosalie turns out to family things and smiles and does as she's told and gets her share of his allowance, but I'll bet she gives Timothy one hell of a time when she does it,' and he laughed, but the sound was snatched from his lips by the wind blowing around the service forecourt.

She settled into the car and he pulled it back on to the blacktop and settled again to a steady fifty miles an hour in the fast outside lane, and she sat brooding for a while, thinking about all he had told her and then said carefully, 'And what does your mother say to that? To Tim and Rosalie fighting? Or does she –'

'Listen, Mother's no fool. She knows when not to interfere. And she never interferes when they spat. Anyway, everyone always spats in our house. You ought to hear Betty-Jane go at Maureen. That really is something.'

'Betty-Jane and Maureen –'

'They're my oldest sisters. Bernie and Cathy – they're the younger ones – they're easy enough. No trouble to anyone. But BJ and Maureen are like Kilkenny cats. You'll see –'

Yes, she said inside her head, I'll see. And I think, so will the other Mrs Kincaid. She needn't think she can bully me the way she bullies everyone else. Not me. Not now I'm a married woman, and Jay's mine. She won't get away with a thing. Just you watch me . . .

But her certainty began to waver, just a little, when they got to the hotel, a rather ferociously decorated country place with much evidence of the sea about it, from the fishing nets draped

155

over the check-in desk to the glass bubble floats in vivid colours strung over the bar. They had checked in and gone up to their room and she stopped at the doorway of their bedroom, as the bellboy went on ahead with their luggage, and said softly to Jay, 'You ought to carry me over the threshold. It's not our home, I know, but it's all we've got to be getting on with –'

He looked blank and she laughed again. 'It's what all married men are supposed to do with their wives – carry them over the threshold to make sure they belong to them! And I'm not that heavy.'

He bent and picked her up as the grinning bellboy stood and held the door, carried her in and threw her on the bed before tossing a coin to the boy and sending him away.

'There,' she said with great satisfaction, still lying on the bed where he had thrown her, and laughing up at him, 'now I really *feel* as though I'm married –'

'I don't.' He grinned down at her. 'I feel as wicked as ever I did, screwing a girl as mad as you are –'

'But of course you should feel married! I mean, look –' and she showed him her left hand, wagging her long elegant fingers at him and still laughing.

But he shook his head and turned away, pulling off his tie. 'Well, it's not as though we went to church, is it? A nuptial mass, now – that must make a man feel married! So let's make the most of it, hon, and go on being a wicked immoral pair. It's a hell of a lot of fun, that's for sure –' And all the time he spoke he was pulling off his clothes.

That was the first time she made love as a married woman. And the first time she didn't climax.

17

October 1950

They drove into Boston on a morning so bright and cold that it hurt her eyes, sweeping along the broad highway and past the grey scatter of buildings in a haze of morning sunshine and she felt her chest tighten with apprehension and knew she was nervous only because he was.

For the past few miles they had sped along the highway in total silence, as he became more and more abstracted, but now as they passed a board that read 'Welcome to Norwood', he said abruptly, 'I'll take the Yankee Division Highway and then turn east on the Worcester turnpike. We'll be in Brookline in about a half-hour or so, maybe less, depending on the traffic. Okay?'

'Mmm? Oh, yes, I suppose so. That's fine –' she said, and stole a sideways glance at him. He looked particularly handsome this morning, with his hair burnished to a rich golden sheen and his profile jutting against the passing scenery with all the glamour of a film star's and she felt the sheer pleasure of him lift inside her and shivered a little and said, 'Who'll be there when we get there? To your house, I mean?'

'Who can say? It could be everyone or no one. I –' He stopped and scowled as he overtook a huge articulated truck which had been roaring its exhaust fumes behind it so that they swirled into the car and made them cough. 'As a matter of fact, they don't know we're coming. I didn't let them know. So there's no reason why anyone should be there at all right now.'

'You didn't – why not?' She turned in her seat and stared at him. 'Why didn't you tell them we were coming?'

He made a face. 'I thought it be easier to explain it all when we got there,' he said and slid his eyes sideways to glance at her. 'Don't glare at me like that, for God's sake! It's no matter, after all. We can explain when we get there. I told you.'

She sat in silence for a long moment and then said dully, 'They don't even know we're married, do they? You didn't tell them that either. No telegram, though you said you'd send one. You just didn't send it, did you?'

'I *told* you! There'll be plenty of time when we get there –' He sounded sulky now. 'Why start a whole drama for no reason? It'll be fine when we're actually there, believe me. So I send a wire and what happens? Mother gets into a panic, Pa hits the roof, everyone starts screaming and shouting. They're like that, my family . . .'

'They're my family too, now,' she said. 'Don't you think you might have made it a bit easier for me if you had told them? Even at the risk of screaming fits? I mean, I'm your wife, Jay! I'm entitled to a bit of consideration, aren't I?'

'Christ, you sound like my mother already! What happens to women when they get wedding rings on their fingers? Do they find out how to nag the same moment?'

'I'm not nagging, I'm just – I'm scared,' she said and wriggled down in her seat to hide her face in her fur collar again. 'It's – I'm a long way from my own family and I wanted so much to be loved by yours, that's why. I love you and –'

He glanced at her uneasily. 'Don't start to cry, for God's sake.'

'I'm not going to. I just wanted you to know how scared I am –'

'Oh, for God's sake, no need to be scared! They aren't ogres. Just my folks. A bit on the – well, they get a bit excited sometimes. But then so did your father. I remember, believe me. He gave me one hell of a going over once or twice.'

'I dare say he did,' she said in a small voice. 'But that was in the way of business. This is family – it should be nice and – oh, what's the use of talking about it? You didn't tell them so you didn't. I'll have to manage as best I can.'

The curious thing was she didn't feel nearly as apprehensive as she had. Now she knew the situation, and knew too how nervous he was, it seemed to have made it better. Indeed, more than better; exciting. The prospect of meeting a whole crew of people who didn't know that she had scooped up their son under their very noses and making them like her – and she would, she vowed; she knew she could and she would – was very exciting. It was a challenge and she sat with her mouth and nose buried in fur, staring out of the window and pretending to be a sad little thing but feeling the pleasure and drama of it all bubbling inside her.

Equally curiously, her show of anxiety seemed to have put some muscle into Jay, for he stopped being so anxious and silent and began to talk to her of the scenery they were passing.

'That's the Charles River – see? There on the right. It flows on right into the middle of Boston and into the harbour. It's a beautiful river. Now, this area's called Newton Upper Falls and there ahead – see? – that's where we turn right in to the turnpike – home any minute now –' And now his mood changed and he became like a child, eager to get home after the long term away at school.

The road was still a major highway, but now the buildings they were passing became larger and more imposing and the roads that ran off on each side showed very elegant big and comfortable houses with large front lawns and she grinned into her collar even more widely. This was going to be a lovely place to live. Soon, she and Jay would have just such a house as any one of these, all to themselves, and need not worry at all about his family. Not once they were living as a married couple ought to live, in their own house, and she let her mind drift away into a happy fantasy of a house full of busy servants and Jay and she in the middle of a beautiful drawing room and somewhere in the upper reaches of the house perhaps a couple of pretty babies – it was a very delectable image and she almost jumped when Jay said, 'Okay. This is Boylston and here is where we turn left into Brookline –'

'We're here then?' She sat up sharply and stared out of the window.

'Not quite,' he said. 'This is just Brookline Avenue. We live on Commonwealth, so we have to go on, up there till we get to Beacon and then we're there. You can almost see the house –'

It was undoubtedly a handsome house, quite as handsome as any they had passed. Red brick with an imposing front and a pillared entrance of considerable splendour that looked like any of the old Georgian houses she had seen at home in England, and a large expanse of front lawn sliding down to the road. There was a large red car parked in the driveway and she stretched her neck and said, 'Looks as though there is someone home, after all.'

He had pulled their hired car into the drive behind it and now he switched off the engine and sat staring out, making no effort to move, and after a moment she opened the door and got out herself, leaving it to him to follow.

It was pleasant enough outside, though there was a nip of cold in the air from a sharp easterly breeze and she lifted her face to the thin winter sunshine and took a deep breath. It smelled clean and fresh, with an overtone of salt in it, and it invigorated her and she turned back to the car to run round it and open the door on Jay's side and urge him out.

There was a sound of hurrying footsteps on gravel behind her and a voice roared, 'And who do you think you are, then?' and she turned to see a large woman in a calico apron and with her hair tied up under a scarf thudding down the path from the house. 'You can't be just puttin' your car there, with himself ready to go out in no more than a minute or two now – you be movin' at once, or we'll have him chewin' up the grass, I'll tell –'

Maddie wanted to laugh. The accent the woman had was so weird, such a thick mixture of stage Irish and cinema American that she felt it must surely be put on for her benefit, but the woman went on and on about the car, and it was clear that this was as she was. There was no element of pretence at all, and Maddie bit her lip and turned to the car once again to urge Jay out.

But he needed no urging, for now he was out and leaning over the top and staring at the shouting woman with his face split into a huge grin, and at last she turned away from Maddie and looked at him and at once the tirade of abuse dried up and she stared and then threw her arms wide and came scuttling round the car to throw them around him and hug him till Maddie could almost hear his ribs crack under the brawny arms.

She stared almost in horror. Whatever else she had expected of Jay's mother it hadn't been anything like this, and for a moment she was nonplussed. But she regained her composure fast and stepped forwards and held out her hand.

'Hello,' she said and produced her most winning smile. 'It's so good to meet you.' And as the woman turned to look at her she smiled even more widely and leaned over and kissed her cheek. She smelled of soap and polish and sweat and beneath that of beer and cigarettes and Maddie fixed the smile on her face with even more determination and wondered wildly if she'd ever be able to cope with such a mother-in-law.

Jay was still looking delighted and now he grinned at Maddie and said cheerfully, 'Well, you've met the most important person in the house, now! At least, we know she is, eh, Mary Margaret? Never mind Pa or Mother – this is the one who keeps the place going. Have you missed me then, you wicked old devil?'

'Missed you? Never a bit of it!' The woman turned back to him and beamed. 'Glad to see the back of you imp of mischief, that I was. And who might this be, then?' And she jerked her head over her shoulder towards Maddie.

Maddie was almost giddy with relief. How she could ever have imagined this woman was the mother of whom Jay was so patently in awe was beyond her, but in doing so she had clearly wrought better than she knew, for obviously this woman was a force to be reckoned with in the Kincaid household. There could be no mistaking the affection Jay felt for her, old nanny that she is, Maddie thought, who brought him up. And still loves him best of all – and I kissed her. Oh, thank you to whoever it is who was watching over me! I'd never have kissed her if I hadn't thought she was his mother, and it couldn't have been a better thing to do –

For Mary Margaret had turned and was now looking at her with a critical eye, but there was no hostility to her, just an appraising interest, and after a moment Jay said almost with embarrassment, 'Er – well, to tell you the truth, Mary Margaret – this is my wife.'

'I thought as much,' the woman said and grinned, displaying unlovely tobacco-stained teeth. 'There's an air to her that shows she's got you by the short ones. Well, well, and where did he find you?'

'In London, Mary Margaret!' Maddie said, and smiled again, but more demurely now, and then glanced at Jay. 'We met when Jay was working with my father –'

'Jesus, you're English then? That'll go down great with madam your mother and I don't think,' Mary Margaret said but she didn't look at Jay. 'Your Pa now, he'll be taken with you. Always did like pretty girls with curly hair, he did, the old devil. Well, you'd better be coming in, then, out of the cold –'

'Are they home, Mary Margaret?' Jay was slowly taking luggage out of the car, not seeming at all anxious to go inside. 'And the girls, where are they?'

'Your Ma and Pa just finished their lunch, they have. I suppose I'll have to be rushin' about fetchin' vittles for you two now. Oh, the way you all run me off my poor old feet is a sin and a crime, but what can you do? You'd all starve if I didn't. Your sisters are out some place, don't ask me where for all they ever tell me, the pair of madams they are. Bernie and Catherine, they're still away at college, o'course. We don't see them till Thanksgiving, and God knows who'll they'll fetch along with them when they do come. Like yourself, that pair. Never know who they're takin' up with next –'

'And Timothy?' They were walking up the drive now, Mary Margaret carrying most of the luggage and Jay walking behind her with a couple of small cases. 'Is he here?'

She sniffed. 'By a miracle he ain't at the moment. He's here a deal too much for a man with a wife and a home of his own, but what can you do? No one tells him what to do, never did. He's at the office, I dare say, though there's no guaranteein' it. Goin' by himself this mornin' he's a sight fonder of bein' where he wants to be than where your Pa wants him to be, but there, I dare say you'll be no different now you're back. You wasn't before you went away, was you?'

She jabbered all the way into the house and Maddie stopped listening, staring around at all there was to see with a sort of hunger. She wanted to make no more mistakes of the sort she already had with this servant; as it happened it had been a good mistake that could rebound to her benefit. It was obvious that having Mary Margaret as an ally in this house could be useful. But her next mistake might not be so profitable and she needed to keep her wits well about her to avoid it.

They came into the house through the back door to which Mary Margaret had automatically made her way, and past a vast kitchen where another woman was briskly washing dishes and on through a dim corridor to a door at the far end which led into the main hallway of the house. Here any similarity with the sort of Georgian houses she had seen in England vanished, for there seemed to be no other internal doors, apart from the one which led to the back part of the house. The hallway led by a couple of steps into a big comfortably furnished sitting room full of great vases of flowers and on the other side into a dining room, equally doorless, while the stairs ran up the centre into a gallery above, off which she could just see there were some doors at last, and she took a deep breath and felt, just as she had in New York, that she had walked straight into the set of a film. This was the sort of house inhabited by Myrna Loy or Greer Garson in all those stories about happy marriages threatened by misunderstandings and interlopers, and the sense of strangeness that thought gave her made her want to laugh.

'Have you got rid of whoever it is, damn you?' someone roared and she whirled towards the source of the sound and saw at the far side of the stairs a man standing in the opening that led to the dining room. A tall man, well muscled and with a long thin face that was very like Jay's, surmounted by white hair that was as glossy and thick as Jay's own golden thatch. He was holding a napkin in one hand and was glaring furiously as Mary Margaret stepped forwards, out of the lee of the staircase where they were standing and shouted back at him, 'I did, at that, I did. He'll move the car when you're fit to go and that'll not be in such a hurry after all, not once you see who it is —'

Maddie didn't wait for Jay to make his move and join Mary Margaret where his father could see him. Moving swiftly she dodged past him and ran round the bulky figure of the servant and towards the old man. Her coat, which she had unbuttoned, swung open to show the sleek red woollen dress she had on and which she knew showed off her shape to advantage and she lifted her chin and gave her smile every bit of sparkle and excitement she could and held out her hand and went purposefully towards him.

'Hello,' she said and she kept her voice interestingly low. 'I'm Maddie. How are you?' And then she added very deliberately, 'Pa,' and did exactly what she had done with Mary Margaret. She kissed him.

18

November 1950

'As long as we're all right, I can handle anything,' Maddie said. 'Jay? Believe me, we'll be all right. Only stick with me, back me up. If you start taking sides against me, I don't know what I'll do.'

'You can't call it taking sides when I listen to my own folks, for God's sake,' Jay said, and turned over in bed irritably, thumping his pillow to get it comfortable. 'You pull me all over the place, Maddie, you know that? I told you we'd have to take things easy, give it time, let Pa and Mother get used to what's happened. Then it'll be okay –'

'It won't,' she said, and slid into bed beside him, stretching her bare body against his back, and reached over his shoulder to play with the lobe of his ear, which always pleased him. 'Because they're nervous about me. They're not sure they can trust me. Well, of course they can – why can't they see that? Things won't get any easier till they do. They have to understand . . . When you love someone as much as I love you, it's obvious I can be trusted – and if you tell them that, if you show them by backing me up all the time, it'll all be fine and they'll feel good with me.'

He turned over at last, and she slid under his arm so that she could push her head into the soft part of his shoulder, just above his armpit, and his hand slid down to hold her left breast. At last she felt comfortable again, the way she ought to feel. It was dreadful when he turned his back on her.

'The trouble is, they think it's all money. They don't understand you – they think you're like Rosalie.'

'Me like that silly – huh!' and she snorted. 'She's as wet as they come. I'd be ashamed to be such a whiner as she is –'

'Don't misunderstand that one,' Jay said. 'She's crawling round Mother the way she is because she wants to stay in this family a hell of a lot more than Timothy and we now want her to be here. If he had his way he'd pay her off once and for all and she'd go away and never come back. He doesn't care that much about being married and there're plenty of girls who'd enjoy being around him once she'd gone. But the way she hangs around here – it cramps the guy's style.'

'Not as much as he cramps yours,' she said softly. 'It's not just Declan who's getting your share of what there is, you know. I've been listening and watching. Timothy's not exactly your best pal, you know.'

His arm tightened around her and she winced as his fingers bit into her breast. 'What do you mean?'

'Well, I keep my ears open when I'm with your father –'

'And you're with him a hell of a lot, one way and another,' he said. 'I've never seen the old man so taken with anyone.'

She grinned in the darkness. 'I made sure he would be. Like I said, I listen, and I know that it's Timothy you need to watch as much as Declan. He's not the brightest, Jay. You're much cleverer than Declan is, and he thinks you're the best of the lot. He'd do anything for you. If you got Timothy out of the way and ran the business with your Pa, then Declan'd do things to please you and you'd really be laughing.'

'How do you mean?' He was very interested now, and she slid out of his grasp and turned on her belly to peer down at him in the dimness.

'Look, that whisky deal from Scotland – isn't it funny how it's always whisky when it's you and me, hmm? Well, I heard your Pa on the phone and then I heard Timothy telling your mother something and – well, Timothy left his briefcase in the dining room last night.' She chuckled softly. 'Silly thing to do, wasn't it?'

He was silent for a moment. 'So?' he said at length.

'So, half the profit went to Kincaid and Sons Inc., but the rest went to a building set-up in Cincinnati. Where's Cincinnati, Jay?'

'It sure as hell isn't in Boston,' Jay said wrathfully. 'The bastard! Just let me get my hands on him – and when Pa finds out –'

'Hush.' She set her fingers over his lips. 'Don't be silly, my darling Jay. Listen to your Maddie. The last thing you do is say a word to your father.'

'What? When he's been skinning me the way he has? It's as much my money that goes to Kincaid's – I'm one of the sons, too, remember. Timothy isn't the only one. And I thought it was Declan doing the dirty on me – the bastard –'

'Tell your father and where do you end up? No better off. All he'd do is scream and rant and fight with Timothy – and take the money in his own hands. You've got little enough access as it is. If your Pa thinks one of his sons is cheating him, he'll get suspicious of all of you, and then where'd you be?' Maddie said softly. 'Better to get the deals away from Timothy, hmm? Stop it at source the way we did in London. I can't do as well here in Boston as I did in London for you, my darling, but if you back me up here in the house, and let me do things my way, you'll be amazed at what I get out for you in the way of information.' She stopped then and laughed, rolling over on her back. 'Rosalie. That's the answer, Rosalie.'

It was his turn to roll over now and he did, covering her and setting his elbows on each side of her and crushing her breasts under his body.

'How?'

'She wants to get Timothy back. She won't, of course – he's had enough of her, and I don't blame him. Those drippy blondes – they're all the same. Do nothing but whine and then wonder why people can't stand 'em. Well, I'll stand her. I'll make a fuss of her, and you know something? She'll do anything I want after that. She's scared and she's lonely. That's why she comes here so often even though they're supposed to be separated and don't get on. She says it's to see your mother, but I'm not so easily fooled as your mother is –'

'My mother easily fooled? You must be crazy.'

'Believe me, she is. She's so full of herself and her own good works and her own virtue it never occurs to her she might be wrong. And that means that anyone who sucks up to her looks to her to be sensible and anyone who thinks for themselves is out in the cold. That's why she doesn't like me. But never mind, Rosalie will like me, and I'll get what I want out of her, and that means you will and then – oh, Jay, it'll all be lovely, you'll see. Wasn't I right before? Haven't I always made it work for you before? Well, I will again. Only for God's sake, back me up. Do what I want you to do, follow my lead and it'll all be fine –'

'You are one crazy kid, Maddie,' he said and at the sound of the familiar words she smiled, softly and slowly in the darkness and lifted her arms and linked them round his neck. He always said that before they made love now; it had become part of their loveplay, so much so that when he said it in the dining room or the sitting room when they were all there she knew it was an invitation and would produce gargantuan yawns and would say her goodnights demurely and wander up to bed, knowing he would follow as soon as he could.

Now he wasn't willing to waste time in more loveplay than those few words and as he pushed himself into her and pulled her knees up on each side of him she let her thoughts slide away, letting her body respond to him and not bothering to think about her own sensations much.

It was still good to make love, of course it was, but not so much because of the directly physical way it made her feel, as it had been at the beginning. Now it was an affirmation of her possession of him, a reminder to him as much as to her that he was now hers and only hers, and that was gratification enough. So, as he rose and fell rhythmically above her now, grunting a little with pleasure, she didn't need to think about what he was doing. She could think and plan things.

It hadn't been an easy four weeks at all. She had felt like a cat in a room full of broken glass, treading deliberately here and there, going round in wide circles to get to where she wanted without injury, but it had been worth it. She had them pretty well in her eye now, knew how they operated, understood the rhythms and currents of life in the big luxurious house which was in reality far less comfortable to be in than it seemed.

Pa, the autocrat who wasn't, seemed to run everyone according to his own whims but was himself so much under his wife's baleful eye that he had been forced to become devious and sly. He spent as much time evading her control and criticism as he did on business. She hadn't lived with as sharp a businessman as Alfred Braham all her life without learning to recognise a sharp operator when she met one – or a sloppy one. And there was no doubt in her mind that old Timothy Kincaid was sloppy in his dealings. There was major profit to be made from the fact, and she had soon found ways to do so.

Building and booze, they were his main concerns, the ones

that brought in much more cash than all his other interests, which ranged from South Boston taverns to North End restaurants via dairies, fruit warehouses, liquor stores, car dealers and shoe stores. It was an odd mixture of interests, she had thought at first, until, while listening and chatting artlessly to the old man to unbutton his own gossip, she had discovered the link between them. He had an odd and uneasy partnership with a group of Italian businessmen as well as with the obvious Irish cronies a man such as he would be expected to have. Dubious Italians too, she thought shrewdly, and far from the simple honest small businessmen they seemed, for when their names came into their conversation the old man became uneasy, and sheered of.

'Why do I deal in fruit and shoes?' he would say, twinkling down at her over his cigar. 'Why, you chatterbox, because people need shoes and fruits. Why else? Now tell me, did your Daddy ever tell you of the time we got hold of thirty-seven geese at Christmas 1917 and then sold them as Christmas dinners for Douglas Haig's staff and after that sold them three times over to the French army staff and to a bunch of French civilians? They all paid up and we sent them all to the same place to collect their geese – oh, it must have been rich! I wish I'd been there to see their faces –'

'No, he didn't tell me that. But he told me about the cellar full of wine you found near Château Thierry still there after the offensive –'

He had slapped his leg with enormous satisfaction. 'Jesus, yes! I'd forgotten that! Now what did he tell you? And I'll put the record straight.'

And so it had gone on all through the weeks since they had arrived and been installed in Jay's room, into which Mary Margaret, with some muttering and complaining, had shifted a double bed. It was she and only she who had made any effort towards their comfort; certainly his mother hadn't and Maddie had not been at all surprised by that fact.

From the moment she had first seen her, when she had come out of the dining room behind her husband the afternoon they had arrived, Maddie had known she was a formidable adversary. Tall and thin, with fair hair so faded it was the colour of old straw pulled back into tight waves across the top of her head, she dressed in clothes as muted and as understated as could be found. Beside her husband, who exuded colour and vigour and life she seemed to disappear, to become little more than a rosary-clutching shadow (for she never seemed to be seen without one, as far as Maddie could tell; she wondered if she took one with her into the bath but knew that to ask such a question would cause great offence so she said nothing). But that she was powerful was undoubted. She had looked at Maddie through her gold-rimmed glasses as round as buttons, and said quietly, 'How do you do,' when Jay made his nervous introductions and then had reached up and hugged Jay with an eager hunger that was almost embarrassing to see, and Maddie had thought – take care. This won't be easy.

It wasn't. That Blossom Bryan Kincaid was implacably opposed to Maddie's presence in her house was soon clear, even though she never said a word against her, and always addressed her with meticulous politeness. But she never invited Maddie to come with her to church as she always did everyone else in the house (including Mary Margaret who always gave the same retort, 'Ah, the Good Lord knows there's as much virtue in sweepin' a room as in runnin' to church. I've work to be done. I'll be there Sunday for mass and he'll settle for that much of a view of me. You be on your way.'). Nor did she invite Maddie to sit with her when she read her day's portion of religious tracts, as again she always asked her daughters and her other daughter-in-law.

But that did not worry Maddie. She knew better than to waste efforts on people who would not respond. That had never been her way. She cut her losses and got on to the next thing – and in this case, the next thing was Rosalie. She was the key to dealing with Timothy Two and Declan and it was a key she would use.

Timothy Two and Declan, she thought now as Jay, his head stretched back and sweating heavily, began to move more rapidly so that her head was banged rhythmically against the head of the bed. I need more time to get to know about them. Aloof, that was the word for them. They had been introduced to her that first evening when they had returned home for family dinner, and had shaken hands politely, showing little surprise at the fact that she was now their sister-in-law, and had from then on kept their distance. They would need a little more effort, she told herself, if I'm to get everything right for us, the way it ought to be. Right for *all* of us, and as Jay at last finished and rolled off her she smiled sideways at him in the darkness, and said softly, 'Jay, my darling, I have to tell you something.'

'Mmm?' he said sleepily and turned away, ready to fall asleep, but she pulled him back so that he had to look at her.

'Jay, darling, I have to tell you I wasn't quite as clever as I thought I was. I should have had a period last week, and I haven't. And I've been regular as long as I can remember. I think, maybe, there's going to be a new generation of Kincaids in this house. Unless we get one of our own soon.'

19

January 1951

She couldn't risk being sick, Maddie decided, so she wasn't. She felt sick enough, heaven knew, hardly daring to get out of bed in the morning for fear of throwing up, but she was well aware with a deep certainty that if Jay were to see that happening he would be so alarmed that he'd back away from her. And right now that was the last thing she wanted. So a strong effort of will was essential.

Actually, it wasn't as hard to control the way she felt as she had feared it might be. As long as she took plenty of time over getting up in the mornings, and took no more for breakfast than clear tea and a little dry toast, the waves of nausea would recede until she felt well enough to cope. She would slide into the pattern of the days without leaving a ripple to disturb anyone and certainly not Jay.

He seemed to have returned to the life he had lived before he had been sent to England without any difficulty at all, sinking into the mud of his home waters with even less of a ripple. He went to the State Street office of Kincaid and Sons each day with his brothers Timothy and Declan, leaving his father to follow later when he had spent the morning reading the papers and listening to his favourite radio commentators and then taking lunch with his wife and daughters – and now Maddie – after which all three men came home to the big house together to sit over the vast dinner that Mary Margaret and her staff of two thrust in front of them.

The house ran like an oiled turbine under the big noisy woman's care; Maddie hardly ever saw the other two servants though she knew they were there, for she heard Mary Margaret swearing raucously at them often enough. There was certainly nothing for her to do, any more than there was for the daughters of the house. Their daily pattern was similar to their father's; late rising, mornings spent about their own affairs,

171

mostly getting dressed, and then disappearing after lunch to, as far as Maddie could tell, spend the whole of the afternoon shopping in Newbury Street. Even though she could be a dedicated spender of money herself, Maddie couldn't imagine doing that. Not every afternoon, every week.

She had, during her first days in the house, tried to talk to Jay about the provision of a home of their own. It had never occurred to her that he would not set about making such arrangements as soon as they had reached Boston and greeted his family. They did not have a great deal of money behind them, of course, but he had his salary from Kincaid and Sons, and she had ideas about improving that. So there was no reason they shouldn't have their own home, in which she could be the supreme person, as Blossom Bryan Kincaid was in this house. But Jay had just listened and said nothing when she had broached the subject, and then had talked deliberately of other things, so she had said no more. It was clear that he would settle for no home smaller than this family one, and since they could not afford such a house for themselves, then the only thing to do was to live with his parents. He saw no loss of dignity in that, so why should she?

But she did. Perhaps, she would think sometimes, later on, perhaps if I had had something to do, a place to call my own, I wouldn't have let it all happen. I wouldn't have had the time to do it, apart from anything else . . .

But she did have the time and her pregnancy, rather than making her somnolent and willing to loaf through the winter days – and they were bitingly cold in a way she had never met cold before – made her edgy and eager, as though she were filled with a sense of urgency she could not control. Things had to happen, and if they did not happen of their own volition, then she, Maddie, had the responsibility to make them happen.

So, she set to work. It would be a waste of time, she knew, to try to get anywhere with Blossom. It would be equally pointless to try to influence her sisters-in-law, Maureen and Betty-Jane. They were little more than ornaments, seeing themselves as having only one function in life, which was to find themselves suitable husbands. Maddie had a hazy notion that they were getting anxious about their advancing ages since they were twenty-six and twenty-five, but at the same time were very pernickety in their tastes and that between them they had turned down half the eligible men in Boston, seeking partners who were as romantic and exciting as they wanted them to be, as rich as their father expected them to be, and as pious as their mother insisted they be. There were, Maddie gathered, sadly few left who came up to the required standard. But that was their problem and Maddie could not have been less interested in it.

It was Rosalie who drew her attention, Rosalie who timed her visits to her mother-in-law carefully so that she never saw her husband, who had moved back into the family house leaving her in possession of the smart apartment on Tremont Street, beyond the Common, to which they had gone when they married. Twenty minutes after the brothers had climbed into the car each morning, to be driven by Liam, Mary Margaret's nephew (a man as taciturn as his aunt was loquacious) to the offices down by the harbour, she would arrive, slipping silently into the house by the side door to sit by Blossom and read with her and listen to her murmurings and to go with her to church. She always slipped away equally silently at lunchtime, preferring not to see old Timothy, but back she would come as soon as Liam had taken the old man downtown, and renew her vigil by Blossom's side.

But Blossom dozed in the afternoons. She wasn't that old, Maddie knew, but she chose to behave as though she were, and an afternoon nap, taken sitting bolt upright in her chair with her head neatly arranged against the petit point cushion set behind it, was part of that pose. So, that was the time that Maddie chose to take over Rosalie for herself.

It was not difficult. The first thing she did, after persuading the girl in a whisper to come and sit with her while Blossom slept, was confide the facts about her pregnancy. She had no intention of telling anyone else yet; it was her ace in the hole, she decided. Later, if necessary, she would use it as a way of putting pressure on all of them to arrange that the Jason Kincaids had their own house; they would not want a squalling infant around, she was sure of that. But there was time to wait, to see whether she needed that sort of weapon to deal with them. But it was a useful one now for Rosalie, and after swearing her to secrecy she confided the details to her, whispering into the small ear beneath the wispy fair hair and then leaning back with a nice air of weariness, to watch the effect of her news.

It was as she thought it would be. Rosalie was one of those women who made a strength out of her weakness. She never hit out at anyone or displayed any rancour or hurt. She would sit and look pathetic and wait for the people she cared about to feel first embarrassed and then irritated, and finally guilty enough to do something about her obvious misery. It was a technique Maddie had seen others use and she had always despised it. Her friend Audrey at home had been just such a one with her parents, drooping and weeping if she was refused anything, but never asking or arguing or demanding as Maddie always did. And eventually Audrey had always got what she wanted just as Maddie had, but with the expenditure of much less effort. Maddie had learned a lot from Audrey. And now she put the lesson she had learned into action with Rosalie.

'I don't know what to do,' she said now piteously. 'Jay isn't making enough out of the business to get us our own house, and I can't nag him, can I? I think the trouble is that he just doesn't know much about what happens there – if he could have more responsibility then Pa'd see he ought to have more pay and we could move out. But as long as your Timothy is there, what chance has Jay got?'

'I wish he were my Timothy,' Rosalie murmured, bending her head forwards so that the sheet of fair hair swung forwards to hide her face. 'He isn't. He's *theirs* – especially Blossom's. She's like that with all of them – wants to hold them and make them do things her way because they're her men. All of them, not just Pa. It was she who wanted Timothy to come back here and leave me, you know –' And she lifted her head and her pale blue eyes were oiled with tears.

'But you come here and sit with her and –' Maddie began and then stopped and smiled. 'I see. If Blossom likes you and decides it's all right for Timothy to live with you, then she'll make him go back to you –'

Rosalie said nothing, sitting with her head bent again as the tears dripped on her hands, clasped in her lap.

'You're very sensible,' Maddie said firmly. 'It's the only way you can get what you want, isn't it? And if you want to have a baby too, like me –' and she saw Rosalie's shoulders tighten as she said it and knew she was right in her estimation of the effect of her news '– then you have to get Timothy to come back. Unless you want to divorce him –'

Rosalie threw her one shocked stare, and then bent her head again. 'Oh, no,' she whispered. 'That couldn't – Blossom wouldn't . . . No, that's not at all possible. We're *Catholics*, you know that.'

'But you do want him back?'

'Of course I do.' Rosalie sniffed lusciously. 'Oh I do, so much. I do love him.'

'If I tell you how to get him back, will you help me and Jay to get what we want? Our own house? And soon? I'm only a couple of weeks pregnant, really. If you and Timothy get together again soon, you could be having your baby not that long after me –'

Rosalie still sat with her shoulders sloped with sadness and her head drooping but then slowly she looked up and turned her head so that she could look into Maddie's eyes. There was an expression there that was familiar and Maddie stretched a little, almost catlike, as she identified it. That was how that silly Bobbie had looked at her, when she had been a sixth former in her last term at school, Bobbie who had been fourteen to Maddie's seventeen and who had adored her with so much passion that it was almost frightening. But very useful too, for Bobbie had been so willing to do anything her angel Maddie wanted that Maddie had come out of school with much better exam results than she had had any right to, considering how little school work she had done. She had left it to Bobbie to deal with her notes and her essays for prep. Bobbie had won her a respectable class placing, and here was Rosalie, who would do something just as useful and for the same reason.

'But what can I do to help you? If there was anything I could do for you, I would gladly. You're – you're so kind and friendly to me. But I'm not a brave person like you, Maddie. I daren't even talk to my own husband –'

Maddie leaned forwards confidentially. 'I've been talking to Jay about your husband. They're not as close as I thought –'

For the first time Rosalie showed a flash of spirit. 'He's always been jealous of my Timmy –'

'Jay says it's the other way about – oh, Rosalie, it must be awful to have too many brothers and sisters and always be jealous and have to fight them for what you want! I think I'll only have this one baby, you know, to save the misery for him or her –'

Again Rosalie looked shocked. 'That'd be a sin, Maddie, you know that. You can't not have babies just to suit yourself.'

'But you were married a while before Timothy left and you've no babies,' Maddie said with an air of innocence, knowing full well why.

Rosalie reddened painfully. 'I had some miscarriages. I was too – I didn't rest enough –' And she went brick red and looked at Maddie with a scared glance and then down at her hands again. 'Timmy, he's such a passionate man, and even when he knew I was pregnant he – well, he said it shouldn't matter in a healthy woman, but I was always delicate – and so there it was, you see, a miscarriage. But the next time the doctor says I'll be fine, just fine. If there's a next time –' And she looked agonised again.

'There will be,' Maddie said confidently. 'Now, listen. Like I said, I've been talking to Jay about his brothers. Not asking, you know, just chatting –'

Rosalie's eyes glinted for a moment and Maddie thought joyously – she isn't that bad after all. She can laugh, too, when she understands, and she grinned at her. 'Well, you know how it is with men. They're too daft to know what it is you're after half the time,' and now Rosalie managed to produce a smile of real amusement and for a moment a bubble of amity hung between them like a tangible thing.

'The thing is, Jay told me your Timothy likes the idea of politics.'

Rosalie seemed to catch fire for a moment. 'Oh, my, yes. He makes the best speeches you ever heard! So fiery you know, and so – he wrote the best paper of all his year at Harvard, when he was starting his law degree, all about why America shouldn't mix in foreign wars and they thought very highly of him, but then the war happened and well, it sort of wasn't right not to want to be in it. But then he wrote another paper, more like a little book it was, and his Pa got it published for him, and they talked a lot about how much political wisdom he'd developed. The papers, they were full of him for a while then. But then –'

Her face clouded. 'Then Pa did something to annoy the papers. I don't know — I never did get that clear in my head, and the people who'd been so interested in Timothy for election sort of lost interest. But it's what he wants. It's always been what he wants —'

'He couldn't stay with Kincaid and Sons if he was elected as something or other, could he?' Maddie said sharply, trying to dredge her memory for what she knew of the system at home in London. Local councillors and MPs there could still be businessmen — she'd met several who were, but she had an idea it was different here.

'Oh, no, Timothy hates the business, he says. He's good at it, and knows how to make money, but he says Pa's already got so much it's boring to make more and if he had gone into politics then Kincaids would have bankrolled him and he'd be able to concentrate on what he was doing in Washington.' She looked wistful then. 'But I can't see how that'll ever happen now, since Pa lost those people who used to back him —'

'But you have a family too, Rosalie,' Maddie said gently. 'Jay tells me that your family has always been very busy in politics.'

'Well, yes,' Rosalie said. 'My daddy used to be very active. I never quite knew what it was all about but he used to be out a lot. My mother always said if he put half the time in at home he did in the South Boston taverns drumming up votes we'd be richer than the Kincaids, and they're lousy rich.' She went pink. 'That was what my mother used to say.'

'She was probably right. Is your father still in politics?'

'Oh, he died three years ago. Before I married Timothy. He'd never let me marry Timmy. He was a Democrat, my father, and Timmy, he wanted to run on the Republican ticket.'

'Does it matter that much which sort of ticket they run on, as long as they get in?'

Rosalie looked startled. 'I always thought it did.'

Maddie shook her head firmly and spoke from the depths of her total ignorance of the matter. 'Of course it doesn't. It's the same at home in England. If a man wants to be a Member of Parliament, what matters is getting elected, and if the only way you can do that is by joining a particular party then you join it. I dare say it's the same here. What's the difference between Republicans and Democrats, anyway?'

Rosalie looked disapproving. 'I never talk politics. My mother hated it and said no girl ever should. It bores the men if you do. Leave it to them.'

'Well, I dare say someone'll tell me eventually,' Maddie said and lifted her chin as she heard a faint sound from the dining room across the hallway from where they were sitting in a corner of the big living room. 'Listen, before she wakes up and you have to go back to her, the thing is, there must be people *you* know, who your father knew, who are still involved with elections and the rest of it?'

'My brother Joe,' Rosalie said. 'He works for the Democrats in Washington.'

Maddie looked triumphant. 'Then you talk to him! Make him see to it that Timothy is invited to join them. It's all you have to do – or introduce me to your brother, and I'll see to it he gets the idea –'

Rosalie was staring at her with her mouth half open. 'I don't understand what you mean,' she said at length. 'What has that got to do with me and Timothy being together again?'

'Everything!' Maddie said. 'If Timothy wants to be a serious politician he has to have a wife and a family, doesn't he? I think politics are boring, but even I know that. Wives and children, they're as good as votes for a man, and separation and divorce are as good as votes for the other side. Isn't it the same here?'

They heard the sound again as Blossom pushed back her chair and got to her feet, and at once Rosalie leapt from the low stool, where she had been sitting beside Maddie's armchair, and hurried across towards the hallway.

'Will you talk to him, Rosalie? To your brother Joe? If he can persuade Timothy to take a chance on the idea, then I'll start to work on Pa. I've listened to him a lot, and he's a very ambitious sort of man. If he gets the right prodding, we might be able to get your Timothy out of the office downtown and into Washington. He'd have to take you with him then –'

'Yes,' Rosalie said, and then turned her head to look as the sound of Blossom's footsteps on the parquet floor came thinly out of the dining room at them. 'I'll try. Joe's a good brother to me. He'd do a lot for me. I just never thought to ask him this –' and she threw another glance at Maddie, who leaned back satisfied.

She hadn't thought so drippy and silly a girl could look so alive, to tell the truth, as Rosalie had at that moment; there is no doubt, she told herself as she wriggled back into her armchair and reached for her magazine, that I'm on the right tracks. Timothy is the log that's jamming things here and Rosalie's the lever that will fetch him out. Rosalie and Pa, of course. I'll start work on him tomorrow.

20

January 1951

Working on Pa was ridiculously easy. She started by sitting beside him as he read his newspaper and asking him to explain things in it to her. At first he was irritated, and merely rattled the pages at her, but she sat there quietly and timed her questions carefully, so that he was not as aware of being interrupted as he might have been, and slowly he thawed and began to talk and once he had started, and discovered the pleasure of having a rapt audience who clearly respected and admired him and never questioned his opinions, went on talking.

She would sit beside him, carefully choosing the same low stool on which Rosalie had sat beside her, knowing how appealing it was to have someone sitting looking up at you, and would hug her knees and rest her chin on them so that she had to keep her eyes even more upturned, and he clearly found her very beguiling indeed. She would laugh often, too, as they talked and he became more expansive than ever, trying little jokes and sallies for the pleasure of hearing her laugh again, and slowly and easily she threaded him on her line and pulled him in.

Blossom became aware quite soon of what was happening, and took to coming into the sitting room, instead of remaining in her favourite place in the dining room, to talk to her husband, but he became gruff when she appeared and returned to his reading, and after a while she would go away again, clearly put out but unable to do anything about the situation. Maddie would sit there demurely, smiling at her and leafing through a magazine that she kept beside her in case she needed it and, baffled, Blossom would take herself and her missal and her rosary to the dining room, leaving the two of them alone again. And after a while the old man would look over the top of his paper at Maddie and glint at her and she'd grin back and they'd return to their discussion of the day's news. And if Blossom came back they would lapse into silence again until she went away. It really became a most diverting game.

Maddie concentrated on politics after the first few days of the game, chattering artlessly about her inability to comprehend and he would set his paper on his knees and give her an account of how the American political system worked which, though she pretended to find it too complicated, she understood well enough to know that it should not be all that difficult to get Timothy Two out of the family business and involved in public life.

But it was not so easy to bring the subject of Timothy into their conversation. Any attempt to talk about family business made the old man shut his lips and she would have to be very adroit to get him talking again on the innocuous subject of American doings in the world. Until she hit on the idea of asking him questions about his own history. 'Tell me about Boston,' she said to him. 'How you started, the sort of people who live here, how it was for you when you were young –' And then he was away.

He did not in fact tell her anything that was outside his own experience. He said nothing about the city or its history as part of America; he only spoke of Boston as part of him. He talked of what it had been like in the nineties growing up in the streets of South Boston as a first-generation American, the third son of an Irish immigrant who had arrived from County Tyrone with no money, no skills apart from his experience as a barman in a tiny country inn, and huge ambitions. He told her how his father Eamon had worked his way up from being a barman, in a tavern that was not all that unlike the one he had left behind three thousand miles away, to owning four taverns of his own within ten years. He spoke of his mother, Katy, as illiterate and as hungry when she arrived as old Eamon himself had been but who had made herself genteel and respectable with great speed ('Lace-curtain Irish, she became,' Timothy said. 'As fast as bloody lightning, too.'). He chuckled as he described how she had dragged her children from the streets to the church, only to have them escape back into the excitement and glamour again, but had gone on doggedly trying. He boasted of how he had been educated in spite of himself and eventually set up by his

181

father in his own tavern when he was nineteen and heart-set on marrying the daughter of the man who was Eamon's most disliked rival in the South Boston politics in which so many immigrants became involved. And he ended with great relish telling her how, as the years had gone on, he had worked and slaved to make a living for himself and his family – only to explode into riches when the government in their wisdom had brought in the Eighteenth Amendment just at the end of the Great War, as he came home again from his army service, and made his fortune.

'Oh, Maddie, Maddie, I tell ye, it was a gift from heaven! There were all those good thirsty men everywhere and the government saying it was prohibited to take a drink! It was a mad business, crazy to let it start, but if the government wanted to be crazy, who was I to stop 'em? I just set to work and well enough I did.' He leaned forwards confidentially. 'Do you know how much I made that first three years of Prohibition? Three million dollars, that's how much. I counted up my assets on Armistice Day, 1922, when my first son was born, Timothy Two, and it was three million. Three million.' And he chanted like a litany over and over again, 'Three mil-li-on dollars. Ther-ree! Ther-ree mil-li-on –'

'You must have worked very hard,' Maddie said, not sure what response was expected from her, and he stared at her for a moment, his eyes wide and startled and then threw back his head and laughed as though he had never heard so witty a remark, till tears ran down his face and she was seriously alarmed that he would choke.

'Worked hard!' he managed to splutter at length. 'Worked hard! I should say I did – but there's not many as sees it that way, my dear, and that's the truth of it! I've been called a lucky old sod, and a wicked old villain and the devil's own, and a sight of other much worse names, but you're right! I was a hard-working businessman, and I still am.'

He cocked an eye at her then and grinned wickedly. 'Not working as hard as I did now, not as hard as I did. Don't need to, you see. Place runs itself, don't it? Great big office we got there, close on fifty people signin' on the payroll every week – and doing little enough to earn their money, I can tell you – what need for me to go there? Anyway –' and he sighed gustily,

182

'anyway, it's not the gas it was. It used to be good fun, you know, the best there was, getting in a consignment, seein' it on its way, gettin' past the coastguard and the state cops and the rest of 'em – oh, it was a man's business in those days. Now I own all these shops and fruit warehouses and dairies and the rest of it, and building all over the place, and it's no joy at all. It makes money, but the only use for that is to keep people working and even that gets boring –'

'Maybe you and the boys ought to stretch yourselves even more? Do more exciting things – make even more money –' she said and grinned at him and decided to take a chance. 'I'd like to see my Jay making a lot of money. It'd be nice. I'd really like that.'

He laughed again, but not quite so uproariously this time. 'I'll be damned sure you would! What woman wouldn't! There's my wife wanting to spend all she can get her hands on on her damned church and orphanages – no, we'll have none of that. Keep the money in your own hands when you've made it, and you stay on top. I'm not lettin' those lads of mine loose on the business – they do a fair enough job, but they can settle for their wages. The rest goes where it's meant to go, into a trust for them – they can wait till I die for it.'

And again he laughed and looked at her sideways, wanting a reaction, wanting to needle her. 'They can wait till I die for it, you hear me? And that'll not be for longer than any of you think. My old father only died last year, well over ninety he was, and all his brothers and sisters at home in Ireland still, and his cousins and the rest of 'em – they all live a long life too. Here's me only sixty yet – you and your Jay'll have to wait a good deal yet to get your hands on my money.'

She smiled lazily. 'Oh, I don't want your money, Pa. I want my own –' and this time his laughter was once more filled with real amusement.

'And how do you plan to get it, then? You a girl and all? Sitting on a fortune every time you sit down, that's for sure, but that don't put money in your pocket when you want it. Or does it?'

And he leaned forwards to pinch her cheeks and leer at her and she became suddenly aware of the fact that the old man was flirting with her. More than that; he was making a definite attempt to grope her. His hand which had been apparently hanging nonchalantly over the arm of his chair was actually reaching under her skirt.

For a moment she wanted to jump up and shriek; that this old man should behave so was as disgusting as if her own father had and the sense of sudden desolation that filled her as she thought that made her feel even more the need to jump up and away and cry her protest and her fury.

But she didn't. She sat tight and stared at him, her eyes wide, willing him to back away, and after a long moment his hand faltered and then withdrew and he leaned back in his chair, and rested his head on the back so that he could stare up at the ceiling. His thick white hair made an aureole round his head, and his cheeks beneath were plump and rosy. It didn't seem possible that he had behaved as he had. Yet she knew she hadn't imagined it.

She sat very still for what seemed a long time, trying to think what to do or say next. Her pulse was beating thickly in her ears, for she had been genuinely frightened. There had been something very brutal about the way he had slid so suddenly into that lascivious mode; she felt soiled as though he had in some way actually abused her, even though in fact his fingers had done no more than touch her thigh and slide beneath the top of her stocking. But mixed with her fear there was a great anger; she shouldn't have to do things like this, crawl round a dirty old man to get what she needed for herself and her husband – and her baby, she thought almost tearfully – shouldn't have to tolerate such things as his hateful gnarled and veined hand beneath her skirt. She was entitled to better –

The thoughts came and went so fast that when she spoke it was as though there had been no lapse of time at all and she said as smoothly as she could, 'How do I plan to get money for us? Why, by persuading you to do more for my Jay.' Her voice was soft. 'It shouldn't be hard for you, now, should it? There he is, your own flesh and blood, someone you can trust. Why not let him do more in the business, let him make more money? He'll be the best help you ever had, if you give him the chance. And me of course.'

She smiled with great sweetness. 'I'm family now, aren't I, Pa? Just one of the family? Things ought to be nice in families, everyone happy and comfortable, no one telling tales to anyone if they get upset, no one bothering Mother – I want the family to be like that, because it's *my* family now. Isn't it?'

'Ah, Jay's well enough,' the old man said gruffly, still lying back in his chair, not looking at her. 'He's got his wages, and he knows when the time comes he'll get his share of the trust money –'

'You don't want your own family wishing you dead for want of a little cash, now, do you, Pa?' she said even more softly and leaned forwards and rested her hand on his, where it lay on his knee. She felt it tighten beneath her grip and wanted to smile, feeling her triumph. But she didn't, keeping her expression of earnest good sense.

'Not that I'd ever let him be so wicked, but you can't help human nature, can you? There's Timothy and Declan too, all as anxious to be successful as you are, and what chance have they, all together there in State Street? It ought to be done differently, Pa, didn't it? The way it was when you were a lad and making your own way – with chances for everyone to make their mark in their own special way.'

He lifted his head now and looked down at her hand, still resting on his, and she smiled back at him and lifted one brow slightly and then let go of his hand and sat back further on her stool. And looked over her shoulder towards the dining room where Blossom sat and then back at him, still smiling, and though she hadn't said a word he seemed to understand.

'I'll talk to Jay, then,' he said, still gruffly. 'Give the lad another chance. He made a fair old mess before he went away but he seems to have done well enough in London with your father – and came back with you, and you're no fool, are you? No, you aren't – well, I'll see what I can do. But don't go getting any big ideas, now. I'm not as daft as I look, nor as easy to push around –'

'Of course you're not. You're just my dear Pa, aren't you?' And she got to her feet and leaned over and very deliberately kissed his mouth, and was away from his reach before he realised what she had done. 'It's great to have you to look to, now I've left my own Daddy so far away. I'll tell Jay what you said tonight –'

He was staring up at her and the pupils of his eyes were so

185

dilated that they looked black, and his mouth was partly open and his lower lip lax. 'And while you're talking to Jay, Pa, you ought to give a bit of thought to Timmy. He's not happy, you know. You ask Rosalie – he has so many ambitions! I'd let him do what he wants to do, you know. Jay'll do well enough for you if Timmy isn't there. You'll see. He'll have me to watch over him, do you see –'

She straightened her back and turned to go, still smiling down at him and then, as she turned her head, she saw Blossom standing at the top of the shallow steps that led down into the sitting room and staring at her with her face so blank of expression that it could have been carved in wood. There was nothing else Maddie could do but smile at her and say, 'Hello, Mother. Have you had a pleasant rest? Shall I see if lunch is ready yet? Pa and I have been having such a nice talk together!'

It took rather less time than she had feared it would. Rosalie, clearly much struck with the value of having her beloved Timmy in need of a respectable family life, lost no time in talking to her brother Joe. She actually went to Washington to see him, sending Blossom a message that she wouldn't be able to visit for a few days since she had to be away. Maddie, who knew where she had gone, was greatly amused to see how put out Blossom was. She had made it clear to everyone that she merely tolerated Rosalie's visits because she was sorry for her and had made no effort to show her any real liking, but now she wasn't there to dance attendance and to fetch and carry, Blossom was annoyed.

More than that, she was angry with Maddie's presence, and though Maddie had played with the idea of slipping into Rosalie's shoes and being charming to her mother-in-law, she soon realised what a wasteful effort that would be. Much better to have her mother-in-law loathe her; then perhaps she too would put pressure on Jay to get a home of his own so that he could take his wife out of Blossom's way . . .

So Blossom moved about her house more blank-faced than ever and had more disagreements with Mary Margaret than ever – who became even louder in consequence, if that were possible – and Maddie went on sitting beside Pa each morning, and sometimes into the afternoon too, when he chose not to bother to go to State Street today – 'as it's so cold, you know, damned cold,' he'd say to Liam when he brought the car – as Blossom became more and more angry.

But all her efforts came to fruition on one Friday evening over dinner. It had been a dreadful day, with the snow falling relentlessly from a steel grey sky, and the brothers had been late getting back from the office, even though Liam had put the snow chains on the car and driven with greater speed than was considered safe in such treacherous conditions. Their lateness made Mary Margaret more fractious than ever, for she had baked a steak pie 'and it don't stand easy' she shouted at Blossom, furious when she told her dinner would be delayed by half an hour and that neither of the girls would be in for it, for they were staying downtown to go to a theatre with the latest of the young men they were considering. That in turn made Blossom icier than was even her wont, so by the time they sat down at table the only people who didn't look uneasy were Maddie and Pa, both of whom were well pleased with themselves.

They had been plotting all week, and now their plans were coming right. The old man had so enjoyed the way, as he said, he was putting one over on that old Blossom Bryan that he seemed to have lost sight of the fact that the plans were all Maddie's, and that he himself was having one put over on him. But that didn't matter, for he was livelier and happier than he had been for some time, and it showed. Watching him, as he put his knife into the pie that Mary Margaret set in front of him, and then grinned at his sons and said, 'Wait till you taste this – it's the best she's made for years, the old besom – you'll see,' she wondered why she had been so angered by the way he had tried to make a pass at her. What did it matter, after all? He'd done her no harm, and she'd more than got her own back, as they were all to find out, any minute now.

In fact, half an hour later, as the last plates were being swept up by a muttering Mary Margaret and the coffee was brought in, Timmy coughed and said, 'Pa, have you told her?'

Blossom lifted her head. 'Told who? Told what?'

'You, Mother,' Timothy said after a moment and pushed his chair back from the table and tilted it on its back legs so that he could stretch himself a little. His heavy square face, already showing signs of jowls though he wasn't yet thirty, was glowing with anxious sweat in the bright light from the big central chandelier and there was a glitter of reflection of the silver and crystal on the ridge of his nose that made Maddie want to giggle. But she didn't. She just fixed her gaze on Blossom instead.

'Well?' Blossom said, staring at her son. Her eyes looked wide and somehow hungry, Maddie thought, as she watched her. As though she wants to eat him.

'Mother, I'm going away,' he said and looked round the table uneasily. 'It's all fixed so I want no fuss from anyone. I've talked to Pa, is all, and he says – well, it's all arranged.'

'Going away?' Blossom's voice sounded flat and dull, but there was a world of expression in it, of fear and anger and an indefinable something else. 'Where?'

He seemed to swell a little as he lifted his chin and stared back challengingly at his mother. 'Washington. I'm going to work with Joe Flannery.'

'Joe –' She swallowed and started again. 'Rosalie's brother? Doing what?'

'Oh, Mother, you know perfectly well. If it's with Joe Flannery, it's the Democrats, isn't it? No, don't look like that. I've a better chance with them and it's what I want. Joe says, another year, maybe two, they can put me forward as a candidate somewhere. That's better than the Republicans ever offered me. I talked to Pa and he says he can do it. The money's there to be used, so why not?'

'It's there for *me* to use,' Pa said and slammed his coffee cup back in its saucer. 'Never you forget it, Timmy! You'll stay there in the politics game only as long as I choose to pay for you to do it. But –' He grinned then and stopped trying to look so fierce. 'Why not, after all? It'll be good fun, a real gas, to see the old excitement comin' back. Kincaid all over the papers – it'll be better this time than it was last. You'll show the bastards where they were wrong, eh, Timmy? That you will –'

'Indeed I will,' Timmy said gratefully and then grinned at his brother Declan. Anything rather than look at his mother, Maddie thought shrewdly. 'So, there you are, Declan, you young devil – you can have that corner office after all. No need to bellyache any more over it –'

'I'm taking that office,' Jay said smoothly and Maddie threw a brilliant smile at him and he smiled back.

Of course he was having the best office, Maddie thought. I gave him plenty of warning of what was happening, so he had time to get it all organised. Oh, Jay, it's going to be so wonderful, now!

'Pa agreed this afternoon that I'm taking over the whole eastern section – yes, I am –' he shouted as Declan suddenly roared and jumped to his feet. 'It's no use you screaming at me, Dec – it's all agreed. Pa says I do, so I do. It's a big section and it takes a big man to run it. Not a kid like you. You've had your own way for far too long as it is –' and again he grinned at Maddie.

'And there's something else, Mother. You ought to be pleased about it,' Timmy said above the din and Declan subsided as his father leaned across the table and thumped his fist down in front of him. 'I'm – Rosalie and me. We're going to try again –'

'Much good that'll do you!' Declan roared. His face was red with fury and so sulky that he looked even younger than his twenty-four years. 'After the way you whined about her and complained how useless she is in bed, and you're going back to her? You're a bastard, you know that? You don't give a shit about her –'

'Be quiet, Declan!' Blossom said loudly as at the same time Timothy leaned forwards, dropping his chair to its front legs with a crash.

'We all know you had your eye on her,' he shouted. 'Well, take them off, right now. She's my wife, okay? My wife and we're going to Washington together and there's an end of it.'

'When?' Blossom's voice was thin and tight and glancing at her Maddie could see the anguish in her face. To let any of her sons go was clearly agony for her, and Maddie bent her head and thought, wait till she hears that we're going too. She thinks she's got Jay back, but she hasn't. We're getting away from here – we must. It's hell here with them –

'First of February,' Timothy said. 'It's a while yet, Mother. We have to get a house there and shift our stuff from Tremont Street –' He leaned back in his chair again, taking it back to its precarious position. 'Oh, I can't remember when I've felt better about anything! Ain't it great?'

'To be going away from me?' Blossom said and bent her head to stare down at the table before her. 'I must have been a wicked woman to suffer so at the hands of my children. A wicked woman —' And she reached into her lap for her rosary and her missal, which she carried with her even to the table, and got to her feet. 'All I ask of life is to have my family about me, to live a decent good life and have my children beside me, and now —' She shook her head and turned to go, leaving Timothy Two staring at her with his face twisted with uncertainty.

It was, Maddie decided, a dangerous moment. Much as he wanted to go to Washington, she knew that for Timothy his mother's demands came high on his list of essentials. It would take very little effort on Blossom's part to persuade him to reverse his decision and then where would they all be? Something had to be done.

So she did it. She told them she was pregnant. Even Blossom couldn't compete with that.

21

July 1951

It was, Maddie decided, a small miracle of timing to give birth to her son as she did on 4 July. She lay in her hot bed in the small hospital room as the contractions jacked themselves up to a great creaking fierceness, hearing the squibs and the Catherine wheels and the firecrackers and squealing rockets outside as she sweated through each wave of pain, and told herself it was worth it. It was *worth* it, it had to be, and to have her baby on Independence Day was a sign, a promise of good things to happen to her and to her Jay and to the baby too, when it arrived.

But by the time it did, late in the evening as the fireworks too reached a crescendo of noise to match the crescendo of her pain, she almost hated it, and certainly did not care whether good things happened to it or not.

They showed her the child, wrapped in a bloodstained towel, its face a furious red streaked with a revolting yellow waxiness and she stared at it, turning her sweat-soaked head on the pillow to do so, and felt nothing. No concern, no worry, no excitement and certainly no love or awe or any of the emotions she had been expecting to feel. Not even any interest. She just turned her head away again and said hoarsely – for her throat hurt from the way she had been shrieking her reaction to her pain – that they should take it away, she was tired, take it away and let her sleep.

But next morning it was quite different. She woke to a gleaming hot day – it was always hot now and she wouldn't have dreamed she could loathe summer weather as much as she did here in Boston – but the humidity had blessedly dropped a little so the air was fresh and breatheable. Not as clean and crisp as English summer weather, for which she had so often longed during the past burdensome weeks of her pregnancy – but at least tolerable.

They bathed her and settled her against clean comfortable pillows and then brought the baby to her. And this time some feelings were there. He had lost the ferocious redness and the waxy streaks and looked agreeably baby-like, and she touched his hand and the small fingers closed convulsively on hers and she found herself grinning from ear to ear with pride and delight.

Jay, when he came later that afternoon, carrying a large and singularly ugly bouquet of crimson peonies, seemed less excited by him. He peered down on the infant when the nurse brought him for his approval and said, only, 'Oh – it's a bit creased, isn't it?'

'Oh, Mr Kincaid!' the nurse said, all arch disapproval. 'How can you say such a thing? And you his dear daddy. Why he's just darling, the dearest little baby! You should think him the most beautiful child in the world, shouldn't he, Mrs Kincaid? I'm sure *you* do –'

'Yes, of course,' Maddie said and tried to look adoring. That she was fascinated by the baby and pleased with her success in creating and bearing him was undoubted, but did she think him the most beautiful child in the world? She knew she did not, and it was a little worrying that that should be so; but she said nothing about her doubts. It was safer to keep her own counsel.

She had become very good indeed at keeping her own counsel. The last month had been a minefield for her, as she had tacked her way to and fro through the choppy Kincaid waters, trying to get where she wanted to go without having any head-on collisions, and she had managed it; but mainly by dint of keeping her mouth shut. And of course her ears open.

It really had been rather like it had been in the old days at home, when she had worked in Daddy's office and helped Jay to make some useful deals on the basis of her inside information. She had started to visit Jay downtown in State Street once it had been agreed that they would have their own home. She had persuaded the old man to release some money for them (and when she thought of just how rich he was it infuriated her that he was so very mean about allowing them enough to buy the sort of house she wanted, but again she bit her tongue and said nothing. It was safer that way) and the spending of it had devolved heavily on to her. But, knowing as little as she did about house prices and the geography of Boston, she needed guidance; hence the visits to Jay so that she could get necessary decisions and information from him during office hours when the realtors were available to talk to. And there was too the matter of building work and renovations when they did get their house, a small but pleasant one at the Massachusetts Avenue end of Beacon Street. Where else would she seek workmen but through her husband's family firm?

So it was a rare weekday that did not find Maddie bedecked in the most elegant maternity clothes she could buy from Saks or Bonwit Teller, sitting in her husband's office or outside in the main reception area, as the work of Kincaid and Sons surged around her. And she listened.

Sitting now in her hospital bed, watching Jay trying to cope with the baby the nurse was so determined he should hold, she remembered with satisfaction how useful those days had been. It had been worth the effort and the weariness as her body became ever heavier and more cumbersome to have heard the things she heard and worked out how to use them. She looked at Jay fondly, at the thickness of his hair curling over his ears and the smooth broadness of his shoulders and could have burst with the delight of just being with him. The way she felt about him had not been reduced in any way by the strains of living in his parents' house or of moving into their own. The loss of her girlish shape had mattered to her only inasmuch as it mattered to him and when she had found that his need to make love to her was not in the least diminished by the way her breasts and belly bulged and got in the way, she had been hugely relieved and loved him all the more. To see him now holding the baby she had made for him and knowing that their bank balance bulged with a good deal of money she had also made for him by dint of using her ears and her wits around the office made her feel wonderful. Much better than being a mother made her feel, that was certain.

When at last the nurse had gone and taken the baby with her, she had pulled Jay to sit on the bed beside her and had nestled against him contentedly and he had talked about the last deal he had done for the firm, to supply the materials for a building that was to be put up at Wollaston Beach in Quincy this autumn.

'It's going to be one hell of an operation,' he said with great satisfaction. 'It'll cover three-quarters of an acre, and have every damned facility in it you can think of. The holiday business is one hell of a business, if you ask me. Hotels, resorts, they're all making money like tomorrow'll never come. It's beautiful.'

'Did you do it the way I said, Jay?' she asked, sleepily now. It was getting hot again and her body still ached a little from yesterday's efforts.

'Mmm? How do you mean?'

'I told you!' She pulled herself up, sharpened by the tone of his voice. 'Oh, Jay, you did, didn't you? All you have to do is pad the estimates by five per cent. No more than that! And if the supplies are put through the subsidiary company we'll have no problems getting it out again –'

'I told you before,' he said a little sulkily, 'I don't like it. Suppose the old man does one of his checks? You know how he can be.'

'I know perfectly well how he can be – and I also know perfectly well that good at dealing as he is, the one thing he hates is reading complicated bookkeeping. You do it the way I said, with a lot of documentation, and he won't know whatever sort of check-up he does. Nor will anyone else. Not even Declan, and we all know how he noses about – and I'll bet he's picking up plenty on the side for himself. It's not difficult for you, Jay! And you're entitled to it – you work hard enough.'

He looked at her broodingly for a moment and then nodded. 'Yeah, I do, don't I? And Declan getting only a coupla thousand below me – and what the hell does he do anyway but screw the stenographers every chance he gets and stay out to lunch till it's cocktail time? Goddamn it, the old man ought to check up on *him*! That'd make him think a bit –'

'So you'll do it,' she said softly and he grinned at her and said, 'Crazy kid, Maddie,' and she smiled and snuggled down against him again. That was great. Not just Jay happy, but another fifteen thousand dollars at least into their own private account by the end of the year. Getting some real money together was going to take time, but if he listened to her they could do it, and then it wouldn't be Kincaid and Sons any more for him, but his own company Kincaid Inc. Or perhaps Jay Kincaid and –

She lifted her chin. 'We'll need a name for him,' she said. 'Have you thought?'

'Hell, what do I know about names?' he said and then added, 'I dunno – Jay Two maybe?'

'No,' she said and pushed her head even more into his chest. 'Next time, maybe. This time, box clever. How about Timothy? Timothy Kincaid the Third. Isn't that something that sounds good? And wouldn't it be useful?'

'I don't know,' he said dubiously. 'It sounds – maybe you ought to talk to the folks first.'

'Why should we? He's our baby, so it's our choice. And he is the first grandchild, isn't he? So he has the right. They ought to be very pleased he's here. Timothy Kincaid the Third. Only we'll call him – what shall we call him?'

'Buster,' Jay said after a moment. 'He looks like a guy I used to play ball with in college. Buster was a good fella, too. A real pal –'

'Buster it is then,' Maddie said contentedly, not caring at all that it sounded a silly name to her. If Jay wanted it that was good enough.

'I would not have come if I had not been told of your choice of name,' Blossom said and stood ramrod-straight at the foot of the bed, refusing to sit down, refusing to look at the baby who was in a crib beside Maddie. 'This child cannot be called by the name you have chosen.'

'Oh,' Maddie said and folded her hands on the counterpane in front of her. Her eyes were glittering a little and were narrowed too, as she stared at her mother-in-law. 'And why not? He's the first grandchild you have, isn't he? He's the third generation of the family –'

'It's no grandchild of mine. It can't be,' Blossom said and stared at her with the same blank look on her face and for a moment Maddie did not understand the import of what she was saying. And then she did and her face flamed.

'What did you say? Are you daring to suggest that I – that this baby is not Jay's?'

'Oh, of course it's of Jay's getting!' Blossom sounded contemptuous. 'The way you are around him, like a bitch on heat, even when you're as pregnant as a farmyard sow, makes it obvious.'

Maddie stared, her face as blank as Blossom's own for a moment. To hear that sort of language from a woman who rarely had spoken of anything but saints and feasts of obligation and the virtues of Father Mulcahy of Our Lady of Sorrows Church on the corner of Sewall Street was amazing, and even more than that – it was exhilarating. She felt the laughter lift in her and then put her hands to her face as it burst out.

'Yes, you would laugh, wouldn't you?' Blossom said. 'It's all you're fit for. Laughing in the face of God will take you to hell as sure as you sit there in all your sinfulness. Your sins will be paid for so I needn't worry over them. But you are not to name your bastard as you said you would, and as Jay has said you are. I will not permit it –'

'You can't prevent it,' Maddie said softly. 'And why should you? For he is not a bastard. He is the legal child of our marriage – do you want to see the certificate we have from City Hall?'

This was an old argument; she had heard Blossom rant on before about the speed in which her pregnancy had followed her marriage, though not in the coarse way she had this afternoon. She wasn't going to be upset by it, she wasn't, no matter what the wicked old bitch said.

'City Hall certificates.' Blossom almost spat it. 'What do such things matter to me? That's no marriage. You are living as a fornicator. You have seduced my good son to forget his Catholic soul and taken him into fornication. But God won't be mocked. You'll see what will happen to you and your bastard!' And now there was expression on her face, for it had developed red patches over the cheekbones.

'Timothy Kincaid the Third,' Maddie said in a reflective way, and smiled sweetly at her, feeling better and much calmer now that Blossom had let her composure crack. 'It sounds good, doesn't it? Timothy Braham Kincaid the Third. That's his name, and you can go to your own private hell and burn for all you can do to change that.' And she laughed, a soft contented sort of laugh, designed to make Blossom even angrier.

'You can't,' Blossom said then and seemed to droop a little. 'It's Rosalie's right to have that name for her baby. Rosalie and Timothy Two. It's due in just another month – for God's sake, be decent and let her have the name her child is entitled to have. They had a decent nuptial mass, they live a decent Catholic life. You can't come along and steal their name from them –'

'My son is the first grandchild to Pa,' Maddie said. 'So, he's entitled to be called as I've named him. It's not Timmy's right at all. Anyway, Rosalie's going to have a girl. You've only to look at her to know that –'

'She's to have a boy!' Blossom almost wailed it. 'I've prayed and she has prayed – it's to be a boy –'

'A girl,' Maddie said implacably, and laughed again as Blossom half turned to go. 'Oh, giving up already? I am sorry. Well, do come here and see your little grandson before you go –'

'I will go when I'm ready!' Blossom said, and turned back to her. 'Not until I get your promise you won't use my family's name for your bastard –'

Maddie took a deep breath in through her nose and leaned back on her pillows to close her eyes. There had been other such arguments before with Blossom, if not couched in quite such vituperative language. She had shown her loathing for Maddie more and more obviously as the weeks had passed, but never in the presence of anyone else. If any of the family were within earshot Blossom either ignored her or spoke with icy politeness, but when she got her alone, oh, it was a very different thing then.

· Maddie looked back over the long weeks of her pregnancy and saw herself standing against the attack much as the people of London had been described as standing firm during the Blitz. It had felt like that, in many ways: a bombardment of cold loathing that had threatened sometimes to make her crack and turn and run away.

But she couldn't run away and leave Jay – and there was the painful core of her situation. For Jay could not, would not, believe that his mother disliked her. She had tried to tell him of what happened when he and his father and brothers weren't there, had tried to enlist his support, but had known when to give up. In Jay's eyes, as in Timmy's and to an extent in Declan's, Blossom was all that was good. She was alarming, someone to be catered to and placated and worried about rather than someone to love in a comfortable and easy way, but she was *good*. Of that there could be no doubt in her sons' minds, and Maddie had squirmed and tried to escape from the trap into which his attitude to his mother had pushed her and could find

197

no escape. To bring the struggle with his mother on which she was engaged into the open could destroy their marriage. Jay loved her, but he revered his mother and if there was one skill Maddie had developed over these past few eventful years, it was the ability to recognise when to stop fighting. So she had stopped fighting with Jay. But not with Blossom. She was still an adversary and always would be.

And now she stood at the foot of her bed looking at her with a venom that Maddie could recognise even with her eyes closed, and willing her to buckle under the onslaught.

But she didn't. Because now she had a trump card; she was the mother of a baby that old Timothy was very happy to have in his family. He had come to visit her on the baby's second day of life, bringing chocolates and flowers and a bottle of champagne and had leaned over the child and admired him and spoken approvingly of his tough lungs when the baby, woken by the old man's noisiness, had bawled his alarm. There was no doubt that Pa was well pleased with his grandfatherly status, and much less put out by the fact that his son and daughter-in-law had been wed in a City Hall rather than in a church. So Maddie had a new weapon to use against Blossom, and she wouldn't hesitate to do so.

Now she opened her eyes and looked at Blossom and then, slowly, smiled. 'Why do you hate me so much, Mother?'

'You may not call me that!' Blossom snapped. 'I'm not your mother. If I had been, you'd have been a decent God-fearing girl and not a fornicating bitch on heat who steals from good souls –'

'If I'd been your daughter I'd not be here. I'd be out man-hunting and getting desperate with it,' Maddie said and lifted her brows insolently at her. 'And as for stealing from you – I've stolen nothing. I wouldn't soil myself –'

'You have stolen my son Jay! You have stolen my son Timmy! Do you think I don't know that it was your doing with that stupid Rosalie, sending her to her brother, stealing my son away to work with him? Do you think I don't *know*? And fornicating with my husband, an old man like my husband – you're a foul and evil creature –'

The words rolled on and on, and again Maddie closed her eyes. Once Blossom was set on one of her tirades there was no point in interrupting her. And it was good in a way to hear it all with its new development of violent language and wild accusation; it showed Maddie just how much she had managed to get her own way and how much she had got under Blossom's skin since she had been pitchforked into this hateful family. Not all hateful. Not my Jay. But, oh, I want to go home to Daddy! And for a moment tears threatened to crawl out from beneath her eyelids.

But she could not let Blossom have the satisfaction of knowing she had penetrated her defences in any way and now she opened her eyes and pulled herself up to a sitting position and reached into the crib beside her for the baby, who had woken and was whimpering.

'It's time for Timothy the Third's feed,' she said loudly and with deliberate movements, unbuttoned the front of her nightdress and pulled it back over her shoulders with a langourous movement so that she was sitting there with her breasts fully exposed. 'He's a greedy little darling, too –' and she lifted the child towards her, and at once he turned his head and began nuzzling her bare skin.

It worked as she had known it would. Blossom stared at her and then with a sharp little sound of revulsion that was almost a retch turned and went, slamming the door behind her, and Maddie was able to put the baby down on her lap and rebutton her nightdress before ringing for the nurse to bring his bottle.

It might have been worth breastfeeding after all, she thought, as the nurse came and took the now furious baby and started to feed him, if it was going to upset Blossom so much. It would be nice to sit and do it in her very own sitting room during the regular Sunday visits to Commonwealth Avenue on which Jay insisted. But oh, it would be nicer still to have someone here as well as Jay who loved her and would take care of her and wouldn't be so hateful and suspicious of her. And now the tears did come as she lay on her pillow and thought about her father.

22

June 1987

'The trouble is, we're running out of time.' Gresham's tone was one of sweet reason, all regretful common sense. 'That ward has only seven people left in it, Miss Matthews! How can we go on like that with costs being what they are? It isn't reasonable. The contractors need to get down to it, and if we don't put a move on we'll be in breach of contract and that could lose the whole sale. I'm afraid I really can't do much about it. She'll just have to be sent somewhere – anywhere I can get her in –'

'She's not fit to be sent away!' Annie said. 'Not yet. Give me a little more time and maybe she will. Joe, can't you get across to him that this is ridiculous?'

Joe came over to Gresham's desk from the window out of which he had been staring. Below him the grass was being cut and the smell of it, rich and fresh and soothing, came drifting into the room on the warm June breeze.

'It's not his fault, Annie. It's the system – he's no happier about it than you are. Right, Gresham?'

'Hardly,' Gresham said feelingly. 'Once we're finished here I have to up my stakes and go half across the country to start again. There won't be any job here for me, so I have to go where the work is and drag my family with me. Wolverhampton, would you believe . . . ? No, Miss Matthews, it is not my fault. In fact I've used your Maddie as an excuse to delay things much more than they should have been. But they're running out of patience. So we'll just have to put a move on.'

'Joe, what can we do?' she appealed to him with all the passion she had. 'You can't let her be sent away now. I'm just beginning to get somewhere at last. She's really unbuttoning. She's been pouring it out – about how it was when she lived in Boston, all sorts of stuff. I've started writing it all down, so that I don't forget – I'll let you see it as soon as I've knocked it into some sort of shape. But stop her now and I hate to think how

200

she'll be. She'll go back to being as she was. Worse, maybe –'

'I wondered about the hostel on the Larcombe Estate,' Gresham said. 'But Sister B raised hell at that. Says even though she's so improved she couldn't take the responsibility, not till the nurses' locker arguments are sorted out anyway. Would you believe it?'

'I'll believe anything about Sister B,' Joe said. 'But actually she's right. Maddie wouldn't be happy there. Look, Gresham, I have a couple of beds to play with in the acute ward. I'll put her there and see if I can get in a couple of sick people from the other major units on the patch to back it up. If I have long-term heart or kidney problems to look after there, they won't be able to rush us out, right? And it's well away from the main blocks so the contractors will be able to get on. It could give us another few weeks.'

'Well, some, I suppose,' Gresham said dubiously. 'They're behind on the work they're doing on the East Pavilion, so perhaps – will you be able to get away with that? Keeping her in an acute medical bed for any length of time won't be easy.'

'Watch me,' Joe said. 'But God help you, Gresham, if you tell anyone what I'm up to. I could be in real soup with the Medical Committee if they think I'm playing ducks and drakes with their precious beds.'

'Not a word,' said Gresham fervently. 'Just get Maddie out of the West Pavilion and let me put the contractors in. I'll have the other six patients disposed of by the end of the week, and the men can start on Monday. Thank you very much, Dr Labosky, and you too, Miss Matthews. I knew we'd find an answer that'd please everyone if we tried.'

'I doubt it'll please Maddie too well,' Annie said as Gresham got up to go. 'She mightn't find the change all that much to her liking. She's not used to changes, after all. She's lived in that ward for almost forty years now. It'll be a hell of an uprooting for her.'

'She'll manage,' Joe said, and put his hands in his pockets to stop himself from touching her. She looks marvellous today, he thought, alive and alert and almost pretty, with that hint of make-up on her face, and her hair a little longer than it had been used to be but still short, curling over her ears. 'She'll manage because the most important factor in her life won't change.

You. As long as you're around, she'll cope very well indeed.'

'I wish I could be so sure,' Annie said. 'I know how moving from a place you're used to turns you upside down. Looking back on it now, I think a lot of the bad way I felt last winter was because of moving to the flat as much as anything else. I did hate it so –' She stopped then and looked sideways at him. 'I suspect I was hateful to be with around that time.'

'Oh, you were,' he said cheerfully. 'Ghastly.'

'Oh!' She was nonplussed by his bluntness. 'Well, I'm sorry.'

'No need to apologise,' he said, still cheerful. 'Just be glad you're through that stage and out the other side. But you could be right up to a point about Maddie being a little more difficult for a while after we move her. But you can handle that, can't you? I'm beginning to think you and Maddie together can handle anything.'

July–October 1951

She would not have thought it possible that she could feel quite so dreadful. She had always been full of energy and eagerness; when her girlfriends had wilted and cried off from parties, it had been she who had chivvied them and teased them until they had made the effort, she who had been able to keep going night after night and party after party on the minimum of sleep and the maximum of excitement.

But now it was all different. She came out of the hospital with Buster, who was proving to be a difficult baby, according to the nurses, much given to waking in the middle of the night and demanding large feeds only to throw them up again as soon as he was put down to sleep, to return to the new house on Beacon Street. Jay had not been able to take her home; he had to go down to Quincy, he said, to meet with Cray Costello, who was financing the whole project.

'It's really exciting, Maddie!' he had told her the night before she was to leave the hospital. 'He's putting up two million – not all his own of course, nothing like it, but he has access to a lot of good money – and getting him to work with us has to be good news. He makes a bad rival, know what I mean? Pa and him, they've been after the same business for years, and sometimes

Pa got it, sometimes Cray did – but this time, it's between us. Him with the loans, us with the goods. Very pretty. We can make a nice deal. So I've got to go tomorrow to meet with him. He wants to walk the site, look at the survey and the quantities we've assessed –'

'Did you explain it was the day I was to come home?' she said, suddenly not caring about business. She had imagined it night after night since Buster's birth; riding back with him, walking up the front path of their own house, Jay settling her comfortably in her sitting room, seeing to it the girl they had hired to help with the baby was ready to take him and look after him, and then to go to bed again together – for sleeping alone this past ten days had been misery; she needed his closeness more than she needed food and drink – it had all been very important to her. And now he was telling her he wouldn't be there.

'That's the way of it, Maddie!' he'd said cheerfully as he kissed her goodnight. 'Come on, honey, you understand the business as well as I do! If I want to make anything useful out of this deal I've got to be there. D'you want I should send Declan instead? Exactly! Listen, I'll be home about eight, nine maybe. No need to make anything fancy for dinner. Tell the girl she can broil a steak when I get in. Take care of Buster, now!'

So she had gone home alone in the taxi he had sent for her ('Can't send Liam,' he'd told her on the telephone. 'Declan and Pa have taken him over to Walpole to check out the Friary Fruit markets. Pa reckons they've been slicing the top off the profits – the taxi'll see you're okay.') and it had been a shabby taxi, and a smelly one, because the driver smoked heavy old shag in a filthy pipe and by the time she got to the house, she felt queasy and shaky. And then when she had let herself in the shock of what she saw made her knees buckle.

The builders had been supposed to fix the kitchen while she had been in hospital. Some faulty work in the first place had resulted in water seeping through one wall, but ten days, Jay had said, would be plenty of time to get the job done, and it'd all be as good as new when she got home. He'd stay with his folks on Commonwealth, he'd told her, while it was going on, so there'd be no one in the workmen's way.

But clearly his plans had gone hopelessly wrong. The hallway and the way that led through to the kitchen were bare, with the carpet rolled back against the walls. The floor was sodden and she picked her way gingerly over the mess, leaving Buster bawling in his Moses basket by the front door, to see what had happened. Clearly there had been some disaster in the work, and water had flooded in, for the whole kitchen was a mess of floating debris and dripping walls, and the living room and dining room which ran off each other out of the other side of the hallway were piled high with furniture from the hall. The whole place looked dreadful and anything but welcoming, and she sat in the middle of it and wept as she remembered how pretty it had been when she had finished the decorating, and thought about how long it would take to get it clean again.

It was at that point that she realised that there was no one else in the house but herself. The girl Jay had told her he'd hired to help her with Buster and to look after her: where was she? There was no sign of her and, wearily, Maddie dragged herself to her bedroom, which was at least as she had left it, if somewhat dusty, and gave the baby the bottle the nurses at the hospital had prepared for him, before curling up miserably on the bed to sleep.

Jay came home not at eight or nine but at ten, rosy with the convivial dinner he had shared with Cray Costello, and found her there. Far from being abject at the sort of homecoming she had had – and she would have been comforted, she told herself later, if he'd shown he was at all sorry about it – he had lost his temper spectacularly, cursing the stupid builders he had hired who had obviously made the mess-up, and then run away for fear of reprisal, and the hired girl who hadn't showed up. But most of all he was angry with Maddie.

'Why in hell did you just sit here feeling sorry for yourself?' he roared. 'Why didn't you call my mother? You should have gone over there in a taxi; she'd have looked after you –'

After that she could do nothing but weep. She couldn't explain to him, couldn't tell him how impossible Blossom was, could do nothing but cry and though at first he had shown some compunction and tried to comfort her, she knew that he became irritable after a time and wanted only to go to bed and sleep.

And when they did, Buster woke and screamed and neither of

them had much rest. They started the next day with Jay in as filthy a temper as she had ever seen him and she herself feeling worse than she ever had.

It got no better. Within two weeks Jay had found new builders and had the kitchen put to rights, and Rosalie, who had come to visit and stayed to hover over her and murmur over and over again, 'Oh, you poor dear, you poor dear,' until Maddie thought she would scream, had found her a new hired girl. But somehow Maddie never was able to pick up her energy again. Each day she woke as soon as the sun rose, and sometimes even while the sky was still pearly grey at dawn. Each afternoon she found herself dragging her weary bones around the house and night after night found herself weeping helplessly into her pillow, trying to disguise the sound for fear that Jay would hear. Because there was one thing about which Maddie was quite certain: Jay must not know how miserable she was. If he did he would leave her.

She had no obvious reason to think so, no sign from Jay that he was thinking of any such thing; indeed, he was so totally absorbed in the business, so eager to get to the office each morning and so late coming home that he had no time or energy for anything else. But she remained certain. Her need for him, her longing for him, had now grown to such proportions that she felt desperately unsafe. The more her passion for him consumed her, the more she doubted her ability to hold him. And the more she doubted, the more desperate her love became, and the more fearful she was of letting him know how she felt.

Yet she managed to keep her misery out of sight. The hired girl turned out to be reasonably sensible, and was at least willing to stay in at nights and look after the baby once Jay did get home. They could be together then without worrying about Buster or his needs and that helped a little. The evenings Jay was home were the best times in the bad times, Maddie thought. By nine o'clock the worst of her lassitude seemed to have worn off, and she could push away the bad thoughts that came to her, the hatred she sometimes felt for Buster for coming to spoil everything the way he had, and the even greater hatred she had for Blossom who had made her so angry and so fearful.

Because that had become an obsession with her. Blossom would find a way to persuade Jay to leave her. She would sit and watch him eat his dinner and listen to him compare the food the hired girl had provided with the sort of fare he had from Mary Margaret, and feel sick with terror that somehow Blossom's baleful influence would come snaking towards them from Commonwealth Avenue to suck him away and swallow him up. It was as though Blossom wanted to take her son back into her own body again, and hideous images would rise before Maddie's mind's eye as the thought came to her.

And then there were the thoughts about her father. She would lie on her bed each afternoon, ostensibly taking a rest while the hired girl took Buster out for a walk in his buggy, and toss and turn as she thought about him. She would see the flat in Regent's Park, see the rooms empty and dusty and then see her father slumped dead in a chair, with no one to know because she wasn't there to look after him. Or she would see the office in Great Portland Street and watch helplessly as he came out of the door and went to the head of the stairs and tripped and tumbled down them to lie dead and broken at the bottom, until she was weeping great desperate sobs and was almost out of her mind with fear. It was the way that her thoughts ran away with her, and ugly images came and went of their own volition, that terrified her most. She was out of control of her life and she didn't know how to get it back into her own hands again.

And no one knew what was happening. She went through the times when other people were around her with a fixed smile on her face and an air of calm insouciance and showed no sign of her hidden misery and turmoil. Rosalie admired her new slimness – which was entirely due to the fact that Maddie had no appetite at all – and said she hoped she'd be able to get her figure back as fast as darling Maddie had, but then she didn't have Maddie's great willpower! and she would droop heavily in her chair with her hands looped across her vast belly and stare at Maddie with her great adoring eyes and beg for reassurance that it wouldn't hurt too much having her baby, and then cry, 'Please, please Maddie, be with me. I need you so much, what with Timmy being in Washington –' And Maddie would smile brightly and assure her she'd be fine and remind her she had her mother to rely on, and after all wasn't that why she was in Boston and not in Washington to have her baby? So that she could be near her mother? And Rosalie would subside with a few tears and say, 'Well, yes – I suppose so,' and say no more. Until the next time when she would trail out the same old plea.

Maddie even managed to hide what had happened to her feelings for Jay. She still adored him, with a fierceness that never wavered, still wanted to be with him and only him, still felt renewed when he came home and abandoned when he left to go to the office, but she no longer wanted his lovemaking. That deep aching for sex that had been so intrinsic a part of her feeling for him had gone as though it had been a candleflame someone had blown out. When he touched her she felt at first nothing and then a crawling distaste that made her grit her teeth and breathe deeply to control the nausea that rose in her. She wanted his love and his support more than she had ever wanted anything, but she did not want his body. He, on the other hand, seemed as eager as ever; it was a rare night when he didn't grope for her almost as soon as they got into bed, and sometimes he started the day in the same way, waking with an urgent need that allowed him no time for any finesse or even an invitation. She would find he had reached for her shoulder and flipped her over on to her back and was thrusting himself into her almost between one breath and the next; but curiously she didn't mind that as much as the night-time lovemaking he wanted. She was at her lowest ebb in the morning, but at least it was quick and easy then. He demanded no more cooperation from her than her body's presence. At night he demanded cooperation and what was more, enthusiasm, which she did her best to simulate.

But he didn't know. He would talk to her of the baby, of work, of the house, and show no awareness of any of her feelings and for that she was grateful. It made her feel safe and that was what she needed most of all.

Summer limped, sweaty and heat-shimmering, into a rich golden autumn and still she felt no better. She was almost gaunt now and Jay had begun to comment on it, complaining in a heavily jocular fashion about the way her breasts had diminished in size, and she made an effort, forcing herself to drink milk and to take extra vitamins and minerals from the drug store and that helped a little. The baby on the other hand was growing at a great rate, as the hired girl became more and more attached to him and showed her affection by filling him with quantities of extra sugar in his bottle feeds. Maddie watched him grow bracelets of fat and thought, at least he's all right, though somewhere at a deep level she suspected he needed better care than he was getting. But she was too weary and too miserable to care.

It was late in October, when the work on the new site at Wollaston Beach had been under way for several weeks, that she began at last to feel better. Not a great deal better, but at least she wasn't waking so early in the mornings now, and the thoughts that had so frightened her seemed to have receded a little. She still thought about her father, still had visions of him dead or dying and alone in London and all because of her wicked abandonment of him, but the fear those thoughts had created in her seemed less biting and less icy.

She even found the energy one day to go and buy a new dress at Bonwit Tellers, something she hadn't bothered to do since the baby had been born. She left Buster with the hired girl and spent the afternoon in Newbury Street, even buying new shoes too, and then on an impulse, went to the State Street office to see Jay. It was time she made more of an effort to be interested in what was happening, tried to see if he was doing as much as he should to look after his own interest. She had some fears that perhaps he wasn't making as much money as he might be, and with her interest in shopping renewed, that mattered. Time to talk business was what they needed. So she came out into Newbury Street with her purchases and hailed a cab and was driven through the hazy October sunshine to Jay's office.

23

October 1951

The office looked different. She came out of the elevator on to the seventeenth floor and stood in the lobby and stared. The place had always looked good but now it looked palatial. The carpets were new and thick, the reception desk was the latest in heavy chrome and everywhere was the glitter of glass and mirror. The girl sitting behind the reception desk was new, too, and just as glossy, and Maddie walked past her soundlessly across the deep crimson carpet, and felt her hackles rise at the sight of the perfection of upswept hair, long red fingernails and frilled blouse.

'Hey there!' the girl called after her, and her voice was high and nasal and that made Maddie feel a little better. She was one of those who was fine until she opened her mouth, she decided, and she turned and fixed her with an icy stare. 'Are you talking to me?' she said haughtily.

'I ain't talkin' to the cat,' the girl retorted. 'You can't go in there if you ain't got no appointment.'

'I don't need one,' Maddie said contemptuously, and turned to push open the doors that led into the interior offices just as the elevator doors sighed open again and a tall dark girl, wearing a very long Canadian fox tie in the richest of glinting silver over a most elegantly cut grey flannel suit, came drifting out on a wave of expensive scent.

'Good afternoon, Chrissie,' she said to the receptionist who at once grinned and nodded a greeting and pressed a button near the edge of her desk and the doors towards which Maddie had been walking immediately buzzed open and the tall girl in furs swept through. The doors closed before Maddie could follow her and by the time she reached them and tried to push them open, they were locked.

She turned furiously to the girl at the desk. 'Did you lock that door?'

'I sure did,' the girl said and gave a high cackle. 'We got the most up-to-the-minute stuff here, lady. We don't let no one just go walking in.'

'You call my husband at once,' Maddie roared furiously. 'You hear me? You call Mr Jay Kincaid and tell him his wife is here. And open that bloody door.'

The girl stared at her with her mouth half open and then said uneasily, 'How do I know you're his wife? I ain't never seen you here before —'

'Open the bloody door, do you hear me?' Maddie shouted and leaned over the girl's desk and put her face close to hers. 'Or do I have to make you?'

Now the girl looked terrified and she scrabbled beneath her desk edge and behind her Maddie heard the door buzz and with one last withering look at the receptionist she turned and went, her head high and her colour blazing in her cheeks, through the doors and to the corner office which she knew now belonged to Jay.

She pushed the door open and stood there, taking in in one comprehensive glance the fact that this room too had been made over. There was another new carpet, a rich blue this time, and a vast rosewood desk, and buttoned furniture in dark grey hide. And in one of the deep armchairs the girl who had come drifting in was sitting with one long silken leg draped over the other with a considerable display of knee and thigh, while Jay sat on the front edge of his desk, the phone in his hand.

'It's all right, Chrissie,' he said into it. 'She's here.' And he hung up and got to his feet and came across the room with both hands out. 'Maddie! What are you doing here?'

'I was shopping,' Maddie said shortly, the anger which the receptionist had set alight simmering even even higher at the sight of the interloper in her Jay's office. 'And I thought I'd drop by. Who the hell is that creature you've got outside? And why this business with remote control doors? I never saw anything so stupid in my life! Have you started employing prisoners here or something?' Her colour was still high and her voice was peremptory as the anger bubbled sickeningly inside her.

He laughed, a little uneasily, and glanced at the girl in the chair. 'Hell, no, Maddie! We just decided to have all the best equipment we could have. Cray Costello showed us the sort of gear we could get and Pa fancied dictating machines instead of stenographers – now we got just typists – and electric typewriters, and these door controls. Keeps out the riff-raff and makes sure we know who's around. I'm sorry you were stopped – the girl's new too and she didn't know you. Now, let me introduce you. Maddie, this is Gloria Costello. Her dad, Cray, is working with us on the Wollaston Beach development, you know?'

'I know about Wollaston,' Maddie said, and smiled brilliantly at the girl in the chair. 'How nice to meet you, Miss Costello. I'm sorry if I'm breaking up a business meeting –'

'Not at all –' Jay said hastily, just as the girl got to her feet in one smooth easy movement and said in a rich drawl, 'Why, no, Mizz Kincaid, I don't believe you have.'

'Because I'll go at once if so,' Maddie went on relentlessly. 'I just thought after I'd done my shopping I'd come by and maybe you could get away a little early, Jay, and we'd go together –' She looked at her watch. 'It's almost six.'

The girl was walking over to the door, and Maddie tried not to look at the way her buttocks, rounded and pert, seemed to bounce a little with each step. She herself was so thin now it seemed sometimes as though her clothes hung on her instead of making the best of her, the way this girl's suit did.

'I must go,' Gloria said, and the drawl was still very pronounced. 'I guess I'll find Poppa with your Pa, Jay? Glad you found the drawings useful. Goodbye, Mizz Kincaid. A real pleasure knowing you.' And she went, letting the door close softly behind her, leaving behind a wash of her scent. Chanel Number Five, Maddie thought knowingly. Just the type who would.

'What drawings?' she said sharply as Jay moved back to his desk and she followed him.

'Hmm? Oh, her father wants her to be involved in the internal decorations on the development. She was at art school, got a few ideas. So of course we said sure. It's no skin off our noses, and she's Cray Costello's daughter. Important lady in this business, Costello's daughter.'

The wave of jealousy that had risen in her when she had seen the girl sitting so nonchalantly as though she lived there, began to ebb away and Maddie let her shoulders slump and went to sit

211

in the chair the girl had vacated. It had been the receptionist Chrissie who had made her feel so bad, she told herself; don't be stupid, don't make a fuss just because of that. This was supposed to be a good evening I'm planning. A time to talk . . .

'Jay,' she said, 'I fixed it with the girl – she's not doing anything tonight, so she'll be with Buster. We're free again. How's about dinner out, hmm? We could go to the Circus Room at the Copley Plaza, eat clam chowder, dance maybe – I have a new dress, too. Right here.' And she patted the parcel she had dropped beside the chair. 'I could change here, and then we could have some fun. What do you say?'

'Well, Maddie, it's a lovely idea – but why didn't you call me? As it is, I have a date with Cray. We're supposed to be going out to dinner so we can go over the newest estimates –' He looked at her with his face smooth with regret. 'I'm really sorry, honey. Maybe tomorrow or the night after? If you'd just called me . . .'

She stared at him for a long moment and then produced another of her brilliant smiles. 'Cray Costello's here, isn't he? I bet if I ask him he'd let you off the hook. He's in with Pa. That girl – what's her name – Gloria, she said he's in with Pa. Just you watch me –' And she was on her feet and out of the door so fast that he couldn't stop her, though she heard the cry of protest that followed her.

Pa's office had not been made over, and she stood in the doorway and looked round at the furniture, carefully not looking at the three people in the room. The same old roll-top desk, cluttered and shedding papers everywhere, the same old calendars with pictures of half-naked girls pinned on the walls, and the same shabby old chairs with the battered cushions.

'Hello Pa,' she said then and looked at the old man sitting in front of the desk with his feet up on it. He grinned back at her, his white head seeming haloed by the light that came from the window beside him.

'Hey there!' he said and brought his feet to the ground with a little crash. 'How's my grandson then? You brought him here?'

She shook her head and laughed at him. 'Bring him here, Pa? Why, I wouldn't dare risk it – he'd pick up terrible habits from being around you, he'd be smoking his head off before he was a year old if I let you get to him, and having whisky in his formula.' She slid her eyes sideways and smiled even more brilliantly. 'You must be Mr Costello,' she said to the man in the armchair alongside old Timothy. 'I've heard so much about you.'

'Nothing but good, I hope,' he said and got to his feet. He was a small man, in terms of height, about the same as Maddie's own five feet five, but he had size about him. He looked big and strong without being fat and for a moment she was puzzled at the illusion, and then realised it was his stance. He held his arms slightly away from his sides as he stood there, in the way heavily muscled boxers did, and there was a faintly menacing air about him. Yet he seemed friendly enough, grinning at her from a round rosy face which was fringed with long side whiskers and crowned with a gleaming dome of a scalp that was almost entirely bald, save for a small fringe of grey hair just above the ears.

'Oh, everything good,' she said and stepped a little closer. 'So good in fact that I'm going to risk asking you a great favour.'

She felt rather than heard the door open behind her and knew Jay had come in and before he could speak she said quickly, 'You see, Mr Costello, I'm being a tiresome wife. I came into the office after an afternoon in Newbury Street to persuade my husband to take me out to dinner at the Copley Plaza. But he says he has an engagement with you –'

'An engagement! How d'you like that, eh?' Costello said and looked at old Timothy. 'Real limey talk, eh? I got an engagement, have I?'

'To look at the new estimates.' It was not Timothy's voice which cut in but Gloria's and Maddie looked at her briefly, in her chair opposite her father, and then away. 'I brought in my designs for the bigger units, Poppa. You said you'd let J – Mr Kincaid use them if they didn't cost too much.'

Costello looked at her and then at Timothy, rolling his eyes comically. 'Hey, kids! More trouble'n a squad of bricklayers and all the Teamsters' Union put together!'

'Oh, Poppa!' Gloria said and again got to her feet with that same easy movement and came to stand beside him, overtopping him by at least three inches, and bending to kiss his bald head. 'You know you don't want it any other way.'

'Listen to this, and listen good, Mrs Kincaid,' Costello said and laughed again. 'That baby o' yours'll be twisting you round his little finger any minute now. You have 'em and they're cute little devils and you let 'em get away with murder on account they're so cute and you barely turn round and look what you got! A great thing like this and still getting away with murder!' But he looked up at his daughter fondly and she grinned back at him and Maddie felt a shaft of pure loathing for both of them. Daddy, she thought confusedly, how are you, Daddy?

'Well, there it is, Maddie,' Jay said easily and came and slid his arm through hers. 'We'll have to go out tomorrow night, I guess –'

'Ah, the hell you will!' Costello said and turned to pick up his hat, a wide-brimmed affair in rich black that looked almost as expensive as the astrakhan collared coat he wore slung casually over his shoulders. 'We can talk estimates another time. We'll make another engagement.' And he laughed fatly at that and turned to Timothy. 'Tell you what, old man, *we'll* go and tie one on. Like the old days, hmm? Get really stinko –'

'Great for you,' Timothy growled. 'You're a widower.'

'And you're the boss around the place!' Costello retorted. 'Or I thought you were.'

'I'm the boss,' Timothy said. 'But I'm a tired one. I don't want Blossom nagging the ass off me, you should forgive me, Gloria, just for the pleasure of a hangover. Tomorrow, I'll come with you and Jay, okay? Then we talk money and we have a few beers and it'll be very nice. Hey, Maddie – I'm glad you're here. I got something to show you –'

'I'll be on my way,' Costello said. ' 'Night, Jay. 'Night, you old villain. C'mon Gloria. We'll go eat some place too –'

'But not the Copley Plaza,' Gloria said, her drawl even more marked in contrast to her father's staccato voice. 'We don't want to intrude on the lovebirds, hmm, Mr Kincaid? Goodnight all, see you tomorrow –' And she led the way out of the room with her father close behind her and after a moment of hesitation, Jay went too.

Maddie looked after them and then back at the old man who was scrabbling on his desk amid the mass of papers there, and decided it would be more politic to stay and wait for him than to follow the others. And anyway, she told herself as at last the old man swung round with a strip of newsprint in his hand.

Anyway, I'd make a fool of myself if I did. I've got what I wanted. We're going out tonight . . .

'Listen, you heard from your father lately?' the old man said. 'I didn't ask. I reckoned you'd tell me if there's anything important, and since the baby, who's got time to talk, eh?' He peered at her now, and there was in his milky blue eyes a look she hadn't seen before. Not the lascivious one she knew all too well, nor the watchful one he had when Blossom was about, but a simpler, kinder look. He's worried about me, she found herself thinking with some surprise, and that made her feel warm suddenly.

'No, we haven't much spare time now that . . .' she said, and then abruptly, 'No, I haven't.'

She shifted her eyes and looked at the paper in his hand and saw the heading on it and felt a wave of cold rise in her belly. It was the London *Times*. 'Why? What's that you have there?'

He bent his head and smoothed the cutting under his rough fingers. 'It was sent to me by someone I got in London watching my interests. Since your little trouble with your father – and don't look at me that way! You think I didn't find out what you did, running out on him that way? I tell you, I got friends everywhere – since then, I thought, better not to deal with him so close like I used to. So this other guy, he sent me this. Listen, I don't think you should pay too much attention. It's the way with newspapers – they get it wrong, they blow things up – they could be wrong, but I thought I should show you, when I got the chance. And you coming in like this this afternoon . . .' His voice drifted away and the silence hung around them like a curtain.

She took it and bent her head to read it. A bleak account of a road accident after a prison escape involving a fast car. Two people severely injured, one not expected to survive. And the names slid off the page into the margin and danced there giddily as she stared.

After a while she lifted her gaze. 'Is this all you've got?' Her voice was husky.

'That's all. I phoned once, tried to find out more, but no one seems to know. Listen, how old is he, this brother o' yours?'

'Six years older than I am,' she said dully and looked at the cutting again. 'Twenty-six –'

'A kid, a boy!' Timothy said. 'He'll be all right. It takes more'n an argument with an auto to kill a boy. An old man, now, that'd be different. But a kid – he's younger than Jay, for God's sake. He'll be okay. I wouldn't have said anything if I didn't think so. I thought, maybe it's time you called, hmm? Your father'll have got over it by now, you running out. He's a grandfather now, after all! He has a right to get in on the act. He'll forgive you.'

She lifted her head and looked at him and he said again, 'He'll forgive you. Believe me.'

'How can you be so sure?'

'Because I've known him longer than you have, and I'm a grandfather too,' the old man said. 'Okay? So go phone your father, write a letter at least –'

'I wish I could see him,' she said looking down at the paper again, as she heard Jay push the door open behind her. 'The phone's not the same.'

The old man tilted his head and looked at her and then at Jay and after a moment slapped his knee awkwardly like a bad actor playing a character in a children's Christmas show. 'You're right! Why not? Listen, you go – eh Jay? You take this girl of yours, she should visit her old man, make sure her brother's okay. The Wollaston business is doing all right, there's nothing there I can't handle. Me and Declan, we can deal with it. You take your wife back to London, take your baby, let him see his other grandfather. The man's entitled, for Chrissakes. Then come back, eh, Maddie? You'll be good friends with him and you'll feel better. Better'n you've been this past few months, eh?'

She looked at him and felt the tears lifting in her eyes, but it didn't really matter. For the first time since she had come to America she felt someone cared about how she felt, and understood her. Jay loved her, of course he did, but their closeness was a different sort of thing entirely. Jay was about passion and need and possessing, but what she was now getting from Timothy was a sense of concern, a protectiveness that she hadn't realised she missed so sorely. All the feelings and fears she had had about her father for so many months came flooding back into her, but they didn't make her feel sick and ill as they had done. She felt instead a great rush of warmth and she hurled

216

herself at the old man and flung her arms round him and cried thickly, 'Oh, Pa, thank you! You're so kind to me!'

'Ah, the hell with it,' Timothy said, patting her shoulder awkwardly but clearly enjoying the encounter, for he held her close with his other arm. 'You're just a kid yourself, not much more'n a baby, and you with a baby of your own! You've been looking peaky – go home and see your Pa and then come back and it'll all be better. Hey, Jay?'

'It's not a good time, Pa,' Jay said and Maddie felt the warmth that had filled her begin to drain away for he sounded wooden. Not angry or sulky exactly, but not happy. 'I'm just beginning to get old Cray to see things our way. I need to see this through. Declan'll make a complete balls of the whole thing, you know that –'

'But I won't,' Timothy said and his voice was sharper now. 'And I've made up my mind. I was thinking about it anyway. Your mother's been giving me a bad time,' and again he patted Maddie's shoulder and she stiffened a little at the mention of Blossom. 'It'd be a good idea if you're both away for a spell. She's got Rosalie and her baby to fuss over, and Timothy coming home for Thanksgiving, and the girls – she'll be all right. You take Maddie. Come back after Christmas, okay? Let her see how things are with her family, and she'll be all right. And Blossom, well, you heard me. You get a sailing as soon as you can. Out of Boston if possible, but New York if you must. I got some business I want you to do in London, anyway, Jay. I'll give you all the details, but not now. Right now, I'm heading home. You two go to your Copley Plaza. I'm having Mary Margaret's corned beef and cabbage and I'll be better off for it. Now get out of my way, the pair of you. I've made up my mind, and that's an end of it.'

24

July 1987

'It's like when I was a kid,' Joe said. 'If I said I had a headache or a toothache, so that I could bunk off school, you could count on it I'd get the real thing the next day. I claimed she was physically ill so that I could get her in here and –' He shook his head. 'It's been a nasty few weeks for her.'

'It hasn't been a great deal of fun for me either,' Annie said tartly. 'I caught it too, you know. From her. Even though I'd had that stinker already.'

'So did I,' he said mildly. 'Half London had it. But at least she's a good deal better now, and seems settled enough. Not that dear old Gresham got off so lightly.' He laughed then. 'It is not an agreeable trait to take pleasure in another's downfall – what's it called? *Schadenfreude*? But I have to admit to being deeply grateful for Gresham's sick leave. It's kept all the fuss about getting the hospital cleared out of our hair for a while.'

He looked down the ward, at the serried rows of beds on both sides, each humped with an occupant lying tidily under the red covering blanket, and shook his head. 'This ward never used to be so full when the whole hospital was occupied. To see so many of these poor old souls wheezing and coughing like this is depressing.'

'Flu's depressing,' Annie said shortly. 'Maddie was hell for a while there, quite apart from her sniffing and snorting.'

He looked at her shrewdly. 'Yes, and it's knocked you back a bit again, hasn't it? And don't give me a display of aggression just to prove it. A simple yes will do.'

She had opened her mouth to protest but now she managed a thin grimace of a smile. 'Yes,' she said.

'If it's any comfort to you, I've been feeling like a little heap of something very nasty,' he said and got to his feet. 'But it's an interesting experience. Every psychiatrist ought to get depression sometimes. Therapeutically valuable.'

'It won't make most of them any the less arrogant when they get better,' she said. 'They'll still stuff their patients full of pills instead of listening to them.'

'You sound like a lecturer at an alternative medicine symposium,' he said after a moment. 'Very boring and even more arrogant than the people you're castigating.'

She stared at him and then, surprisingly, laughed. 'That's better!'

'What is?' He was scowling and it looked faintly comic on his agreeable face, surmounted as it was by his untidy frizz of curls.

'You, biting back. It's been driving me potty, your placidity. No matter what I said, no matter how bloody I was, you did your damned psychiatrist thing and came on like Pollyanna, all sweetness and light and joy through strength. Boring at best, and unbelievably irritating.'

The scowl had faded. 'I'll remember in future to be a pig then. Clearly, you like men who behave badly. No nasty modern equality for you.'

'Pah!' She made a soft little noise of disgust. 'What's equality got to do with it? It's passivity I can't stand and that can drive me mad, whatever the gender of the person who shows it.' She looked past him to Maddie's chair, by the window. '*She's* another. She was so much better – starting to snap back when I had a go at her instead of sitting and sopping up all the abuse and saying nothing at all. But this flu seems to have sent her right back.'

'Not all the way back.'

'No.' She allowed that. 'Not all the way. She is still talking, at least.'

'Can you give me an update? Or do I have to wait for the notes to come down? Not that they're bad notes, mind you. In fact, they're damned good. It's like reading a particularly absorbing novel. Great stuff.'

She went pink with pleasure. 'I'm glad you like them,' she said gruffly. 'Yes, I can give you – how far had you got in your reading?'

'Marriage. Life in Boston. The wheeling and dealing over the business of getting her brother-in-law out of her way.' He shook his head admiringly. 'She was a sharp operator, wasn't she?

"Whatever Maddie wants, Maddie gets," ' he sang softly, seeming to have quite forgotten his moment of pique, and he grinned at her again with his usual amiability. 'Is there more? I thought she'd been feeling too lousy to talk?'

'I've got a bit more. She came back to London when she found out her brother had been involved in a police chase. It sounds like a film, the way she tells it, but you have to believe it. It's all so –' She shrugged. 'It's just true. I can tell. He was sent to prison for his black-market dealings, it seems, and because he was a first offender it wasn't a difficult prison. An open one, I gather. Anyway, her father got him out, using some villains or other, Maddie said, and they were speeding to get away when the police caught up with them. The police chased them off the road, the driver was killed, the other two men escaped and ran for it and her brother Ambrose broke his neck. Died six weeks later – he was twenty-six at the time.'

'And this was because of black-market dealing? Oh, Christ, what a world this is. To kill people because of crimes against possessions. Did it matter that much?'

'It did to them, I suppose. I wasn't around at the time so I don't know how much people cared about crimes like black-market dealings. Maybe they thought people who profited out of shortages were wicked enough to die young? Anyway, no one much seemed to care, it seems. Her father, Maddie said, tried to get action against the police, claiming they'd done it deliberately, that they weren't trying to stop them so much as knock them off the road, but he got nowhere. And then he had a stroke.'

'Not all that surprising,' he said. 'There's a direct link between emotional stress and CVAs.'

'Mmm?'

'Sorry. Cerebro-vascular accidents. Strokes.'

'Then call 'em strokes. You all love your jargon, don't you? Maybe that's why you like my notes. They're written in ordinary straight English and not medical gobbledegook.'

'I like them because they're written by you,' he said. 'And you're good. So, he had a stroke. What happened after that?'

'Maddie had a bad time,' she said and looked over at the slumped grey figure in the chair again. 'I have to say she's coming out of all this as a frightful twister – she used people like shoes, you know? Fancied them, got them, broke them in and then went looking for new ones. But it wasn't all her fault.'

He was looking at her with bright eyes, watchful and eager but she wasn't aware of that. She was still looking at Maddie. 'Well?' he said softly after a long pause. 'Whose fault was it then?'

She shrugged. 'Oh, I don't know. Her father, maybe. He spoiled her as surely as if he'd set out to do it. Told her she could have the world if she wanted it, and gave her some of it – and then sent her out to get the rest for herself. He made her believe that if she didn't go after what she wanted, and get it, she was useless and wet – and she was proud too, I think. She wanted to do things the way they ought to be done. She had such a thing about her house in Boston, you see. It had to be right – it was the way it looked as much as the way it was. So she was like that about what she did with people. It all had to be her idea of what was right. Except with Jay. She loved him, poor pathetic object that he was. She loved him –'

'You don't like him?'

Again she shrugged. 'How can I say? I never met the man. But he sounds – the way she tells it, he sounds like the most selfish and stupid of men, and she's telling me he was wonderful and how she loved him and needed him. But the man was a bastard. It comes out in all the things they did together. A total right royal bastard.'

'Strong words,' Joe said and sat down again. He ought to be somewhere else, but this was too important to miss, he told himself. And, anyway, I want to be here. 'What sort of bastard?'

'Every sort. He simply thought of no one but himself. When her father was ill and she felt so bad about him and blamed the whole thing on herself – and she had shopped him, of course, hadn't she? And her brother? Sending that cable to the police from the ship – she felt bad. And she was pregnant again. But what did he do?'

'I don't know. Tell me.'

'Nothing.' She invested the word with so much scorn it seemed to crackle in the air between them. 'Nothing at all. He sulked, I think, because he had to leave Boston, though God knows why. From all she says he didn't have all that wonderful a time at his father's hands there. Nothing like as much money as Maddie said he got in London, and it's obvious to me that money was the only thing that man ever got excited about. *Really* excited. But look after his wife when she was going through such a rotten time? Not he, not that bastard –'

'Annie,' he said softly, 'why are you getting so angry with him?'

She turned her head at last to look at him and her eyes were very dark because the pupils were so enlarged. 'What?'

'You're red and your forehead is sweating and you're furiously angry. Over a man you never knew, and are never likely to. Why, Annie? Try and tell me.'

She stared at him and slowly the flush died down and she shook her head, but he leaned closer and said, 'Talk to me, Annie. You must talk to me. Tell me about Colin.'

'Colin.' There was no question in her voice. She just repeated the name dully.

'Colin Matthews, Annie. Your father – another right royal bastard, wasn't he? No, don't pull away, for pity's sake. Tell me! Tell me now –'

She was still trying to pull her hands away, because he had taken hold of them and was gripping tightly and for a moment he thought she would manage to escape and the chance would be lost, but slowly she stopped tugging and relaxed. And then, even more slowly began to speak.

'Yes. He was a bastard. He made me one, but he was much worse than I am.'

'You were an accident of marriage and birth, Annie. But he was selfish and unkind from choice, wasn't he? We're not talking about his birth certificate when you say he was a bastard, are we? We're talking about his behaviour. Tell me what he did.'

'The stupid woman adored him!' Annie said, and she shook her head. 'Just like that stupid one there – adored a man who was too selfish and too stupid to understand what was going on. He used her, sucked out of her all he could get, made her do whatever he wanted, when he wanted, and what did he give her? Nothing. Nothing at all. Just a stupid grand passion to talk to herself about, to dream about, to make stupid schemes about. Scheming to be with him, to make him care for her, to –'

'Annie,' Joe said very quietly, 'who are we talking about? Maddie's Jay, or your mother's Colin?'

She shook her head piteously, and her eyes filled with tears, but she said nothing.

'Go on,' he said and put up one hand to touch her cheek. It was a friendly gesture but she turned her head away and he let his hand fall. 'Go on, Annie,' he said again, as though she had not moved. 'Talk about it. You need to.'

'You're doing it again,' she said dully and now she did manage to pull her hands away. 'Treating me like a patient. I'm not a patient.'

'No,' he said. 'Just a friend.'

But the moment had gone. She had her anger under control now, and the tears had not spilled over and she stood up and moved away towards Maddie.

'Anyway, there it is, up to date,' she said as lightly as she could. 'You'll see the notes as soon as I can get them typed. But you may have to wait a while. I've got a lot to do at the flat and anyway Maddie isn't talking so much these days.' She looked down at the bent grey head. 'Are you, Maddie? So the next chapter of the tale is one you can't have for a while. But we'll get round to it, I dare say.'

He was on his feet too now. 'Thank you,' he said. 'And I hope you feel better about —'

'Please, don't start talking about me,' she said. 'It isn't only your Pollyanna-ing that drives me potty. It's your meddling too. I don't want to talk, all right?'

'No. It isn't. It's time you learned to be a little less selfish yourself, you know.' He seemed to flare up quite suddenly, and she blinked in surprise as his voice rose, and even some of the elderly women in the red-covered beds turned their heads to look. 'When people offer friendship, it's not just yourself you're depriving when you reject it. I don't create my concern for you out of the air, and if you stopped to think for just a moment about other people apart from yourself, you'd realise that. You'd realise that I talk to you as I do because I *care* about you, damn it. I told you once before that I like you. Can't you see what it all is, or are you too wrapped up in your own misery and loving it, to give a damn about anyone else? I'm a determined man, Annie, and when I build a set of feelings, I don't jettison them that easily. But go on as you are and you'll make even me despair. And that could be the worst thing that could happen to you. So give just a little thought, will you, to what you are and what you're doing with your life and other people's? You might surprise yourself if you manage to be honest enough.'

And he went, walking down the ward with the long loping strides she knew so well and out of the door at the end, without looking back, as she stood and watched him go, feeling curiously deflated. She wasn't angry – the emotion with which she was most familiar – and she wasn't surprised or miserable or anything else identifiable. She just felt that half of her inner structure had gone, leaving her like a sagging wrinkled weakened nonentity. And it was a very uncomfortable way to feel.

'Annie.'

She was still standing staring down the ward to the far end where the double doors were just stopping the swinging action he had left behind as he went sweeping out, and did not answer. Until it came again.

'Annie. Come and sit here.'

Slowly Annie turned her head. Maddie was sitting in the same position but her chin was up and she was looking at her, and as Annie's eyes met hers, she put out one hand.

'Come and talk to me, Annie. I want to talk to you,' the cracked old voice said and Annie said irritably, 'Cough, for heaven's sake! You don't have to sound as croaky as that.'

Surprisingly Maddie laughed, opened her little black cavern of a mouth widely, and then she coughed, deliberately, and swallowed and coughed again, and then said, 'Will that do?' Her voice sounded clearer and stronger and after a moment Annie came and sat down beside her on the window seat.

'What do you want?'

'Did you mean all that?'

'All what?'

'The things you said about Jay.'

Annie looked at her and considered for a moment, and then said, 'Yes. Yes I did. I think he treated you badly when your brother died. Don't you?'

'No,' Maddie said. 'Nothing he did was ever as bad as what I did.'

'What did you do?' Annie felt alertness creep into her. The

deflated feeling thinned out and disappeared as interest came to fill the space Joe had managed to create in her. 'He was dreadfully selfish and unkind. You must know that. How could you have been as bad to him as he was to you? When you loved him as much as you say you did?'

Maddie was staring at her with her eyes wide and very dark. 'I can't tell you. Not ever. I'll tell you some of what happened. But I won't tell you all of it.'

'Why not? Isn't it better to be as you are now, better than it was last year, when you never talked to anyone?'

'No – yes. No. I –' Maddie shook her head and hunched her shoulders a little. 'I was all right as I was. Just thinking of the good parts, the happy days, the wonderful things that happened to me. Never the other – Jay was wonderful. I loved him so much –'

Slowly the rocking began, at first almost imperceptibly, and then more and more definitely, and Annie let her shoulders slump. She knew what this meant: another panegyric about Jay and his good looks and his wonderful lovemaking and the joy he gave her. It would go on for an hour or more before Annie would be able, slowly, to persuade her to change tack and talk of the events in her life instead of about her feelings. When she did that the truth about Jay always emerged. The man she described and gloated over was a very different one from the man who came snaking his way out of her stories, and it was that man Annie wanted to know about. Now, she looked over her shoulder out of the window to the dampness of the dull July afternoon outside and decided it was worth trying, just once more at least, to get more out of Maddie, including the 'bad things' about which she had hinted and then refused to speak. And she turned back to her and reached out and touched her rocking shoulder and said what she had said so often during the long months since she had embarked on this damn fool exercise.

'Tell me what happened next, Maddie. Tell me all about it.'

25

May 1953

'I won't have it,' Jay said. 'I've told you, Maddie, and I don't want to talk about it any more, for God's sake. I won't *have* it.'

'It wouldn't make any difference to you,' she said, trying to sound reasonable rather than wheedling. 'I promise you, you'll never even see him. I'll have the room fixed up so that he can stay there all the time. I'll get a nurse in at night as well as for the day, it won't make any difference to you –'

'Nurses at night, as well as – listen, that costs money! It's crazy. Leave him where he is, Maddie. He's okay there.'

'Money! Jay, for God's sake, we can pay for that much for him! The business is his, after all –'

He whirled on her then. 'The business belongs to the person who does it, right? And who is doing all the work right now? Is he, that – is *he* doing the work? No. *I* am. So don't give me any stuff about how the money gets spent. It's mine. I make it. And if –'

'All right, all right!' she said and put up both hands. 'I meant no harm. I only meant that he started it and –'

'And I'm carrying it on. Listen, what's the matter with you, Maddie? I know you're a crazy kid, but this is getting ridiculous.' He came and sat down beside her and slid one hand up her leg under her skirt in a conciliatory fashion and the bright green felt lifted and eddied over her knees as she leaned a little closer to him. 'His brains have gone like scrambled eggs, he doesn't know what time it is, for God's sake. What difference will it make to him to have him here at the house? None. But to me? A lot. It won't be nice for the boys – they shouldn't have to be around an old man like that – and he's in good hands there at the hospital. They take good care of him, we visit often – you're there as much as you're here sometimes – leave him in peace, honey. Don't go spoiling things here.'

It was hard to concentrate on what he was saying. Lately her physical need for him had increased and deepened; it was not at all like those dreadful grey days after Buster's birth when all her hunger had gone out like a candle. Almost from the moment that Danny had been born she had been desperate for Jay, had wanted to make love at every possible opportunity, and now, a year later, it was still the same. She wanted him at any time she could have him and now she slid down on the sofa a little so that it would be easier for him. But he just laughed and kissed her nose and then stood up and went back to the fireplace.

She sat and looked up at him and opened her mouth to start again and then closed it. It was a dreadful situation to be in, but what could she do? If Jay was so certain it wouldn't work, then it wouldn't. Big as the house was, she wouldn't be able to keep Daddy out of his way, and if Jay got angry he'd just go out more and that was not to be thought of. She shouldn't have mentioned it this morning; she should have known it would annoy Jay. But Daddy had been so particularly miserable last night that she had had to promise him she'd try to arrange something. So what else could she do? She felt like a piece of meat being torn between a pair of lions, so all she could do now was smile brightly and say, 'All right, Jay. But at least let me arrange for his own nurse there for him. It won't cost too much and that might help him to feel a bit better –'

'That's a pleasure,' Jay said handsomely. 'Believe me. I don't want to be mean, but there are things that are possible and there are things that are not. A nurse is possible. Look, I want to talk to you about the business of the bleachers. I got the offer of two blocks, down the end of the Mall. What do you think? Should I take them? They want a bloody fortune – and how much can I ask for 'em if I do?'

She sat up straighter and tried to set her mind to business. Ever since they had got back from Boston and discovered just what a tangle Alfred Braham's affairs had been allowed to get into, while he struggled to deal with Ambrose and his problems and then had become ill himself, Jay had been like a new man. All the way over on the ship from Boston, he had been taciturn and remote, spending every day playing poker and coming to their cabin so late and so drunk that there had been no loving at all, only head-holding and vomiting and a good deal of stertorous sleeping, and she had been frightened then, very frightened. Had the bubble burst? Had their wonderful marriage, for which she had struggled so hard and done such dreadful things to her family, gone sour and died on her? She had spent the six nights at sea weeping into her pillow, terrified to think of what was to come, sickeningly aware of the fear that she was pregnant again, so soon, and worn out with the way Buster woke every night as soon as she managed to drift into a shallow sleep. It had been a hell of a journey.

But once they had arrived and moved into the Regent's Park flat and he had gone to the office in Great Portland Street to see how things were, he had been galvanised.

'The place has just been ticking over,' he had told her jubilantly when he had come back to find her in a heap on the sofa, having just come back from visiting her father in hospital. 'Just ticking over with a half-witted secretary fielding phone calls and any amount of business waiting to be done –' And he had gone rushing away again, to immerse himself in it all without even asking her how her father was.

How her father was. Sitting now and staring out at the dripping garden while Jay went to find the map that would show her the stands he had the chance to get on the Coronation route, she thought of her father and again the ugly tightness came into her throat. It was like a band of thick gristle that pushed a lump into her gullet so that sometimes she almost felt sick with it, and it came whenever she thought of him.

Alfred, the swaggering, cigar-puffing Alfred of the gleaming ridged black hair and the tramlined forehead, Alfred, so muscular and strong and so very *Daddy*, to look as he did now, collapsed in a wheelchair with his head poking forwards like an old tortoise and his eyes, once so bright and shrewd, looking dead and milky blue and leaking with gummy matter, while his lower lip hung open so that he drooled a little on the right side where all the lines had been smoothed out until he looked like a sagging old doll that had been left out in the sun too long – she shuddered as she thought about him, and then, as Jay came back into the room, pushed the thought away. Later, when Jay was busy, later she'd think about Daddy.

Together they sat in their big living room, on the tasteful white leather sofa, poring over the map that Jay spread on the smoked topaz glass coffee table and decided they would take the stands that had been offered to Braham's Export Agency Ltd by one of Alfred's old business cronies who had an in at the Ministry of Works, and resell them to American tourists at three times the recommended rates.

'It won't make me any big money,' Jay said contentedly. 'But it'll make a few bucks, enough to cover expenses. And I'll lay on something special in the way of refreshments and see to it that Declan sends the people we want to do good business with. It can be a real investment –'

'Then why not have them as guests? Why make them pay for the seats? Let 'em come to the Coronation for nothing,' Maddie said.

He shook his head at her, half amused, half irritated. 'I thought you were a businesswoman, Maddie. Listen, what matters most? Something you get given or something you have to pay big for? I know the answer to that if you don't. I'll get 'em all over here, the Flannerys and the Martyns and the Costellos and those guys Pa did so well with a couple years back – who was it, they were brothers, Italians – Giovale. That was it, the Giovale brothers –'

Maddie's brows creased. 'The Costellos?'

'Yeah, you remember Cray Costello, don't you? Guy we did the beach development with at Wollaston? According to Declan that's well on schedule. About four months, it should be operational and then the money'll really start rolling in –'

'You'll just ask Cray to come?' She hoped she sounded casual.

He shrugged. 'Whoever. I'll leave it to Declan. I'll send him a cable tonight then, as soon as I get confirmation I got these bleachers for sure. Listen, I've got to go. You'll be in the office later?'

'You want me there?'

It mattered to her to be told, suddenly, how important it was to him that she worked beside him and she sat there with her green felt skirt in a circle around her and looked up, hoping her beseeching need didn't show on her face. It might irritate him to know how much she wanted his approval.

'Of course I do! That stupid cow Murchison is off sick again. That woman has three periods a month, I swear to you. If I could only get someone better – it's crazy, the way it is these days, no decent help to be had anywhere. Listen, I'll be back from lunch about two-thirty, three – I'm eating with Perry Burns, he's got a load of stuff, all sorts of things, coming in from South Africa and I can do a nice deal with him. You be there when I get back, okay? Then we can settle this business and one or two other things. So long, honey.'

And he was gone, his long legs in their beautifully cut grey flannel trousers almost twinkling with his haste and she followed him out of the living room into the broad hallway and stood on the step as he climbed into the Bentley and drove himself away with a casual flip of one hand out of the window. She waved back and then as the car disappeared round the corner with a spit of gravel under its wheels, stood on the porch staring out at the dripping front garden. Behind her she could hear the day really getting going; the hum of a vacuum cleaner from above as the daily from the council estate started on the stairs and Buster's voice shouting something at Jenny, truculent and shrill, and she tried not to listen. Buster was not the easiest of children at the best of times, and this new nanny seemed to threaten to be as bad as the rest of them, overly keen on her own way and not at all interested in dealing with small boys as high spirited as Jay encouraged Buster and Danny to be. She smiled then as she thought of Jay with the boys. He was undoubtedly all a father should be, as far as the children were concerned. They would land on him squealing and shouting, even two-year-old Buster pretending to box with him, and Jay would let them roll him on to the floor and wrestle and box back as the nanny stood stony-faced and disapproving at such lack of control and then would scoop them up and take them away, shouting and wailing, when Jay had had enough. But he was a good father and he loved them. She was sure of that.

And he loves me too, she whispered inside her head, staring out at the laurels and the rhododendrons that lined the gravel drive, with their leaves dripping mournfully in the eternity of rain that had ushered in the year. Floods everywhere according to the papers. All the preparations for the Coronation and nothing but rain – and she wrenched her thoughts away from such trivial nonsense and tried to deal with the bad feelings she had, pushing the thoughts around her head to try to uncover their roots.

Jay's refusal to let her bring her father here to their house in Stanmore to be looked after was a particularly painful one. But that was nothing new. She had been trying to persuade him to agree to that ever since they had moved here a year ago, but he had never been anything but adamant. She had been stupid to start again this morning; she had only done it because Daddy had been so piteous in his pleadings when she had gone to see him in his nursing home yesterday afternoon, so incoherent with his hatred of the nurses and the routine of the place, so desperate to get out that what little control he had over his speech was lost altogether and he had babbled and shouted and babbled again. Of course she had had to ask Jay. And of course she had known he would refuse.

And had known too that she wanted him to. That was the worst part of it; she wanted to take care of her father, wanted to do something to ease the guilt that was always there hovering just below the surface when she saw him in that state, wanted to be rid of the conviction that it was all her fault, but she knew she couldn't bear to have him in her house with them all. Jay was right about that. It would never work.

And anyway, she thought confusedly, it says it in the Bible doesn't it? People have to cleave to their spouses, not to their parents, and never mind that commandment about honouring fathers and mothers; and she almost shook herself with irritation. What was she doing, for pity's sake, thinking about religion of all things? She'd better watch it. She'd get as bad as Blossom if she didn't take care, and that would be to get as gaga and revolting as Daddy had become. Oh, indeed, indeed, Jay was right. He couldn't live here.

So it wasn't that that made her feel so wretched this morning; it must be the weather, she thought, and turned to come back into the lounge, shutting with a thump the big studded oak door that tried so hard to pretend it was Jacobean, and then going through to the living room to look around it critically. The style she had chosen for it was right, she told herself with satisfaction for the umpteenth time; the white leather sofas she had had specially made had been worth the vast price she had to pay for them. And why not? When she thought of how much money Braham's was making under her and Jay's control, they had a right to spend some. And she had her inheritance from her mother now, too, so there was no cash shortage. It was pouring in, that was what it was doing; she had every right to be a little extravagant, and she walked across the thick carpet, only one shade darker in its off-whiteness than the sofas and armchairs, and went to the kitchen to talk to the au pair who did the cooking in the middle of the most lavishly equipped modern kitchen in tasteful greys and reds that she could provide for her. Only nursery lunch today, and no dinner tonight because she and Jay were to go to a charity ball at the Grosvenor House, so the girl needed to be warned not to get over-excited about what she could make.

But all the time as she went through her normal wife-and-mother routine, going on after leaving the kitchen to talk to Jenny about the children's day, she worried away at the back of her mind for the source of her uneasiness. And eventually found it.

Of course she had known what it was all the time, but had been trying to ignore it. Had Jay been genuinely casual when he had spoken of offering tickets for the Coronation to the Costellos? Had the name been dropped in among those others as a matter of unimportant course? Or was he thinking about the tall girl she had seen that afternoon, all that time ago, on the day when she had first heard of what had happened to Ambrose? It was crazy, she told herself as she dressed to go up to town to the office, stringing pearls around her throat so that they filled the scooped-out neckline of her skinny black sweater and pulling on her oversized coat, the one she had bought from Jacques Heim when she had last gone to Paris, collecting her long-handled umbrella without which no one was dressed this year, leaving the house in a flurry of last-minute instructions, quite, quite crazy. Why worry about a girl three thousand miles away and all that time ago in Boston when there was so much else to worry about?

Grimly she threaded the roads down through Stanmore village and on to the Edgware bypass that would lead her into the Finchley Road and on to Great Portland Street, and tried not to think about what was behind such a stupid notion, and eventually, as her white MG was caught in a traffic jam at Swiss Cottage, gave up the struggle. The fears that were really trying to beat at her awareness at last came pushing out of the morass of other thoughts with which she had tried to suppress them and stared her bleakly in the face.

Barbara Morton had told her so casually, at a charity dance last week, with so little malice, almost as a by-the-way, that she had seen Jay in Bond Street having tea at Barbellions with a girl with red hair, 'and my dear, the most pointed breasts I have *ever* seen in *all* my life. *Do* ask him who she was so that I can ask her where she buys her brassieres,' she had said and gone bopping away, leaving Maddie feeling cold and sick.

It wasn't the first time, that was the trouble. There were other tales other friends had told her, some casually like Barbara, some with that edge of mischief that gave them so much pleasure and her so much fear. Mostly she managed to ignore them, for wasn't Jay as eager in bed as ever he had been? However difficult he might be about timekeeping, however often he came home so much later than she had expected, or not at all, phoning casually later to say he'd gone on to dinner on some sort of business deal, she had always had the comfort of knowing that as soon as they were in bed, Jay was Jay, wanting her and making sure he had her. There could be nothing at all to worry about, she told herself again and again. Not with the business doing so well. Yes, there was Daddy's illness, which seemed to drag on and on unendingly – and she pulled herself away from the implications of that thought very smartly – and the ever-recurring problems of finding new nannies for the boys, but that was all.

The business was thriving and the house was lovely, exactly what she had always wanted with its five big bedrooms and its three bathrooms and its big downstairs rooms, all surrounded by a beautiful garden; the children were well, and so was she; grimly she counted her blessings as the traffic jam at last loosened and spewed her out into the West End to look for somewhere to park. And not least of the blessings was Jay, who loved her so dearly and so often. She really had nothing to worry about. Nothing at all.

26

June 1953

Maddie was edgy and tired even before they left the house. The children had woken ridiculously early with the excitement of it all and had been bawling and shouting vigorously since before dawn, and the relentless rain had done nothing to lift anyone's spirits. Jay was irritable with the children which made them even more bad-tempered and even Daphne, the new nanny who so far promised to be the best they had ever had, lost some of her sunniness and ability to keep the boys in check and became a little snappy.

They left the house just after six o'clock, piling into the Bentley with blankets and packets of rusks and flasks of the children's favourite drinks. ('There'll be plenty of food in our suite at the Savoy, for God's sake,' Jay said. 'Can't they make do with that?' 'No sir,' said Daphne sweetly. 'They have to have their special blackcurrant and their special biscuits. Vitamins, you know.') and joined the steady stream of traffic already clogging the roads into town. It took them twice as long to get there as it should have done, even with Jay's special knowledge, provided by his friend at the Ministry of Works, of the route they were to use.

By the time they reached the nearest point they could, which was along the Embankment – and they only managed to get that close because of Jay's purchase from the same Ministry of Works friend of a special windscreen sticker – the children had settled a little, as Daphne had told them stories all the way up, and Maddie began to feel a bit better. Her early-morning headache had subsided under the onslaught of the aspirins she had swallowed in recklessly large doses and Jay, though quiet, seemed his usual self.

She slid a sideways look at him and decided she had been worrying needlessly; he wasn't at all in any special sort of state about the visitors. He'd said last night when he'd come in late from having dinner with them all at the Savoy only that they were comfortably settled and looking forward to the fun, and that had been all. He'd said nothing at all about who made up the party, and showed no special excitement himself. So, she had assured herself, she was worrying needlessly. She could have gone with him last night to meet them after all. He'd suggested it, and she had meant to, but the headache had been a sick one and had made her temples throb so dreadfully that she could not have lifted her head from her pillow, let alone gone out to dine.

But now she felt better and knew she'd been a fool to worry herself into such a state. The headache had been all her own fault, she thought as she stood in the rain, peering up from beneath the edge of her dripping umbrella at the lowering grey sky; all she had to do now was relax and enjoy the fun of the day and be charming to the American visitors. They were worth money to them, via Kincaid and Sons Inc., and that made the effort well worth while.

'Maddie, you take Daphne and the boys and get through to the bleachers, okay? Here's your permit – and if you have any trouble get a policeman to sort it out. Eddie told me there might be a bit of trouble with people trying to help themselves to booked places. I'll collect everyone at the Savoy and we'll follow you, okay?'

'Can't we all go together?'

'It's simpler this way. I've got nine people to collect. If we all try to go around in one big bunch we'll look like some damned army and they'll arrest us. It won't take me more than a half-hour or so to round 'em up – we'll see you there.' And he bent and kissed her cheek and cuffed Buster and went loping off westwards leaving her with Daphne and the boys, both of whom broke into wails as their father disappeared.

'How do you mean, nine? You didn't say there were nine –' she called after him, but he was out of earshot and all she could do was shepherd the children and Daphne along the side street that led steeply up to the Strand to start the long walk down to Trafalgar Square and on to the Mall just beyond Admiralty Arch.

They shared out the packages between them, the rugs that Daphne had insisted were essential, the bag of food and drink

235

and the children's spare sweaters, and the umbrellas, and began the effortful trek, pushing their way through the crowds of people who were slowly moving along the pavements, arm in arm and plentifully bedecked with Union Jack hats, scarves and even trousers and shirts, and blowing the noisiest hooters and tin whistles they could find. It was a long and difficult journey and by the time they got to the Mall she was drenched – having long ago given up all hope of using her umbrella in the hubbub – and red-faced and her clothes, which had looked neat and attractive when she started the day, seemed to her to be unkempt and therefore cheap and shabby. Her full skirted grosgrain silk coat was a sopping rag and her hair curled in untidy tendrils on her wet cheeks.

And her appearance wasn't helped by the fact that, as Jay had suspected, squatters had attempted to take their double block which gave them a dozen seats. When she showed the interlopers – a group of very noisy and half-drunk sailors and their girls – her tickets and told them they'd have to move, they got abusive, and jeered at her and even more so at Daphne who was wearing her nanny's uniform, and whipped up support for their right to stay put from the surrounding crowds, who took immediate and noisy umbrage at the sight of bleedin' toffs tryin' to push Our Brave Boys about. Maddie got redder and hotter and more and more dishevelled as the argument went on, and knew she looked a mess, and that didn't help. It was all sorted out eventually when Daphne managed to scramble down through the pushing crowds to fetch a policeman, who grumbled, but at last came, inspected their tickets and then turned out the sailors with dispatch, but the argument was still going on when Jay arrived, leading his party, and called her name loudly above the din.

She turned to see, and there he stood, with Cray Costello on one side of him and Gloria on the other. She was wearing a pencil-slim black skirt over her incredible length of very silken legs and wonderfully high-heeled little shoes and over it a broad-hipped tight-waisted three-quarter coat in dark green ribbed wool and silk, the whole surmounted by a cheeky forward-tilting flat pancake of a hat which held her hair well in check in front, while at the back the thick heaviness of it was wrapped into an elaborate chignon. The rain seemed to slide off her, leaving her looking only more dazzling and cool and altogether stunning and Maddie ran one hand through her own mop of now hopelessly untidy curly hair and wanted to burst into tears.

He hadn't said she was here; if only he had she could have been ready for her, could have made sure she looked as cool and as gently amused as Gloria did; she could have competed. But as things were she felt she looked what she was: a distracted and far from efficient mother of two unruly children – both of whom were now bawling again, while Danny's nose was running unappetisingly as Daphne struggled to prevent him from hurling himself off the high stand into the crowd below – who looked and felt squalid.

'What's going on, for God's sake?' Jay said, and he sounded amused, but there was an edge in his voice that told Maddie just how irritated he was to find her in such a state. 'I told you, get the police to help if you have any problems.'

'We did, but it wasn't that easy,' she retorted and then managed a smile. 'How great to see you again, Mr Costello! Welcome to London. I hope you enjoy the little show we've arranged just for you.'

'Hello, Mrs Kincaid! It's great to see you too!' He came forward, his coat, a fur-lined Burberry, Maddie noted, which must have cost a small fortune, flapping over an expensive cashmere and silk suit, and planted a tobacco-scented kiss firmly on her mouth. 'It was real good of you and Jay to fix things up so we could get here. Worth every penny, too, even though it's so godawful cold. How do you people here live, for Chrissakes? Such weather and no damn central heating – it's a good thing I brought my own,' and he winked and patted a hip pocket which bulged neatly to show the shape of a large flask.

'Hello, Mizz Kincaid.' The slow drawl in the soft husky voice couldn't be ignored and Maddie turned and smiled brilliantly at her.

'How lovely to see you here!' she beamed and leaned forwards and set her cheek against Gloria's and kissed the air. 'And do call me Maddie, please! I'm so glad you were able to come – and isn't that Ellen Flannery there? It is! Lovely to see you again, too. We met once at the office in State Street in Boston, you remember? When you came in with your husband

– and is this your little boy? How nice to meet you – Dwight, is it? Yes, lovely to have you here. Come and meet my boys, now. They're a bit young for you, I know, but –'

She covered her wretchedness in a flurry of welcomes and Jay picked up her cue and began introductions. There were of course the Flannerys whom she'd met before in Boston, John James and Ellen, and she knew he was the owner of a string of taverns and bought all his liquor through Kincaids, and there were Mr and Mrs Martyn. 'Benny and Rose to you, Maddie. Benny and Rose,' said the woman boomingly, holding out a claw of a hand and grinning at her ferociously. 'I'm so sorry we never got to meet in Boston. Your dear mother-in-law is one of my greatest friends, or was, till she got so all-fired religious. She sure ain't the Blossom I was a girl with –'. And she cackled like a parrot, which she greatly resembled, dressed as she was in the most vivid of reds and yellows and greens and having a nut-brown and exceedingly lined face. 'Since we went to live in California,' she chattered, 'it ain't been so easy to keep in touch, except through business, but with my Benny sending out all his peaches and grapes and tomatoes through Kincaid's to the New York markets, we manage to hear what's going on. We keep in touch with old friends – it's the way we are. And are these your cute little boys then? Oh, aren't they just darling!'

And she went scrambling up the stand with an unnerving display of skinny wrinkled brown legs to sit beside the boys and start them off bawling again.

'We haven't met, Mrs Kincaid.' A short square man in a neat double-breasted suit and very colourful tie over a shirt so white it made her eyes water, held out one hand. 'Gian Giovale. It's a pleasure to meet you. My brother Umberto is over there, talking to Benny Martyn. You must talk to him later – he and your father used to know each other way back. Did some business, you know, before the war – old friends. I'm sorry to hear your father is sick and in the hospital. I'd like to have an address, so we can send a small remembrance to him.'

She took his hand and it was surprisingly warm and dry against her damp cold one and she felt the first moment of pleasure she had since the party had arrived. He was a cheerful man and he radiated friendliness but it wasn't that. She was puzzled for a moment and then realised that he made her feel good because he bore a fleeting likeness to her father as she remembered him rather than as he was now, the same ridges of glossy black hair shining with brilliantine and the lined forehead that made such friendly patterns when he lifted his brows. And she tightened her grip on Gian Giovale's hand and said almost fervently, 'How lovely to meet you! I'm so glad you could come!'

'I wouldn't have missed this for the world,' he said, and stood back to gesture her on to the stand, where the rest of the party was with much chatter and laughter arranging itself, deciding who should give the two small boys a lap since there were seats only for the eleven adults and ten-year-old Dwight (a large child who, clearly, Maddie had privately decided, ate more hot dogs and hamburgers and ice cream than suited his metabolism). Gian seemed determined to sit beside her, and she found herself on the end of a row of seats, with him beside her, while Jay, she saw as she leaned forwards, was sitting in the row in front between Cray and Gloria, with Daphne beside Gloria. And then she grinned a little wickedly, for Buster, with great determination, was climbing over Daphne's feet to get to his father, and was clearly intending to scramble over Gloria. That, she told herself with satisfaction, would be a far from happy experience for someone in such a stupidly tight skirt. And such fragile stockings, too, she added gleefully inside her head as she saw Buster's shoes thump against the expanse of nylon perfection that was all too visible.

She leaned back against her seat and smiled at Gian Giovale, who smiled back. 'Well?' he said. 'Can you relax now? The children are settled, so you can settle too, hmm? It's not easy being a Momma.'

'It certainly isn't,' Maddie said and her tones were heartfelt. 'They had to get up so early today, it made them a little tired and cross and I do so hate it if they upset people –'

'Listen, Mrs Kincaid, never apologise for babies. These two little men of yours – they are special, hey?' He too turned his head to look along the line to where Buster was now sitting firmly on Gloria's lap, swinging his legs so that his heels hit her shins with a thumping regularity. He seemed happy enough to be there, within touching distance of his father, and again Maddie smiled, seeing the look of discomfort that Gloria was barely able to conceal as Buster started wriggling as well as kicking. Maddie, who had had her share of Buster's wriggling, sat back again, well satisfied.

'Oh, yes, Mr Giovale. They're special.'

'Call me Gian,' he said and closed his warm hand on hers again, lifting it and putting it down on his knee. 'I can't tell you how I envy you and your Jay. All I ever wanted was a wife and children of my own, but there, it wasn't to be.' He shook his head a little mournfully and she saw his eyes were glittering with tears. 'My Momma was a magical lady, Maddie. I can call you Maddie, hmm? She was magic. She loved us and she cared for us and she brought us up good to show respect to her and to remember that there ain't no one like a mother. Umberto and me, all we are is what she made us, and me, I never forget. And I give to all mothers the same I gave her, respect and any help they want and at any time. You never forget, hey? You have any problems with your lovely little men and you come and tell me and I'll look after you and them.' Again he lifted her hand and made that patting gesture and she smiled at him, enjoying his easy sentimentality. There was something endearing about this bulky little man in the neat suit, and it was not just the fact that he had a likeness to Daddy. It was his earnestness, she decided, and gave him the widest and warmest of smiles she could.

'I won't forget,' she promised. 'Now tell me about yourself. You are a friend of my father-in-law?'

'Old Timothy and Umberto and me – we are like that,' Gian said solemnly and twisted his two forefingers together into a tight knot. 'For years we worked together. We go back to before 1933, you understand me? Before the Twenty-first Amendment.'

She looked blank for a moment and he grinned. 'You English. You don't know nothing, do you? The Twenty-first Amendment, Maddie, that was the end of Prohibition, right?'

'Oh!' she said and laughed. 'Of course – it must have been a very exciting time, Mr Giovale.'

'Call me Gian,' he said again and once more made his patting movement. It was getting uncomfortable and Maddie wanted to pull away, but didn't want to offend him, so she held on.

'It must have been an exciting time, Gian,' she said obediently.

'It was a profitable time, I'll tell you that much!' And he

laughed and beamed at her and she had to respond to his joviality and grinned back.

'Hey, you two!' Jay's voice came to her out of the rumbling of noise that was all around them. 'Pay some attention here! Listen, we have the hampers – we're taking a vote. Do we crack open some bottles now and have a little extra breakfast, or wait another while until just before the procession starts?'

'Now,' Gian said promptly and Buster, still in Gloria's lap, bawled gleefully, 'Now, now, now!' kicking vigorously and bouncing hard on each word.

'You heard your answer, Jay!' Benny Martyn cried loudly and reached for the hamper that was at the end of the row on which he was sitting. 'Here, let me help.'

The next few hours seemed to Maddie to be interminable. They ate a great deal – Jay had arranged for rolls filled with smoked salmon and cream cheese to be provided to give his American guests, he said, a taste of home, and the champagne, though warm from its long stay in the baskets, was plentiful and Jay was generous with it. The children ate their rusks and drank their blackcurrant – narrowly escaping spilling it all over themselves and everyone within reach – as below them in the road the police and the crowds and excitement became more and more noisy and intense as the time for the procession came closer.

By the time it started, to deafening cheers and an outburst of waving and jumping that made the stands they were on sway terrifyingly, most of the party were very happy indeed on their champagne. Only Maddie seemed to have been upset by it, she decided as she massaged her temples discreetly and scrabbled in her handbag for more aspirin. At least she hadn't to worry too much about the children. Danny was now fast asleep on Daphne's lap, his thumb firmly in his mouth and his plump legs spread wide and helpless – and she melted a little at the sight of him; he was always so very endearing when he was asleep – and Buster was at last sitting still, curled up on Jay's lap now. But even as Maddie watched, and saw his eyelids beginning to droop, a fact for which she was deeply glad for the child was getting far too fractious and excited and needed a rest – he lifted him gently sideways and deposited him back in Gloria's lap.

But this didn't disturb Buster, who simply pushed his head

into her shoulder, and closed his eyes and copied his infant brother, pushing his thumb into his mouth and falling immediately and happily asleep. And now Maddie did not feel nearly as pleased to see Gloria with him. She caught a glance the girl threw at Jay, a sideways little smile, and a pang of the old jealousy came bursting up from the root of her belly like a hot knife.

'I must rescue Miss Costello,' she murmured to Gian, and got to her feet and with some difficulty passed him and Ellen and Dwight at the end of the row in front, to reach Gloria.

'I'll take him,' she murmured as she got there, reaching for Buster, but Gloria smiled up at her dreamily and said, 'Oh, don't you worry yourself, Mizz Kincaid! He's no trouble at all, none in the world. It's a pleasure to have him here. Just you go and relax and enjoy yourself, now. You have him all the time – let me share him for a while, hmm?'

'That is nice of you, Gloria!' Jay said heartily, turning back from Cray with whom he'd been in close colloquy. 'Isn't that great, Maddie? Hey, look – is that the Queen's coach? I do believe it is! Look, back there, they're just coming round that mess of statues in front of the Palace – hey, will you listen to them shout! Jesus, but who'd ha' thought it?' And he jumped to his feet as did half the rest of the stand's occupants as they all waved to the coach that even on this grey drizzling day managed to glitter like tinsel in a pantomime as it passed just below them.

And Maddie went back to her seat beside Gian Giovale, and tried to take pleasure in watching the Coronation procession of Queen Elizabeth the Second instead of worrying about Gloria Costello.

27

June 1953

Getting back to the Savoy Hotel from the Mall after it was all over, and the noisy procession with its columns of red-uniformed guardsmen, glossy head-tossing, harness-clinking black horses and the eternity of gleaming glittering carriages led by brass bands had returned to the Palace, was even more difficult than getting there had been. The crowds were now milling around everywhere, organising impromptu dancing along the pavements, climbing lamp posts and bouncing in and out of the overcrowded pubs and cafés and coffee bars in eddying groups that made a steady forward passage hazardous in the extreme. But somehow they managed it, steaming gently as their efforts heated them up and sent the damp their clothes had collected from the relentless rain back into the grey air, and humping their rugs and the empty hampers and the weary children and each other along with as much cheerfulness as Jay could muster in them with encouraging hails and grins and waves as he led the way.

But once they were there the day picked up again. Jay had gone to considerable trouble to entertain his guests, renting a suite on the river side of the hotel in which he ordered champagne and afternoon tea for them all – much to the American visitors', especially Rose's, shrieks of delight at the sight of the little sandwiches and the scones and jam and cream – and booking a big table for them all at the dinner and ball that was to be held at the hotel that evening. After they had all fallen on the food and drink, Daphne and the boys were scooped up by Rose and borne away to her suite on the third floor where they could be dried and changed and take much-needed naps, for which Maddie was deeply grateful, and Gloria too disappeared to her room, drifting away with murmurs about nose powdering, while Cray and Benny Martyn and the Giovale brothers sat at a table in the corner of the suite and settled to

243

some serious drinking of Cray's whisky and the Flannery family, especially Dwight, enjoyed the remaining food and seemed happily oblivious of everyone else. For the first time Maddie felt she could talk to Jay – and didn't know what to say.

She knew what she ached to say. Why had he asked the Costellos rather than other Kincaid customers? And having asked them, why had he not told her they were coming? And why Gloria anyway? Her father was the important Kincaid contact, surely; if Jay wanted to impress some of his father's most important business colleagues why waste a place on a stupid girl who didn't matter? Unless, of course, she did matter –

'How come your folks and Declan didn't come, Jay?' she managed at last, and complimented herself on her tact. 'Didn't you suggest it? It would have been nice to see them all.' And she smiled at him brilliantly to hide her mendacity. The only good thing about the situation was the absence of Blossom.

'Pa's not fit to travel,' Jay said. 'I asked him to bring Mother and the girls but he said *he* couldn't, so he sure as hell wasn't going to pay for Mother and the girls to whoop it up if he couldn't be around too. As for Declan –' He scowled then. 'Someone has to mind the store. He gets enough benefit being there in Boston all the time. He doesn't have to come here and get in the way. The people who are here are all important – they have money. Lots of it. And they spend it with us. I make a nice piece out of their business. Not as nice as I'd make if Declan weren't there, but nice all the same.' He paused then and reached for a plate of sandwiches. 'Most of it comes from Costello, of course. Once the Beach project's done, I'm hoping to get him going on some of the redevelopment here. Christ knows it's needed. He's got the money to invest, people here want the buildings – if I can sort out the permits and the money exchange business it could be very pretty. I have to be very nice to Cray – and thank God, Queen Elizabeth was willing to give me a hand.' And he grinned at her and even though his mouth was full of egg sandwich, and he was a little dishevelled from the day's damp efforts, he looked so young and so wonderful that she felt herself melting, and she reached for him and lifted her face and kissed his cheek.

'Anything Queen Elizabeth can do for you, I can,' she murmured. 'If you want me to charm the man out of his tree and prove to him what a great place London'd be to build in, just say the word –'

He laughed. 'You'd better get yourself sorted out first,' he said. 'Have you looked in a mirror since we got here?'

She pulled back from him, her face scarlet. 'For Christ's sake, Jay! What do you expect with two kids to deal with and weather like this and –'

'So? Leave them to Daphne, for God's sake. She's the first decent girl we've had – *use* her. Go and get yourself changed, hmm? There's some sort of reception here at half after six, then there's the dinner and the ball. It's cost a godamn fortune to set it all up, so I'm counting on you to make it all look good. You too – what are you wearing?'

Mollified by his interest she said, 'I'm not telling you. Not in detail. You don't think I don't know it's important to look right tonight, do you? I've got a new dress. I've had it for weeks. It's from Worth. I warn you, it cost a bomb.'

'Where is it? You don't have to go home to dress, do you?'

She shook her head. 'Don't be daft! I'm going over to Marianne's flat in Covent Garden. It's all been arranged for ages. I can walk there and back, and I'll be fine, even in this weather. It'd be easier if you came too, of course –' And she looked at him sideways, hopefully. But he shook his head.

'I'm changing in Cray's suite. My tux is up there already. Okay, Maddie, go and sort yourself out. I'll change later – I want to have a word with Flannery before I go up and dress.' And he patted her rump and dropped a swift kiss on her cheek and went across the room to sit down beside the still eating Flannerys and start talking to them.

She sat for a while longer watching and then slowly got up and slipped away to go and find Daphne and the boys. There was no need to worry, she told herself as she padded damply along the thickly carpeted corridors towards the lifts. No need in the world. It's all fine. He's like me, cares only for the business and money. And me. She repeated it inside her head and then said it aloud. 'And me.'

Daphne was indeed the best nanny they had ever had. Both

the boys were asleep in Rose's big bed, and Daphne was occupied in drying out their clothes and packing up the baskets they had brought.

'Don't you worry about us, Mummy,' she said in her jolly Northern voice, full of relentless cheerfulness. 'I've got everything organised,' and indeed she had and Maddie relaxed, not minding as much as she usually did Daphne's refusal to address her as anything but Mummy, which, since Daphne was half a head taller and a good deal heavier, did rankle.

'Will you be able to get back to the car with the boys without trouble?' she asked. 'It'd be a pity to wake them yet to take them home, but unless we go now, I can't go with you. I have to go and change for the ball —'

'I told you, don't worry about a thing,' Daphne said brightly, and smoothed her apron smugly. 'It's all arranged. Mr Martyn says he can miss part of the reception on account of he doesn't like standing about much, and he'll come with me down to the car and then I'll take the boys home and you can stay and enjoy yourselves, you and Daddy —'

'It is essential business entertainment, Daphne,' Maddie heard herself sounding apologetic and was annoyed and that sharpened her tone. 'If I had my way I'd gladly come home and spend the evening quietly watching television, but as it is, we have to be here.'

'Of course you do,' Daphne said, managing to sound both soothing and jolly at the same time. 'And you need to have a rest first yourself. Go over to your nice friend's flat, now, do, and take your time dressing. And the boys and I will see you in the morning.'

So she did, and it was an oasis in what was proving to be a wearing day and not just for the most obvious reasons. Marianne was, as she knew she would be, out, and she let herself into her racy little flat in Henrietta Street with its rather outrageous, indeed decadent, decor and ran a bath in the round black tub and filled it with handfuls of Marianne's most expensive bathsalts. There was, she told herself, little point in having as expensive and lavish a friend as an actress like Marianne if you didn't make the best use of her you could, and she wallowed in the scented water and tried to think of agreeable things like her new dress that was waiting to be put on and the smell of the bath and the sense of silken hot water on her body. Anything but think of that girl and Jay . . .

I'll bet she hasn't got stretch marks, she thought lugubriously as she climbed out of the bath and stood watching herself dry her now pink and glowing skin. She tried not to look at her body but it was impossible since the bathroom walls were completely mirrored as was the ceiling and even the back of the door, and what she saw fed her uncertainty. And she stopped for a moment as she rubbed her feet dry and thought, when did that happen? I never used to worry about how I looked or what people thought of me. I was certain and excited and everything was so easy and right – I knew what had to be done and I did it. Why can't I be like that now?

Because you are older and have two children and the stretch marks they gave you and your breasts are softer and lower than they used to be, a part of her mind answered, and she felt the most bitter pang of regret she had ever known as she straightened up and looked at herself properly. I didn't know I was beautiful when I was, she thought. Now I look and all I see is what has gone; and tears started in her eyes and she had to sniff hard to hold them back. It was almost the way she had felt during those dreadful months after Buster's birth, and she shook her head to clear it of such foolish thoughts and went padding out of the steamy bathroom into the cool of the bedroom, and threw herself on to Marianne's purple counterpane to lie staring up at the ceiling with its drapes of matching billowing purple silk and take a series of deep breaths.

This was all nonsense. She was far from being sensible in being so obsessively suspicious of that silly vapid Costello girl. She meant nothing to Jay. Jay cared only for his business and his family and certainly never worried about such minor items as stretch marks, and Maddie smoothed her hands over her soft belly as she lay there stretched out and remembered last night's lovemaking and felt good, and a little sleepy too. It was a much pleasanter way to feel than she had been.

She woke suddenly and stared up at the ceiling in amazement, totally disoriented and then turned her head to look at Marianne's clock and nearly fell out of the bed in dismay as she leapt up and rushed to dress. It was gone six and she'd promised Jay she'd be back at the hotel in ample time to receive all their guests at the reception. She had just twenty minutes in which to dress, make up, repair her hair and get through the crowds down to the Strand and into the hotel. And she almost wept as the spring of anxiety inside her tightened inexorably as she rushed herself into her underclothes and into her new dress, a sheath of dull bronze taffeta pulled to the right hip in a great sash bow, and held over just one shoulder. It looked marvellous, and once she had it on she felt much better, and in a moment of inspiration brushed her hair up into a great aureole of curls and riffled through Marianne's bottles and sprays to see what she could find; and discovered bronze sequins in a small box and, using a plastic bottle of hair lacquer she had seen Marianne use once, managed to stick some of them to her hair. It looked odd and interesting and she stared at herself and thought triumphantly – match that, Mizz bloody Costello, match that if you can.

She was only ten minutes late getting to the reception, and she stood in the entrance to the main ballroom looking round and saw him standing against the wall, talking to Cray, and smiled at the sight of him. He had said he was wearing a tux but had gone one better and she admired him for that; clearly he'd taken himself to Moss Bros and found a well-fitting set of tails and he stood there with one hand in his pocket so that the tails drooped elegantly behind him, with his dark gold head bent over the stocky man beside him and Maddie sighed deeply with pleasure and moved across the room towards him, knowing she looked good, and also something that was better than good; she looked striking. She knew that from the way people's heads turned as she passed and she curved her lips into a little Mona Lisa smile of self-satisfaction as she drifted to his side.

And was well repaid for her efforts for he turned and looked, letting his gaze slide from her feet up to her head and back again and then smiled.

'Great!' he said. 'Just great. What have you done to your hair? Sequins? Wow – you look fantastic – you really are one crazy kid, Maddie. And that dress – well worth waiting for.'

'I told you it was a Worth dress,' she said and laughed softly and Costello laughed too, loudly, chucking back his head to display his appreciation of the joke.

'And you'll see how much *you're* worth by the time you've

paid for it, hey, Jay? But it's a lovely dress, Maddie. You look as good as the Queen herself –'

'And so does your daughter, Mr Costello,' she said graciously and smiled and turned to make room for Gloria. She had seen her as soon as she had arrived, of course. She looked pretty, Maddie decided, if a shade obvious, in a froth of pale blue silk chiffon skirt and the skimpiest of strapless bodices embroidered with glass beads, and she was trailing a very long chiffon stole with it, quite in the very latest style. But Maddie knew it to be a girlish look which had none of the sophistication and excitement of her own and she felt there was no contest. And her spirits lifted and bubbled and she turned back to Cray Costello and started to chatter vivaciously at him as the rest of their party joined them and the day's ubiquitous champagne, now spiked with brandy and served in sugar-frosted glasses to make cocktails, appeared at their sides, borne by Savoy waiters on their best behaviour.

'It's been the greatest day ever, Jay!' Benny Martyn boomed at them all, holding his glass high and then draining it at one draught and looking round for more. 'The greatest. To be here at such a historical business and to share it with you British – and you're so witty about it, too. I just heard a guy over there saying someone asked who that little guy was in the same carriage as Queen Salote of Tonga – you remember, that fat black broad who waved so much? And Noël Coward was there and he said, "The little guy? That's her lunch, I guess." ' And he swallowed his second cocktail and laughed so hard Maddie thought he would choke. But he recovered and slapped Jay on the back, and roared even louder. 'I tell you, the greatest day. Worth every penny it cost – you're a great guy to fix it for us, eh, Rose?' And Rose screeched and chattered something in a loud parrotty squawk and then everyone was chattering and laughing as the cocktails came round yet again and the vast room filled up.

Benny really was right, Maddie declared. It *was* a magnificent occasion. Heaven knew they were not unused to such events, she and Jay. There were the over-elaborate Masonic Ladies' Nights to which they were so often invited by business contacts, the charity dinners and balls they supported to placate some business contact which were much like this and held in the great

London hotels like this, but this evening was special. People had taken extra trouble to dress well, and the whole atmosphere bubbled with money and excitement and optimism. The bad years, the evening seemed to say, were really over. The Festival two years ago had been the start of it all, the birth of the new Britain where there was fun to be had and work to be done and above all money to be made. No more austerity, no more post-war misery, no more making do and skimping. From now on it was to be growth and expansion and a truly new and truly Great Britain, and she smiled again at the thought of how much that could mean to she and Jay, with their thriving business which was so much bigger and so much more successful than its shabby and understated Great Portland Street offices would ever suggest. We're well and truly on our way to being millionaires, Jay and I, she thought as the brandied champagne swirled delightfully around her head. Well on the way. No need to worry, no need to feel uncertain. Just be ready to work and make it all wonderful; and she drifted into dinner on Jay's arm and ate her way through its six courses, and chattered her way through its three wines as full of happiness and self assurance as a bubble is of air.

The bubble burst when they were dancing. All through dinner he had talked with Cray and only Cray across Gloria, who had been sitting between them (and Maddie had not been able to disguise the pleasure she felt when she saw how bored the girl looked, as she sat there crumbling her bread roll between her fingers for want of something better to do) but once they had reached the dessert stage and conversation had become general, he had concentrated on everyone else at the table. And that, of course, had been exactly as it should be, and she had followed his lead, being the perfect hostess, as busy in her chatter with their guests as he was.

But now, at last they could talk to each other and she slid into his arms gratefully as the band swooped into a syrupy medley of the songs from *Kismet* with 'Stranger in Paradise' to start with, and rested her head against his shoulder and let him lead her as he chose.

They danced for a minute or more as she hummed the tune softly and then he said, 'Maddie, I have a problem.'

'Mm?' It really was remarkable how rested and floaty she

felt, and she went on humming '– lost in a wonderland, a stranger in Paradise –'

'It's Declan.' He sounded sombre and she lifted her head and looked up at him, aware of the dazzle in her vision, and said carefully, 'Declan? What about him?'

'It's always the same,' he burst out, as the song ended and the band went immediately into a sprightly rendition of 'Baubles, bangles and beads'. 'As soon as I turn my back that bastard's got all four feet in the trough. Cray's been telling me – he's milked a cool forty thousand out of the business this past two years, he reckons. And he should know on account of he's the money man in the conglomerate, right? He says it ought to be sorted out for my good. Pa's not able. He's well past it, Cray says, and someone else has to be in charge. No use looking to Timothy Two – he's got himself bogged down in Washington, Cray says, it's amazing he ever finds time to take a crap, so it's no use looking to him to do anything useful –'

'What about your sisters?' she said, lifting her chin to stare at him, feeling the excitement and delight in the evening begin to flatten inside her. 'Can't they help?'

He snorted at that, turning her into the swirl of the dancers yet again as they reached the outer edge of the dance floor. 'The girls? Be your age, Maddie! What good is a girl in business? Women like you don't come more'n once in a blue moon, believe me. I can't get any help from them –'

The excitement and the delight bubbled back in all its glory and she slid her hand from his shoulder to his cheek. 'Darling, I do see the problem – but what can we do? Will Costello be able to sort it out for you?'

'Come on, Maddie! It's not his interests that are at stake! He knows perfectly well that Kincaid's is entitled to its share of the profits. He's not complaining about that. He just wanted me to know that too much of that money isn't going into Kincaid's, but being filtered straight out to Declan. So, Pa and me and the girls – and Mother, of course – lose out. That's why he told me – it's no goddamned skin off his nose. He's just a good guy, Cray. Best friend I could have over there, and that's a fact.'

'Then –' she began and stopped, knowing all too well and too painfully what was to come.

'Then I've no choice, have I?' he said savagely. 'I've got to go and sort the bastard out. I've had enough of this and I have to get it clear once and for all. Declan has to learn and no one else can teach him. I'll have to go back with them all, Maddie. It's a bastard, but what else can I do?'

'We'll come with you, the children and I —' she began but even as the words came out she knew it was impossible.

'And who takes care of what happens here in the meantime? I've got Dave Catterick and the Poundsley fella dealing with a lot of the stuff, but you know as well as I do they can't be trusted without being watched. Catterick's good, gets a lot of stuff set up, but he only hangs around for the pleasure of seeing where he can cut us up. I let him have a little just to sweeten him, but on his own? No question of it!'

'Then I have to stay here —'

'Like I said before, someone's got to mind the store. With Declan minding my other store the way *he* is what can I do? I'll try not to be away too long, Maddie. Goddamn it, I've got so many sweet little deals cooking up nicely here it's a bastard to have to leave them —'

'I know,' she said dully. 'The hospital development in Kent and the German shipping deal —'

'Yeah,' he said. 'And there's the spade work I've started to put in on that distillery in Ireland. Can you handle that? I have a good deal of the documentation already.'

'If you've time to show me before you go, I can manage,' she said and then as the music ended with a flourish of drums let her hands slide down his elegant tailcoat and tried to smile at him.

'I'll miss you, Jay,' she said huskily and stared at him with her face quite still, in spite of her efforts to look agreeable. 'How long will you be?'

He shrugged and turned to lead her back to their table. 'How can I know? I'll be back as soon as I can manage it. D'you think I want to be away? You know I don't. But what choice have I?'

'None, I suppose,' she said and followed him, her feet dragging a little. Any more than I have, she thought miserably. I have to let you go, whether I want to or not. And then as his broad black back moved away from her line of vision and she could see the table, and saw Gloria look up and smile a welcome to him, it all came rushing back, the jealousy, the doubts and the anger. And she stood there and stared at Cray

Costello sitting so complacently beside his daughter, with his round face and his elaborate gold jewellery and expensive clothes and then at Gloria again, and felt herself so consumed with hatred for both of them that had they been within reach, she might even have hit out.

But all she did was sit down again, and try to imagine how she would cope with Jay in America without her for the next couple of weeks. It was a horrible prospect.

28

June–August 1953

But it wasn't two weeks. It wasn't even four. It was for much longer than that, and she spent a lot of time at the beginning dreaming of the day he would be back.

He had gone by sea, travelling on the *Queen Elizabeth*, and that had irked her when he had first told her, for it would have been swifter by air. But as he had pointed out reasonably enough, there would be little point in getting back before Cray Costello. He had promised to help Jay deal with Declan, so what else could he do but travel with him?

'I thought of waiting till they were back in the States, and then going by air,' he had said to her, that night after they had got home and were lying in bed talking into the small hours, 'but I didn't think that'd be good politics. Cray wants to help me – so I have to be seen to be making an effort for him, right? I'd rather stay here another week, fly there, sort it out and be back before the end of the month when the Irish meeting's due, but there it is, I have to go now. But I should be able to fly back and that'll help, hmm? I'll miss you, Maddie, quite apart from business –' and he had turned and nuzzled her neck and they had made love and that had been important to her; not because it was so wonderful (it wasn't, but then that happened fairly often now that she got so tired, what with the two boys as well as the office to worry about) but because it had been comforting. As long as Jay needed her as much as he was now making patently clear, she had no need to worry.

But just dreaming of his return would not be enough to keep her even tolerably content. She needed more than that to cushion herself against her loneliness, so she took to filling in the waiting time with work. The children had settled so well with Daphne that at least she didn't have to worry about them. There were no more tantrums and scenes when she went out, no panics because the nanny had left in a huff and the daily help had to phone and insist she come home immediately. All that was now forgotten as the house and children settled into a smooth easy-running system under Daphne's care and Maddie could pour all her energies into the affairs of Alfred Braham Export Ltd.

So she did work, much longer hours than she needed to. She would get to the office well before nine so that she could deal with the post and be ready to get the secretaries and clerks busy as soon as they arrived – and by being so early herself she made sure that they learned to come in well on time – and then had more opportunity to oversee the other two men on the staff. Catterick, who was Jay's immediate deputy in normal circumstances, and Poundsley, a young man who was bright and eager and was being trained to take on more work, seemed willing to let her lead the way, and were as energetic in doing as she told them as they had been in obeying Jay's lead; which was a comfort. So often, in her experience, men took umbrage rather than orders from women bosses. It was good that these two men were more sensible than that. But she discovered very soon that in fact Jay had not been a good boss at all, and it might have been that fact that made the two men welcome her so willingly. He had clearly not been working as hard as he might have been, as far as she could tell, having spent large parts of the working day lunching or having meetings with potential clients at which there was more emphasis on conviviality than useful work.

She herself had come into the office to help whenever she could, but the demands which her last pregnancy and then the care of the boys had made on her had made sure that these occasions were too few and too scattered to make her really aware of the way the business was running. But now she could find out and was irritated.

They were not personally short of money, or didn't seem to be; Jay paid their way comfortably as far as she knew, but they were by no means as rich as she had been led to believe. She had seen herself and Jay as a millionaire couple on Coronation night; now she knew they were a long way from that – but she also knew that they could rapidly become one with a good deal more effort. So she made it.

June slid away in a series of twelve- to fourteen-hour days

and long meetings well into the night as she mobilised the two men – and the extra staff she later took on – to be much more vigorous in their hunting down of new contracts, new clients, new possibilities. It wasn't difficult; the optimism that was everywhere this Coronation year lingered well after the event itself. People were eager to do business and particularly eager to do it with a firm that seemed to be quick and thrusting and ready to take on major jobs without implying they were doing anyone a favour.

So, before Jay had been away a month, she had landed no fewer than five major new clients and had three big projects in hand. The company had begun to diversify into much the same sort of avenues as the Boston company and now a carefully engraved plate, reading 'Braham's Construction Co.', joined the brass plate that was already beside the modest street door that led up to the third floor from Great Portland Street, and Catterick spent most of his time rushing about the country tracking down suppliers of bricks and mortar, timber and glass, plumbing fixtures and roof tiles and all the myriad things needed to build a hospital, albeit a small one.

It really was surprising, she discovered, how well she felt on her new regime. She would get home much too late to see the boys awake but would creep into their nursery to look at them and to melt at the sight of the starfish hands wide flung on their pillows and the long eyelashes shading their cheeks, and then would fall into bed, exhausted, but feeling well for all that. She missed Jay dreadfully, of course, she would tell herself sleepily, but it was nice to be able to keep her body to herself a little; and she would drift off contentedly and sleep better than she had done since before Buster's birth.

They spoke on the telephone once a week, each Friday night, just before she went to bed and Jay went to his folks, he would tell her each time, to eat dinner.

'I'm sorry this is taking so long, honey,' he would bawl at her through the crackling line, his voice fading and reappearing and then fading again. 'It's more of a mess than I knew – there are things here that have to be dealt with that I just can't polish off in a week. Maybe the start of July I'll be back. How goes the Irish business?'

'Fine, fine,' Maddie shouted back, not wanting to waste their precious time detailing just how fine; she had bought in to the new distillery at a remarkably favourable price and already the market in the shares was rising fast. She had managed to persuade the board there to let Braham's do some building for them too, and had already signed a contract for a £250,000 job; but she'd tell him all that when he came back. She was looking forward eagerly to being able to sit at a desk with him and go through all the documents and show him just how well she had done for them all while he'd been away. Now, on the phone, there were more important things to discuss.

'How much do you miss me?' she shouted and heard the faint echo of her own voice on the line, '. . . miss me . . . miss me . . .' and then Jay, remote and disembodied, crying, 'What did you say?'

'I miss you,' she shouted even more loudly. 'I miss you, and so do the boys – a hell of a lot –'

'I'll talk to you next week, honey. Keep on going, kid. I can't hear you tonight – sleep well. Talk to you next Friday . . .'

All very unsatisfactory, and yet she managed somehow, because of the office and its demands; and it was really remarkable just how much comfort there was to be found in work. She spent her Sundays driving down to Kent where their first major building operation was beginning to see progress to check the state of the site and generally to reassure herself that all was going as it should, and every other day of the week, including Saturday, on the telephone or checking ledgers or head to head with their accounts and insurance people to see where they could pick up more equity and grow their money faster. It was an exhilarating, dramatic and curious time, for she felt as though she were operating fully on just one cylinder, while the other, the one that was Jay and happiness at home and peace of mind, had shut down altogether. Yet she forged forwards because that one working cylinder was so very powerful.

But July limped into August and she began to get more restless, in spite of the pleasures and successes of work. Jay had been gone almost eight weeks now. He had warned her after the second week that it would take longer than he'd hoped; Kincaid's, he told her on the phone, were to have a new corporate set-up, and to make that work all the family had to be in the

State Street office at the same time to sign the necessary documents. His sisters could be rounded up well enough in the next month — but there was no way they could get Timothy Two out of Washington until the end of a committee on which he was sitting and which, according to Timothy, was the greatest thing in his life since it could lead to his nomination for a winnable seat in Congress.

'He won't come till August's end at the earliest,' Jay bawled on yet another bad phone line. 'So hold on to your hat, honey. Is it still going well? You can manage? Is Catterick seeing that things are ticking over?'

'We're ticking over,' she said and grinned to herself as she tucked the phone more closely to her ear to try to hear him the better. Wait till he comes home and sees just how well; oh, but it was almost worth being without him for the joy of that prospect. 'We're doing fine. I miss you, darling —'

It was in the second week of August as work slowed down everywhere, with most of Britain on holiday and refusing even to think of overtime let alone doing any, which was what Maddie most wanted from her own and everyone else's staff, that a message was sent from the nursing home about Alfred. 'Would Mrs Kincaid,' the secretary said, 'please call them as soon as possible —' and had added no, she didn't know why, and no, they hadn't said it was urgent, or at least she didn't think they had.

Maddie was in the middle of a complex discussion with Catterick, sorting out a new bonus scheme she had dreamed up for making sure he was as honest as it was possible for a man dealing with someone else's money to be. She had devised it with the accountant who had complimented her on her sharp mind, while looking at her rather woodenly as he contemplated the deviousness of her ideas, and it seemed foolproof. If Catterick worked hard and closely supervised Poundsley, he could benefit more from honesty than from milking the job in the time-honoured way was what it amounted to, and as she sat there with him and described it as simply — and as tactfully — as she could, she forgot about the message from the nursing home.

She had in fact given sadly little thought to Alfred lately. There was no point in making herself miserable about him, for there was nothing she could do to improve his situation, so she had deliberately stopped herself from thinking about him. As a result he had become more and more morose and more and more unwilling to talk once he had realised there was nowhere else for him to go than the nursing home. Her visits to him had become agonising hours spent being as bright and cheerful as she could, doling out delicacies and chocolates and little bottles of brandy from her bag while he sat and glared balefully at her and said nothing. It had been inevitable that with the new pattern of her life, office-centred as it was, he would slip into the background of her thoughts so easily.

And so he died on the fourteenth of August, the morning that the nursing home matron phoned to warn her that her father was very ill, that he had slipped into a coma and if Maddie wanted to see him alive she had better come now.

That had been what the Matron had intended to tell her as soon as she phoned back, not feeling it right, she told Maddie later in her most self-righteous manner, to discuss private family matters with a mere employee like a secretary.

But Maddie didn't get round to phoning until late afternoon, and by that time Alfred Braham was dead.

It was a dreadful week. She cabled Jay, swallowed up in a great wave of guilt and loneliness so vast that she wanted him and only him, but all he could do was telephone and offer his condolences and tell her he couldn't get back in time for the funeral, which was to be on the Sunday immediately after the death, at Golders Green Crematorium.

'Listen honey, sure I'd like to be there, to take care of things, pay the old man my respects, but what can I do? If I left here right this minute, I'd be too late, and I'd still have to come back here. It'd be crazy. I send you all my wishes in your sorrow and that but, come on, honey, he was a sick old man! It was a blessed release – it'd be a sin to wish such a one a longer life than he had. Talk to Barney about the will, okay? He'll see to the probate and so forth. You are the only beneficiary, aren't you? Yeah – so, that'll be okay. Leave it to Barney. Lawyers understand these things – he'll take good care of you.'

Barney had, but it hadn't been the same as it would have been having Jay there, and she stood in the small bleak chapel at the crematorium with half a dozen men in dark suits and bowler hats who had emerged from the shadows of her father's past to see him on his way and murmur their condolences to his sole surviving child, and then drove herself home again to Stanmore through the heavy clamminess of the lowering August day and wanted to weep and couldn't.

Daddy, she thought, and made herself remember him as he had been when she was young, with his glossy dark hair and his grin and his loud talk, but not a tear could she force through her eyes. They remained stubbornly hot and dry as she pushed the MG through the Sunday quiet roads, past the houses with their gardens full of tired roses dripping their thick cloying scent, and took her mind even further back to her childhood, to the time when her mother had died in that air raid. That had been something she could rely on to make her cry, once.

But it didn't now. All she could do was stare out at the world from her hot dry eyes, behind her hard still face which felt as stiff and expressionless as if it were made of cardboard, and think and remember and feel nothing whatsoever. It was a horrible way to be.

Daphne fussed over her agreeably when she got home, fetching her hot milk and brandy to drink, which she loathed but she tried to drink it to please her. The girl had become ever more important to her over the past couple of months, taking as she did so many of her domestic burdens from her, and she was grateful to her, and needed her too; and now she lifted her head and looked at her and said huskily, 'Thanks, Daphne. I don't now what I'd do without you. You've been great, you really have –'

'That's all right, Mummy, you don't have to thank me! I know how it is. I know what happened when my granny died. I cried for a week and I thought the world'd come to an end, I did that – it were awful. Oh, I know how you feel all right, Mummy –' And she patted Maddie's shoulder and pushed the hot milk towards her invitingly.

And at last Maddie cried, at the thought of this large and relentlessly cheerful girl weeping for a week over her granny. The image of Daphne with her jolly round face twisted with tears rose in front of her and she felt her own cardboard face soften at last and twist itself into runnels and channels down which tears could run, and then they did, like a shower of pain that left even more pain behind it. Daphne's granny was dead –

it was a dreadful pitiful thing, and she had to cry for it; Daphne's granny —

'There, there, my duck, just you let it go, then,' Daphne said in high satisfaction. 'It's better out than in, that's for sure. You just have a good howl there — you'll feel the good of it, you see if you don't —' And hearing her granny's voice masquerading as Daphne's, Maddie cried even more and with increasing abandon until even Daphne became alarmed and started to try to soothe her and persuade her to go to bed.

But still Maddie wept on, and at last Daphne said, 'Eh, I don't know — perhaps I ought to phone Daddy in America, tell him it's made you so poorly, losing your Dad, that he'd better come home —'

Maddie managed to shake her head at that. 'I — he can't —' she managed. 'Business — he's got to stay there. He can't come home —' And then she wept even more, but this time it was because Jay couldn't come home, rather than because of Daphne's granny.

'Well, then, maybe you ought to go to him then,' Daphne said and patted her shoulder again. 'It's not right you should be on your own at such a time. Why not take some time off and go and see Daddy, then? The boys'd love it, you know. They miss him as much as you do, Mummy — and it'll be a little holiday to be in a ship, wouldn't it?'

At last the tears began to ease, subsiding slowly as the image created by the words in the flat Northern voice began to form and then strengthen before her eyes. She and Jay, together. That was what she most wanted. And if he couldn't be here, then why indeed should she not be there? And the image wavered a little as she thought of Pa and Blossom and then strengthened once more as Jay moved into the middle of it. And she lifted her head and said huskily, 'Me go to Jay? Oh, Daphne, do you think I could?'

'I don't see why not,' Daphne said and beamed at her, clearly delighted with herself that she had managed to hold the storm. 'It's where you need to be right now, 'nt it? Families ought to be to-gether when they've been bereaved. It's only natural. You go and see Daddy, Mummy. It's what you *need*. And it'd be nice for the boys too, wouldn't it?' And she set her head on one side and smiled winningly. 'If you feel you'd like to take us with you, that is.'

29

August 1953

She considered flying, to get there as fast as was humanly possible, but that really would have been difficult. It wasn't just the thought of the cost, high as that would be for two adults and two children – about five hundred pounds – it was the sheer misery such a journey would mean. Ten hours, even in one of BOAC's much vaunted stratocruisers, with two restless boisterous children – its discomfort and misery could be imagined all too clearly; and when she heard that there had to be a two-hour stopover at Gander as well as at Prestwick, that settled it. Even at the cost of spending five days on the journey it had to be by sea.

She managed to get a large double cabin, into which cots could be put for the boys, on the SS *Media* out of Liverpool on 25 August, the following Saturday, and that meant a massive effort to get them away. She left the packing of everything, not only for the boys but also for herself, to Daphne who was in a fever of excitement at being taken to America, and concentrated on the office arrangements. She was deeply glad she had started the new scheme for Catterick; leaving him in charge would be not only safe but effective. He had as big a stake in the success of Braham's Construction as she had now, and she made sure he had meticulously detailed instructions on what to do and when to do it, and how to cope in any foreseeable emergency in her absence, however long it turned out to be.

And then caught the boat train from King's Cross in a welter of luggage and last-minute parcels of objects with which Daphne was sure the boys could not possibly travel, and collapsed into her corner seat to face the four or more hours of inactivity that lay ahead of her. For the first time since Alfred's death she had time to think, and she took a deep breath and closed her eyes against the hubbub the boys were already kicking up, leaving Daphne to cope, and relaxed.

And then, of course, the doubts began. Perhaps she should have called or at least cabled Jay to tell him they were on the way? The idea of surprising him had seemed so attractive when it came into her mind that she had not queried it; she had just agreed with herself that that was what she would do. But now, as the train grumbled its way furiously over the points and went roaring northwards out of London through Finsbury Park and Edmonton, past the soot-encrusted chimneys and the brave if twisted trees and shrubs beside the line which bent their heads against the combined onslaught of the summer heat and the engines that spewed great gouts of steam over them, the uncertainty came boiling up in her.

Would he understand why she had felt so desperate a need to be with him? Would he be angry with her because she had not stayed to deal with the legal aspects of her father's death? But there was no need for that, she told herself defensively. Barney Copeman, their solicitor, had assured her that he could look after it all. He had all the necessary signatures, and the will had been a well-prepared document; she was not needed in London. And, he had added reasonably enough, Boston wasn't the end of the world. She could get back soon enough if she was really needed.

But all the same, maybe a surprise won't be all that agreeable to him, and she opened her eyes to stare out of the grimy window at the fields fleeing past and thought, I'll cable from the ship. Then he won't have to wait so long once he knows until we arrive, and it will be a bit of a surprise, if not a total one. And satisfied with the decision, she fell asleep.

That kept on happening all through the journey. They made the exchange from train to ship without too much drama, taking into account the fact that Buster chose to run off and disappear for almost fifteen minutes in the great echoing luggage shed, and settled into the cabin with dispatch, thanks to Daphne's efficiency. She had then taken the boys off to explore, as she put it, and left Maddie to relax, and she had promptly slept again. And had gone on sleeping through most of the days that followed, taking morning and afternoon naps and spending long nights in deep slumber.

It was clear she had been badly in need of the rest, she told herself as at last the ship moved over the glassy green heave of water towards the pier in New York, and she stood at the rail watching the Lady and her lamp slide past while the children leapt up and down beside her; that was why this crossing had been so somnolent, compared with the last one she had made. And her lips curved as she remembered how it had been that last time she had made this journey, the way she and Jay had spent so many hours in their lifeboat, and then, a little alarmed at herself, pushed her erotic memories away as Buster tugged at her dress and shouted, 'Mummy, where's Daddy? Is Daddy here, Mummy?'

She turned and picked him up and hugged him, suddenly full of excitement and happiness for the first time since she had left London.

'Not here, darling,' she said. 'Not in New York. But I dare say he'll meet our train in Boston when we get there. I sent him a cable yesterday to say we were coming. He'll be very surprised and very excited — just like us.' And she hugged him again until he refused to stay in her arms any longer and demanded to be set down beside Daphne once more.

Daphne was now not quite as effective as she had been. The bustle and excitement of New York seemed to overawe her and she stood a little helplessly beside the luggage once they were disembarked, clutching Danny and with Buster holding her skirt, looking very alien in her English nanny's uniform coat and sensible hat, pulled well down over her forehead, and stared around with her mouth half open at the newness of it all. It was Maddie who had to organise the porters, the tedious shuffle through Customs and the finding of a cab to take them uptown to Pennsylvania Station.

But she managed it, and as they ate dinner in the train, speeding through Connecticut, she tried to relax once more and recapture the sense of happy excitement she had felt as they had come steaming up to the pier at Manhattan, and could not. She felt only a sense of foreboding, dull and heavy in her belly, and she pushed her chicken salad around her plate, trying to control the feeling. It was silly, she told herself firmly, perfectly ridiculous, to be so anxious. She was on her way to meet her husband, and he would be as excited to see her as she and the boys were about seeing him; she knew that. So why feel that weight of fear and doubts pulling her down? It was unnecessary and nothing to do with Jay at all, probably. It was just a left-over feeling of grief for Daddy, and she thought hard about Daddy, to see if that made the feeling worse. But it had no effect at all. It just stayed there, cold and lumpy in her chest like a palpable object.

But when they reached Boston's Back Bay Station at last, and the porter had hefted their luggage out and left them standing there, the children grizzling now with fatigue, the feeling at last went. Because he was there, hurrying along the platform towards them, and now she knew why she had been so anxious. Deep inside herself she had been afraid he would not be glad to see them, that he would make no effort to meet them, and she was now filled with a vast gratitude, and also much compunction at her own wickedness at harbouring such a notion.

'Jay!' she cried and dropping her bags heedlessly went running along the platform to meet him and hurl herself into his arms, and he held her close as she wept into his neck, and patted her back and made soothing noises as she began to chatter at him, her grateful relief spilling over into a cascade of words.

'Oh, Jay, I'm so glad to see you – it's been so miserable. When Daddy died I felt so awful – were you angry? You weren't angry, were you, that we came? It seemed the only thing I could do. Are you all right? How is it all turning out? Can we go home again soon? You're not angry with me for coming, are you? The boys were so excited to be seeing you – oh Jay, it is *good* to see you –' And she hugged him even closer and pressed her face against his, surprised to find her cheeks so hot and wet. She hadn't realised she was weeping.

'Hey, now, cool down, honey! No need for all this – sure you're tired, but don't make it worse – calm down or you'll set the kids off – there, you see?' For now the boys were wailing and Buster was standing beside them pulling at Jay's jacket, demanding to be picked up and Jay disentangled himself from Maddie's grip and bent and hauled the child up and hugged him and then set him astride his shoulders, so that he could hold on to his hair and whoop his excitement from his superior vantage point.

'Hello, Daddy,' Daphne said and simpered a little. 'It's been a long time, hasn't it? You look ever so well, though –'

And indeed he did. Maddie, who had been scrubbing her face

dry with her handkerchief, gave her nose one more blow and looked at him over the edge of the cambric. He was deeply tanned, and his hair had been bleached to an even richer gold so that he almost seemed to have a halo, it gleamed so brightly. There were white lines around his eyes where he had squinted against the sun, and his hands, emerging from the sleeves of his cream summer suit, were as brown and lean as a boy's. She shivered slightly at the sight of him, feeling all the old desire for him lifting in her, and that made her feel marvellous. It had been some time since that had been so important to her. To find it had come back was a bonus she had not expected, and impulsively she stretched out her hand and said, 'Oh Jay, you'll never know how good it is to see you –'

He looked at her sideways, a sudden blue flash of a glance and grinned and then reached for Danny, taking him in his arms to hold him against his chest where Buster's swinging legs could do him no harm, and then he looked away and it was almost as though he were embarrassed and Maddie felt her physical need for him rise even higher. He's feeling the same way I do, a secret voice in her mind sang. He feels just the same way I do – and she looked around for a porter among the crowds of passengers and meeters still swirling around them, impatient to be on their way, to get the children settled and to be alone with him.

'Will you be able to get everything into the car, darling?' she said as at last a porter with a trolley emerged from the crowd. 'We could check some of this and fetch it home tomorrow if you like.'

'We're not going to the house,' he said and turned to start walking along the platform to the exit as the porter, his trolley now loaded, followed them with Daphne scuttling along beside him and staring round at everything with the same excited look of amazement at the brave new world in which she found herself that she had had ever since they had docked in New York. 'I booked rooms next door at the Copley Plaza – a suite with a small bedroom for the boys and Daphne.'

She almost stopped walking in her surprise, but he was striding ahead so she had to run to catch up.

'Not going home? Why not?'

'There wasn't time to fix things up. You know we had everything put under covers and the house locked up. It takes a

266

lot of time to get straight and I thought, it won't be worth the cost and effort. It's not that you're going to be here all that long –'

'Oh, Jay, can we go home again soon, then? Oh, that'd be marvellous, just marvellous! How long do you think? Oh, I should have called you, and then you could have told me when and – but you don't mind us being here, do you? You are pleased to see us?'

'Daddy's pleased to see us. Daddy's pleased to see us,' Buster sang and swung his legs again, deliberately trying to catch Danny with his heels, and Jay shook him firmly but affection-ately enough and said, 'Sure I am, you young villain. Mind where you're putting those goddamned feet of yours, if you don't want my hands where you don't want them. Come on, now, porter, take that stuff through to the Copley Plaza, okay? We'll collect it all from you at the check-in as fast as we can – come on, Daphne! No time to stand there!' And Daphne, who had been standing gawping at a display of cars that had been set up on the big concourse, giggled and came scuttling along behind them.

All the time they were checking in and settling themselves into the suite he concentrated on the children, chattering at them and teasing and tickling them till they were in a state of towering excitement that made them bouncier than even they usually were, and Maddie watched indulgently as she hung clothes in the closets and arranged her make-up on the dressing table, glad for them that they were together again. The boys needed their father, she thought; they spent too much time with women. They'd have to talk about it, she and Jay, make plans so that he could spend more time in future with their sons, rather than be as immersed in the business as he usually was – and as she had been lately.

When it was time for the boys to be bathed and put to bed they screamed their demands that Daddy should do it so loudly that good-naturedly Jay pulled off his jacket and pushed up his shirt sleeves and took them, one under each arm, into the bathroom, and Maddie followed. His arms looked like hot buttered toast, she thought, for the skin was as deeply tanned there as on his face and the fine hair on them was bleached to a bright gold, and at the thought she felt a sudden stab of acute nostalgia. It wasn't now, the middle of 1953 in a hot sticky Boston summer, but a foggy and chill New Year's Eve in London in 1948, and she was seeing him for the first time and falling suddenly and violently in love. He was as beautiful and adorable as he had ever been, more so in fact, and while he seized each naked small boy, as Daphne pulled their clothes off them, and dunked them in the bath and splashed and soaped them, she leaned against the door and watched, dreamy with contentment and love.

Eventually the boys settled on the understanding that Daphne would sit with them till they slept, and Jay pulled on his jacket again and smoothed his hair, which the boys had ruffled considerably, and said over his shoulder as he reknotted his tie in the mirror, 'We'll go down to the coffee shop for some supper, okay? Unless you want to go to the Circus Room?' And he cocked an eye at her clothes, and she looked down, suddenly self-conscious. She was still wearing the travelling suit she had put on that morning on the ship, a costly green linen confection from Paris, but it was sadly creased now and looking over his shoulder in the mirror she saw how dishevelled she was.

'I ate on the train, darling,' she said. 'But you must be hungry. Let me change and then we can go wherever you like – it won't take me a few moments –'

'You'll do as you are,' he said and smiled at her and turned away from the mirror after one last tweak at his tie. 'We'll go to the coffee shop and I'll have something to see me over. I lunched at the Ritz, anyway, so there's no risk I'll starve.'

He went over to the bedroom door and put his head round the jamb. 'Daphne,' she heard him hiss, 'call room service for anything you want. We'll be back in an hour or two, okay?'

'That'll be fine, Daddy.' Daphne came creeping out of the room, on exaggerated tiptoes. 'They've gone out like lights, the poor little devils. All that excitement! Not good for them, you know.' She shook her head in mock reproof. 'You mustn't let them get so full of themselves again, now, Daddy. It's natural enough tonight of course, but on other nights, you really must be more –'

'You're right, Daphne,' he said and patted her shoulder. 'It's great to have you to tell us how to go on. You're going to be a great hit here in Boston, I can tell you that! Come on, then,

Maddie. We'll go down. There are things we have to talk about –'

The coffee shop was quiet with few people at the wicker tables and she looked at her watch and was amazed to see how late it was; gone ten, and she shook her head, a little bemused. Such a long and full day, and she stifled a yawn and told herself joyously, no sleep yet. Jay is here, no sleep yet, and felt a little frisson of pleasure as she thought of going to bed with him.

He ordered a steak and french fries and she shook her head at his invitation.

'I'll just have iced tea,' she said. 'I've eaten enough for one day. And it's too hot for food. I'd forgotten just how hot it can be in Boston in August.'

'That's why everyone's at the beach,' he said a little absently and began to butter a roll, keeping his head down as he concentrated on it. 'I've spent some time there myself these past few days.'

She grinned. 'That's no secret. Not with a tan like that. Honestly, you look as though you've been kippered. It suits you, though.'

He glanced at her and a tendril of the uneasiness that had been with her on the train began to wriggle its way back through the happiness that filled her now. 'Does it?' he said. 'Nice of you to say so –'

'Is something wrong, Jay?' She leaned forwards and put her hand out on the table. Usually when she did that he covered it with his own, but now he seemed not to have noticed her gesture and went on smoothing butter over his roll, making no attempt to eat it.

'I've been busy with this and that,' he said. 'You know how it is. And we're still trying to get Timothy out of Washington to sign those goddamned papers about the new incorporation. Everyone else there has gone off for the summer, but not him. No, he has to hang around his damned committee. They're writing up a report or some such crap –'

'Oh,' she leaned back and looked at his bent head. 'Does that mean we won't be able to go home again for a while?'

'I can't do anything till this is all fixed up,' he snapped and this time he did look at her and the tendril of fear grew and thickened like smoke over a fire that is taking a sluggish hold.

'Jay, don't be like this —' she said, and her voice was low and reasonable. 'So snappy and — well, snappy. You're bothered about something. Don't pretend you aren't. This is me, remember? Tell me what it is.'

The steak arrived and he leaned back and watched as the waiter set his plate in front of him and offered mustard and salad and added a side order of fries, and she watched him, staring at his impassive face and feeling fear lifting higher and higher. There *was* something wrong, dreadfully, appallingly wrong. She knew it. And she braced herself to be ready for what was to come as at last the waiter took himself away and left them alone.

30

August 1953

And when it did come she could not believe it. It was like a scene from a bad film, she thought wildly at one point. I'm not experiencing this. I'm sitting in the dark frowstiness and watching a screen on which all this is happening. If I drag my eyes away to one side or the other, I'll see the signs glowing amber in the darkness, saying 'Exit' and I'll be able to get up and run away from it all, because it's so dreadful and so terrifying and it isn't really happening.

But it was true, and it was happening. There were no convenient exit signs to look at or run to. Just Jay, sitting cutting up steak and then chewing it, and spitting out the words, the casual words that were destroying her.

'I never intended it to happen, believe me I didn't,' he said. 'As far as I was concerned I love you and only you. I mean, really love. There are the boys too, of course. And I still love you, Maddie, you know that. You're my crazy kid and I do love you in a crazy sort of way. You taught me how to, that was the thing. I kept remembering all the time how you had been, back there in London all that time ago, and —' He shook his head and then grinned and wiped his mouth with a napkin that looked achingly white beside his brown face. 'Maybe if you'd been here it would have been better. To tell you the truth, it never entered my head when she was there in London. But she is here and — well, there it is. And it's all so silly, really. I've thought a lot, Maddie, and I know how it can be so we'll all be happy. It's silly to make a big thing about it.' And again he had grinned at her and she had stared at him through eyes so hot and raw they felt as though they were set in holes that had only just now been torn out of her living flesh.

'You say this was — that it wasn't something you wanted to happen,' she managed at last and was amazed at how ordinary her voice sounded. Flat and dead, and ordinary.

'Believe me, Maddie, as sure as I sit here!' and he set his fork down on his now empty plate and pushed it to one side so that he could sit with his elbows on the table and lean closer to her. 'It was one of those things that sort of – well, they just happen, you know?'

'I don't know,' she said, and still her voice had that level deadness. 'Tell me.'

He sighed and looked down at the tablecloth. She did too. It was a pale green coarse-textured linen with patterns of willow leaves woven into it and as he talked she let her eyes follow the pattern the leaves made, in and out, twisting and repeating just as the words twisted and repeated themselves in her mind.

'It was Cray who said it first. Or maybe it was my mother – oh, I don't know. It just sort of *happened*. We were down at Cray's place, you see. Did I tell you he has this great summer house down at Osterville? It's on the elbow of Cape Cod right near our house at Hyannis, a *great* place. The fishing, the surfing, the sailing – the greatest. And we were there and Ma had been saying –' He reddened then so that his tan took on a coppery sheen. 'Hell, you know how she is, Maddie! Religion means a lot to her – a hell of a lot. And she was on again about how we weren't really married. What with it being at City Hall and all –'

'Not married,' Maddie said and tried to close her eyes, but couldn't. 'Not married, with our home and our children and working together in our business and – not married? When we have the certificates and – she's mad, you know that? She's totally mad.'

'Talking my mother down won't help, Maddie,' he said and now there was an edge of sharpness in his voice. 'I told you, she's religious. It matters a lot to her. It mayn't be any great shakes in your life, but it's the start and finish of hers and you've no right to insult her for it.'

'I, insult her? Christ!' Maddie said and wanted to laugh. Not that she could. The sound wouldn't come out.

'Well, that's the way of it. To her, we aren't married. Dammit, how could we be? A Catholic marriage means a nuptial mass, the whole shebang. Sneaking off to City Hall like some sort of tavern trash –'

'That's what she said I was?' Maddie said. 'She said that and you didn't –'

'Not you!' he said and looked genuinely surprised. 'Me – it was *me* she was mad at. She said we weren't truly married, that we were just fornicating. She's always said that, you know what she's like! But she went on and on about it there at Cray's that time and Cray –' He moved uneasily in his chair. 'Cray, he listened to her and then he came and talked to me after.'

Now she sat very still and silent. She was used to Blossom's abuse and bigotry and insults. That was what Blossom was about. But Cray Costello? How could he have any involvement in that mad old woman's religious mania?

'He's a widower, you know that? His wife died when Gloria was born.'

'Gloria,' she said softly and then took a deep breath, knowing now how it had been. She had heard what was to be told to her now, knew the whole story as clearly as though she had grown up with it. She had grown up with it in a sense, she thought then, as Jay leaned back and tried again to get the right words together in his head before he spoke them. And as she watched him, and all the time as he talked, she saw another vision inside her head, of another man like Cray, but not Cray, of another girl like Gloria, but not Gloria.

'She's the most important thing in his life, that's the thing,' Jay said. 'Anything that girl wants, she's always had. Only had to ask – it's a lovely thing to see, you know?' And he sounded almost wistful. 'Me, I like to see it. I got so many damned brothers and sisters I couldn't even breathe when I was a kid. There was always someone standing in my place, always something getting in my light, everything I wanted I had to fight for so damn hard it made me sick. And all of them always trying to put one over on you. If you run a race and win then that goddamn Timothy has to do it too and then Declan, the whining little bastard – but Cray, he just had Gloria. Lucky devil, her –'

'Yes,' she said dully. 'Lucky devil, her,' and looked down the long corridor of her mind at herself, sitting on her father's lap and staring at Ambrose and hating him.

'So when he said it at first I thought – hell, this is crazy. But he kept on saying it, over and over. And there was Ma – and Pa just laughed when I asked him and told me he didn't give a damn either way, that all cats are grey in the dark –' Again his face took on that coppery sheen and he looked at her directly for the first time since they had sat down. 'He meant no insult, you know, Maddie. It's just that –' He shrugged. 'He's always been like that. First girl I ever brought home when I was at Harvard he knocked up, or damn near. He just laughed at me when I told him that I – he just laughed and said when it came to it a man's no man who can't look after his own prick – hell, you know how Pa is! I'm just telling you what he said –'

'You're still not telling me what I've a right to know,' she said and now she could close her eyes so that she didn't have to look at him any more. It hurt too much to see those blue eyes blazing so vividly. It's all wrong that he's so tanned, her secret voice complained almost pettishly. It makes him too beautiful to be true –

'But I did, Maddie, I did! I told you, Cray came out with it straight. He said if I'll go to Reno and then have a proper church affair, the nuptial mass which is what Gloria wants, then the day we do it, the whole business gets handed over. He keeps control and use till he dies, of course, but it's all mine, mine and my kids –' He slid his eyes away then. 'Gloria's kids, I mean –'

'And all this happens just by going to Reno,' she said softly and opened her eyes and stared at a point somewhere above his head. 'You go to Reno and you drop me into the bottom of nowhere just so that you can get a business, a lousy business –'

'Hey, Maddie, don't be crazy! This isn't just any business, you know! This guy owns half of Massachusetts, I swear to you. And a fair part of Vermont and Pennsylvania too, one way and another. Not obviously, but he owns it. I mean, his name may not appear on all the companies, but they're his all right – and their money. He's worth so damn much – and he's only got Gloria to care about, and if – listen, Maddie.' And now he put both hands out to grip her above the elbows, pushing the table's contents aside so that the ketchup bottle tumbled over and the cap fell off and ketchup began to ooze out on to the cloth like a pool of blood.

'Let go of me,' she said and bent her head to look down at his hands on her arm. '*Now*.'

He let go as though she had bitten him and stared at her, and then said, almost aggrieved, 'Hell, Maddie, you don't have to be this way! Am I being nasty? I'm not. I'm just trying to explain to you. Let's be civilised about this, for Christ's sake. There's no need to make any great drama over it. I mean, think of it as a business deal. It's all it is —'

'A business deal?' She lifted her chin to look at him. 'A business deal? You let this man Costello buy you for his dear little girl, she wants you, so all she has to do is say "Hey, Daddy, get me one like that. No, not just *like* that — get me *that* one. I don't care who he belongs to, just buy him for me." Is that what you call a business deal?'

'He does,' he said after a moment. 'That's the point. *He* does. Cray. So I do too. Why can't you?'

She began to laugh then, a subdued and controlled little bubble of sound, but at the sight of his face, sulky and boyish as he sat and stared at her with his lower lip thrust forwards, the laughter grew and pushed and finally broke its bounds until she was leaning forwards with her hair flopping over her face and tears streaming down her cheeks as peal after peal broke from her. People around them turned and looked and grinned in sympathy at the sight, though some looked disapproving at the noise, but she cared neither way. She just laughed until he leaned forwards again and pinched her hand sharply to stop her, and slowly the hysteria damped itself down until she was doing little more than producing an occasional hiccup.

'It's not so funny,' he said. 'It happens all the time, for Christ's sake. Do you imagine that every time a rich man's daughter gets married it's all hearts and flowers? Like hell it is. It's contracts and settlements, that's what it is. You saw what happened when *you* ran off. Didn't your father try to get you back, try to stop you, hey? Don't you think if he could have got to me he wouldn't have tried to buy me off to leave you alone?'

She took a deep and shaky breath. 'Would you have let him?' she asked, and stared at him and after a moment he grinned, a wide transparent sort of grin that had no subterfuge in it.

'Listen, Maddie, I don't know and that's the goddamned truth of it. I'm not like you, all passion and — I mean, I love you

275

well enough. As well as I can. But I don't go in for all this eternity with hearts entwined guff. I just don't – and at the time, if your Pa had turned up with enough dollars, who can say what would have happened? Sure, I wanted you. You were – you still are – a great kid. You're crazy and you're fun and I'll tell you, you're a great lay. It's not every man can say that about his wife after damn near four years. Most of the guys I know, by this time, they're screwing around like – well, you know what fellas are like! It's business I'm interested in – Kincaid and Sons, and here's Cray Costello offering me on a plate of parcel of equities that'd make you dribble. It's solid gold, Maddie! I've found what I've been looking for all my life. You can't expect me to give that up for hearts and flowers, now can you? Cray Costello's like me – he knows what matters and he reckons that him and me together can build a set-up called Costello Kincaid into the biggest conglomerate these United States have ever seen. The big one, Maddie, the golden one. All I have to do is go to Reno and then march off to mass with his daughter. He says it himself – he's a fool for her. But that's the only way he's a fool. He gives her what she wants but in doing it he gets what he says is one of the best wheeler-dealers in the business.' He seemed to swell a little as he said it and grinned at her. 'This last couple of months, Maddie, I've pulled off some sweet deals here, I can tell you. And with Cray to back me up I can do some even better ones. All I have to do is let his girl call herself Mrs Kincaid. It's no big deal, dammit.'

'No big deal,' Maddie said and the laughter threatened to come welling up again. 'No big deal. I lose my husband, my children lose their father, and you say it's no big deal –'

Again he leaned forwards in that confidential way and reached for her but she stayed well back so that he couldn't.

'Listen, Maddie,' he said earnestly. 'Would I be talking to you this way if I meant any such thing? I don't. I can't pretend you haven't made me jump the gun a bit. I was going to hang on here a bit, sort it all out, go to Reno, then come back to London and explain it all. But you turning up this way – well, there it is. You're here and we had to talk. I knew you'd find out on your own, anyway, now you're here. Enough of the old biddies are talking about us, as it is.' Again he shrugged. 'So here I am telling you. But it won't make any difference to me. I told Cray that out straight. I have two boys, Cray, I said. Timothy Three and Danny. They're mine. I don't just dump 'em, and never you think it.'

'Bloody good of you,' Maddie said savagely.

'I don't dump you either. Listen, we just go on as we always did! I'll see to it the boys don't go short of a thing. They'll come here to go to school as soon as they're the right age, and then go to Harvard – Kincaids always do – and I'll take good care of all of you. Not that you have problems, really. Now your old man's dead – and I'm sorry about that, but like I said, it was all for the best really, wasn't it? And it means that now you have your own business. And I want nothing from it, not a damn thing. All the work I did, forget it. It's all yours, every penny. You should be sitting pretty – the house, the cars – everything in London is all yours. And –'

'Big of you,' she said, still savagely, 'seeing the whole thing is now in my name, anyway. Braham's is mine, and what little you did for it wasn't worth a row of beans –'

He bridled at that, and the sulky look came back into his face. 'Hey, I know you're mad at me, but there's no need to be wicked about it! I worked damn hard there in London – and what for? It's like dealing with a bunch of pussycats, they've got so little get up and go. Christ, what a country! What a bunch of layabouts. Useless, the lot of them –'

'Useless?' she murmured and her eyes narrowed. 'Not so useless. Just you listen to this –' and she began to tell him of all she had done while he had been here in Boston, of the new clients, the big new development, the creation of Braham Construction Ltd, the share of the new distillery in Ireland, all of it, and he listened with his eyes bright and alert and then, when she had finished, laughed, throwing his head back with real pleasure.

'You see what I mean?' he crowed. 'A bunch of layabouts, to let a woman, one woman on her own, put that sort of stuff over on them! Oh, Maddie, why are we arguing, for Chrissakes? You and me, we're both cut out o' the same piece of cloth. We understand each other. What do you care about nuptial masses and the rest of that stuff? What if I do this? It won't make any difference to us, you and me and the kids, any more than it would if I had an affair with the woman! I don't give a damn for

277

Gloria Costello, whatever she thinks of me. It's just her father I care about, believe me—'

'*Have* you had an affair with her?' she said and held her breath waiting for an answer.

His eyes slid away from hers. 'Aw, come on, Maddie, what's the sense of –'

'Have you?' Her voice rose, became more shrill and someone at another table turned and looked and he frowned and leaned forwards and spoke softly, as though dropping his own voice would make her do the same.

'Listen, Maddie, what do you expect? The girl's got the hots for me – and you know me. I'm no monk. It's something that matters to me, as you know better than anyone – and here I was, and you weren't – what do you expect?'

'So while I was breaking my heart over you in London, alone and bloody lonely and working my guts out, you were screwing yourself stupid here –' Her voice was still high, and he looked uneasily over his shoulder again. But no one was paying any attention any more. Just another marital spat to them, she thought drearily. What do they care that my life is being shredded before my eyes, that every bit of the solid ground I stand upon is melting away beneath my feet? What do they care that I'm dying?

'So what if I was?' he leaned back now, looking sulky. 'It's not as though I was doing anything different – I'm the guy I am, Maddie. I've always been the guy I am and I'm not about to change. I married you because you – do I have to tell you? Remind you? You wanted me and boy, did you make sure I knew it! You laid it on the line twice over and more for luck and couldn't see that that was what made me – well, it worked for you, so it does for other women too. It's not as though I never came back to you. I always did, didn't I? You've never had any cause to complain; I kept quiet, behaved like a gentleman, which is more than a lot do. What more do you want?'

She was staring at him with her eyes hotter and wider than ever. 'Are you telling me that you've had affairs before – since we were married, before this bitch now and –'

He frowned sharply. 'Calling her names won't get you any place. Sure I've had affairs.' He lifted his chin now and stared at her challengingly. 'What do you think I am, for Chrissakes?

Caspar Milktoast? I'm a man, goddamn it all to hell. I've got needs, so I deal with 'em. I did in London and I do here. Big deal – but I always came home to you, right? Did I ever see you go short of anything, you and the boys? Haven't I been all a husband has to be?'

'That red-headed girl –' she said, and her lips felt stiff. There seemed no need now to speak loudly any more and her voice was dull and with no resonance in it at all.

'Who? Who – oh, yeah, her.' His lips curved reminiscently. 'Yeah, her and one or two others. So what? Has it hurt you? Of course it hasn't. Any more than this will hurt you. Listen, Maddie –' And now he leaned forwards again with that confidential smile of his and looked deeply into her eyes. 'Let's not make big dramas out of this, what do you say? I'm a lousy husband. No better than my old man. He screwed around all his married life and never cared what it did to my Ma. He's only stopped now because he's a dried-up old prune. That's why she's so religious, if you ask me. But I won't treat you the way he treated her. I'll do the decent thing by you, always. You'll never go short. You'll get your Dad's business, of course – and good luck to you. We can do some nice deals together maybe, who can say? Costello Kincaid Braham – it sounds good for a subsidiary, hmm? We'll talk about it. But like I was saying, you have the business, we get a quiet divorce, Gloria gets her wedding and Cray is happy. I'm happy, you're happy, so we're all happy –'

'You amaze me,' she said after a long pause. 'You really think I'll be happy with this sort of arrangement?'

'Why not?' He gave her that blazing boyish grin that was usually so good at twisting her chest into knots. 'Why not? Okay, we won't be married – but we'll still be us. We'll still have a great time. You and me – *we'll* be the affair, not the boring married couple we've turned into. We'll see a lot of each other, we'll have fun, we'll find out what loving can really be like. Let her have the headaches of being married. You and me, we can do better.' He looked deeply into her eyes, and smiled again. 'And you're a great lay, Maddie, you know that! There's no one like you. We can have a hell of a good time, you and I, as long as you see the sense of this –'

'And the boys – how do they see the sense of it? Do they

become an affair too?' Her voice was scathing and he made a face at the sound of it.

'It'll make no difference to them, I told you. They'll get all the money they need, all the education they need –'

'But not a father who is married to their mother.'

He shrugged. 'So? It's no big deal, not these days. Every other kid on the block has a divorced dad and mom and stepmothers and stepfathers galore. It's nothing special – they'll never give a damn. They're so young they'll never remember it being any other way by the time they grow up a bit.'

'But I will, Jay,' Maddie said. 'I'll never forget.' And she pushed the chair back and stood up, moving very carefully to make sure her legs would obey her. She felt curiously light-headed and her muscles seemed not to be interested in working as they should.

He looked alarmed. 'Where are you going?'

'I'm going to bed. I'm very tired, and I'm going to bed. Goodnight.'

He jumped up and followed her as with a control she would not have thought herself capable of exercising she walked out of the coffee shop and into the broad lobby of the hotel towards the elevators banked on the far side. 'Hi, Maddie, so what do we do? Do you agree? You see the sense of it?'

'I can see nothing,' she said and walked into the elevator as the doors sighed open. The boy who operated it stood aside to let Jay in and reached for the button as she murmured, 'Eleven.' Jay stepped forwards to join her, but just as the doors began to close she put her hand in the middle of his chest and pushed hard so that he almost fell backwards. The last she saw of him was his amazed expression as he regained his balance and the doors finally closed and she was alone in the elevator with the operator. Who, well trained as he was, stared woodenly at the blank doors as they travelled upwards so that he wouldn't have to notice that she was crying.

31

Maddie was sitting bolt upright in her chair by the window and had her eyes tightly closed. She wasn't asleep, however. That was very clear both from the stiffness of her posture and the way the shape of her eyes could be seen behind her lids, steady and fixed. Annie had noticed that and shuddered slightly; it was as though Maddie were able to stare through the opacity of her own eyelids and could watch her, Annie, while being unobserved herself. A silly notion, a downright stupid one, and she shook herself slightly and turned her head to look at Joe.

He had been crouching in front of Maddie for some time now, trying to rouse her, at first with words and then with touch, applying first a slight pain stimulant with a pin he took from the corner of his jacket lapel and which he used to prod gently at the back of her hand, and then the deeper pain stimulus, pinching down firmly on the flesh between her thumb and forefinger. But she had responded to none of it and now he pulled himself to his feet a little stiffly, and stood staring down at her with a frown between his brows, his lower lip caught contemplatively between his teeth.

'You say it happened suddenly?'

'Yes,' Annie said. 'I was trying to get her to go on talking. She'd been rattling away for – oh, ages, talking about all she did before she went back to Boston with her two children and the nanny in the summer of 'fifty-three – just after the Coronation. It was fascinating stuff, like living my own life again, and she just poured it out, like – like a rainstorm. The year before I was born, it was, the year Jennifer first started going around with Colin.' She stopped then and after a long pause went on abruptly. 'They met at the side of the road, in Whitehall, you know. She was working there then and had a place to see the procession and he came and pushed in and that was the start of it all. And of me – it was like listening to my own life, listening to Maddie talking about it.'

'You liked what you heard?'

'Not a lot,' she said harshly and flicked her gaze back to Maddie. 'They're all the same, these bastards. There wasn't much to choose between 'em, her Jay and Jennifer's Colin, bastards both, quite different in every way, but exactly the same. She talked about him the way Jennifer used to talk about Colin, thinking she was saying only good and not knowing how his hatefulness showed through like dirt on a window. He was a selfish lousy bastard –'

'Jay? Or your father?' Joe said softly, and let his gaze slide back to Maddie. He ought to concentrate on her, on the sudden change in her condition, but Annie needed him too, and was as deserving of his attention. And to make it worse, he was more interested in Annie – and he tried to put his professional self before his personal one and knew that he had only succeeded in melding them, as he heard his own voice repeat its question.

'Jay? Or your father?'

'I'm not rising to that again. You tried to make me talk about that before and I won't,' she said sharply. 'Tell me about Maddie. Why did she suddenly go into this state? She's like a board, she's so stiff, she won't move, she won't – she hardly even breathes, for God's sake! She hasn't eaten anything for the last twenty-four hours. Don't you have to do something about that? What happens now?'

'Too many questions,' he said abstractedly as he turned back to Maddie, trying to get his ideas clear in his own head before he spoke of them. He leaned forwards to lift one of Maddie's eyelids and the eye glared out at them both, fixed in its forward stare, the pupil so dilated that she looked almost black eyed. 'One thing at a time –'

'Well? What do you *do* about her? You can't leave her like that.'

'I know that perfectly well,' he said, suddenly irritated. 'You don't need to nag me.'

She opened her mouth to remonstrate and then shut it again as a staff nurse came towards them from the office at the far end of the long ward.

'Dr Labosky, I have Dr Moffatt on the phone again. He says he really has to push about this post-natal depression of his. He says she's suicidal, that she's already got quite severe wrist wounds that have to be dressed every day and as she's supposed to be breast feeding and has developed a breast abscess, they don't want to put the baby into care. So he really has to have a bed for her this morning. And this is the only one available according to Mr Gresham. So what do I tell him? He's holding on.'

Joe looked at Maddie again and rubbed his chin and then, as though he'd made a decision, nodded sharply. 'I'll come and talk to him,' he said. 'I'll put Mrs Kincaid in the side ward, nurse, so if you could get a second bed in there, please. It's only temporary. I'll take her to the old ECT unit this afternoon to try an abreaction session. That should get her out of this fairly quickly. And then we can send her out –'

'Where to?' Annie said and the staff nurse echoed the question, but he wasn't there to answer them, his long legs already taking him in loping strides down the ward to the office telephone.

Annie looked at the staff nurse who was bending over Maddie and rearranging the blanket over her knees with brisk and totally unnecessary movements, for the blanket had been neat enough over those unmoving knees, for all practical purposes. 'Staff Nurse,' she said, 'what is an abreaction session?'

'Mm? Can't say, I'm sure – it's really up to Dr Labosky. I can't discuss his patients with anyone else –' the nurse said and Annie made a soft noise of irritation between her teeth.

'I'm not asking you to discuss Maddie,' she said as politely as she could, knowing how little cooperation she was likely to get from the woman if she was sweet-tempered, let alone if she were to display her annoyance. 'I just didn't understand the words he used. I'm not very well informed about medical things, and I like to learn. I thought you might know. If you don't, of course –'

The woman rose like a fish to a gnat. 'It's rather old-fashioned,' she said, disapprovingly. 'They used to use it a lot when I was a junior, but nowadays they prefer group therapy and so forth. But you can extract a lot of material, especially in very withdrawn people, if you put in some Amytal or Pentothal and then talk to them. People who knew no better used to describe them as truth drugs, but that was just silly newspaper stuff. You can't guarantee the truth, can you? You can just try

283

to get 'em to talk, that's all. Sometimes you can do it with hypnosis but you need a cooperative patient for that. This one –' She looked down at Maddie and almost, but not quite, sniffed in disapproval. 'This one is hardly likely to cooperate. She's a great one for acting, of course, but she won't act sensible –'

'Acting?' Annie shifted her gaze sharply to Maddie and then back to the nurse. 'What makes you say that?'

'Experience,' the woman said crisply and then bent down to put one finger under Maddie's wrist and lift it. 'See that? There's conscious resistance there. That isn't a true catatonic state. With those they're the same all over – in spasm, pretty well. This one, she just won't talk. Her stiffness is uneven, I reckon. But she'll chatter enough with a shot of something in her arm, I dare say, and that's what he's going to try. As long as we get her out of this ward as soon as possible, that's what matters. It isn't right to have one of these old chronics cluttering up acute beds like this –'

'I thought you didn't discuss Dr Labosky's patients with anyone?' Annie said and grinned maliciously as the woman reddened slightly.

'I wasn't,' she said huffily. 'I was trying to explain what it was you wanted to know. But there, some people just can't understand whatever they're told,' and she went away, rustling her over-tight nylon uniform self importantly as she swung her hips between the beds.

Joe came back after a few minutes and stood beside Maddie for another while staring down at her and then looked at Annie.

'I'll have to discharge her from the ward tonight,' he said. 'I really have no choice. She can't go back to the West Pavilion, to be sure. It's cleared of patients now, and the wards have been stripped. The bulldozers go over there next Monday. I can't send her to a hostel – I'll have a nurses' riot on my hands. And there's nowhere else.' He turned and looked at her very deliberately. 'Will you take her, Annie?'

She gawped at him. It was the only word to describe what she knew to be an open-mouthed stare.

'What? Take her where?'

'To your flat,' he said patiently. 'You've got the space. I can arrange this afternoon to get a bed and linen sent over – we can lend you that for her – and if you like I can arrange a care allowance of some sort too. We still have the Greenhill Fund, and we can use it at our discretion –'

She flushed. 'If you think I want money for what I'm doing for Maddie –'

He looked tired suddenly. 'Dammit, I know you don't. I was just trying to get across to you that we need to find the right place to send her for the time being, and that we'll – *I'll* do all I can to make it easy for you if you'll help me by making it easier for me. You've done so well for her already, Annie, it'd be a wicked waste, wouldn't it, to dump her in one of those damned geriatric units where she'll be lucky if they clean her up when she wets herself, let alone if they talk to her?'

'Take her to the flat –' Annie said and tried to visualise it. The flat was now neat and tidy, with the boxes emptied and disposed of and the furniture arranged, and she tried to think of it as home, but that was difficult. It was a dead sort of place, with no feeling of homeness about it; the old house, cluttered with those awful hateful gewgaws that Jennifer had so loved, hadn't been to her taste, but there had been no doubt in her mind that it was a home, a place where people lived and breathed and experienced themselves and each other. But her new flat wasn't like that, not at all; and she tried to see Maddie melting out of her present iciness in it, tried to imagine the effect the flat would have on her and found herself shaking her head. It wouldn't help her at all. She needed a real home, a place where there was not just furniture and a roof and warm radiators but where the breath of life filled lungs and the food of comfort filled bellies.

'Damn it all, Annie, when will you stop being so full of yourself!' Joe's voice was low and controlled but the anger in it made her blink and jerk backwards as though he'd roared at her.

'What?' she said stupidly.

'I told you, it won't be for long – a few days is all I need to find somewhere to get rid of her for you. She's served her purpose for you, hasn't she? Given you something to amuse yourself with while you got over the worst of your depression, but now when it's time to give her something in return you don't want to know –'

'But it isn't like that!' she said, protesting, needing him to know how wrong he was. 'I wasn't refusing – I just –'

He stared at her. 'You were shaking your head,' he said.

'Because I couldn't imagine her there. The place is so – it's so cold and miserable.' She needed him to understand, wanted his approval in a way that amazed her. She who had never cared for anyone's approval, to need his, of all people's?

'But you've got central heating.' He sounded genuinely puzzled. 'I saw the radiators – and I told you, we can cover the cost if that's a problem, though I didn't think it was, actually.'

She waved a hand to dismiss that. 'Of course it isn't. And I didn't mean physical warmth like that. Of course the heating's there and it's often too hot because I keep it turned up – no, it's just that it's so dull and dismal. I couldn't see her being anything but worse there with only me –'

He was red now, obviously embarrassed and he put out one hand and touched her shoulder.

'Oh, God, what is it about you? I feel like the proverbial ass who finds his foot in his mouth every time he opens it. I'm sorry. So you will take her?'

'I can't,' she said after a long moment. 'I daren't. I wouldn't know how to cope if – if she was like this, and wouldn't eat and –' To her horror she felt her face crumple. 'What would I do if she got worse?' she said piteously. 'I'd be so afraid that she'd – I know I looked after Jen, but that was different. I knew her when she was well, and anyway she wasn't like this. She wasn't – it was an illness she had, a physical illness. She wasn't like this, hiding away from whatever it was that happened to her, hiding away so deeply that she's fit to die of it.'

She hadn't noticed when it had happened but he had his arm across her shoulders and that felt comforting and she let her own tense shoulders relax and let her head sag a little so that she could rest against him. That felt a good deal better than she could ever have imagined.

'She won't come to any harm with you,' he said gently. 'Quite the reverse. It's places like this that make people ill.' He lifted his head and stared down the long ward with its tall windows and the red-blanketed beds between them. 'Look at the place – they built it a hundred years ago and it hardly looks any different. Being here would make anyone ill.' Now he looked

286

down at her and lifted his other hand to touch her cheek, and then seemed to think better of it and dropped it again. 'Being with you will be good for her – believe me.'

'But how can I help her if she won't talk?' Annie said and lifted her head and tried to pull away a little, suddenly embarrassed at the childishness of her posture. 'It's all right here, I can get her chattering away here – or at least most of the time I can.'

She moved forwards now, hiding her embarrassment and intention to escape from his side behind concern for Maddie. 'Look at her! What went wrong, for heaven's sake? She was so different – but now she's even worse than when I started. She wasn't stiff like this, then. And she did eat and –'

'Look, if I can start her talking again this afternoon, will that make a difference? If I can get her over whatever it is that's blocking her now, will you let me take her home with you? I'll keep a close eye on you both afterwards anyway – I'll visit you on my way in here each morning and probably come in the evenings too. Just to be on the safe side –'

She flashed a glance at him over her shoulder. 'Would that be the only reason for coming?'

He was silent for a moment and then smiled at her, rueful and oddly shy. 'You know damned well it wouldn't, don't you? You know I like you?'

She turned back to Maddie. 'Yes,' she said and then burst out, 'I can't think why.'

'Neither can I, sometimes. You make it very difficult – look, do we have a deal? I'll see what I can do to restart her engine, and then we'll decide about whether or not you take her on at home after that?'

Again she was silent and then reached out and touched Maddie's shoulder. It was still unyielding, and still the round shapes of her eyes could be seen staring ahead through the eyelids, unmoving. And then she said unwillingly, 'Yes. All right. If she talks.'

He sighed softly, a faint movement of air that was hardly perceptible but she heard it and turned back to him and said with her chin up, 'But I want to come and listen to what she says.'

'What?'

'This abreaction session – when you give her the injection. Can I be there and listen?'

'Don't you trust me to tell you what happens?' He tilted his head slightly and looked at her, almost smiling but not quite.

'Oh, of course I do! But it's not the same, being told what someone says and actually hearing it yourself. I want to hear it. It's more like living it, then –'

'Are you living what she says?' He sounded surprised.

She was surprised herself; she hadn't realised quite what she had said and she pushed her mind back to think about it and then nodded. 'I rather think I am. She starts to talk, and she goes round in circles a little, and repeats herself, but it doesn't matter, because I don't just hear it all. I see it happen. When she told me about being in the ship for the first time, when they made love in the lifeboat –' She went a sudden rich crimson. 'Well, other times too. When she told me how she arrived at Back Bay Station in Boston, with Daphne and the boys, and he met her, I could see him walking down the station platform towards her and – he was madly good-looking, you know.'

'Was?'

'Hmm?'

'You said was. As though he were dead.'

Again she was surprised. 'Did I? I don't know. She hasn't said so. It's just that –' She turned and looked at Maddie again. 'Even a bastard like that couldn't leave her here for so long in such a state if he were alive, could he?'

'He might if he didn't know she was here,' he said. 'Maybe he's still in the States? Maybe he didn't know she came back – or why? And there are the children too. The little boys. From what she told you they must be men of – how old are they now?'

'How – I'm not sure. They must be –' she did a fast computation and then laughed. 'It's odd to think of. I just see little boys – awful ill-behaved little boys, too – when she speaks of them. Nice-looking babies with chubby knees and dirty faces. But they must be well into their thirties, older than I am. Buster – Timothy Three – must be around thirty-six or so –'

'And is probably in the States. With his father. We've still got a lot to find out, haven't we?'

'Yes,' she said. 'Such a lot to find out – so I can come and hear?'

'Yes,' he said after a moment. 'You can come and hear.' He turned his head then and looked down the ward. 'Staff Nurse!' he called and the woman came bustling up, all efficiency and apparent willingness.

'I'm taking Mrs Kincaid to the old ECT room this afternoon. Do me a tray please, with sodium pentothal – and put on an ampoule of amytal too, will you? I'll decide later which I'll use. You needn't send anyone down with the patient from the ward. Miss Matthews will help me.'

The staff nurse looked singularly wooden. 'Oh. I didn't know Miss Matthews was trained staff.' She stopped then and added pointedly, 'Sir.'

'She isn't,' Joe said cheerfully and grinned at her. 'But she's next of kin, so to speak, and she can help take notes perfectly well. I'm quite capable of coping, you know, with just one patient.' And he too paused and then added firmly, 'Staff Nurse.'

The woman sketched a shrug and went away to get the tray and together Annie and Joe lifted Maddie into a wheelchair – a task that took several effortful minutes, for without any cooperation she was a dead weight – but by the time the nurse had come back with the tray, covered with a dressing towel, they were ready to go.

And Annie followed Joe as he pushed the chair out of the ward wondering a little nervously what the hell she had let herself in for.

32

July 1987

She had tried so hard, and had failed. And she didn't know which caused the most pain, the fact that she was forced to remember, or the fact that she had failed to forget.

She had dug the deepest hole she could in her mind, lying there stiffly, forcing herself to see the great gaping space inside her head into which it was all going to be buried, the pain and the anger and the sick desolation. She was going to make it the deepest hole there ever was, and put all the hateful feelings in and weigh them down with great rocks and then fill in the hole and get on with living. There was the business to run. There were the boys to look after – there were the boys and there were friends to be made and other men to be found and loved and –

But she failed. As fast as she dug the hole so did its sides fall in. As hard as she pushed the bad feelings down, so did they ooze up all round her to engulf her again. The rocks she wanted to use for weights turned into soggy pastry which slid through her fingers and then crumbled into dryness and finally dust which blew away, and her fingers themselves became brittle fragile sticks with which she could do nothing. And all round her the darkness throbbed and heaved like a sullen black sea and she felt so sick and so ill she wanted to die, to disappear for ever into that black hole and leave the miseries outside. Just to be buried and to die – it would be peace and comfort and no more pain at all and – but remorselessly the memories came and pushed up at her from beneath, thrusting her up and out and back into the middle of it all and she opened her mouth in the darkness and shrieked her fury and her hurt at whoever was there to hear.

'What is it?' Annie whispered, staring at Maddie's sweat-scattered face and her wide staring eyes which clearly saw nothing that was in this chilly little room with its elderly couch and its battered trolleys and chairs. 'Why is she so – she looks terrified – what's in that drug, for God's sake?'

'It isn't the drug,' Joe said, never taking his eyes from Maddie's face. He was sitting beside the couch on which she lay, her right arm held firmly across his lap so that her hand was under his arm and the big syringe nestled in the crook of her elbow. He was easing off the tourniquet on her upper arm with almost imperceptible movements of his left hand as he let the drug drip very slowly into her vein. 'It's what is already there inside her. The drug just lets it free. Maddie.' He leaned closer to her. 'Maddie, where are you? Tell me where you are, Maddie. Maddie, where are you? And what are you doing? What are you doing, Maddie?'

August 1953

The blackness thinned, flattened and became a square of dull light that made her squint, and she peered out through her swollen eyelids, trying to collect her thoughts. Where am I? She'd heard it inside her head, deep inside, muffled but clamorous. Where am I? What am I doing?

Somewhere she heard the children shouting and then there was a long wail from Danny and a shout of fury from Buster and she dragged herself up on one elbow and peered round the room, and as she stared at the unfamiliar furniture and the wide window with the blue curtains through which the sunlight outside glowed to make patterns on the strange carpet she felt a great wave of fear, because she had no idea where she was, or why she was, or even for one crazy moment who she was.

And then as Danny shrieked again it all came back in a vast wash of memory and she fell back on the pillow and managed to put her hands up to her head and press hard on the throbbing temples.

She had drunk three glasses of whisky last night. She, who hardly ever used alcohol, had come into the quiet suite with the scatter of half unpacked luggage across the sitting room and the sound of Daphne's heavy breathing coming from the room she shared with the boys, and had sat down and quite deliberately swallowed three glasses of whisky. How she had done it without being sick, she didn't know; she disliked the taste of it even more than she loathed the smell, yet she had pushed it down and then gone to her room, to that big double-bedded room that she was to use alone, and dropped her clothes where she took them off and crawled into bed, unwashed, the taste of the whisky rank around her unbrushed teeth, to try and sleep.

And somehow had, after weeping furiously for what had seemed like hours, but had dreamed and dreamed, and she tried now to get hold of what she had dreamed, to expunge the bad feelings the dreams had caused by recalling them, but it was impossible. They were gone like the night itself and she opened her eyes again and stared round at the unfamiliar and therefore unfriendly room and felt fear rise in her once more.

He was leaving her. He said he wasn't. He said he was going to marry Gloria just for practical reasons, that he would still love her – but what did it matter what he said? He was leaving her, leaving her, leaving her –

Somehow she pulled herself out of the bed to stand swaying a little beside it and then pulled at the counterpane and wrapping herself in it, awkwardly, went padding across to the door on the other side of the room. She needed a bathroom badly. A bathroom offered a lavatory to be sick in and a shower and perhaps some aspirin for the agony of throbbing pain behind her eyes.

The door actually took her into the sitting room. Daphne was sitting at the table in the window space with the boys, feeding them, and Danny, sitting in the high chair, was banging his heels against the legs of it, with a monotonous thumping sound that made Maddie wince.

'Hello Mummy!' Daphne looked up and gave her a wide arch grin. 'Well, you and Daddy did sleep late, didn't you? You must have had a very late night – here we are having our nice dinners, and you just getting up. Say, "Yes, Mummy, nice dinners" –' and she spooned a greenish mass into Danny, which he promptly spat out.

Maddie felt her face go grey as her stomach rose into her chest. 'Jay's not here –' she managed. 'I'm going to take a shower –' And she moved across the room towards the other side where the bathroom door stood half open.

'Oh, men!' said Daphne cheerfully. 'Don't they make you furious? They can go and have ever such a good time and have ever so many little drinkies and wake up bright as ninepence and go off to work as usual. It's not fair, is it, mmm? Danny, tell Mummy it's not fair –'

Danny shrieked again and gratefully Maddie reached the bathroom door and slid inside and closed it against the din, just in time. She was going to be horribly sick and the one thing that would make it even worse than it was would be Daphne's clucking commiseration. And she hurled herself at the lavatory basin, for once grateful for the noise the boys made, for it covered up her own.

She emerged from her bedroom an hour later, showered, dressed and carefully made up. There was still a pallor beneath the applied colour, but it helped her feel less vulnerable to have made the effort and she was able to face Daphne, who was sitting in the window, now sewing.

'That's better, Mummy,' she said heartily as she came across the room. 'You look much more tickety-boo! The boys are asleep at last – they do so hate their afternoon nap! – but I was wondering, where shall we take them for their afternoon walk when they wake up?' And she looked over her shoulder out at the street with unmistakable longing on her face and for the first time Maddie was able to think of someone other than herself, and experienced a stab of compunction.

'It must be very boring for you here,' she said huskily and coughed to clear her throat. It felt raw and painful, and she knew it came from the tears she had shed last night. 'I'm sorry –'

'Oh, that's all right, Mummy!' Daphne said and turned resolutely back to her sewing. 'I know how it is when family matters are pressing.' And she kept her head bent studiously over her flying needle, and Maddie could feel the curiosity oozing out of her, prodding at her pruriently, aching to know why Jay wasn't here, where he had gone, why she looked so dreadful. And the moment of concern she had felt for her shrivelled and died.

'I hope you called down to room service for all you needed for the boys,' she said now. 'Just keep a note of all you order, will you? So that we can check the bill –' She had meant to say, 'So that Mr Kincaid can check the bill,' to cover up the fact of Jay's absence as though it were a temporary matter, but the words had stuck in her raw sore throat. 'And you'll have to do it a good deal, I'm afraid, on your own. We have – um – business affairs to deal with, so we won't be around as much as we'd like. You can cope, I imagine? Of course we'll pay you overtime, double time, for the loss of your off duty –'

'Oh, that's all right,' Daphne said, still with that dreadful adamantine cheerfulness. 'I can't go anywhere, after all – I mean, I don't have any friends to go about with, and it's no fun on your own, is it? So I don't mind just being with the boys all the time –' She looked up then and added hastily, 'Though a little extra cash always comes in handy, of course.'

'I'll see to it you have it,' Maddie said wearily and then moved over to the window to look down into the street. The scene there, with its chrome-dripping cars and trucks and brightly dressed people and the shouting shopfront signs and windows, looked exotic after the last years at home in England, and yet was still deeply familiar to her. It was as though she'd never really been away from Boston, as though the intervening time at home had been a dream. She felt isolated and alien, as though she did not belong here or anywhere else, and that it would be the same if she were to go back to London right now. She would feel as alien there. And she half whispered a phrase she had heard someone use on the ship to describe the sort of people who forever shuttled between America and Britain and who, wherever they were, were always homesick for the other place: 'Lost citizen of Atlantis . . .'

'What did you say, Mummy?' Daphne said brightly and Maddie turned away from the window and tried somehow to get herself together again. There must be no hint to those watchful lascivious little raisin eyes staring at her from that roly-poly face that she was anything but her usual self, the secure, the settled, the beloved wife of Jay Kincaid –

'Nothing – just thinking of all the work I have to do. I must, I'm afraid. There are deals to be fixed up between our company here and the London end –' and she waved her hand, trying to be airy, apeing the busy woman dismissing the labour ahead as something she could easily deal with once she got going. 'So you'll have to be patient – now I'm going out.'

Suddenly she had to. She had no idea where she would go or what she would do when she got there, but she could not stay here another moment, of that she was certain. It was too stifling and too much effort to be with Daphne.

'Take the boys out, do. There's a nice place you can go to – the Public Gardens. There's a lake and there are the Swan boats – you can take them there and they can sail on the lake. Get a cab downstairs and ask him to take you to the best entrance, I can't remember if it's on Arlington or Charles, but the cab driver will know –'

She was gabbling over her shoulder as she went back to the bedroom to collect her bag and a thin coat, and was halfway to the door as she pulled it on. 'Whatever it costs, let me know, and I'll settle up with you. I've left fifteen dollars on the dresser in my room – use that to start off with but don't stint yourselves. There are ice-cream sellers and the rest of 'em there at the Gardens and the boys'll enjoy that.'

'But Mummy, won't they be going to see their grandma and grandpa after their walk?' Daphne called and she stopped, the doorknob in her hand. She had almost escaped, but now she had to stop and go back for a moment.

'Oh,' she said and didn't know what to say next. She just hadn't thought about that. That had been part of the original plan, of course, when she had left London. To remind old Timothy and more particularly Blossom of the boys' existence, and especially of Buster, Timothy Three. She had thought of showing them to Rosalie and Timothy Two as well, had even considered the possibility of persuading Jay to take them to Washington for a visit so that she could prove to them all what special boys she had. But now she was a woman who was about to be divorced with ignominy, the mother of children whose father was about to –

'There's plenty of time for that,' she said now, and walked through the doorway. 'Plenty of time. Just take them to the Gardens today, and see they go to bed at a reasonable hour. And there's a TV set here for you to watch tonight if you like. They'll show you how to use it if you call down to the desk –'

And now she could escape, at last, and she pulled the door closed behind her and almost scuttled for the elevators, needing to be away and out so much that she could feel the urgency pushing inside her like a physical lump. And the lump was still there when she reached the lobby downstairs, bustling still with lunchers even at this time of year when so many people were out of town on holiday and ringing with the cries of satisfied Bostonians meeting each other to display their delight in belonging to what they knew without doubt to be the most important place in the entire world.

And at the sight of them her feelings shifted and twisted and became something quite different. The people she could see milling round her all looked so well, so tanned and so golden. The long Boston summer had toasted even the dullest of them to a rich glowing healthiness, and everywhere she looked there were the familiar self-satisfied brown faces and the glinting fair hair of the deeply comfortable, the deeply complacent, the deeply committed money-makers of whom Jay was so typical an example. At home in London he had seemed an exotic creature, a person of such rare beauty that people – women, at any rate – turned their heads to look at him pass in the street. But here he was just one of a genus, a good example of it, if a somewhat more beautiful than most example, but still just another rich, well-pleased-with-himself Bostonian who regarded the world as his private cow, a place to be used and milked and used again as and when he chose.

And she hated them for it, each and every one of them. How dare they stand here in their Brooks Brothers suits and button-down collared shirts and their magnificently cut hair and perfectly smooth-shaven talcum-anointed faces, looking as though they had a right to do whatever they wanted? How dare they think they could use people's lives and loves the way they used their dollars and their buildings and their equities and bonds?

And the feelings that had made her so sick and so frightened began to stiffen and to take on shape and hardness so that what had seemed like a thick swirling vapour became a cold liquidity and then a gel, and finally a hard solid mass that settled inside to join the lump already there, and lay lurking like a threatened animal, waiting to jump out at anyone who came near.

She had at last more rage than pain in her and it gave her the strength she needed. And she lifted her chin and took a breath and walked composedly across the lobby to the desk to ask if there were any messages for her.

There were not and she nodded as though that were the

response she had not only expected but welcomed and moved away to the great revolving doors and out into the street.

Where the heat hit her like a buffet from a high wind, making her gasp and stand still in the centre of the pavement as she felt the sweat start out on her upper lip and brow. Oh, but she had forgotten, quite forgotten, the heat of Boston in August, and in her belly the crouching animal lifted its head and hated the heat as well and added that hate to the store it already had, and subsided, muttering at her.

She began to walk, slowly, keeping in the shade of the buildings wherever she could, and let her mind begin to think. She did not direct it; she just let the thoughts come and arrange themselves. She could trust her own mind to decide what to do, and how to do it, and she felt her lips curve as the ideas slid neatly into place, quite unbidden by her.

First, to State Street, to see old Timothy. There were things being done by his sons to his business that he knew nothing of. He must be told and turned into her ally again. And she remembered the way he had been in the house on Commonwealth Avenue when she had first come to Boston, all that time ago, and he had shown her just the sort of man he was. Oh, she knew how to handle old Timothy, the randy devil, she knew how to handle him.

And he would see to it that this mad Blossom-inspired notion that Jay was playing with was scotched, immediately. For that, Maddie told herself as the angry animal inside her settled to a slow silent sleep, was what it was all about. It had to be. A mad notion that he could be talked out of. There would be no further trouble, once she had talked to Timothy.

33

August 1953

She came out into State Street and stood there on the pavement as the last workers took themselves home, eddying round her as though she were a boulder in the middle of a brook, their collars unbuttoned and their jackets, hooked over their forefingers, slung over their shoulders and she tried to get her head clear.

She had walked in there quite certain that she could sort it all out and had gone on being so certain as Timothy had come hobbling out of his office, both hands extended, to welcome her.

'Well, well, well, and here she is then, the girl herself!' he said and laughed. 'And wasting her time coming to see the likes of me! Who'd ha' thought I'd deserve it!'

She had smiled at him smoothly, her eyes wide and sparkling. 'Still as bad as ever, Pa!' she said. 'Still pretending to be old – you're looking very well –'

'Ah, well, what's well? A bit of brown on me from the summer doesn't make me well. It just makes me look more like the piece of crap I feel,' and he had laughed and led her into the office and looking round she had been afraid suddenly. It looked different, somehow, as though there were a faint sheen of dust over it, even though in fact everything looked well cared for, and she tried to pin down her uneasiness. And then, as she looked at the big desk behind which Timothy was settling himself with some muttering about his stiff legs, she knew what it was.

This was not a place where any real work was being done. The desk had a few well-arranged oddments of paper on it, together with the blotter and the requisite telephones and dictaphone and there was an in tray and an out tray, both with one neat file in them, but they looked what they were; mere set dressing. There was no reality in the place. It was a shell of a room, a place that had been left behind when its real tenants –

busyness and activity — had passed on. Old Timothy sat here like an ailing crabshell, as discarded himself as his furniture and his phones were. And she shivered a little.

But still she had to try, and try she had.

It had taken time, of course. Timothy was not one to be hustled and it was clear he was delighted to have a visitor. He sent for coffee and doughnuts — which in fact she was glad of, she discovered somewhat to her surprise, for she hadn't eaten all day — and insisted on talking for a long time about her father.

'Good old Alfred,' he said, and leaned back in his chair, and some of the coffee dribbled on to his already stained necktie. 'Wicked old devil — the deals we pulled, he and I! Did he ever tell you, now, of the time we pinched the motorcycles and then had to sell 'em back to the owners on account we couldn't get the gas? Oh, 'twas a great jape. It was like this —'

And off he had gone on a long rambling tale that she had to tolerate as best she could, as she sat and sipped coffee and listened with all the attention she could to the other sounds outside the office, to which he had blessedly left the door ajar. Was he here, Jay? Would he walk in, and smile at her and tell her that last night had been a bad dream, a bad joke, a bad everything and forget it all, they were of course to be together for always and —

But there was no sound from outside other than the sluggishly whining voice of the receptionist — a new one since she had been here last — and the rattle of the elevator doors and the ringing of telephones. No male voices to be heard at all, apart from the old man's, droning on and on —

And she had eventually managed to interrupt him, deflecting him from yet another reminiscence about her dead father, by talking of the children.

'They're looking so well, Pa, and I'm dying to show you the little one, Danny. He's a sweetie — you'll adore him. I think he looks more like you than Timothy Three does, you know.' And she had bitten her lip knowing that neither of the boys looked at all like the Kincaid family; they had taken most of their inheritance from her, with Buster already showing a marked likeness to dead Alfred.

'Yes,' he'd said then and his eyes had slid away from hers and he had reached for another doughnut.

'When shall we bring them over to you, Pa?' she said then, a little sharply, recognising uncertainty in him and he had muttered, 'Hmm?' sputtering a little so that he sprayed sugar at her and she had leaned back in her chair and said even more sharply, 'When shall I bring the children to see you?'

'Oh, hell, Maddie, that's hard to say. Blossom's down at the house on Cape Cod. You remember, we have this place at Cape Cod? And I have to go down there tomorrow, on account she just don't trust me back here – thinks I'm screwing all the help –' He had laughed then, his face twisting into a lascivious leer. 'I tell you, in this weather, I'm lucky to get a twitch of any kind, let alone getting any further! I need a bit of chill for that, I do – I was always at my best in the winter – so I have to go down there tomorrow and I dare say I'll stay a week or two this time. There ain't a lot happening here, that's for sure.'

And he had scowled at the room and for a moment she had seen looking out of his eyes the bleak stare of a frightened ageing man who saw himself being left behind as useless, a relic that his sons no longer wanted.

'So we'll have to see –' he had ended vaguely and then had brightened. 'Now, tell me, my dear, who was at the old devil's funeral? Was there anyone I'd recall from the old days, now? And –'

And so it had gone on, he dodging and diving, refusing to let her talk of any other personal affairs and at last she had given up in despair as Liam had come, wooden-faced as ever, to collect him to take him back to the house.

'We can't take you anywhere then?' he had said as Liam helped him to his feet and set his straw hat on his head, and helped him into his thin jacket, for he had been sitting in his shirt sleeves. 'You can take a cab to your hotel? Ah well, then, be sure to call and say your goodbyes before you go back to London –'

And he had gone, leaving her standing there in the middle of his dead office with her pleas unspoken, her plans to use him as her ally against Cray Costello in shards. They had done their work well, Jay and Costello, destroying not only her happiness and her life but the old man's, too. He was impotent now, she could see that, impotent in every way. A useless old man who had had his balls torn from him by his son and his son's allies;

and the animal inside her woke and stretched and began to glow again with its icy anger.

She picked up a cab that was cruising at the end of the block looking for a fare and told him to take her to the Public Gardens. There was a chance she might find Daphne still there with the boys and they could go back to the hotel together; suddenly the thought of returning there herself, on her own, was more than she could face.

But at the Gardens she realised she was being ridiculous. To search so vast an area for a girl with two small children, even a girl as oddly dressed as Daphne in her nanny's uniform would seem here in Boston, was absurd and she turned to call the cab back.

But it was gone and there was no other in sight and after a moment she began to walk. It didn't really matter in which direction, as long as she didn't stand still, and she pushed the hot stones of the pavement away beneath her thin-soled shoes, concentrating her mind on the heat that came up into her feet to sting them. That was better than paying any attention to the skulking creature in her belly which was sending ever more frequent waves of anger up into her chest.

And then it all became strange. She stopped feeling she was going anywhere or needed to go anywhere. The walking became an end in itself, something that she wanted to do, not to get to any particular place but just for the sensations it gave her, muscles tightening, muscles softening, feet thudding down, feet lifting up, muscles tightening, muscles softening – and so it went on, hour after hour as she moved through the city, somnolent now with the day's heat and slowly darkening from the brassy blueness of the stifling August day to a rich indigo.

And still she walked, mile after mile, along Boylston Street to the Back Bay Fens, and then curving down the Fenway and back along Huntingdon Avenue, muscles tightening, muscles softening, feet thudding down, feet lifting up, muscles tightening, muscles softening – Huntingdon Avenue to Trinity Church to Holy Cross Cathedral – and she passed the Copley Plaza Hotel and yet didn't stop as she moved on that leg of her relentless journey and still she went on, moving like a sort of machine with no awareness of fatigue or pain, even though a part of her mind knew perfectly well that she was experiencing it.

And all the time she thought of him, of his cruelty and his wickedness and his hardness. Of his body and the way it made her feel and the way it had been in the beginning, of making love with him on the ship and in their own little house on Beacon Street in Brookline and at home in Stanmore far away in North London and then again of his wickedness to her.

But that was not all she thought of. She thought of Gloria Costello, seeing her as she had looked sitting there beside Jay on that grey day in June – was it so short a time ago? – in the Mall, with Buster on her lap as they watched a Queen go by . . .

And the anger congealed even more and filled not just her belly now, but all of her.

Quite when it was she remembered Gian she wasn't sure. Was it as she walked up Tremont Street in the direction of the Common, or later, when she wheeled on to Eliot Street to walk towards Chinatown where the neon lights glittered and winked and the passers-by looked even more exotic? She had been thinking of Gloria at the Coronation, that was it, and how Gian Giovale had sat there beside her at the end of the row and told her solemnly that Mommas were special people who had special little men to care for. She could see him suddenly, that crinkled head and corrugated brow that was as familiar and as friendly as Daddy's had been and for the first time in many hours she stopped walking. She stood there staring along Kneeland Street and saw his face superimposed against the vivid colours of the restaurant signs and the restlessness of the stuttering neon. And almost heard his voice too.

'You never forget, hey? You have any problems with your lovely little men and you come and tell me and I'll look after you and them.' A silly sentimental creature, she had thought him there in London on a rainy afternoon in June.

But this was not London in June. This was Boston in August and the air was thick with heat and tension and inside her there was pain and fear and an angry beast and a desperate hollow loneliness and Gian Giovale did not seem now to be in the least sentimental. He seemed to be a promise of peace and comfort, a champion, a bulwark, and she struggled to find the words she needed to describe him to herself and failed.

She began to walk again, or try to, but now it was hell. Her legs seemed to shriek at her and her hips ached abominably and she remembered suddenly, vividly, the same ache after Danny's birth which had been so prolonged that she had had to spend over three hours on her back with her legs slung up on stirrups. After that her hip joints had felt just like this, except that this was worse.

She almost dragged herself to the nearest restaurant, unable to think of anywhere else she could go to sit down, and pushed the door open to a smell of soya and frying ginger and onions that made her suddenly dreadfully aware of how long it had been since she had eaten any real food, and she stood there, her vision hazy and glittering, and blinked to try to see more clearly.

The space before her shifted, shivered and split and a Chinese face appeared and she stared stupidly, for he seemed to be something out of a bad film, wearing as he was traditional ancient dress, and framed in the strands of the glass bead curtain which had obscured the entrance.

'You wish a table –' the man murmured, looking at her doubtfully, and she nodded dumbly and managed to push herself forwards and to pass him and go into the restaurant.

'A table – yes, for one, please,' she muttered and then managed to straighten her back, which was also shrieking pain at her now. 'But first a telephone. And the telephone book. Important –'

The old man seemed as though he were about to turn her out, he looked so dubious, but then he nodded courteously and went away and fetched her a phone book and with her fingers shaking she began to look at the Giovales. And felt sick, for there were page after page of them. But then she found it, amazingly, remembering the address he had given her on his card when they had parted in London, and she ran her finger along the line and somehow managed to circle the number with the pen the old Chinaman had lent her.

'Please,' she said and her voice croaked in her own ears. 'I must call him. Urgently –'

'Phone out back,' the Chinaman said and she managed to get to her feet and follow him, horribly aware of the curious glances of the other customers at the tables they passed, and then at last was offered a tall stool on which to perch as she used the phone.

There was of course no reason why he should be there. She sat with the earpiece pushed against her head, very aware of the way her sweat made it slippery against her skin, and listened to the distant ringing and told herself, he's like everyone else, gone to the coast. He's got a place in Cape Cod like everyone else and that's where he is. In Cape Cod . . . he won't be there and I'm still alone and I still don't have anyone to care for me or –

The ringing stopped and the thin voice clattered, 'Yeah?' at her and she sat and stared dumbly at the red wall in front of her, unable to believe it.

'Yeah, who is it?' the voice said impatiently and now she managed to talk. 'Mr Giovale?' she said at last, and her voice croaked. 'Is that Mr – Gian Giovale?'

'So who wants him?' the voice rasped and she caught her breath in sudden hope, recognising that sort of suspicion as so much a part of the man, just as it had been so much a part of her father's, to whom he bore so warm a resemblance.

'I – this is Maddie,' she said. 'Maddie Braham Kincaid. I'm – I'm Timothy's daughter-in-law and you said in June, in London, if I ever needed help not to forget you.'

She was weeping. Not because of the fact that she had found him. Not because of Jay and Gloria, but because she hurt so dreadfully. Every fibre of the muscles in her legs and buttocks were shrieking their revenge at her for the way she had abused them that evening and she could hardly sit with the misery of it.

'Hey, where are you?' The voice had changed, lost its rasping suspicion and become concerned. 'Are you calling from London, for Chrissakes?'

'No – no.' She managed the ghost of a laugh. 'I'm here in Boston. I'm –' She squinted at the wall where a copy of the restaurant's menu was pinned. 'I'm in the Jade and Ivory Garden Restaurant on Kneeland Street. Don't ask me why I'm here – I was so – I didn't know what to do, you see, I just walked and walked and then I remembered you said if I ever needed anyone to help me and the boys I should – so I walked in here and – oh, Gian, what am I to do? It's all so dreadful!' And now she could no longer speak at all, for the tears had choked her and drowned her voice and she sniffed hugely and heard him say only, 'Stay right there. I'll find you. Don't budge now, you hear me? I'll be right there.'

And the phone went dead and buzzed in her ear and for the first time since she had woken from her whiskied sleep that morning she felt it was possible that someone could perhaps bring some sort of order and comfort for her out of the chaos into which she had tumbled.

34

July 1987

'If I give her any more she'll just go out cold. In bigger doses it's an anaesthetic. Hold on. It's all we can do. Hold on and see if she'll start again.'

'I never heard her talk so before,' Annie said, and whispered it. It seemed wrong to speak loudly, after the sort of sound with which Maddie had filled the little room. 'So vicious, so bitter . . .'

He nodded. 'I told you. She's reaching some very painful material. There's something here that's very powerful. That's why she's been the way she has for so long. She couldn't cope with whatever it was that —'

'Of course she couldn't!' Annie said, irritable suddenly. 'How could any woman cope with such a — such a betrayal. That man — how could that man be so —'

He shook his head then and leaned forwards to peer into Maddie's face carefully before straightening his back once more. 'It's not that. At least I don't think so. It's more than that. Yes, he behaved appallingly — not that I'm all that surprised. It's amazing what some people regard as perfectly reasonable behaviour towards others.' He looked at her sideways and grinned a little, the corner of his lips curling at her. 'At least, it's amazing in my terms. But then I'm a different sort of bloke, I suppose.'

'No one could think it reasonable to treat a woman like that, a woman with his children and —' She stopped abruptly and was silent for a long moment, and then said slowly, 'My father did.'

'Yes,' Joe said and looked at her, still sitting there with Maddie's arm across his lap, still holding the syringe firmly in the crook of her elbow. 'Yes. But would that have made your mother withdraw from everything the way Maddie has? *Did* it? You know it didn't.'

'Jen and Maddie are – were – different women. What one can cope with perhaps the other can't. And Jen had me – 'She shrugged then. 'Hell, how can I know? How can you?'

'You're quite right. No one can. Everyone's very different, but all the same I think there's something more here than the fact that her husband treated her badly. Much more. What she's resisting is a memory that is so explosive that –' He shook his head. 'She's very frightened. Look at the sweat – and her pulse is strong, but it's much more rapid than the drug would justify.'

'Yes,' Annie said and then suddenly moved round him to crouch beside the bed and leaned forwards and set her cheek against Maddie's. 'Poor Maddie. It's all right, Maddie. Never mind, my love. It's all right.'

And she began to croon softly as if to a child and Joe sat very still looking down on them both and wanted to shout his delight aloud but didn't. It was as though something in Annie had given way at that moment, as though a sheet of ice had thinned, shivered and then dissolved to nothingness so that she could feel warmth on her own face again and wanted to pass it on to someone in greater need of it than she was herself.

For a long time it seemed Maddie was not going to respond, but then, slowly, her head moved and her lips twitched and then parted and Joe, moving with great care, leaned over and touched Annie's shoulder with his other hand, and she lifted her head and looked at him and then again at Maddie and scrambled to her feet to stand behind him in her old place again.

Gently, with infinitesimally delicate movements, Joe let some more of the drug slide into the vein in Maddie's arm and she turned her head on the pillow and shrieked, 'Oh, God. Oh, my God, what have I done?' and tears, great oily tears, began to push from beneath her eyelids to fill the sockets above her cheekbones.

August 1953

'I can't think about it,' Maddie said and closed her eyes tightly as though shutting out his face would have the effect of shutting out his voice as well. But it made no difference. He went on talking, his voice low and agreeable and oh so reasonable, and slowly she let her lids rise and watched his face as the words went on. And on.

'I don't see why,' he said and smiled winningly. 'Here's the problem. The man has behaved to you like a bastard, a grade-A copper-bottomed bastard. But you're a woman. A real warm loving woman, so what do you say? Get this man off my back, get him out of my hair, screw him for every penny he has and then get rid of him, the way a man who'd been treated that way would? No, not you, on account of you're a warm lovely woman. You just say to me, "Gian, help me. Get him back for me." And I want to help you.'

He smiled again now, more widely than ever as he caught her glance. 'I want to help you, believe me. But I have a better notion of how to help you than you have.'

She shook her head. 'It can't be that way,' she whispered it, partly because of fear of what she had heard and partly because of the way her voice had become so unreliable. She had swallowed some hot soup — he had insisted on feeding her before he allowed her to say a word — and had managed to eat some of the noodles he had ordered for her, but even so she still felt very shaky and her back and legs and hips ached abominably. Above all, her voice could not be trusted. 'It can't be.'

'Why not? It don't hurt your precious Jay —' He reached forwards now and patted her hand. 'I tell you, a woman like you, a price above rubies, to love a man so much when he's treated her so bad — it's a beautiful thing to see. Beautiful. I wish my Momma had known you. She would have understood you, and she would have loved you like a girl should be loved. And she'd have told you I'm right. "My Gian is right," she'd say. "You listen to him, *cara*, my Gian is one who knows. Take advice from an old woman, listen to my Gian." That's what she'd have said.'

She shook her head. 'It's impossible,' she whispered. 'You can't expect me even to consider it.'

'Why not?' He sounded all sweet good sense. 'Give me one really good reason why not and believe me I'll listen. Gian Giovale always listens.' His face split into another of his great grins. 'This is the way I've learned so much and got so much, *cara*. I listen. So I'm here, listening. Tell me one good reason why not.'

'It's — it's wrong,' she said and coughed a little, experimentally, needing to see if she could trust her voice yet. She couldn't.

'That is no reason,' he said strongly. 'What he's done is wrong. What he's planning to do is wrong. You ain't wrong, and I ain't. *He* is. To say you're not married, to a lovely little Momma with two such lovely little men you've given him, to dare to say you ain't married on account you went to City Hall and not to mass? This is a load of bullshit, you should excuse me. All he has to do if he feels bad about that is to take you to church. End of problem. No. *He* is wrong. He's using the Church –' and here he crossed himself devoutly '– like it was his shoe rag. For a convenience, for an excuse. So don't tell me what I say I'll do is wrong. It ain't. It's paying a debt like it should be, and what's better, it's solving a problem.'

Again he gave her that winning smile, tilting his head beguilingly at her. 'So, give me another good reason.'

'I – it – you'd get into trouble.'

That made him laugh, and he threw back his head to do it, opening his mouth widely so that she could see the glint of gold in his teeth.

'I said a reason, *cara*! This is not a reason! This is a –' He waved one hand. 'This is just non-existent. You're talking to Gian Giovale, not to Joe Soap. Believe me, it's good of you to worry. I appreciate it. But there's no need. Try again.'

She stared at him and then shook her head, almost despairingly. 'I don't understand,' she said at length. 'How can you even think of – and why should you be so willing to – to do such a thing? I don't understand.'

There was a little silence and then he leaned forwards, and put both his hands firmly on hers on the table. His fingers were square with highly polished and carefully filed nails and the backs of his hands were thickly dusted with hair and she stared down at them, fascinated.

'Listen, I'll tell you. When I met you in London –' he gave a gusty little sigh, 'I tell you, I committed a sin. I saw you, another man's wife and I thought – ay, ay, Gian, why didn't you meet this lady long ago? I never saw a lady I liked the look of better. You're lovely, you know that? A beautiful lady, with two beautiful little boys – I loved you the moment I saw you. But I tell myself, I am not a man to steal another man's wife. I am

309

Gian Giovale, a good man, well brought up by a great Momma, a lady like you. I don't do such things. But when I say I love someone that is for life. I can't ever hope you'll care for me, but I won't ever change. And that means, when you want something, I want it.'

He leaned back again, well satisfied with his speech, releasing her hands and staring at her with his eyes glistening with unshed tears of emotion and suddenly, dreadfully, she wanted to giggle.

There was this square little man with the overfussy clothes and an air of self-importance as ridiculous as a bullfrog's, whom she had found agreeable simply because he looked faintly reminiscent of her dead father, here he was vowing his love for her, casting himself as some sort of latter-day Abelard, and all she wanted to do was laugh at him . . .

And then she remembered the calm way he had told her what he could do to help her and the laughter spluttered and died in her throat and was replaced by tears and she shook her head, miserably, letting the tears slide unheeded out of her eyes, and he looked at her with his own eyes brighter than ever as his feelings bubbled up, obviously deeply gratified by her response.

'There, my dear Maddie, there, there!' he said and patted her hand again and then, clearly well satisfied, leaned back.

'I can't let you do such a thing,' she said huskily, and reached into her pocket to find a handkerchief. 'I mean – it's the maddest thing I ever heard and –'

'There's nothing mad about it,' he said sharply and she glanced at him and then away, startled by the new note in his voice. So far he had been all she could ever have wanted in his attitude to her; warm, concerned, tender, always polite, even when he had outlined in the most chillingly casual terms his remedy for her dilemma. But now he sounded irritable and she felt a little stab of apprehension.

'There's nothing mad about it. It's an answer. This man Costello and his daughter have made trouble for you. So, we deal with this. Is this mad?'

'No, Gian,' she said. 'Of course I didn't mean mad – I just meant, it's so extreme.'

At once he was all charm and tenderness again. 'Extreme? I like that. It sounds so English – so refined, you know? I don't think it's any more extreme than what they're trying to do with you. They want to end your marriage to a man you love and make your little men into bastards? *That* is extreme. What I am saying will stop them. And make sure they never try it again –' He laughed then, cosily, as though he were talking of some sort of practical joke, no more. 'And make sure they never try it again – and like I told you, I've had a few business problems with Costello. I ain't saying I couldn't handle 'em, but this may be quicker and I'd get an extra benefit out of it as well at the pleasure of being of service to you. So why not?'

She stared at him with her eyes wide, fascinated now. The longer he went on about it, the more reasonable it sounded and she knew that she was being dazzled. The combination of her aching muscles and back, the way her feet screamed their resentment of her abuse of them, the empty-headed sensation that still bedevilled her, all added together to rob her of all her common sense. Or so it seemed, for she heard her own voice speaking now, a little more strongly, and was amazed.

'How would you – I mean, what sort of –' she swallowed, 'what would you do?'

'That's better,' he said softly. 'Now you think like a person, and not only a good loving lady. It's right you should be such a lady, of course, but sometimes a person has to be sensible and not so good. Are you sure you want me to tell you? Wouldn't it be better I just arrange it all and let you know afterwards?'

'I haven't said yes, yet!' she said, alarmed, and he laughed again and shook his head at her.

'I know you haven't! And I promised you I wouldn't do anything without your agreement and Gian Giovale keeps his promises. As a matter of honour – okay, you want to know what I do?'

He tilted his head and thought a while. 'There's a lot of possibilities. Cars is always good.'

'Cars?' she said.

'Huh hmm. Cars. A little attention beneath the bonnet, the long run up Pilgrim's Highway – anything can happen.'

She shook her head. 'I can't – I mean, suppose it doesn't? Suppose that it goes wrong and the car – the car crashes, but the people in it –'

'Yes,' he said judiciously. 'Yes, this is a problem, so it's not a way I like. This time. But there are other possibilities.'

311

She watched him, still fascinated, unable to believe this was happening. She was sitting here discussing with this little man the way to get Cray Costello and his daughter Gloria out of her way for always. That, he had said with every air of practical common sense when she had told him the cause of her distress, was what had to be done. There would be no sense, he had pointed out, in trying to buy Costello off; he was too rich. No sense in trying to appeal to his better nature, because he hadn't got any of that. Gian had been very certain and his face had hardened as he had spoken of his past dealings with him. So what was left? Just get rid of the pair of 'em, he'd finished calmly. 'What else can we do?'

And in spite of her first horrified rejection of the notion, in spite of the way she had refused even to think about it, here she now sat over delicate china cups full of pale amber jasmine tea, talking about it as calmly as they might have talked about getting mice out of a kitchen or cockroaches from a cellar. It just didn't seem believable.

'I don't like ways that make the police interested. Even the most efficient ways. Once they start putting their noses in it upsets people, you understand? Better they don't get involved. And there's no skill in just popping off with pieces either. Anyone can fix this. From me, you expect other ideas, hmm?' And again he beamed at her and this time she managed to smile back. Why not smile, after all? He was being so kind, so caring, so helpful.

She picked up the little cup and began to sip her cooling tea, glad to have something on which to concentrate. Holding it still, getting the edge of the cup to her lips, all this took effort and while she was doing that she couldn't think of other things. Like the pain in her muscles and her back and the fact that this man was sitting opposite her and planning to kill two people simply because they had made her unhappy and were trying to rob her of the most important person in her life. And she raised her eyes to look at him and saw again that resemblance to Alfred and thought muzzily, Daddy, Daddy always takes care of me. I was so wicked, Daddy . . .

'Better ideas,' he said again and slowly began to smile. 'Right?'

'Hmm?' she said a little dreamily. The fatigue in her was

beginning to make her feel as strange as last night's whisky had done, though without the sense of sickness.

'I have one. It's summer – such a difficult time, summer.' His grin widened. 'Everyone down at the beach, all the extra pressure on the local people and the services. It's difficult. So, so hot –'

'Very hot,' she agreed, wondering lazily what he was talking about. Was he still making his plan, still offering to get rid of Cray and his hateful daughter? And suddenly, quite unbidden, Gloria's face came into her mind's eye as clear and as sharp as if she had been standing right in front of her. There was the glossy complexion and the droop of the carefully painted mouth and the hair pulled back into such a classically elegant style and – she shook her head and put down her cup so sharply that it tipped on the table and spilled its contents into a little pool.

'This time of the year,' Gian was saying, 'is not a healthy time. For houses, you understand me? Fires happen all the time. It's a bad thing, fires. They spread so fast in these seaside houses.' He looked at her then, very seriously. 'They're timber-framed houses, you see. Clapboard. Pretty, old and pretty, but all the same –' He shook his head regretfully. 'If they catch from a cigarette end or a forgotten TV set or a barbecue not put out right it can go up whoosh – like that –' And he threw his hands up in a quaint little gesture that made her smile.

He looked at her benevolently and then said, 'You like that, hmm?' and she thought again of the gesture he had made and smiled even more widely.

'Mmm,' she said. 'You're so funny, Gian. So funny and nice and kind –'

He patted her hand and then, purposefully, pushed back his chair. 'I won't be long,' he said and went away and she sat there at the table staring through the now almost empty restaurant to the window, beyond which the street signs and the cars still livened Kneeland Street, even though it was so late, and didn't think of anything much.

Her head was spinning still, and she felt as though she weren't here at all really. She had split into two separate people, and one of them was sitting here, trying to keep her exhausted eyes open and the other one was curled up, fast asleep, somewhere high in a corner of this odd room. And she lifted her eyes and stared round at the dusty cornices and the tasselled Chinese lanterns and embroidered silk pictures, trying to see that curled-up self.

'There we are, then,' he said and she blinked and focused her eyes on him again as he came and settled himself at the table once more.

'What?' she said stupidly.

'Not another thought,' he said happily. 'Don't give it another thought. I fixed it, I told you. I have my ways. Not another thought do you need. Have some more food, *cara*. You ate nothing. A little egg Foo Yong, maybe, a piece of their lemon chicken?'

'Fixed it,' she said, still stupidly, and then more sharply, 'fixed it?'

'I have people at Orleans. It's not that far from Osterville. Half an hour in the Packard maybe on a good night. Small country roads, you understand how it is. But not far. They'll sort it out. Now, let me call the waiter and —'

She put out one hand and gripped his like a vice. 'What have you done?'

'What I told you I'd do,' he said and smiled at her. 'I fixed it so Cray Costello and Gloria will not be a problem any more. Soon you'll hear. They don't waste time, my friends, you know? It doesn't do to waste time. A day or so, and you'll hear. They'll sort it all out and your Jay will come back to you and I —' He sighed and looked at her with his eyes once again bright with emotion, tears of self sacrifice hovering there on the lids, 'I'll go back home and think about you and your little men, happy again, and that will be enough for me. It'll be enough I could help you.' And he closed his hand on hers and smiled in her eyes, 'Because you're a lovely lady, a lovely little Momma and to help you is my pleasure.'

And she sat and stared at him and thought, it's not true, it can't be true. Only a madman talks such rubbish. It isn't true and it's time I went back to the hotel and to bed and got rid of him. I'll talk to Jay tomorrow, sort it all out tomorrow.

So she smiled at him and said only, 'Please, Gian, take me back to the hotel. I'm so tired —'

35

August 1953

Again she needed whisky to get to sleep. She should have been able to lie on a pin and sleep, she told herself, exhausted as she was, but once she got back to the silent suite with its litter of toys and the faint sound of Daphne's snoring coming from behind the closed door of the room she shared with the boys she was so tense she couldn't imagine lying down anywhere.

She stood in the middle of the sitting room and looked round and tried to pretend that nothing that she saw was real. All this was a dreadful dream, and she was really at home in her bedroom at Stanmore, Jay asleep beside her while she dreamed these horrors. And she folded her arms across her chest with a convulsive movement and pinched both her upper arms hard until she winced. And it wasn't a dream, none of it, and after that whisky seemed the only answer.

When she woke late the next afternoon, it seemed to her that she was experiencing bad dreams in layers; last night with Gian Giovale had been another nightmare to add to the one she had already been having and now she was seized by another, and she lay on her back in the vast rumpled bed, tasting the sickly sourness of the whisky on her furred tongue and tried to remember all Giovale had said and what she had said in response. And was so appalled when she did remember that she couldn't bear to think of it at all, and struggled out of bed and went padding off to the sitting room to find Daphne and the boys. She needed them suddenly, needed their noise and their fussing because they were normal everyday things that would drag her some way out of this horrible sensation of being not quite real.

But they were not there. She stood in the middle of the sitting room, her toes curling against the thick carpet and clutching to her chest the sheet with which she had wrapped herself and felt tears rise in her throat. She wanted her boys and they weren't here and she was dreadfully alone and dreadfully miserable, and she lifted her head and let the feelings erupt into a howl.

'Maddie, Maddie, it's all right –' Annie cried and reached for her, but Joe pulled hard on her arm and made her fall back.

'No,' he said softly, 'don't stop her. If you try to make it easier for her she'll refuse to dig it out. It's got to be faced, however much it hurts. Leave her be –'

'But how can you be so cruel? Look at her! She's in a dreadful state.'

'The more dreadful the better,' Joe said grimly and held on to her so hard that his fingers dug into her arm. 'Let her suffer. If she doesn't suffer now, it's all wasted. Let her *suffer* –'

The shower helped and so did getting dressed and then she went downstairs to sit in the lobby and try to think. Sitting in the suite was horrible, bleak and empty as it was, and there was always the chance Daphne would get back soon with the boys and she could see them coming into the lobby through the great revolving doors. She'd wait for them there, she thought, and then, when they came in, take them for an ice-cream soda. That would be fun, to take her two little boys for an American soda, even though Daphne would look disapproving, and she managed a small private smile as she imagined Daphne looking at her and saying in that loud bossy voice of hers, 'Really, Mummy, they'll never eat their suppers!' as she took them, jumping and laughing, to the soda fountain. My two little boys, she thought, and suddenly heard Gian Giovale's sentimental tones in her ears: 'Two little men, such lovely little men'. And she shivered and got to her feet with a sudden movement to walk round the lobby and the desks and shops instead of just sitting there. It would give her something to do while she waited; while she was looking at things she couldn't be thinking . . .

But thinking was unavoidable. All the time as she loitered past the shops the vision of Jay and Gloria Costello sitting together, walking together, being together, snaked in and out her thoughts, slippery and swift, and she had to make an almost physical effort to stop herself from crying her rage and distress aloud again as she had upstairs in the empty suite. There it

316

hadn't mattered, but here where people would see her and hear her – somehow she had to hold on to the shreds of her normal self, somehow had to look and be like other people.

It was when she reached the car hire desk that the idea suddenly came to her. So far she had thought of various people she could turn to to help her deal with her pain, two in particular who could intercede for her with Jay, or with Costello, and put an end to this sickening nightmare. And they had failed her hopelessly, being either impotent or mad with crazy dangerous ideas. But there was one person, and only one who really could make things right for her, and she wondered, as she stood there staring at the poster that had caught her eye from its commanding place behind the desk and stared at the wide Cape Cod beach and the white clapboard houses of a small town it depicted, why she had not thought of him before.

He had been pleasant enough to her when they had met in London, had seemed a reasonable enough sort of man, she told herself. Maybe he was besotted with his horrible daughter, but that didn't mean he was not approachable, did it? If she went there to see him, took her little boys with her, discussed the situation with him calmly and simply and honestly, wouldn't he see how absurd it all was? Wouldn't he see too that she was as good a businesswoman as anyone would want to deal with? There she was, with her father's business safe in her own hands at home in London, and thriving too, and that meant she had something to offer him.

And offer it she would. She stood there in the lobby of the Copley Plaza Hotel and saw herself standing beside Jay, her Jay, and telling him she had given up all she had for him. Her business in London, her inheritance, all her assets, Costello could have them all in exchange for what she had a right to hold – her own husband. And Jay would laugh down at her with those blazing blue eyes of his and say, 'You're a crazy kid, Maddie, you know that? One crazy kid and I love you for it.' And the nightmare would be over for ever –

The girl at the desk was remarkably helpful. A car to rent? Of course. What would she like? A Packard, a Plymouth, or maybe a Lincoln? She had a nice convertible available this morning, a very fast good car, ideal for runs to the beach. Ah, with small children? No, then better not a convertible. A Studebaker or –

no, the best would be the Plymouth. On Mr Kincaid's account? Of course, no problem.

And then the girl took all the time Maddie needed to help her work out how to get there. Looked up the Costello address in Osterville in her collection of telephone directories and then showed her the route. Leave the city on Hancock, join the Southern Artery and then out through Weymouth and Rockland and on down to Kingston, Plymouth and Sandwich, and Maddie felt a great wave of optimism wash over her as the familiar English place names rang in her ears. It was all going to be all right. She wasn't an alien in a strange unwelcoming place that hated her and treated her like a nothing, that tried to rob her of the only person who mattered in her life. This was after all the real world where people understood and things could be sorted out with a little simple wheeling and dealing. Hadn't she been doing that successfully all her life? Hadn't she shown what an excellent businesswoman she was? Well, she could be just as excellent a businesswoman in her private life. If a business had to be fought for and finagled for and bargained for, so did love and so did husbands. And she would do it.

And she folded the map with its careful pencil marks which the girl had given her and took the keys for the car and went down to the garage to see it, a handsome dark red Plymouth, and patted its bonnet as though it were a living thing and went back upstairs to wait for the boys. She would still give them their sodas but after that they would set out for Osterville; it was just a two-hour drive, the girl had said, in that car, with a little speeding, 'But watch out for the cops. They get nasty on that road south sometimes, especially on Fridays. But if you keep a sharp eye out you can get away fast enough. I do it often –' So that was what she would do. And she went and sat in the lobby, to wait for her two little boys and their nanny.

By eight o'clock she was angry still, but also very frightened. She had been merely irritated at first, as the afternoon had crept on round the clock and the people in the lobby had ebbed and flowed around her as though she were an inanimate thing, and then had castigated herself for her own foolishness. Daphne was the best nanny she had ever had, and the fact that she found places in this strange town to take her small charges to enjoy themselves instead of sitting cooped up moping in a hotel room, neglected by their mother, was something to be grateful for, not to find annoying.

So she went to the coffee shop and made herself eat, ordering a bacon, lettuce and tomato sandwich. But when it arrived it was so vast and the amount of trimming that came with it in the form of salads and potato chips so lavish that the sight of it sickened her, and all she could manage to swallow was some of the toast. But it used up time and after she had finished and paid, she made her way, loitering a little to make assurance doubly sure, back to the suite, certain that Daphne and the boys would be there.

But they were not and the clock crept even more slowly onwards, and by nine o'clock she was so alarmed that she was ready to call the police and put out searches. Daphne had always been so punctilious about the boys' bedtimes. Six o'clock for Danny, seven o'clock for Buster, unless he had been naughty (which was fairly often) with a special stay-up-late treat at the weekends sometimes. But nine o'clock? She would never keep them up so late, let alone out in the streets . . .

But for some reason she couldn't pick up the phone yet, and after a moment she went across the room to the bar and took some more whisky. It nagged at the back of her mind that this was the third day running she'd taken the stuff, she who never drank. Everyone knows that in times of stress people need strong liquor, but all the same – but she ignored her inner doubts and poured a large glass of the stuff and splashed in some soda and drank half of it in a single swallow. It steadied her nerves a little, and made it easier for her to control her fear, but she set the glass down on the bar so sharply that it splashed some of its contents on to her, and she swore softly and dabbed at the stain, knowing it would mark, and then lifted her head sharply as at last she heard a key in the door.

Daphne came in, alone, and Maddie stood there beside the bar, holding on to the edge of it and stared at her, startled, and was plunged again into it, that dreadful feeling of unreality that had so plagued her yesterday evening. Once again she felt like a half person, with the most important part of her curled up somewhere above her head, watching with a beady-eyed stare all that was going on.

And then she closed her eyes and shook her head a little and opened them again and knew why she had felt so strange. She had only once before seen Daphne out of her uniform, for which the girl clearly had a great affection. That had been on the day she had come for her interview for the job, and she had worn a civilian coat and hat, but it was not all that unlike the uniform ones she had always worn thereafter. She had appeared dull and ordinary and that had been one of the most comfortable things about her. She had looked what she was: reliable.

But now she was wearing a tightly fitted red suit in heavy linen which was rather crumpled and which looked less than ideal on her plump figure, straining at the very seams every time she moved, while perched on the top of her head was a red hat with a scrap of dotted veiling which hung over her eyes and made her look slightly cross-eyed. She was smiling a little with inexpertly painted lips and she had blue eyeshadow smudged over her lids.

Maddie caught her breath and Daphne turned at the sound and stared at her, obviously startled, and then grinned.

'Why, Mummy, you gave me such a start! I didn't see you. Have you had a good day? Do you feel a bit better? You slept so heavily this afternoon I didn't like to wake you – but you look as right as ninepence now, though a bit peaky. It's the heat, I dare say. It does get to you, doesn't it?'

'Where are the boys?' Maddie said. And then as Daphne stared at her, her voice rose. 'Where are they? And where have you been, looking like that? I've never seen you in such things –'

Daphne almost simpered. 'Oh, do you like it? I couldn't resist it, and that's the truth of it. I found it this afternoon, in a shop on Charles Street. Ever so dear, it was, but I thought – why not? All that overtime money and all, and here I am in America so why not? And they said a hat'd look nice and showed me some and I couldn't resist this one. The girl in the shop was ever so nice, said I should try her make-up and everything and you know me, never one for much of that but it seems all right here, doesn't it? So I went and bought some.' She giggled. 'I've had a lovely time, because then I went to the pictures and I saw ever such a lovely film with Richard Burton, *The Robe* it was, really lovely, and then I had some supper in a nice restaurant – it'd have been nice to have a girlfriend to go with, but you can't have everything, can you? Though it'd be nice to have someone to chat to –'

'Where are the boys?' Maddie said again and her lips were stiff and her voice half choked with the fear that had so inexplicably filled her, but Daphne's tide of chatter went on and on until at last Maddie managed to shout it. 'Where are the boys? Goddamn you, *where are my boys?*'

Daphne turned and blinked at her, her hands ludicrously above her head, as she had been trying to untangle her veil from her hair and she stared, her mouth half open, and then almost gasped with anxiety.

'Oh dear, Mummy, didn't you find my note? I left it on the dressing table in the room – to explain to you. He said not to wake you, so I didn't –'

'Who said – what note?' Maddie's voice was husky now, and she still had to stand there holding on to the bar, unable to move her legs.

Daphne had her hat off now and was hurrying across the room, her thick legs looking wider than ever over the red pumps she had bought and which were clearly rather small for her. 'Here it is!' she called from the bedroom and came out holding a piece of paper in front of her. 'I was sure you'd go in there to see if we were there, and would see the note. I dare say I should have put it in the bathroom but you know how it is when there's a rush on and he was in such a hurry, you know how he is sometimes. So I just left it there. Oh dear, poor Mummy, have you been all worried? Of course you have, I would've been too. Oh, I do blame myself. I should've come back and told you before going off on a jaunt of my own, but it's the first chance I've had since we got here, and I did so want to have a look round the shops and spend a little. And after I'd been given all that extra money and all, I suppose it was burning a hole in my pocket. But it's all right, Mummy. There's no need to fret you.' Her eyes slid down to the bar and the glass of whisky on it and she stopped and then, with elephantine tact, said, 'Well, now, come and sit down, do. I'll make you a nice cup of tea, shall I? I got the hotel to send up the makings. Couldn't be doing with the sort of stuff they sent up when I ordered tea on room service

– just lukewarm dishwater, that was – come and sit down now, Mummy, and I'll soon have you as right as ninepence.'

Maddie closed her eyes in an agony of frustration. 'Where are they, for Christ's sake! If you don't tell me I'll –'

'It's all right!' Daphne said soothingly. 'They're with Daddy, of course. No need to fret. They're with Daddy!'

The wash of relief that came over her was so great that she actually rocked on her feet and Daphne seized her in a practised grip and led her to a sofa, and she stumbled a little and plumped down gratefully. Of course they were all right. There had been no need to panic like this. It had been her guilty conscience, that was the thing. She'd spent no time at all with them since they got here, had left everything to Daphne, no wonder she felt bad about them. But they were all right, they were with their father –

'When will they be back?' She looked down at Daphne, who was now on her knees in front of her, and scrubbing at her skirt with a damp napkin she had brought from the bar, working on the whisky stain on the front panel of the pale blue silk. 'Leave that, it doesn't matter – when will they be back?'

Daphne sat back on her heels and looked at the stain and then up into her face. 'It seems a pity to let it be spoiled,' she said a little censorially, and then looked worried. 'Are you feeling all right, Mummy? It's not like you to – er – well, indulge is the word, isn't it? Can I help? A trouble shared and all that, you know what they say . . .' And she looked up at her with her face twisted with so much sympathy that Maddie could have smacked it.

'I'm all right,' she said brusquely. 'I simply spilled – look, why aren't they back yet? Where did he take them? It's getting on for –' She looked at her watch. 'It's damn near a quarter to ten! They should have been in bed ages ago!'

Daphne laughed merrily. 'I'm sure they are! No need to worry, Mummy. I do wish you'd seen the note – there it is now. That'll explain it all.'

She pointed at the piece of paper which Maddie was still holding and she blinked and then looked down and unfolded it and began to read.

'Dear Mummy,' ran Daphne's big round handwriting. 'Such fun for us! Daddy has said he wants the boys to have a weekend

322

playing by the seaside, so he's collected them to go down to the house where he is staying at Cape Cod (I'll have mine with chips, ha ha!) and he will bring them back on Sunday in good time for bed. I have packed their shorts and the blue striped shirts and plenty of nappies – I should call them diapers! – and the rubber pants for Danny and Daddy says he can get them swimming costumes when they get there, as well as buckets and spades. He says if you want him the phone number is Osterville 722911 but it might be better not. He says to say he sends his love and have a nice weekend. Yours Daphne. PS I thought I'd pop out too, as Daddy has given me the time off. I should be in around nine or so.'

'There,' Daphne said. 'You see? Nothing to worry about at all.'

36

August 1953

Osterville. She read it again and again. Osterville. If it had been anywhere else it might have been his parents' place, but there could be no doubt about this and she lifted her head and looked at Daphne and said dully, 'Did he say who else would be there?'

The girl looked uncomfortable for a moment and then smoothed her face. 'Just people,' he said. I was a bit bothered about the boys to tell the truth — Buster needs to be reminded, you see. If he isn't he gets ever so sore and I'm just beginning to get him trained so I said to Daddy —'

Maddie closed her eyes and said it again, slowly, working so hard at controlling herself that her whole body felt as rigid as a board. 'Who else will be there?'

'It's that Mr Costello's house,' Daphne said after a moment and got to her feet and stood with her head bent, brushing invisible dust from her knees so that she need not look at Maddie. 'Daddy said not to worry about Buster and his potty, that she — that Mr Costello's daughter'd be there and anyway they had a housekeeper and all like that, so I didn't need to go with them.'

She reddened then and this time did look up at Maddie. 'I didn't ask if I could go for my own pleasure, you know, Mummy! I said it was just the boys I wanted to look after, that it was my responsibility and that, but Daddy said —' She stopped. 'He was quite nice about it really, I suppose. He just said he wanted the boys to get to know Mr Costello and his daughter and they couldn't do that so easy if I was there all the time and he gave me the extra money and that and — well, you'd been out all evening, and I didn't like to wake you to ask what to do and —'

Suddenly Maddie wasn't listening to her any more. The realisation of what was possible had broken over her like a tidal wave as she had suddenly found herself thinking of last night with Gian, and she was on her feet and running to the phone, throwing herself at the drawer which held the directory, scrambling through the pages with shaking fingers. It seemed to take her twice as long to find it this time as it had at the Chinese restaurant, but at last there it was, and she seized the phone and somehow managed to dial, misdialling once since she was so agitated, and having to try again, but eventually she was through.

The number rang and rang, bleating away interminably in her ear until she wanted to throw the whole handset violently at the wall, but she managed to control it and dialled again, and yet again, waiting and praying for an answer.

But there was none. There was no way she could get hold of Gian Giovale and make sure that all that rubbish he had spouted last night when she had been so weak and dizzy and stupid with fatigue and fear had been just that; rubbish, and she stood there clutching the phone to her head with white-knuckled intensity, trying to think what to do as Daphne stood and stared at her, wide-eyed and frankly disapproving, clearly certain that Maddie had gone mad. Or was drunk. And Maddie felt her eyes on the stain on her dress and felt her own rage rise and turned her back on her.

And now what? Something had to be done, but oh God, what? And she stood there as the phone in the empty house on the other side of Boston rang on and on, trying to imagine it; phoning Jay, telling him what had happened between her and Gian Giovale, explaining the risk, making sure he got out with the children, didn't stay in the house – and her gorge rose and she literally retched.

But it had to be done and she flung the phone back on its hook, and then ran across the room to pick up the discarded piece of paper that was Daphne's note and smooth it out and find the number on it.

It seemed to take for ever to get the long distance operator to answer, to get her to connect her to Osterville, but then at last the sound came, the steady burring in her ear, and for one mad hopeful moment she thought, there's no one there. It isn't there he's taken them. They've gone somewhere else, somewhere different, somewhere safe –

But then the connection was made and she heard a sudden

burst of music and voices and someone shouted in her ear, 'Yeah? Who is it?'

'I want to speak to Mr Kincaid, please,' she said and knew her voice was still. 'It's urgent.'

'Who? There ain't – oh, Kincaid? Jay – hey, there's a broad here wants Jay. Where is he?'

There was more music and the loud din of voices and she stood there staring unseeingly at Daphne as she listened, straining to hear something beyond the fuzziness of mere noise, and then heard someone else bawling, 'Jay . . . where's that bastard Kincaid?'

And then at last, there he was, the familiar voice at the end of the phone and she gasped, 'Oh, Christ, Jay, thank God – listen, you have to get them out of there, you and the boys, you have to get out of there –'

'What the – who is this?' Jay's voice was cool, a little thick perhaps, and she thought: he's been drinking. That bastard's been drinking and the boys –

'Christ, Jay, the boys! Where *are* they?'

'Maddie?' he said after a moment and now his voice had lost its thickness and sounded just guarded. 'What is it? What do you want?'

'I told you, get the boys out of there – it's dangerous! For Christ's sake, will you *listen* to me. This is urgent –'

'Listen, Maddie, I can't talk now. They've got people here – it's all a bit tricky. Call me in the morning, hmm? Then we can talk, whatever it is. But there's no problem. The boys are great, fine. In bed, asleep, fine. Now just you go to bed and tomorrow we'll talk –'

'No –' she shrieked and grabbed at her own hair with her other hand as the connection was broken and pulled hard in her desperate frustration and Daphne yelled at her and jumped forwards.

'Mummy, please, don't – what's the matter? The boys – what's the matter?'

'He hung up on me,' she cried. 'The bastard hung up on me – I have to talk to him. I have to –' and again she began to scrabble for the phone dial, but twice her fingers slipped and after a moment Daphne leaned over her and said, 'I'll do it, Mummy. Leave it to me. Give me the number.'

Gratefully she let the phone go and pushed the piece of paper at her, still shaking, and as Daphne began to dial the operator, she went across to the bar to get the remainder of her drink. She had to do something to steady herself, had to find some way to stop this awful shaking and she picked up the glass and turned back toward the phone, drinking as she went, to find Daphne's eyes fixed accusingly on her as she held on to the earpiece.

'What are you –' she began but then Daphne held up her hand and said in the special refined voice she tended to put on when she used the phone, 'Is that the Costello residence? May I speak with Mr Jay Kincaid please? It is a matter of some importance. Thank you *so* much –' And she put her hand over the mouthpiece and hissed at Maddie, 'He's coming –'

Maddie hurried towards her, and set her empty glass on the table beside the phone and held out her hand, but Daphne was speaking again. 'Hello, Mr Kincaid? Oh, yes, Daddy, this is Daphne . . . what? Well . . .' She looked up then at Maddie and stared at her, listening hard, and Maddie stood as though frozen in mid-action with her hand held out.

'No, Daddy, not really . . . well, maybe a bit. She's been awfully upset. She didn't find the note I left, you see, and was ever so worried and then when I came in and she found out where the boys were she . . . what? Well, she has –' She turned her back then on Maddie and dropped her voice. 'She has had a *couple* of drinks, I think. Like I said to you last night, it isn't like Mummy to take whisky but she did the night before last and I think last night too, going by the smell and –'

It was more than Maddie could bear for another moment and she threw herself at Daphne, pushing her aside, and grabbed the phone from her hand so violently that the girl lurched and almost fell.

'Jay, for Christ's sake, listen to me. I have to tell you something. Don't hang up or you're a dead man –'

'Maddie, what's gotten into you? Are you crazy?' Jay's voice clacked in her ear full of what? Anger? Pain? No, nothing as important as that. No more than simple embarrassment. 'What are you doing sloshing whisky, for Pete's sake? Do you have to make such a federal case out of this? So we've had a break-up, okay! It happens. It's happened to a lot of people and now it's happened to us. Don't turn into one of those goddamn witches over it. You don't need that.'

'It's not that, it isn't —' she gabbled but he wasn't going to stop this time.

'I've thought a lot about it since we talked, believe me, and I just don't see what you're making so much over it for. People get divorced all the time, I told you. I wanted this to be a good quiet decent arrangement, but you have to make it into a bad scene. Okay, so make it! But I have the right to take my own kids to see their future stepmother if I choose to, without having to put up with a lot of hysterical shit from you over it —'

'It's not about her, for God's sake, I'm not calling about her — it's the boys and you. Jay, I have to tell you I did a crazy thing. I talked to Gian Giovale about this, and —'

'Listen, are you drunk? Daphne said you've been mopping it up a bit. Are you drunk now?'

There was a sudden roar of sound over the phone and a burst of even louder music and she winced as he bawled at someone, 'For Chrissakes, shut the door a minute, will you? I can't hear myself think here —' And then she said breathlessly, 'You're as likely to be drunk as I am. Listen, Jay, I told Gian and he said —'

'Who?'

'Oh, God, Gian Giovale, the man who was in London with us in June and —'

'Oh, him. You talked to him? Why did you — for Chrissakes, will you people shut that lousy door! — Maddie, what are you going on about? Listen, I can't handle all this right now. Call me tomorrow, all right. This is a crazy way to talk, a mad party going on here and all that —'

'He's going to kill you!' she shrieked. 'He's going to kill you —'

'Listen, Maddie, when you start making stupid cracks like that, I've had it up to here. Call me tomorrow, when you're sober — and don't bother to call back tonight. I'm taking the lousy phone off the hook —'

And again the line went dead and she stood there, staring at the buzzing thing, and again the tidal wave of fear rose and washed over her with a great breathtaking roar.

'Oh, God,' she whispered and slowly put the phone down as

Daphne came out of the bathroom carrying a wet cloth in one hand and a bowl of water in the other.

'Now, Mummy,' she said soothingly. 'Let's make you comfortable. Come and lie down and I'll bathe your head and I've got some aspirin here, and we'll get them to send up some ice for a cap and you'll feel much better in the morning.'

She stared at the girl, at her good-natured silly face and her worried expression and she wanted to hit it, to throw her and her concern and her ice and her bowl of water clean across the room. But it wasn't the girl's fault and even in her fevered state of terror, she knew that, and managed to control her own need for violence.

'Thanks, Daphne,' she said, and moved across to the sofa to pick up her bag which she had left there. 'It's not as easy as that. I have to go to fetch the boys. Stay here. I'll be back. I swear I'll bring them back . . .' and she looked at her and knew her face was twisted with anxiety. 'I will, won't I?'

'But they're coming back on Sunday, anyway,' Daphne said, bewildered, standing there with her bowl and her towel like a picture from a nursing manual. 'You aren't going to fetch them back now in the middle of the night, are you?'

'I have to,' Maddie said. 'I have to. If I don't . . .' She swallowed.

'What if you don't?' Daphne was frankly avid with curiosity now and her eyes were almost popping with it. 'What's upset you so much, Mummy? Is he leaving you or –'

'It's nothing to do with him!' Maddie cried. 'It's not the – it's just that it isn't safe for them there. I've got to get them out. The boys and Jay – it isn't safe – I've got to go. What's the time? I've got to go. If I can get there by midnight, it'll still be today and I may be in time. Oh, please – I've got to go –'

And she ran out of the suite, as she scrabbled in her bag for the keys of the Plymouth.

'Here we go,' Joe said. 'Oh, but here we go –' And he pulled the syringe away and took off the tourniquet and then reached out and held Maddie's shoulders firmly as she rolled and twisted and then arched her back and the words came pouring out of her in a fountain, a cascade of emotion, and Annie stood and stared, feeling the fear and horror coming from that twisted anguished shape, letting it roll over her too, and shaking as she listened. It didn't seem possible that just hearing words could create such an electric atmosphere of pain and terror in this small shady clinical room. But it could and it did, and her pulses thumped heavily in her head as she stood and the words went on and on and on.

A black ribbon of road, twisting, rolling, curving ahead of her in the lights, looping and unlooping itself interminably.

Her hands clamped to the wheel, so tightly held that her fingers sang with pins and needles and when she had to change direction her muscles twitched uncontrollably so that the car leapt and swerved and she had to pull it back and over again, so that often she was twisting more than the road was.

Her foot clamped to the accelerator, the other hovering over the brake and her calves aching with tension.

The dashboard, glowing with little lights, and the needle on the speedometer swinging and creeping upwards. Fifty miles an hour, then up to seventy, and down to sixty again as the road began to curve. A sudden plunge to forty on a corner and the tyres squealing their fury at their mistreatment.

Lights coming, tiny pinpricks, starlike and innocent but growing, swelling into a nightmare of dazzle, shrieking their arrival at her, and then sweeping over her in an insulting contemptuous blaze that made her swerve yet again.

The mirror above her head, in which the lights of the traffic behind dwindled and vanished and then grew again as followers came up to her and she had to slow down for fear they were police who would stop her, until they passed and she could speed up again, pushing her foot down to the floor so that the car leapt forwards and roared with anger under its bonnet.

Time crawling round the clock so slowly that it was not possible to believe there was any change at all. Seconds limping like hours and still the black silk of the unravelling road and the hiss of passing billboards that leapt into her lights and dwindled again. And all she could think of was Gian Giovale's voice, that stupid silly sentimental voice. 'Not another thought. Don't give it another thought. I fixed it for you – they'll sort it all out – fires happen all the time. Fires happen all the time, fires happen all the time –'

And then the clock lied to her and it was time she was there, but she wasn't. She had passed Barnstaple, and now the familiarity of the name wasn't a comfort; it was an added threat, somehow, a reminder that this place was alien and cruel and hated her – and Dennis Port and still the signposts for Osterville had not appeared and it was past eleven-thirty and still she had to push and push and push and –

And then it was there. The wheels rattled beneath her and there was a glint of water on each side in the glimmering darkness and a sign that read 'Cape Cod Canal' and then she was on a narrower, rougher road, one that roared rather than sang beneath her wheels and there beside the road she saw it: the sign for Osterville.

A run of trees on her right beside the sea; she could hear the sea now, hear it murmuring and warning her and she opened the window with one shaking hand and the cold night air came rushing in and made her gasp, so that she opened her dry mouth and sucked in the dampness and the salt of it and was grateful.

The trees beside the sea running away ahead of her, and little glints of light showing the other side of the road where now suddenly there were demure picket fences and shaven lawns, black in her headlights as she passed, and mailboxes painted white and gravel paths and always, always the smell of the sea coming in.

And more than that. A different smell that she had to be imagining because she was so frightened, because she had been thinking of it so long, because she had created it inside her own nose.

A cheerful smell. A warm and friendly crackling sort of smell, the sort of smell that made you feel comfortable on cold March mornings and dank winter evenings.

The smell of burning wood.

37

August 1953

The car swerved, almost without her knowing she had turned the steering wheel, and she heard the gravel spurt under her wheels as she went careering through big double gates and up the drive past the trees and bushes on each side which nodded at her in friendly welcome as her bonnet thrust them aside and then, undeterred, pushed their leaves in through the open window, and the smell increased and became so thick it turned into sound, and became the crackling of sticks burning under coal as they tried to make it catch. And suddenly she was five years old again and sitting on her mother's lap in the kitchen of the house in Hackney where they had lived before they had gone to the flat in Regent's Park; sitting there with Mummy and stretching out her feet to the fire so that she could watch the flames seeming to come out of her toes and laugh at them and love the heat on her skin –

But this wasn't the house in Hackney and she wasn't five years old. This was Cape Cod, a million miles from anywhere and her own babies were stretching out their toes to the blaze and – she began to cry in terror, loudly gasping and wailing so that the sound ricocheted around the car and buffeted her ears as she pushed the engine furiously, twisting and turning, rushing onwards, until the last turn came and there in her lights were two men, leaping up and down and bawling with silent open mouths at her, with their arms held out, trying to stop her. And she couldn't stop but sat there with her foot clamped to the accelerator and her own mouth open as she wailed her terror, and they jumped aside as the car hit a barrier, hard, and she felt a sickening blow to her forehead as something came at her out of the glittering lights and blacked them so abruptly it was as though the whole world had died.

Annie stood with her hands over her ears, trying to shut it out, but she couldn't. The wailing was so loud and the pitch of it so high that it was impossible to escape it, and she closed her eyes, hoping that would make it less intense, but in fact it made it worse.

But Joe had an arm across her shoulders now and was speaking to her loudly.

'You can go if you like, Annie, but try to stay. It's all so interesting and –'

'Interesting?' She dropped her hands, as the wailing eased a little and became a high keening. 'You call this *interesting*? To see someone go through this, and to sweat and yell and shriek like that and call it –'

'It's a bloody sight better for her than to sit rocking in silence for another thirty-five years because she doesn't know how to wail,' he said sharply. 'And it *is* interesting. We're beginning to know what it is that she's been avoiding all this time. It's like lancing an abscess – once the pus is out she can start to heal. This is horrible to watch, perhaps, but then opening an abscess is horrible too. They smell disgusting as well. But they get better afterwards then as she's going to get better.'

'Better?' Annie said and moved away from him to go and stand beside the bed and look down on Maddie. She had her eyes wide open, and was staring up at the ceiling, but obviously not seeing anything, and her mouth was stretched in a wide rictus so that all her teeth showed. It was an ugly sight, but an oddly endearing one, and impulsively Annie put out one hand and set it on Maddie's. 'How can this be better? At least before she was contented enough. I wish I'd never got involved – I wish I'd left her alone. It was a wicked thing to do, wicked –'

'As wicked as leaving your mother alone?' Joe said softly, and she lifted her chin and stared at him.

'What? I never left her alone! Except that once, when – why are you so cruel to me? You know I took care of her all the time, all that I could –'

He shook his head. 'I'm not talking about what *you* did,' he said, his voice still soft, beneath the continuing wailing coming from Maddie. 'Why should you imagine for a moment that I'd criticise you on that score? Of course I know you were splendid – you took wonderful care of her. I've told you that many times.

No, I mean what your father did. He left your mother alone, didn't he? Left you and she alone most of your lives, just coming back often enough to make sure so that you could do nothing else but sit about and wait on his pleasure. Wouldn't it have been better if you and your mother had protested like this and then had healed? If she escaped from him, started to live for herself and healed as Maddie is going to? Because she will, you know. All this will leave her and she'll be free again. Jennifer was never free, was she? Always tied to Colin, always dancing to his tune, and there were you, tied to her, and furiously angry about it, and still are –'

'I'm not listening to this! I don't have to! I'm not your patient, and never you forget it! She is, Maddie is, not me – and I don't have to listen.'

But she didn't go. It would have been the easiest thing in the world to do, to walk to the door and open it and walk out, and he wouldn't have stopped her. But she didn't. She just turned and looked at Maddie again and wanted to hug her and rock away her misery.

'I know you're not my patient,' he said and then came and stood on Maddie's other side. 'Do you think I could talk to you the way I do if you were? We're colleagues. She's *our* patient – she belongs to both of us.'

'I wouldn't do this to her,' Annie said. 'It's too dreadful –'

'Then you'd do her a disservice. I'm delighted about this – it's the best thing that could have happened. I should have tried it long ago – though perhaps, before you, it wouldn't have worked –' He leaned down and spoke into Maddie's ear. 'Maddie – where are you? Tell me where you are. What's happening? Tell me, Maddie –'

At once Maddie rolled her head on the pillow and began to wail even more loudly, and as her head shook from side to side Joe looked across at Annie and made a small grimace.

'She's refusing me, Annie. You try, will you? Ask her the same question.'

'I won't – it's all . . .'

'Stop being so selfish! It's her needs that matter, not your sensibilities!' he snapped. 'And *this* is what she needs. She listens to you more than she does me. So ask her – now.'

Annie stared at him for a long moment and then, unable to

meet his eyes any longer, bent her head and looked down at Maddie. And as much to show him that it would make no difference in any way as for any other reason she said quietly, 'Maddie, where are you? What's happening to you, Maddie? Tell me about it.'

'What are you doing, lady, trying to kill yourself?' A thick voice, with an edge of annoyance to it and she tried to open her eyes against the blackness, but then discovered they were open, and there was something over them, and reached up, and tried to push it away.

'Hey, leave that alone, lady – you got to be cleaned up, ain't yer? So's we can see what damage you done – hey, Chuck, come here – this look okay to you now?'

The blackness vanished and a dimly seen face replaced it, a rough, lined face with a stubble of unshaven beard and emitting a gust of cheap tobacco and beer smells, and she grimaced and tried to turn her head away.

'Yeah, that'll do,' the face grunted and disappeared. 'The bleedin's stopped – it's just a scrape. Lucky broad that one. Could ha' killed her stoopid self.'

'Jay,' she said. 'The boys –' and struggled to stand up. It seemed so odd to be lying down on the ground when she was supposed to be driving to Jay and the boys. She didn't know quite why she was in such a hurry to get to them, but that she was on her way to them and it was desperately important she get there, this she knew, and she pushed down on the ground beneath her hands and shoved and the world twisted and lurched sickeningly and then she was sitting up. And staring at a group of men who were wearing hats that looked like the coal scuttle that had been used to stand beside the fireplace there in Hackney when she was small, men with streaked and grimy faces that appeared and then vanished as the light flickered around them, first silhouetting them and then throwing their faces into vivid relief. And she blinked, puzzled, and rubbed her head.

And as she did it she remembered in a single great rush. The boys and Jay were in Cray Costello's house and Gian Giovale had promised to – and somehow she managed to struggle to her feet as the world continued to rock and swirl uncooperatively about her and stood still for a moment to push down the nausea that was rising in her chest.

'I have to find them,' she said and turned and began to walk blindly towards the source of the erratic flickering light and the smell. It was a thicker smell now, less friendly, as chemicals seemed to become part of it and she thought, that's paint. There's paint burning somewhere. It isn't just sticks under coals, it's painted wood. Oh, God, it's painted wood –

Someone seized her elbows roughly. 'Where the hell you goin', lady? There ain't no way through there. You go back to your car and wait for the cops. We've got them coming soon as we can get your goddamned wreck out of the way and get another engine. Not that it makes a hell of a lot of difference . . . Listen, where'd you get off drivin' up here anyway? You oughta know better than to get in the way of fire engines, dammit –'

'My boys are there –' she managed to get out. 'My little boys – my husband – they're there in that house – I have to fetch them out and make sure they're safe – let me go and get my boys –'

There was someone on her other side now, holding her elbow and no matter how hard she tried to escape she couldn't. Her feet scrabbled uselessly against the gravel beneath her shoes as she tried to resist the hard male grip.

'What's that?' one of them barked.

'My boys,' she said again and turned her head, which was now hurting abominably, from side to side, trying to see faces beneath those shovel brims and wanting to escape the smells that were washing over her; not just tobacco and beer but onions and old sour leather and rubber and the thick reek of smoke. 'They're in there, my little boys –'

'Oh, Gawd, lady,' one of the men said, and his grip seemed to lessen a little, though not enough for her to be free. 'Oh, Gawd, lady. I'm sorry. How old's these kids?'

'Buster's two and the baby – let me go, for God's sake! Let me go and get them –'

'I don't know – hey, ask Eddie, will you – see who was fetched out o' there.'

'You know goddamn well who was fetched out. Barbecue, that was who was fetched out –' Someone else had come crunching up the drive from the direction of the house, and now

336

he pulled off his helmet and she stared at him. There was a line on his forehead above which his skin was white and clean, and below it his eyes shone eerily in his blackened face.

'My boys,' Maddie said and her voice was loud and shrill, and she listened to it, marvelling at how controlled it sounded. 'My little boys. My husband –'

The man with the half-white forehead stood very still and looked at her and around her the other three men stood in the same wooden posture and she looked from one to the other as beyond them the sound of voices shouting and the rush of water from hoses came in little bursts, and the light rose and fell like a fairground's invitation. Then one of the other men took off his coal scuttle helmet and after a moment the others did the same and all stood and stared at her, bleakly, silently, and she began to shout at them, to tell them not to be so stupid but to go and fetch her boys at once, now, this minute, and to tell Jay she was here and waiting for him –

One of them moved forwards awkwardly and put his arm across her shoulders. It felt heavy and stiff, and the leather on his sleeve rubbed against her skin, and, grateful for the sensation, she dropped her head sideways and rubbed her face against it, needing to feel the contact because it gave her a grip on reality. Without it all this was a mad, impossible, sickening nightmare, the effects of all the whisky she had drunk – and she seized on that thought, bouncing it about inside her skull, telling herself over and over again that she was just having a drunken dream, that all this misery was her own fault for swallowing that garbage, and she never would again, not ever, ever, ever – and all the time she rubbed her face on the leather sleeve and wept.

'Lady, I'm sorry. There ain't no one can get out o' that place in one piece and that's the truth of it,' the man said gruffly and she thought again, whisky, whisky, this is whisky. But it didn't work. The bouncing ball inside her head which was that comforting thought dwindled and then vanished and all that was left was the echoing void in which his words could jeer at her.

'They couldn't ha' felt nothing, that's one comfort. These frame houses, they go up like goddamned paper, you know? Might as well be paper ones, like they got in Japan, I swear to you. It was all over before we got here, tell you the truth. We just been fetching dead people out this past half-hour. They had a party there, hey? Cray Costello, he was always havin' parties. Goddamn, I been up here myself and been given a drink with the guy. A great guy Costello, and I had to have the finding of him – and a lot of the other people, I didn't know who they was, and that's the way of it. It must ha' been quick for your family – real quick – here, you come and wait in the cabin of the engine there till the cops come and they'll take you back to town, settle you in the hospital with a sedative, huh? Come on lady –'

'How did it happen?' She heard her own voice again, high and loud, and marvelled. She could speak? Incredible. 'How did it happen?'

The man shrugged and she felt the leather of his arm rub her face again, but it wasn't comforting now. Just raw and harsh. 'Could ha' been anything. Ain't the heatin', that's for sure – they ain't started the boilers yet anywheres, it's been rare hot this August. And it couldn't ha' been oil lamps on account of the last party he had when they had dressin' up and he made it all like Paul Revere's time an' all that, with candles and oil lamps – that was when we was all up here and had a drink with 'em on account he was careful no danger and hired us to keep an eye out, you know? Well he'd ha' done that again, wouldn't he, if he was having a party like that? Did your – didn't you know what kinda party it was? Was there a reason why you wasn't here?' And she felt his curiosity focused on her as vividly as she had felt the leather of his sleeve.

'I don't know, I don't know, I don't know,' she said and the repetition helped her. It stopped him talking, stopped his questions, stopped her own thinking. 'I don't know –'

'Cigar butt, if you ask me,' someone said gruffly and she took a breath and stopped repeating the silly phrase and turned to him, needing to know, needing to be told it wasn't Giovale who had done it, that under her prodding he hadn't come here and destroyed her life.

'Are you sure?'

'Can't be sure of nothing,' the man said and shook his head. 'You'd be amazed the sort of fires people can start an' how they do it. But there'd be no percentage in Cray Costello torchin' his own place, would there? Not with himself in it. No man'd kil

338

himself that way. Stands to reason. There weren't no arson here, and no one won't be looking for it.' And he went squelching away in his water-sodden boots back towards the source of the smell and the light, which was reducing; already the flickering had stopped, and now there was just a dull glow coming down the drive between the bushes and the crackling sound had ceased. She could hear the sea again, whispering and then hissing back up the beach, and other night sounds; small creatures moving furtively in the undergrowth and distant cars on the roads and somewhere far off the melancholy cry of a train whistle.

'Come on, lady,' the man beside her said, still gruffly but with an underlying gentleness. 'Come on. The cops is here now and they'll take care of you. Come on, lady. No need to stay here. Ain't nothing more you can do. Nothing at all.'

'Show me,' she said suddenly. 'Show me. I have to know —'
The man peered at her. 'Show you what?'

'My boys — my husband — show me . . .'

He recoiled as though she'd spat at her. 'Lady! I told you — they're like — it wouldn't be fittin'!'

'She'll have to identify them,' someone said out of the darkness, and she turned and stared and saw a policeman. 'Sorry, but someone has to. Want to do it now, lady? I can fix it now if you want —'

'Oh God,' she said. 'Oh, God, tell me what to do! I have to know, you see. I have to know if it is them and I have to know if he did it and —'

'Did it? Did what?'

'If Gian Giovale did it —'

'Hey, lady, what are you saying? Do you know something about this here business what we oughta know?'

'What?' She was staring round distractedly now, and then heard her own voice again, and was amazed at what she said.

'I have to know if my friend Gian in Boston — if he stopped my Jay and the boys coming here. He said he was going to call him, tell him not to come down — I have to know who's here, I have to see —'

The man almost visibly relaxed. 'Oh, sure, sure, I see — yeah, well, come on lady. I'll take you up there. But it ain't nice, I'll tell you, it ain't nice. Hey, Charlie!' he called back over his shoulder. 'Call the station, have 'em send over a woman officer, okay? We're goin' to need one –'

And he began to walk down the drive and she followed him, keeping her head down and staring at the gravel as it spurted up beneath her shoes in little showers of grit, concentrating on just putting one foot in front of the other. How could she have done that? Why did she do that? Why lie to save Giovale's skin? They were dead, her boys and her Jay – they were dead and it was his doing, and she had lied about it. Why, how could she have done that?

Because it was your fault, her inner voice whispered. It was your fault. You who made Giovale do it, all your doing, you killed your children to spite Jay and get him back from the Costellos and in doing it you killed the only person in the entire world who is of any value at all.

The tears that were streaming down her face by the time she was standing in front of the small piles of sacking that were all that remained of the boys were not for them. She knew that. They were for herself. Because she had made it all happen, as she had made so many things in the past happen, and had lied about it. Just as she always had.

38

September 1987

'Have you been watching television this week?' He was asking the question almost before she had the front door open and she gaped at him as he came pushing his way in, his hair even more rumpled than usual and the collar of his rather shabby overcoat pulled high to his ears, for it was a windy, chilly evening.

'Television? Not really. I haven't had time. Why on earth –'

'Good. I mean, I'm glad. I'll have the chance to explain before you see it all. And it might have upset Maddie.' He was shrugging out of his coat, pulling things out of its capacious pockets before he hung it up, a big padded envelope, a battered folder with papers in it.

'What might have upset Maddie?' She led the way into the living room, a little self-consciously because he hadn't been here since she'd made the changes. She didn't really care what he thought, of course, but all the same –

He stopped in the doorway and stared around. And then after a long pause said softly, 'Oh, yes!'

'Yes, what?' She was trying to be nonchalant but it wasn't easy, and she too looked round the room, trying to see it through his eyes. The walls, repainted to a soft lavender; the furniture with its new coverings in deep purple and the cushions piled on the sofa and armchairs in all the shades of red and blue she could find, from the palest pink through to the deepest purple, so that the total effect was of a vast bunch of anemones; the big long glass coffee table in the middle on which she had set the best of Jen's knick-knacks, which looked surprisingly elegant there; and above all the new fire she had had installed. She had always been rather scornful of gas heaters with flames designed to simulate open coal fires, but this one was surprisingly authentic in appearance and it did complete what she knew to be a very pretty and comfortable room. The light of the flames flickered on the walls and the few good pictures she had hanging there, pleasantly supplementing the pools of soft pinkish light from the big table lamps she had set in two of the corners, on low glass tables of their own, and the sound of the Mozart she had playing on her new and very good player, which made the notes sound as though they were being produced right there in the room itself, all added up to an ambience of peace and comfort and, almost, luxury.

And he saw it just as she did, she knew, for he took a deep breath and let his shoulders relax a little and said, 'This is lovely, Annie. How clever you are! May I sit down and just expire peacefully and never get up again?'

She laughed. 'Absolutely not! Dead bodies lying around would quite ruin the effect. You may sit down and wait while I make you some coffee.' And she left him there and crossed her little hallway to the kitchen to put the kettle on.

'I've just remembered I forgot to have any supper,' he called a little plaintively. 'Could you stretch to a dry crust as well, maybe?'

And she smiled to herself but said nothing and went to the fridge to get the makings of sandwiches. There was some of that salmon left from their own supper and enough of the mayonnaise she had made to go with it to create a respectable plate of sandwiches, and she had some good granary bread; and whistling softly to accompany the Mozart, which sounded almost as good here in the kitchen as it did in the living room, she moved happily about, setting a coffee tray, slicing cucumber thinly to garnish his sandwiches, content to be purely domestic just for a while.

When she carried the tray into the living room, he was lying back in her deepest armchair with his eyes closed, his long legs stretched wide and his curly head thrown back against the pile of cushions and she stood and looked at him, thinking in a disjointed way of how comfortable he looked and how much a part of the room and how much she had actually enjoyed making sandwiches for him, and wondering what it might be like to do it often, all the time even; and then, annoyed with herself for thinking such stupidity, deliberately clattered the tray a little as she set it down on the glass table.

He didn't open his eyes, staying in just the same posture as he spoke. 'This is very close to heaven, Annie. The smell of that coffee is pure ambrosia and the music is perfect and I'll never ever want to be anywhere else. Could you put up with that?'

'You'd need too much dusting,' she said, and kept her head down. He was uncomfortably close to what she had been thinking and that was not to be considered. 'When you came in you said something about upsetting Maddie. What did you mean?'

He dragged himself upright and grinned at her and then reached for the coffee she had poured for him. 'What's in those? Salmon? You are a magic lady, Annie. My favourite food bar none. I shall eat all of them, completely, and you shall watch me. I hope you wanted none for yourself, for you shan't have any. I have a bad attack of greedy on me. Yes, I did say something about upsetting Maddie. I don't want to. Where is she?'

'Asleep. She gets tired early, so after supper I told her she ought to go to bed. Are you going to explain, or do I have to nag?'

He shook his head, his mouth full, and patiently she waited.

'No, you don't have to nag. I want to tell you. That's why I came. But we have to decide what to tell Maddie about it. Let me finish this and then I'll show you. Do you have a video machine?' He reached for another sandwich for he had demolished the first at a great rate.

She looked over her shoulder at the television set in the corner. 'Yes. I thought I might as well have one installed when I had the TV put in, though I've never used it. I think I might get rid of it, for all the use I make of it.'

'Oh, you'll get round to using it. We all succumb to technology's artful lures eventually. Anyway, I'm glad you've got it now. There's a video tape in that envelope. Do get it out and put it in the machine, and then when it's ready and I've gobbled up the rest of these delectable sandwiches, I'll explain what it's all about.'

Obediently she took the tape from the envelope, and went over to the video machine in the corner and sat there with the instruction book on her lap, trying to work out how to operate the thing and fiddling with the remote control, and he watched her as he ate, and tried to concentrate only on what he had come here to tell her and not on his private thoughts at all, but it was almost impossible. She was looking so very much better; her hair had settled into its new cut and now framed her face, which was smoother and much less haggard than it had been, in a very attractive way, and her body looked better too, less bony and a great deal more relaxed. She was much too nice to look at altogether, he thought a little gloomily. Damn it all.

She looked up. 'I think I've got it sussed. Now, what is this all about? Shall I switch on?'

'In a moment.' He stretched and lay back in his chair. 'Come over here – you'll get a squint if you sit as close as that.'

She laughed. 'You sound like an elderly nanny,' she said. 'The way Maddie's Daphne would talk –' She stood still suddenly, staring down at him, for she had been on her way to the armchair on the other side of him. 'That's a thought. I wonder what happened to her? She could still be a nanny, I suppose – how old would she be? She was about the same age as Maddie, wasn't she? I think so – from the things Maddie has told me.'

'Has she been talking a lot since she came here?' He looked at her sharply as she settled herself in her chair, her own cup of coffee beside her.

'She hasn't stopped.' Annie laughed then. 'It's been like a volcano, I swear to you. That's why I've seen no television – I've done hardly anything at all but fix the flat and listen to Maddie. Actually, it's been riveting. I've heard more about what the war was really like for people who had to live through it than I would have imagined possible – she was just a kid, you see, and it totally ruined things for her. Her education, her own life, it was all destroyed. Especially when her mother was killed.'

'I imagine it must have been – but is that all she talked about? Nothing about the things she told us that last time? With the injection?'

She shook her head. 'I've not encouraged her. I thought it was bad enough she went through it once. She needs time to recover, surely? Let her talk about the remote past, about being a child and her parents and so forth. Plenty of time to go back over that awful stuff again. You said that yourself.'

'Yes, I did. But now –' He shook his head. 'Now I'm not so sure. It might be that we have to talk to her about the later things. And let her talk to us. The thing is, I set out to find out if it was all true. And it is.'

'But I never doubted it was true,' she said and stared at him. 'Why did you?'

'Because it was such an incredible story,' Joe said. 'Don't you think?'

'Why incredible? She did what she thought she had to. And it led to all that – a dreadful story, I grant you, but hard to believe? Far from it.'

'You can imagine your mother doing what she did?' he said softly and almost held his breath. She had been so much more relaxed an Annie since Maddie had left the hospital and come here to live at the flat, but all the same, there were still difficult areas; but she didn't flare up as he had feared. She just sat and stared at him and then at the flames of her gas fire.

'I don't know,' she said at length. 'Possibly. She had the same sort of madness about her.'

'Madness?' Again he held his breath. Annie, to say that about Jennifer?

She lifted her chin and looked at him. 'Yes. Madness. I used to get so angry if – well, now I don't. It was a sort of madness to stick with him, with Colin, for so long. To lose so much and to – oh, the hell with it. Don't want to talk about it. How did you find out? And what did you find out?'

'What?' He was startled by the change of mood. She had been so willing to talk lately; to find her sliding away in this way was like the bad old days.

'You say you found out it's all absolutely true. How did you find out? And why? *Why* did you doubt it? I thought that what people said when they had injections like that was always true. Didn't they use to call them truth drugs?'

'No matter what they called 'em, they aren't entirely. I've had patients who were so totally gripped by fantasy that even under abreactive drugs they clung to them. That was one of the reasons I wasn't sure about using the method for Maddie. Now I'm damned glad I did, of course, but at the time – I wasn't sure.' He grinned. 'There's something to be said for being an eclectic practitioner after all. Our critics say it's just that we don't know what the hell we're doing so we try any old thing, and we say we're being flexible and open to ideas and responsive to individual patients' individual needs. Sounds better that way, doesn't it?'

'So you doubted it when you heard it, even though she was in such a dreadful state? I don't think I've ever seen anyone so –' She shivered suddenly. 'It upset me a lot. I dreamed about it for ages afterwards. The way she screamed and cried and –'

'You should see what happens with LSD,' he said and grimaced a little. 'Damn it, do I sound like a hardened old medic, couldn't care less about people's feelings? That's not the way of it, you know. We care. It's just that we get good at hiding it. And yes, I did doubt her. There was something – oh, I can't explain, I just needed extra assurance. So I set out to get it.'

She looked sardonic now. 'Private detectives? Seedy little men in seedy hats prowling around Boston and – where was it – Osterville, asking questions of oldies about do-you-remember-thirty-five-years ago?'

'Nothing so complicated. I got it done for nothing. Seedy detectives need seedy money. And I'm just a poor old NHS psychiatrist. All I did was make a phone call to Boston. I did it out of hours to keep it cheap – *and* I used the hospital's phone.'

She laughed aloud at that. 'They'll run you out of town on a rail! Spending government money on patients instead of bureaucracy? What a wicked misuse of taxpayers' cash! Anyway, who did you call? Did you just look up Kincaid in the phone book and call the family? I imagine there are some of them left.'

'Oh, there are some of them left all right,' he said and looked at her sideways. 'One of them you know a good deal about.'

'What?' She stared at him. 'I know about? How? Who?'

'The name doesn't ring bells?'

'Kincaid? Maddie's the only person I know called Kincaid.'

'That's why I asked if you'd been watching television,' he said. 'Switch on that tape, will you?'

She stared at him for a long moment and then reached over to her record player and switched off the Mozart before picking up the video controller and peering at it before pressing the relevant buttons, and the TV screen glowed into life and showed a billiard table and balls being pushed around on it in a desultory fashion and she made a face. 'Now you know why I hardly ever watch,' she murmured. 'Ah, here we go –'

The image shivered, changed and then became part of a news

bulletin, and she watched as the newsreader finished talking about a teachers' union dispute and then moved on to the next item.

'In the United States, activity is rapidly increasing in the run-up to the Presidential elections. Since the naked dancer row over the Senator from Minnesota which led to his surprise resignation from the race, there have been several other new appearances at the hustings. Our man in Washington reports –'

Again the picture changed and there was the usual image of a man in a raincoat standing in front of the Capitol, clutching a handmike and pretending he was talking casually when he was quite clearly using a set of cues from which to read his comments, and she listened as he launched himself into an account of the various people involved in the forthcoming election. And her forehead creased in bewilderment and she looked at Joe and said, 'What has this to do with –'

'Hush,' he said. 'Wait and see.'

She lifted her brows at him, but turned back to the screen. 'A sudden new appearance from a contender is the Senator from Massachusetts who was spoken of dismissively only three weeks ago as a no-hoper, but who has now come on at a very remarkable rate. His opponents have suggested that his family connections have been used to much greater effect than is to be admired, but can't deny that he cuts an attractive figure on the television screens of the nation, where this election will undoubtedly be won – and lost. He has an appeal that is hard to deny –'

And again the scene changed and now there appeared a group of obvious politicians in the middle of the crowd, as one of them shouted into a microphone and onlookers waved and shrieked, though none of it could be heard as the voice of the commentator droned on.

'– Timothy Bryan Kincaid the Second – he always insists on using the numeral, even though some people find it unpleasantly old-fashioned and smacking of an aristocratic attitude that should have no place in modern American politics, is pulling in support so much faster than his nearest competitors that the front runner, Senator Hansell Koenig, has made some distinctly sour comments on his ability as a politician as compared with his charm as a TV performer and –'

Annie was leaning forwards, staring at the screen with her mouth half open with surprise, and quietly Joe reached across and pointed.

'You see the chap they're talking about? The stocky one –'

She nodded. 'He looks too young, though, to be the man Maddie talked about. He can't be a day over forty, surely? And Jay's brother would have been – well, older than Maddie. And she's almost sixty, isn't she?'

'Fifty-seven,' Joe said. 'And this man is around sixty. Never underestimate the power of American dentistry and suntanning oils.'

'Blond,' Annie said and shivered. 'Maddie said her Jay had hair like gold. I wonder if they were alike, the two of them? Maddie didn't say, did she?'

'They are now,' Joe said very deliberately and she turned and stared at him, her eyes wide.

'What did you say?'

'They are now. Look at the chap behind him and to his left – there, beside that thin woman in the mink jacket – watch now.' He had seized her shoulder and had his head very close to hers as he pointed at the screen and she was aware of the warmth of him against her face and, oddly, liked it as she let her gaze follow the line of his pointing finger and saw the man standing behind the speaker, who was still shouting his platitudes into the echoing microphone as his hearers waved and applauded. A bulky man, with hair that was dull, compared with the candidate's, and rather thin as far as she could see, but still unmistakably blond; a jowly face in which the eyes seemed like slits, and certainly gave no hint of their colour, and a fixed watchful expression. The man stood there watching the crowd over the speaker's head, as she caught her breath at that moment because suddenly there it was; an unmissable likeness between the two men. There could be no hint of doubt at all that she was looking at the Jay of whom she had heard so much.

Or could it be . . . and she turned to Joe and said, 'Are you sure?'

'Rewind the tape and look again,' he said. 'And you'll see that you're sure too.'

She fiddled with the control panel and managed to do as he

348

said and then started to rerun it, and again the newsreader appeared to introduce the man in Washington, and she let it run as she said again, 'Are you quite sure? Couldn't it be the other one, what was his name? Declan?'

He shook his head. 'My man in Boston comes in here. No, it couldn't be. He's dead. Got involved in some sort of business scam, apparently, and then died somewhat mysteriously and very conveniently, it seems, in a road accident. According to my chap –'

'Who is your chap? Someone who really knows or –'

'He knows. He's on the surgical staff at Boston General – went down the brain drain ten years ago. I got him to look up the old newspapers there because I knew he'd enjoy it. He used to play at genealogies, for God's sake, always helping people do their family trees when we were students. That's what made me think of him when I wanted to check up on Maddie's story. So I called him and yesterday he called me back and told me. The younger son Declan died, the sisters seem to have married various useful people as far as money and business connections are concerned and now, Dave Mercer tells me, the Kincaid empire is one of the vastest in the whole of the US, if carefully anonymous much of the time. And the man who runs it and controls it and has all the say in what goes on is Jay Bryan Kincaid. It was he, they say, who put his brother into the race for the Presidency and is pushing him hard. I saw another TV programme as well as this one I videoed to show you, in case you hadn't seen it. So there you are. It's all true. Because I got Dave to look at the old newspapers for '53 as well. The fire in Osterville was well covered – it caused a hell of a fuss at the time. Seventeen people – a lot of 'em very powerful people – died as well as Costello and his daughter but some got away. Five of them, it seems. And one of them was Jay Kincaid.'

She turned her eyes back to the screen where once again the tape had reached the stage of showing Timothy Bryan Kincaid the Second at the height of his oratory and as the camera shifted its angle and at last Jay Bryan Kincaid again came into view she leaned forwards to stare again.

'Annie?' The voice behind her was so quiet she wasn't sure she had heard it at all, and she looked over her shoulder to see Maddie standing in the doorway, her dressing gown pulled around her and her hair in a tangle over her sleep-crumpled face.

She was staring not at Annie but at the screen.

'Who did you say that was?'

Desperately Annie fumbled with the control gadget, wanting to protect her, needing time to explain to her before letting her see, but as she tried to find the stop button and press it, her finger slipped and hit the pause button instead.

And the image on the screen flickered, almost rolled and then held. And it had frozen on a direct close-up of Jay, staring over his brother's shoulder out into the room at the three of them.

39

September 1987

'No,' Annie said. 'No, no, *no*. I won't.'

'Why not? What difference does it make to you? Why can't you see how important it is? Why *not*? Please –' And Maddie's voice rose to a wail, and she tried to sit up on the sofa again.

But Annie pushed her back and made her lie still and Maddie lay there, her face so pale that her eyes looked black in it as she glinted up at her, and she could feel the fury and the anger in her – and at the same time something else. There was a calculating look in her eyes, a watchfulness, and Annie sat back on her heels beside the sofa and stared down at her.

It was almost two in the morning, and they had been talking now for what seemed like an eternity, and which had indeed been a matter of some hours. At first Joe had wanted to stay, seeing how Maddie had wept and gasped and wept again, and then he had wanted to give her some sort of sedative to get her through the rest of the night.

'She's likely to go on being pretty uptight for a while, Annie. Will you be able to cope? Dammit, I should have made sure she couldn't hear and be disturbed when I started to show you that tape. It was stupid of me.'

'She had to know sooner or later,' Annie said. 'And I think perhaps better sooner. I can deal with her. You go away and leave us alone. She'll be all right.'

He had lingered at the front door of the little flat, staring over her shoulder at the back of Maddie's head which could just be seen over the back of the sofa. She was sitting bolt upright and rocking to and fro and he grimaced at the sight of that.

'Dammit, I was too hopeful,' he murmured. 'I thought we could really rehabilitate her, living here with you. But if she regresses again now she knows he's alive then you won't be able to – it wouldn't be right to leave her with you. Too much of a burden. I'll have to get her in somewhere, though God knows where. They're emptying the acute unit now. There just isn't a Greenhill left for all practical purposes. Just offices and records, that's all. Certainly nothing that can give her any care –'

'I'll care for her,' Annie said firmly and pushed him to the door. 'Go, for pity's sake. I'll sort her out. Leave her to me.'

And she had been very optimistic that she could sort it out. After the first appalling few minutes when Maddie had recognised Jay, greatly changed though he was, and had wept and then laughed and wept again her huge relief that he was still alive, she had seemed to settle down and become calm. Annie had expected an outburst of – what? Renewed guilt, extra remorse over the boys, anger at Jay because they were dead and he as well as she had survived? But there had been none of that, just the storm of excitement, and then calmness, and at last Joe had agreed to go, and had left the two women alone, and she had gone slowly back to the living room to sit beside Maddie and talk to her.

For a while it had been a little like their very first weeks together. Maddie had sat and rocked and said nothing, keeping her eyes blank and fixed and rocking rhythmically, and Annie had talked and murmured and talked again until she was hoarse, trying to get her to come out of her almost trancelike state. And had just begun to be seriously worried that the shock of seeing that image on the TV screen had sent Maddie back headfirst into the maelstrom of her madness, when she had stopped her rocking and turned her head to Annie and said, 'I'm going to him.'

'I – what did you say?' Annie had peered closely at her face in the low lights of the room, wanting to see how serious she was; surely she was being foolishly jocular, making an incomprehensible bad joke? But she wasn't. Maddie's eyes were blazing with excitement and her face had high patches of colour on it as she said it again. 'I'm going to him.'

'Going to where?'

'To America. To Boston. To Jay. He's mine – I have to go to him. I'll need you to help me – money for tickets, things like that – you can help me with that, can't you? Just a loan – Jay will return it as soon as he sees me. I'll send the money back, or if you like, you can come too. Yes, that'd be better, you travel with me. You come to America with me, and when we see Jay he'll be so grateful to you for bringing me back to him that he'll not just pay the money you spent to get us there, he'll give you lots more. Oh, please Annie, will you arrange it? Right away? I'll need some clothes, too – I can't go to him looking like this –'

And feverishly she had jumped to her feet and run to the bathroom, Annie close behind her, to stare at the mirror and pull her lank hair from her face and stare at herself closely.

'I'll have time for a facial and hairdo, won't I? Yes, I must, and then we'll both go to Boston and we'll find Jay and oh, Annie, won't it be wonderful at last? To be together again and –'

'Shut up!' Annie had roared at her, and gone running back to the living room to hurl herself into an armchair. 'Shut up! I won't listen to this – it's the maddest thing I ever heard – you're not going to Boston! If he'd wanted you, he'd have come to find you long ago. You're a fool to think he gives a damn about you, or wants ever to see you again – you're not fit to go alone, you're not fit to go at all. And I'm not taking you –'

And then it had begun – the pleading, the cajoling, the shouting and the threatening as Maddie tried everything she knew, every word she could lay her tongue to to make Annie do what she wanted. And Annie had sat there refusing steadily until at last Maddie had hurled herself on to the sofa in a flood of frustration and tears.

And Annie had sat and watched and waited, thinking she would weep herself into a sleep of exhaustion and they could both get some rest and regain some sense. But that hadn't happened. Eventually Maddie had rolled over on to her back and started again, not shouting this time, nor pleading, but offering calm reasoned words, simple obvious explanations of why it was the most sensible thing in the world for her to go to Boston and see her husband. Was she not the man's wife? Hadn't he had the same thirty-five years of misery as she, wondering where she was, what had happened to her? Hadn't he been longing for her as much as she had been longing for him? They had to be together – they were meant for each other, he was the centre of her life, the only person who made it worth living. How could Annie keep them apart? How could she? It was only lack of understanding that deterred her; only her own misfortune in never having so great, so vital, so powerful a love; and all the time Maddie's voice was so reasonable and patient. Why not? Why could Annie not see how important it was? It was all so rational, so necessary, so inevitable; why could she not understand?

And finally, at two in the morning, Annie's patience snapped. She looked at the white face on the sofa cushions, framed in the lovely anemone colours of which she had been so proud and which now looked to her sickly and ugly, magenta and puce, not soft lilac and violet, and hated her.

She hated the words she used. She hated the wide-eyed explanations of how deeply she loved this man. She hated the way Maddie explained how much she needed him, how important he was to her.

And she found herself deep inside her own memory, listening to her mother Jennifer, as she stood behind her at her dressing table as she did night after night, brushing her hair, because Annie was to grow up beautiful, like her father, and have lovely curly rich hair like his; and while she brushed she would talk, just as Maddie had been talking, of the way she loved this one man and could never love any other.

Of how important it was for a woman to have so grand a passion in her life. Of the wonder of yielding all your feelings to just one man for ever. Of the way the only women who mattered were those like herself, one-man women who gave a lifetime of devotion where they had given their hearts. Of the glory of suffering for a man who was worth loving . . .

'And one day, my darling Annie, one day you will be a beautiful lady and you will find a man to love as I love your daddy. Maybe you'll be lucky and he will be able to live with you all the time and take care of you but it won't matter if he can't, because you'll have him to love and that's all a woman needs – to have a great passion is to be alive and to be real and to be important –'

And her Irish voice had lilted on and on and Annie, young Annie, had sat and listened and hated her for saying it all, hated what she was being told and felt sick with fear that Jen might be right, that it might be true.

And now Maddie, saying the same things over and over again, pleading to go to a man who had used her so ill that she had lost all sight of the woman she was meant to be and had turned into a manipulating scheming creature who couldn't even see when she had been cruel, who couldn't understand that others had loves and needs and feelings too, who put her own ridiculous grand love above every other person in the entire world and –

And she lifted her hand and swung back her arm and let all her fury and her fatigue and her grief for her mother as well as for Maddie herself come pouring down from her shoulders to her fingertips, and she let all the power she had loose on it; and as her fingers struck Maddie's face with a resounding crack that made her fingers tingle and then burn and which left her muscles all down her arm aching, she felt the flood of her own tears erupt.

'You stupid, wicked bitch,' she howled. 'You bloody fool! He was a bastard and he still is a bastard because they never change – you hear me? They never change – but you're worse than he is, lying to yourself, destroying your life for him, destroying everything because of him, you're wicked, wicked, wicked – I hate you, you hear me? I hate you!' And then the tears choked her and no more words would come and she reached forwards and took Maddie's shoulders in each hand and began to shake her.

'You're worth more than this, you're worth more, don't do it, don't destroy yourself again – don't do it. He's not worth it, he never was, he still isn't, don't do it –'

And then she was holding Maddie close, wrapping both her arms about her and holding her as she wept and rocked, trying to make her understand how much she cared about her, how important it was she should detach herself from this stupid passion she had allowed to consume her all these years, forgiving her for all she had ever done and loving her for what she was; a woman worth loving.

And wasn't all that surprised to find after a while that it had all changed and she wasn't holding Maddie and comforting her and trying to beg her pardon for hitting her and hurting her. Maddie was holding her, and rocking her gently as she wept on her shoulder and let all her grief for Jen, poor sad dead Jen, tumble out on Maddie's dressing-gowned shoulder.

40

January 1988

Maddie, contented. Walking each morning to the town centre with her shopping trolley bumping along the pavement behind her, to buy the things they needed, watching the traffic and the people, the trees and the birds, the dogs and the children, and liking all she saw, however commonplace.

Maddie, working, cleaning the flat and finding it agreeable to polish and wash and iron clothes. Revelling in the long hours spent over a cookery book in the small kitchen while she planned the supper she would have ready for Annie when she came home. Washing up, making their beds, looking after the window boxes, tugging out the weeds, rejoicing when the flowers managed to emerge, grieving when they didn't, and turning over the soil industriously either way. Sweeping the stairs outside the flat and actively enjoying it.

Maddie watchful, anxious when she saw Annie tired, worrying that she was not liking her job, fearful she would lose heart and become depressed again. Rejoicing when she looked happy once more and laughed about things that happened at work, cast down when she was snappy and refused to talk. But always aware of her moods and her needs and her feelings, and liking to be that way.

Maddie laughing, watching silly television shows with Annie and Joe, as they ate Chinese food Joe had brought with him, teasing each other, making jokes. Feeling warm and safe and so right about where she was that sometimes she laughed when there were no silly television shows. She didn't need them.

Maddie wondering, as she saw Joe and Annie so comfortable together, hoping nothing would come to change things and spoil it all, the way it was. Annie was hers now, her person, her passion, her own responsibility, Joe would get in the way and –

Maddie learning. Not the way to be, frightened and jealous. Each week with Joe, having their session, talking of all that had happened, where she had spoiled things, how not to do it in the future, learning, learning all the time, and learning most of all not to be afraid of losing Annie. Because that couldn't happen now, even if she and Joe did get closer still.

Because now, at last, Maddie peaceful.

Sphere now offers an exciting range of quality fiction and non-fiction by both established and new authors. All of the books in this series are available from good bookshops, or can be ordered from the following address:

Sphere Books
Cash Sales Department
P.O. Box 11
Falmouth
Cornwall TR10 9EN.

Please send cheque or postal order (no currency), and allow 60p for postage and packing for the first book plus 25p for the second book and 15p for each additional book ordered up to a maximum charge of £1.50 in U.K.

B.F.P.O. customers please allow 60p for the first book, 25p for the second book plus 15p per copy for the next 7 books, thereafter 9p per book.

Overseas customers including Eire please allow £1.25 for postage and packing for the first book, 75p for the second book and 28p for each subsequent title ordered.